THE FINAL FLIGHT

A COLD WAR THRILLER

JAMES BLATCH

The Final Flight by James Blatch published by Vivid Dog Limited, 4a Church Street, Market Harborough, LE16 7AA, UK

ISBN: 978-1-5272-9075-4

Cover by Stuart Bache

For my mother and father, who lived the lives that inspired this book.

FOREWORD

It begins with nothing.

A space in the sky, silence on a radio channel.

A turn of the head in a control tower; a first inkling that something, somewhere, is not right.

There could be a range of benign explanations.

But old squadron hands sense death quickly.

Events unfold with their own momentum and a predictable narrative.

Somewhere in the countryside, a puzzled farmer stares at a plume of rising black smoke.

Within an hour of the missed radio call, a man in uniform knocks on the door of a married quarter.

He stands in silence, hoping his presence alone will convey the gravity of his message.

It always does.

Families mourn, but the men in flying coveralls must go back into the air.

They bury their friend, then bury their grief.

Away from public view, serious men with clipboards pore over the debris and piece together the sequence of events.

Arguments and compromise precede the publication of an official document on flimsy government paper.

It invariably contains two words. A final insult to young men who had so much of their lives to live but who died in the blink of an eye on a weekday afternoon.

Pilot error.

1966

UNITED KINGDOM

1

TUESDAY 7TH JUNE

The peace of Blethwyn Valley was shattered for thirteen seconds.

The rabbits sensed the man-made thunder first and bolted for their burrows. The sheep, slow to react, scattered only as it arrived overhead, briefly blotting out the June sun. Invisible vortexes sent a buzzard tumbling in the air.

The four engines left a trail of black smoke in the disturbed wake and a deep rumble that quickly faded.

There were no witnesses.

The RAF Avro Vulcan bomber had come and gone on a sleepy weekday in a remote part of Wales.

The Welsh were at work.

And that's how the men of the Royal Air Force Test Flying Unit liked it.

To be unobserved.

Had there been a witness—maybe a farmer turning his head at the sudden and loud intrusion to his otherwise tranquil surroundings—it's doubtful he would have noticed anything unusual about this particular flight.

He may have been able to identify the Vulcan, perhaps because of its distinctive delta wing, but it's less likely he would have spotted the bulge of white casing with a glass-panelled front, nestled under the nose of the bomber.

Although unremarkable in appearance, it was the most secret and significant item of military equipment on the planet.

Inside the white casing, behind the glass, was a laser.

As far as the outside world was concerned, laser was a rudimentary and far from mobile technology.

But then the world doesn't know what the world doesn't know, and the men of the TFU were under threat of arrest to keep it that way.

As the Vulcan exited the far end of the valley, the wings rolled left, and the throttles edged up to eighty-five per cent of maximum to sustain the target speed through the turn. The stick eased back, the rudder deflected left—just a little—as the nose heaved thirty degrees and the jet rolled out on a new heading.

On board, not a single member of the crew had touched a flying control.

In fact, they were discussing the football.

Chris Milford tried to ignore the navigator's drone regarding the England squad for the forthcoming World Cup. He didn't share Steve Bright's concern that there were too many West Ham players in the side. He understood the point about the Hammers being a pedestrian, unglamorous side that didn't produce the type of flair players needed to win a World Cup, but Millie had work to do.

He concentrated on inserting a reel of magnetic tape into a brown cardboard sleeve. A simple enough task on the ground, but difficult when your seat is being hauled through the bumpy, low-level air at three hundred and fifty knots.

After a successful struggle, he scribbled a serial number on the cardboard and dipped into a pocket on his flying coveralls to pull out a small notepad. Millie adjusted the light that hung down on a pipe from the panel in front of him and added the tape serial number to a list. He had to pause as the jet rose and fell, weaving its way through the Welsh hills.

Alongside the serial number, he noted the date, flight number and time. He paused, casting his eye up the list of previous entries, noting the accumulation of flying hours.

So far, so good for project Guiding Light.

Millie tucked the notebook back into his pocket and turned his attention to the switches, dials and readouts in front of him.

Sitting in a well below the cockpit, facing backwards, he studied the converted navigator-radar station.

The Guiding Light panel sparkled orange, electronically generated numbers pulsing as they changed in a rhythm directly linked to the aircraft's proximity to the ground in feet.

Millie watched them carefully.

The display went from 307, to 312 and a moment later 305.

They had asked Guiding Light to fly the jet as close to, but not below, three hundred feet. It was doing a good job of the task.

The veteran engineering officer was still getting used to the marvel of it all. Somewhere behind the switches and dials that surrounded him, electronic wizardry connected the laser's range-finding data to the Vulcan autopilot.

Two pieces of technology in direct communication. Millie hoped they didn't fall out..

To his relief, the captain Brian Hill, interrupted Steve Bright's football monologue with a clipped question over the intercom.

"How many more tapes?"

Millie pulled his oxygen mask over his face.

"That was the last one. I'm out now."

"OK, we'll stay at low-level until we get to the estuary as planned," Hill replied.

With the recorder no longer capturing data from the laser, Millie wondered why they would continue at low-level. But he remained silent on the matter. It would only be a few minutes.

His hand went up to a small black rotary dial beneath the main height readout. He turned it, clicking it through its eleven stops, each a pre-defined position around the nose of the Vulcan.

In fact the system scanned twenty-seven separate locations

sweeping from thirty degrees left and eighty degrees down all the way across to the same position on the right, taking in the view up to forty degrees above the nose.

A design engineer at DF Blackton once told him they began by mimicking how much a pilot's eyes absorbed from the picture in front of him, and improved on that.

Millie noted the twelve hundred feet or so of space to their left and imagined the rocky side of a Welsh hill. He turned the dial back to the number one position, more or less straight down.

Two hundred and sixty-one feet to the unforgiving ground beneath them.

"Do you ever take your eyes off those numbers?"

Millie glanced across to Steve Bright and shrugged.

"Our lives in the hands of a computer with this aircraft's flaky electrical system? Yes, I like to keep an eye on them."

Millie tried to be an amiable crewmate, but it was no secret he no longer enjoyed these trips. Squashed into a flying dungeon with the ever present threat of a sudden end to everything.

He looked back at Brighty; the nav looked bored. A consequence of his job being replaced by a flying computer.

"Hungry?"

Brighty perked up as Millie passed over a sandwich from his flight case.

He unlatched his seat, swivelled it around to face the empty middle position and stretched his legs. They ached from being squeezed under the workstation.

With his oxygen mask dangling under his chin, he muttered to himself, "This is a young man's game." But his words were lost in the perpetual roar as the jet thundered its way across Wales.

He looked up the short ladder to the cockpit, where Brian Hill craned his neck, looking down toward him.

"Getting ready for your afternoon nap, Millie?"

Millie smiled and pulled his mask across his face so his words would be heard on the intercom.

"Would be lovely. Try and fly smoothly."

Hill laughed and turned back.

A third voice piped up on the loop. Rob May, in the co-pilot's seat.

"We're not here for smoothness, my old friend."

Millie noted tension in Rob's voice; the young test pilot was technically in control of the aircraft, although much of the decision making had been ceded to Guiding Light.

Hill drew the curtain back across to cut out the light glare from the windshield, allowing Millie and Bright to see their dials and displays clearly.

Millie turned his chair back to the workstation and again kept a close eye on the height data as it ticked over.

The numbers updated every three quarters of a second. It was hypnotic. He fought the urge to close his eyes.

He reached forward and rotated the black dial once again. Position two showed 1,021 feet, position three showed 314 feet. They were hugging a valley, just three hundred feet from one side.

The computer was showing them what good tactical flying looked like.

He rotated it back to position one. Nine hundred and fourteen feet directly below them.

Nine hundred and fourteen feet. Really?

Suddenly Millie was lifted in his seat.

He felt the aircraft plummeting.

Must be trying to get back to three hundred feet above the ground.

He called into the intercom. "Why are we so high?"

"We're not," Rob May's clipped voice responded.

The aircraft continued down.

Millie grabbed the desk to steady himself.

"What?" he shouted, urgently needing clarification. If they weren't really at nine hundred feet but the jet thought they were, it would try and descend into the...

"What's happening, Rob?" Millie shouted. He glanced at Steve Bright, who stared back at him.

Millie's eyes darted back to the range reading.

803.

"What's going on, Rob? How high are we, for god's sake?"

He needed to know what the picture looked like outside.

"Rob?"

Eventually, Rob replied. "About one hundred feet."

Millie looked back at the reading.

749.

"*Talk to me, Millie.*" Rob shouted.

"Christ, it's gone wrong. Cancel. *CANCEL.*"

They were under instruction not to intervene with Guiding Light unless absolutely necessary. But surely they were about to die unless they took control?

Sweat dripped from Millie's forehead. Why was Guiding Light suddenly blind? Why was the laser looking straight through solid rock?

In the back, they felt a lurch as the autopilot disengaged.

Millie sensed the angle change as the nose raised, but he knew the momentum of the heavy aircraft was still downward.

He looked over his shoulder and stared up into the cockpit; the curtain was pulled open by the g-force.

Millie saw Brian Hill's hands move down to the yellow and black ejection seat cord.

"Oh, shit."

Ejection was only an option for the two pilots. Millie and Bright had no chance of getting out alive at this height.

He closed his eyes and braced for death.

The aircraft continued to sink.

Is this it?

He thought of Georgina, beautiful Georgina. And Charlie. Where was he right now? In a maths lecture, probably. Oblivious to the enormity of the moment.

The aircraft shuddered.

It was almost imperceptible, but the plane's momentum switched from a descending path to a climbing one.

He opened his eyes and looked around again, in time to see Hill release his grip on the cord.

Hill suddenly pointed forward and shouted. "*Trees.*"

The aircraft rolled right and Millie was pinned to his seat as the engines surged to full throttle and Rob May threw them into a spectacular powered, turning climb.

Vibrations rumbled through the fuselage as the engines screamed; the aircraft complaining and creaking under the stress.

Millie groaned as the g-force gripped him, pushing him down into his seat.

They held the gravity-defying manoeuvre for a few seconds, until the wings levelled.

Millie let out a long breath he hadn't realised he'd been holding in.

He looked across at Steve Bright, the nav's eyes bulging wide above his mask.

The throttles eased back and the aircraft settled.

It seemed like a full minute before anyone spoke.

Eventually, the silence was broken by the normally unflappable Brian Hill.

"Jesus Christ."

Millie's eyes rested on the tape data recorder.

It was switched off and empty. Whatever just happened, it had happened after he'd stopped recording the height readings from Guiding Light.

He realised he needed to write down what he'd seen with his own eyes, but he couldn't move.

Too much adrenaline in his system.

He settled his breathing and eventually fished out a pencil.

The system had taken them to within a whisker of a catastrophic crash. The all-singing, all-dancing laser had seen straight through solid earth and told the onboard computer to descend.

How it had happened was beyond him.

It was someone else's problem now. One of those clever boffins at DF Blackton in Cambridge would have some explaining to do.

He added a note to the end of his description of the event.

Guiding Light evaluation suspended.

———

WING COMMANDER MARK KILTON struggled with the acetate sheet. The image in the overhead projector was either upside down or back to front, and now it was out of focus and too large to fit the screen.

The tall and wide American lieutenant general took his seat at the table. "You fly jets better than you operate a projector, Kilton?"

Kilton offered Eugene Leivers III a thin smile and gave up with the projector. He took his own seat at the repurposed dining room table that had somehow found its way into the side office he'd commandeered for the meeting in the station headquarters building.

Paint peeled from the walls of the 1930s construction and the unseasonable heat of an English June made life uncomfortable for the five men in the room.

Leivers removed his jacket, replete with three rows of medal ribbons, and hung it on the back of his chair. He made a dismissive gesture with his hand toward the white screen intended to display Kilton's diagrams, and spoke with a Louisianan drawl.

"Forget it, Kilton. I know what Guiding Light does. What I need to know is, does it work?"

Kilton glared at him. "It works."

"Outstanding."

RAF Air Vice Marshal Richard Mannington stood up and opened the curtains. Kilton winced as daylight flooded in.

"Sunshine," said Mannington, "to illuminate a moment of British engineering triumph."

Kilton turned to the general. "Guiding Light is working and it will change everything."

A broad grin spread across Leivers's face. "Damn straight it will, Kilton." The general leaned forward and banged the table. "Gentlemen, I have to tell you, we've carried out some theoretical simulations using the information you've provided about Guiding Light, and the results have been phenomenal. *Phenomenal.*"

He took a deep breath, lowered his voice.

"What I'm about to tell you will never leave this room. Understood?"

The general's eyes darted between Kilton, Mannington and the two other men sitting at the table. They each gave a nod of acknowledgement.

"Terrain-following radar, the new technology we're both rushing to fit to our new jets, is dead."

"Dead?" Mannington asked.

"Dead, Dickie. The Russkies can detect it."

Kilton tried not to show his shock.

"But we're planning to fit TFR to everything," Mannington said. "The laser... Guiding Light. It's supposed to be a backup."

Leivers continued. "It just got promoted. Instead of helping our boys get in and out of the badlands, TFR will do the opposite. Every Russkie SAM from Berlin to Vladivostok will lock on and blow them out of the sky. They may as well be flying with floodlights and a big arrow that says *SHOOT HERE*. Damn shame."

Kilton inhaled. "Do the Russians know we know this?"

Leivers smiled at him. "No, Kilton. They do not. And neither do they know about Guiding Light. Your silent laser solves a very big headache at just the right time. This goes all the way up the line. And I mean all the way. This is not about winning World War Three. It's about preventing it. Once we have an unassailable advantage over the Reds, it's game over for them." He leaned back and spoke a little more slowly. "And that's why I've got POTUS's attention on this one."

Mannington turned a pencil over in his hands. "What's *Potus*?"

"POTUS is the President of the United States, Dickie."

Minister of State David Buttler cleared his throat. "General. The United Kingdom is not putting Guiding Light on a shelf for sale to all comers."

Leivers balked. "All comers? I thought we had a special relationship, Mr Buttler."

"Of course we have a special relationship, General. But we must remember that Guiding Light is a system that gives us all an advantage only so long as the enemy remains oblivious to its existence. At least until it's fitted to the fleets."

"You don't trust the US to keep a secret?"

"Britain trusts America implicitly. It's just that the chances of the secret getting out are simply higher the more people know about it. How many aircraft are you considering it for?"

The general shrugged. "Two thousand to start with."

Ewan Stafford appeared nonchalant, but Kilton knew him of old and knew damn well the short, tubby managing director was doing cartwheels inside.

"And what else?"

"Excuse me?" said Leivers, tilting his head to one side.

Buttler spoke with patient clarity. "The order for Guiding Light would be substantial, and I'm sure our colleague here from DF Blackton is doing his best not to burst into song. But we'd like to know that our most secret military breakthroughs can be shared both ways."

The general shrugged again. "Well, that's a little beyond my powers, Minister."

"But not beyond the powers of POTUS, I assume?"

"Well, no—"

"And you have POTUS's attention on this?"

The general thought for a moment. "Yes, sir. I do. And I dare say there will be some good deals for both of us in the pipeline. But this is something to discuss when we're ready to talk turkey. So far, we haven't seen this thing working."

Kilton felt the eyes swing back to him.

Stafford spoke up. "Perhaps Mark could give us all an update on the trial work his team have been carrying out for a while now. A very long while."

"As you're aware, Mr Stafford, the Royal Air Force Test Flying Unit will be the sole and final arbiter of Guiding Light's operational effectiveness. We have a detailed trial timetable and it is being executed even as we speak. The two working Guiding Light systems have been fitted to a Vulcan and a Canberra. The Vulcan is airborne at this moment with a TFU crew." He glanced at his RAF issue pilot's watch. "We've flown one hundred and ninety-four hours as of this morning."

"And no problems?" said Leivers.

"No. We're still a few weeks from sign-off. We did agree three hundred hours of intensive airborne time. You want to fit this to two thousand jets and we want to equip more or less our entire Bomber Command fleet. I think it's in all our interests that it's working as advertised."

"Fine," said Stafford. "But I need not remind the room that the longer we wait, the more chance there is of a leak."

Kilton ignored him and turned to General Leivers. "You're sitting in the United Kingdom's most secure RAF station. As long as the project remains under wraps here, there is no scenario where it's rendered ineffective. The Soviets will have no clue what it is or how to defend against it. And when it's operational, and it will become operational soon, NATO jets will for the first time be able to operate deep into Russian territory without giving off any radar energy what-soever. At low-level we will be invisible."

Leivers clapped his hands together and beamed. "That's what we're doing this for. Kilton, you deliver this system and it's not just Mr Stafford's accountant you're gonna make happy. We are gonna be friends for a long time."

"Excellent, Mark," said Buttler. "Very good work from TFU. This won't be forgotten."

General Leivers' hand appeared at Kilton's shoulder. The man from Baton Rouge leaned in close and whispered loud enough for all to hear. "I've dedicated my life to defeating communism, boy. It's a nasty, lethal plague and you, my friend, have its final demise in your hands. Don't let me down."

Kilton nodded. "General Leivers, you have my word."

———

THE MEETING BROKE UP. Kilton reminded the room that they allowed no papers relating to Guiding Light to leave West Porton. The men obliged by pooling their briefing notes into a single pile for him to deliver to TFU's secure cabinets.

Leivers looked suitably impressed with the emphasis on security. "You really do run a secret operation here, don't you, Kilton?"

The air vice marshal cut in before Kilton could answer. "You'd be forgiven for thinking there's no station here at all. At Group we call West Porton RAF Hidden."

"Then I'd suggest we're doing our job properly," said Kilton.

Leivers disappeared out of the room.

Mannington turned to Kilton. "What's that American expression you used once, Mark? *Need to know.* I suppose you think your superiors don't need to know anything."

Kilton continued to shuffle the papers into a brown folder.

"We do need to know something, Mark," Mannington continued. "There is still a chain of command. Just keep that in mind, please."

He walked out of the room; Ewan Stafford followed close behind, offering a tip of his hat before he placed it on his head.

The minister paused for a moment, allowing the others to move out of earshot.

"That was impressive, Mark."

"I thought the same of you, sir. Quite the card player."

The minister smiled and clicked his briefcase shut.

"You realise this project cannot fail. After the mess of TSR-2, we need this victory. Having to cancel a high profile fighter-bomber project was embarrassing to say the least. Guiding Light needs to be a success. As I said, it won't go unrewarded. The PM's always on the lookout for reliable men in the upper echelons of the military. You deliver Guiding Light, we authorise Blackton's sale to the Americans. That's an extremely welcome injection of cash just when we need it. A winning scenario for all of us."

Kilton looked out of the window where Mannington was helping Leivers into his staff car. Buttler followed his gaze.

"And we'll make sure the Americans know who it was who delivered this project. But Mark, if we have another debacle, particularly a leak from TFU, then it's going to be very hard to justify the existence of this unit you've created. You're already ruffling feathers with the RAF brass as it is."

"There will be no leak from here, but I don't like information going up the line to Group." He nodded toward the receding staff car outside. "I start to lose control of who knows what, and that's when it can get leaky."

"I understand. So, how can I help?"

Kilton looked at him. "Allow me to report direct to you, direct to the Air Ministry and cut out Group and the RAF Main Building."

"You realise what you're asking? The men with gold braid on their shoulders won't be happy."

Kilton thought for a moment and shrugged.

Buttler smiled. "I can talk to the PM. I think he'll see the benefit of such an arrangement. Between you and me, he believes most of the RAF now hate him for ending TSR-2."

"They do," Kilton answered quickly. "But then they're mostly old romantics who think we're stuck in the 1940s. Some of us exist in the real world."

"They're a powerful bunch, those old romantics as you call them. Your head's above the parapet now Mark." The minister walked to the door. "You'll find your life was a lot less complex in 1940, shooting down the Luftwaffe and staying alive for another day. I'll talk to the PM. I think we can probably agree you report direct to the Ministry for now. Keeping in tight in the name of secrecy. It would be a tragedy for all if this project failed before that deal was signed."

The minister's heels made a clicking noise on the hard floor as he disappeared, leaving Kilton alone with a brown envelope filled with papers and stamped *TOP SECRET*.

————

MILLIE REACHED FORWARD and flipped a switch marked *DATA PANEL ELEC*. The orange numbers presented by the Guiding Light system went dark as the electrical supply was cut off.

He tucked his flight case back under the navigator station and secured it with a bungee cord. Inside were the four reels of magnetic tape he had filled with height data, recording the flight at low-level. He thought four would be enough to cover the run, but he missed the last couple of minutes, which included the moment when the system went haywire.

But it wouldn't matter, since there were four men on board, and they could describe what happened accurately between them.

The aircraft's wings rolled and he felt the g-force increase, pressing him into his seat. But it was gentle; Rob was guiding the delta-winged jet smoothly onto finals for RAF West Porton. It was a flying style that matched his nature.

A moment later, with a squeal of rubber beneath them, they were down.

Once the aircraft came to a stop at the end of a brief taxi, Steve Bright was quickly out of his seat and opening the hatch. Millie stayed put, but watched as the nav extended the yellow ladder.

It was a warm June day. Millie removed his helmet and oxygen mask, and ran a gloved hand through what was left of his sweaty grey hair, now matted to his head.

Eventually, Brian Hill pulled aside the curtain, looking haggard. He nodded at Millie but said nothing as he descended the steps.

Rob was behind him. Millie winced at the sight of his reddened face with pronounced stress lines, squashed into the helmet.

He looked like a man in his forties, rather than a fresh faced twenty-nine-year-old.

"You OK?"

Rob looked serious. He nodded and continued down the ladder. Millie picked up his case and followed him out, feeling for the metal rungs below him. Everything seemed to take more time these days.

He felt Rob's hand on his back, giving him some help as he concentrated on jumping backwards the last couple of feet below the bottom rung. He landed and wobbled in his cumbersome flying boots, grateful for the support of his friend.

"They didn't make this thing with fifty-four-year-olds in mind," he said, relieved to see Rob smile back at him.

As they turned and walked toward the TFU hangar and offices, Millie instinctively rested a hand on Rob's shoulder.

"You did well. You saved us and the jet."

"I don't know if I did do well, Millie. I was slow to react. You had to shout at me." Rob paused and glanced back at the Vulcan: pristine white, hunched on its landing gear. "I nearly lost it."

"We've been told not to interfere unless absolutely necessary and we've logged, what, nearly two hundred hours? All your experience was working against you. But you got there."

Rob kept glancing back at the aircraft. "It can be overwhelming if I stop to think about it. The jets are large, new, colossally expensive. Three crew members I'm responsible for."

"It's a lot for a youngster, isn't it?" Millie smiled at him. "Look. You did well today. You acted in time, and frankly that's all that matters. Think it through. If you feel you could have done better, work out why and learn. But it's always going to feel messy when things go wrong, Rob. And boy did they go wrong."

"It did go wrong, didn't it? What happened?"

"The laser saw straight through the ground, or at least the computer misinterpreted the feed. Either way, it commanded the autopilot to descend as if we were nine hundred feet not three hundred."

"Can we ever trust it again?"

Millie scoffed. "Not until what happened today is completely and utterly understood and the problem solved."

They carried on into TFU, where they drank tea and didn't discuss the incident with anyone. That was the TFU way. Mark Kilton had made it clear that you only discussed projects with those who needed to know.

But Millie could tell by their colleagues' glances that they knew something was up.

It was such an odd way of operating. In any normal squadron they would be sharing their tale, getting it off their chest, drawing comfort from the looks of horror and empathy from their friends.

But not at Mark Kilton's Test Flying Unit.

After handing in their flying equipment and coveralls, Millie ushered the crew into a side office to debrief.

Once the door was shut, Brian Hill led the questions, all aimed at Millie as the project leader and the man most familiar with the inner workings of Guiding Light.

Millie looked at his hastily scrawled notes.

"I happened to be rotating the selector, checking our general position. When I switched it back to number one position, it showed nine hundred odd feet below us."

"Nine hundred? Christ, Millie, we were still at three hundred," Hill said. "So that's why Guiding Light dived us toward the ground. It couldn't see it."

Millie shook his head in bewilderment. "I suppose it was doing what we asked it to do. Fly us at three hundred feet. It was just trying to get us back down."

"It chose a perfect time to go blind," said Brian Hill. "A state of the art, one hundred thousand-pound system descending a four engine Vulcan jet bomber with four people on board into the Welsh rock? Someone, somewhere better get the sack."

Millie took out the chart and with Steve Bright's help, they did their best to draw the aircraft's track along the valley, marking the spot with an *X* where it had all gone wrong.

"And you definitely didn't have a tape running?" Rob asked Millie.

"No. I brought four tapes based on the low-level run time and I'd just finished the last one."

"Damn shame," Hill said. "The tapes record everything, don't they?"

"Erm, I think so," said Millie. "I've never seen what they do or don't record. They all go off to Cambridge for a mainframe computer to read. But it doesn't matter, does it? If we'd been in a standard fit Vulcan and the autopilot had misbehaved, we'd report it just like this." He motioned to the chart and notes on the table. "Just everyone write it down now while it's fresh and I'll speak with Kilton."

Hill laughed. "Good luck with that, old boy."

"He won't have a choice, Brian. We have to shut it down."

"I agree, chap. But all the same, good luck."

Millie folded up the chart and gathered the notes.

Hill stood up to his full six feet four inches and put his arms around Rob and Steve Bright.

"You know what I need?"

Rob tilted his head. "Does it have something to do with the mess bar?"

"Exactly. Beer. I need beer and I need drinking companions. I've had enough of this malarkey for one day." He led the two younger men out of the room.

"I'll secure the paperwork," Millie said to the empty room.

———

THERE WAS a short queue at the NAAFI shop as Millie picked up a packet of John Player No. 6. Five minutes later, he pushed open the door to the mess bar to discover the usual crowd of men, back in uniform but looking a little dishevelled from the day's airborne activities.

Beers in hand, cigarettes in mouth; tales of flying and smoke filled the air.

Brian Hill, Steve Bright and another TFU pilot, Jock MacLeish, stood by one of the pillars in the middle of the room. Millie went to the bar first, where the white-coated steward was already pouring a scotch.

"I've been here too long," he said as he took the tumbler.

When he arrived at the pillar, Hill was speaking, and he caught the tail-end.

"... anyway, it was damn close."

Millie opened his new packet of cigarettes and screwed up the flap of silver paper folded over the filter ends. He offered the pack around, and Hill leaned forward to take one. When they were close, Millie spoke quietly.

"I hope you're not being indiscreet, Brian?"

Hill shrugged, and tapped his cigarette on the drinks shelf surrounding the pillar.

"We can trust old MacLeish. He's Scottish. The most trustworthy of the Celts, I believe."

"That may be," Millie continued, more quietly than Hill, "but he doesn't need to know."

Hill snorted at the incongruous use of Kilton's new buzz phrase, but Millie continued to look at him, waiting. Eventually, Hill gave a resigned look and nodded in acknowledgement.

In the awkward silence that followed, Millie drained half the measure of scotch, savouring the smoky flavour. The alcohol dulled his senses; it felt good.

He scanned the room, looking for Rob. The bar was filling up quickly as officers came off duty from various parts of the station: air traffickers in one corner, station adminners in another.

An ageing man with sunken eyes raised his glass. Millie lifted his tumbler in return, nodding at JR, a pilot with 206 Maintenance Unit, an unglamorous outfit nestled in the far corner of the airfield.

The rest of the room was TFU. Loud, brash, elite. His colleagues occupied the bar and most tables. What would it have been like thirteen months ago, with 206 MU as the sole flying unit? Rather nice, he suspected, and he suddenly felt a pang of jealousy for aircrew whose only task was the final flight of retired aircraft.

Finally his eyes landed on Rob. He was nestled among the elite of the elite: the chosen few senior test pilots, grouped at one end of the bar.

Millie raised an eyebrow and looked at Brian Hill.

"How did Rob end up over there?"

Hill glanced over. "Ah, the big boys came and took him before you got here, I'm afraid".

Millie studied Rob. On one side of him was Red Brunson, an American on exchange from Edwards. Glamorous and larger than life, he flew with his own grey 'flight suit' as he called it, and a fancy helmet complete with mirrored visor. He looked like an Apollo astronaut.

At the other side was Speedy Johnson, a legend to every schoolboy in the 1940s and 1950s. Kept breaking speed records for the RAF as the jet age blossomed.

"You can't blame him," Hill said and it took Millie a moment to notice he was being spoken to.

"Huh?"

"You can't blame Rob, having his head turned by that lot. He's a promising test pilot."

"Let's hope they don't corrupt him," Millie eventually said.

A round of drinks arrived; as Millie reached for his next glass of scotch, he noticed a ripple of movement across the room.

Mark Kilton had arrived.

This precipitated a stiffening of backs and subconscious opening of groups, hoping he would join them.

Kilton inevitably moved in to drink with the set crowded at the bar. Rob smiled at Kilton, who slapped him on the back.

The room was now heaving. Thick smoke hung in the air, and the heat of the day was making it uncomfortable.

Millie glanced at his watch. Six already. Georgina and Mary would be waiting for him and Rob, impatient to eat and get on with the card game.

He drained his glass, said his goodbyes, and approached the group at the bar. Red Brunson gave him a friendly slap on the shoulder as he arrived. Speedy Johnson exclaimed, "Ah, Milford. Come to talk to us about data?"

The group laughed.

"Well, someone has to look after the computers that are replacing you lot."

This provoked some mock booing from the pilots.

On a whim, he turned to Kilton.

"Boss, can I have a word, please?"

Kilton nodded and they moved off to a corner near the mess piano.

"I was going to brief you tomorrow, and I will, but I thought I should let you know. Guiding Light failed today."

Kilton's expression didn't change at first. Then he looked puzzled. "What do you mean, 'failed'?"

"It went blind, at three hundred feet and three hundred knots, in Wales."

"Blind?"

"Suddenly we were descending. I happened to be looking at the panel at the time. The laser thought there was nine hundred below us. In reality we were still at three hundred."

"So you cancelled?"

"It took a moment for us all to adjust to what was happening, but yes, Rob did a good job and intervened in time. Just."

"Just? How close did you get?"

Millie paused and took a breath. "The tape wasn't running, so I can't be certain."

"You don't have any record of it?"

"I made some notes, but no, the tapes were used up at that point. It was the end of the run."

Kilton stayed silent, studying Millie, making him shift on his feet.

"Anyway, we've no option, boss, but to ground Guiding Light until Blackton can identify the issue and see if they can rectify it. If they can rectify it, I'd suggest we start the trial from scratch."

A flash of anger crossed Kilton's face and Millie took half a step back.

"And you don't think you're making too much of this, Millie, as usual?"

"I'm sorry? With respect, boss, it nearly killed us."

Kilton shook his head. "Put it all in writing and drop it on my desk tomorrow morning." He made to leave, but then turned. "And no discussion with anyone."

Millie nodded. "Of course, boss."

He watched as Kilton joined Brian Hill and Jock MacLeish, rather than go back to the bar group.

Millie went back to the bar and tugged Rob on the shoulder.

"We'd best be getting back, young man. The wives will be waiting for their card game."

"Oh no! Rob's dad's here to pick him up," said Johnson. "Ooh, please, Rob's dad. Can he stay for just one more drink?"

Rob looked at his newly presented pint.

"I might just have this first, Millie. I'll see you at yours later."

———

THE RUSTING WHEELS of Millie's ten-year-old Rover complained as he scraped the kerb outside his married quarter.

"And that's why I'm not a pilot," he reminded himself, clambering out and into the warm June evening.

The sound of laughing women drifted from the back garden as he made his way down the side passage.

Georgina and Mary sat in two tatty garden chairs. Summer dresses, floppy hats, and what looked like gin and tonics in hand. Georgina in her favoured red, Mary in yellow. Millie stood and watched for a moment.

"Darling!" Georgina shouted when she spotted him. "Whatever are you doing lurking in the shadows?"

Millie set down his flight case just inside the open French doors and picked up a third garden chair.

"Just admiring the local beauty."

"Peeping Tom, more like." Georgina lifted herself and kissed him hello. "Drink? scotch?"

"Do we have any ice?"

Georgina thought for a moment. "I don't think so, but I'll see if I can pull something off the inside of the freezer if you like."

"Needs must."

Millie's relief at being home must have shown in his eyes, as Georgina loitered for a moment.

"Everything OK?"

He tried not to glance at Mary; this wasn't the time to say anything about the incident. It was up to Rob and every member of aircrew what they shared with their wives.

"Yes, fine. Just tired."

Georgina looked unconvinced, but then disappeared into the house.

"Well," Millie said turning to Mary, "I thought you might be missing us, but apparently not."

Mary laughed. "The heatwave is so gorgeous. It's just nice to be in the sun."

"No cards tonight?"

"Well, we need four for cards. Did Rob go home to change?"

"Actually, he was still in the bar when I left. I expect he'll be along later."

"Fine, well we can enjoy the evening sun, the three of us." She leant back in her chair and closed her eyes, her shoulder-length brown hair gently shifting in the breeze. Millie smiled at her; so young and pretty and with an up and coming test pilot by her side.

He felt a twinge of jealousy as he recalled the time after the war when he was promoted, and he and Georgina were considered the young ones.

The three of them ate outdoors and remained there in the last of the warmth; it was unusual for it to last so long into the evening.

The Milfords' grandfather clock tolled, its gentle clangs seeping out of the house through the open doors and windows. Ten bells. It was apparent Rob would not be appearing that evening. He was either still in the mess or had headed home, worse for wear.

Millie walked Mary back to their married quarter, two streets away in Trenchard Close.

The house was dark.

"Not here, either." She turned to Millie. "Has my husband forgone us for some new drinking pals?"

"I fear so. We all need to let our hair down every now and again."

She looked thoughtful for a moment. "Yes, of course. A bit rude as we had cards planned. Sorry, Millie."

"Think nothing of it," he said and they kissed their goodbyes on the cheek. "I'm sure he'll be back presently."

Millie sauntered home. Had he missed anything important in the bar of the officers' mess?

It was nagging at him, the brief exchange with Kilton.

Making a bit much of this... Bloody silly thing to say.

He thought of Kilton going over to Brian Hill as he was leaving.

Were they discussing the Guiding Light situation without him?

He looked up as he approached the house and saw Georgina in the kitchen looking at him. He gave a little wave and pushed open the front door.

She was at the sink, apron on, finishing the washing up.

"Let me help you," he said, and he picked up a drying up cloth.

"Thanks. You know what I thought watching you waddle back home?"

"How handsome I look?"

"Yes, obviously, but also how porky you look. You need to lose some weight, mister." She poked him in his side.

"I know, but it's so tedious exercising and, god forbid, dieting."

Georgina stopped washing up. "What happened today?"

Millie smiled. "I can't hide anything from you, can I?"

"Nope."

Millie shrugged and spoke as casually as he could.

"We had a little moment in the air."

"Oh, god." Georgina pulled off her yellow rubber gloves. "Tell me."

"It's fine, it's fine. Everyone's OK. It was just a moment. Briefly scary, but we got out of it and that's all that matters. Actually, Rob was flying and did a sterling job."

"Rob was flying? Is that why he isn't here tonight."

"I think so. Letting off some steam in the mess."

"Fair enough. Did you say anything to Mary?"

"No. That's up to Rob. Everyone's different."

"Can you tell me what happened?"

Millie thought for a moment. "Not really. Sorry."

She reached forward and put her hands on his cheeks. "It doesn't matter. I'm glad you're safe, Squadron Leader Milford."

They kissed and he welled up, the near-death experience catching up with him.

He'd seen it in others: a delayed reaction.

Georgina didn't seem to notice. She released him and walked over to their wall calendar, pinned to a cork board over the table.

"I nearly counted the days today. It's something like one hundred and twenty. She lifted the pages until October showed.

"I'm sorry, what?"

Her finger rested on October 19th. "This is the day, isn't it? October 19th. Your last day in the RAF."

"Ah. Yes."

She let the pages of the calendar fall back down.

"One hundred and twenty days, Millie, that's it. All I ask is that you remain in one piece. OK?"

He laughed. "I promise. Believe me, I'm looking forward to it as much as you are."

"Are you?"

"Yes, of course. I'm going to take up sailing, remember? I'm sure the RAF pension can stretch to the Lee-on-Solent place we saw. Just."

She tilted her head, appraising him. "Good. It'll be fine, Millie. We'll still see all our friends, wherever they get posted."

Millie finished the drying up. Georgina disappeared and reappeared with a tumbler of whisky.

He sat down at the kitchen table and lifted it to his nose.

"Ah, the Glenfiddich."

"Well, I think you need a treat. And it's the posh tumbler, the wedding set. Last one standing."

"The last one? We started with eight."

She smiled. "All things must pass, Millie. Anyway, the attrition rate for glasses in married quarter is pretty high. We've had some pretty wild nights over the years. I think we must have lost three of them in Hong Kong playing that silly game with the cricket ball."

Millie laughed at the memory. "Test Match Sofa was a brilliant game. I was quite the slip catcher when positioned correctly near the piano."

"I'm sure you were, I'm sure you were."

She kissed him on the head and whispered, "I'm glad you're home, Squadron Leader Milford."

He squeezed her hand and smiled up at her.

"Don't worry, our retirement is safe. I'll be getting under your feet every day before you know it."

"Good." She smiled back and headed upstairs, turning off the hall light.

The kitchen light was dim; the midsummer sun had finally set. Orange sodium light from the street lamps filled the window. Millie turned the tumbler over in his hand and let the light glint off it. A beautiful piece of crystal. Such a shame they'd lost the others. But maybe it was a price worth paying for the fun they'd had.

He made a mental note to ensure this tumbler survived into retirement. Something to drink from and remember the glory days.

He drained the glass, suddenly remembering his morning appointment. Nobody came away from a Mark Kilton encounter without bruises.

———

A DRUNKEN TEST pilot played the piano, badly. Rob laughed, still huddled in among the senior pilots.

Kilton watched from the bar, as the pianist beckoned the men around Rob to join in with the song. Most of them sprung up, but Rob remained in his seat, enjoying the show.

The TFU boss picked up his drink and made his way over, choosing the vacant space next to his young prodigy.

"I've been thinking about this nonsense in the Vulcan. I don't think we can let a single uncorroborated incident derail an internationally important project."

He studied Rob, who nodded slowly.

"Its strategic importance cannot be underestimated, you understand that don't you, May?"

The music grew raucous as the men sang a bad version of Cliff Richard's 'Livin' Doll'.

Rob nodded again, staying silent.

Kilton had to raise his voice above the singing.

"Don't you think there was a chance you could have overridden the autopilot with the stick?" Rob furrowed his brow, but Kilton continued. "It won't disengage if you touch the stick. The computer will fight you for a bit until you let go."

"I didn't grab the stick until we cancelled," he finally said.

"Maybe not grabbed it, but it's a tight space, and you may have gently leaned on it or subconsciously pushed it forward while monitoring the flight. You wouldn't have been the first to do that, May."

Rob pondered.

"I mean," Kilton continued, "it would be enormously helpful to me personally to hear that there might be some other explanation. And it's possible. Isn't it, May? You might have accidentally nudged it. That's all it would take at that speed and height to cause a scare."

Rob bowed his head.

"You're not in trouble, May. This is what testing is all about. Now we know how she'll react." He paused and spoke slowly. "It's important you agree that you may have nudged it."

Rob's head came back up and he turned to look at the boss. Kilton gave a small nod of encouragement.

"I suppose it's always possible."

2

WEDNESDAY 8TH JUNE

M illie's burgundy Rover was a luxury car in 1951. Fifteen years later, life had taken its toll. The leather seats were scratched and torn in places, and adorned with occasional strips of black tape from his own running repairs. But it was comfortable, if a little tank-like in its handling. Either way, thanks to a misjudged pension investment and with retirement looming, Millie had little choice but to run it into the ground.

It rolled, rather than turned around corners. It creaked on the worn springs as he guided it along the narrow country road toward the RAF West Porton main gate.

He struggled with the stiff window handle but managed to wind it down enough to pass his identification card to the security guard.

The man in the strange West Porton Security Police cap studied the card carefully. The WPSP were a branch of the military police that appeared unique to this station, as far as Millie knew. He also knew questions about security arrangements were not encouraged.

The sound of jet engines drifted into the car over the breeze. Engine runs after maintenance. Hard working engineers, toiling all hours to ensure Mark Kilton's TFU got a full complement of aircraft to play with every day.

The guard handed back the card, and Millie encouraged the heavy car to leave its moorings and continue on to TFU.

It was quiet in the planning room: no laughter, no excited chatter, just a few murmurs from the men at the tea bar.

He knew something was up and it could be only one thing.

Mark Kilton was in a temper.

He made his way over in search of information.

"Anything I should know about?" he asked Jock MacLeish, looking toward Kilton's side office. The door had a glass pane and there was some movement within.

"Drama in the bar last night," replied Jock in his soft Scottish lilt. "Never seen Kilton quite like it. He and Brian Hill at it full steam."

"What was it about?" Millie asked, fearing he already knew the answer.

"Don't know, as is the TFU way. They ended up in the car park. Obviously we all dived into the anteroom and tried to eavesdrop. All I can say is they had a fundamental disagreement about something. Hammer and tongs, they were."

"The car park? It was physical?"

"Nearly." MacLeish paused and had another look around. "Rumour has it, Brian's gone."

"What? Gone?"

MacLeish shrugged his shoulders. "That's what I've heard. Gone. *Persona non grata.* No longer a serving member of TFU. Went too far with the boss and was shot before dawn, or at least turned away from the main gate and told to await his posting orders."

Millie stared towards Kilton's office.

"Where was Rob in all this?"

"With us. Why?"

"He wasn't involved in the row?"

"Nope."

"*Milford.* In here." A shout from across the room.

Millie exchanged a brief look with MacLeish before heading to Kilton's office; the boss had already disappeared inside after barking his summons.

Just as he got to the door, Rob arrived in the planning room.

"Are you OK?" Millie mouthed.

Rob nodded, but looked worried.

Millie shut the office door behind him and stood waiting while Kilton finished a memo with his black-inked fountain pen. Millie could just about make out Brian Hill's name in the subject heading.

Kilton slashed out the words with short, sharp strokes.

Millie looked through the glass pane in the door; a few faces stared back. Everyone on tenterhooks.

Finally, the TFU boss looked up.

"This nonsense from yesterday is dealt with."

"Nonsense, boss?"

Kilton leaned back and deposited the fountain pen on his desk. "Your attempt to ground the most important military project on the planet with an unrecorded and unproven incident is not appreciated."

An image of Brian Hill's car being pulled over at the security gate filled his mind.

"There were four of us on the jet, sir. I may not have been capturing data but I made notes and each of the other men will corroborate what happened."

Kilton folded the memorandum and placed it in an envelope.

"There are now three of you. Hill overstepped the mark last night and I consider him unstable and unfit to fly."

"Because he argued with you?"

"It wasn't an argument, Millie. He stepped out of line. Whatever happened during flying, it had unnerved him to the point that he was refusing to fly and I don't need pilots who won't fly."

"With respect, sir, was he refusing to fly or simply refusing to fly with Guiding Light?"

"It makes no difference. There's no place for pilots who want to be selective about the trials they carry out."

"With respect, sir, I still believe what I saw. The system fouled up, height readings displayed on the panel were incorrect and it placed the aircraft in a hazardous descent..." Kilton opened his mouth to counter him, but Millie pressed on. "And you are right. I didn't record it and I suppose it's true to say there is no firm evidence. But I've been thinking about this. What if it happened before, and we didn't notice? What if we were at altitude and thought it was turbulence? Or maybe it happened before we had even started engaging Guiding Light with the autopilot? Unless someone was physically watching the entire time, we may easily have missed a similar event."

"Speculation, Millie. Not hard facts."

"But it's out there, isn't it?" Millie pointed to the planning room.

"What's out there? What are you talking about?"

"The tapes. All the tapes we've filled with readings from Guiding Light. Including hours of it before we even connected it to the autopilot. If there's something wrong, it'll be buried in there. We just have to look carefully."

"We don't need invisible numbers on a tape to tell us how an aircraft flies."

"With respect, sir—"

"Stop saying 'with respect'. I have no time for this. Guiding Light trials will continue unabated. If you are refusing to fly with it, then you are free to leave. Retire early for all I care."

Millie's mouth fell open.

He shook off the shock and gathered his thoughts.

"I don't understand, Mark. We're test crews. We're supposed to evaluate in a sober and unbiased fashion and report results. You're asking us to ignore the results?"

"What results, Millie? You forgot to run the tape, remember?"

"I didn't forget. We'd come to the end of the low-level section and I assessed it wasn't worth loading a new tape at that point. It was unfortunate."

"Yes, well, the evidence we do have is of an effective and functioning piece of equipment. If you have any further issues, you are free to bring them up at the project meeting on Thursday."

"I'd recommend we suspend the flying until then, boss."

Kilton snapped forward on his chair. "*No*. Millie. Aren't you listening to me? You will fly the hours as laid out in the trial."

"I'm sorry, Mark. I'm going to say this again, but with respect, you have no alternative explanation for what happened."

"Not true—"

"What was it, then?" Millie interrupted him.

Kilton ignored him. "You've flown more Guiding Light hours than anyone else, Millie. You know it's safe. We can discuss yesterday's events, along with all the reporting, on Thursday. In the meantime, we continue. Is that clear?"

Millie left the room.

As he made his way between the planning desks, he looked at the security cabinets that contained the hours of height readings from previous Guiding Light flights. In the early days of the project, he remembered seeing large green-lined sheets of paper from a computer. The readings from the tape turned into lines of small, typed numbers. Just a few minutes flying filled up a dozen sheets.

Poring through them would be a superhuman task.

He arrived back at the tea bar.

"Everything OK?" Rob asked.

"Mr Kilton doesn't believe there's anything wrong with Guiding Light."

"Yes," Rob said with a nod. "I got that impression last night."

Millie drummed his fingers on the bar. He beckoned Rob away from other ears. They stood by the window, looking out onto the pan. The white Vulcan from yesterday's flight was being towed out of the hangar.

"Look, I can't change his mind today. He's ordering us to continue flying. But Thursday's meeting is crucial. He's got some other explanation for the incident but wouldn't say any more." He looked at Rob. "You and I need to be crystal clear about what happened. Write down your account. I'll get Brighty to do the same. You've heard about Brian Hill?"

Rob paused and spoke quietly. "Yes, I was there, but Millie..."

A corporal approached.

"Look," said Millie. "It's just us now Rob. What we say matters more than ever. We need to stick together."

"I think I should—" Rob started, but the corporal was nearly upon them and Millie cut him off.

"Don't worry, it'll be fine. I've got your back, Rob." He accepted the tasking sheet.

In the project box were the words 'Guiding Light Low-Level Phase III'.

"Here we go, that didn't take long." Millie looked across to the waiting jet.

He checked the crew list.

May (Captain)
Johnson (Co-Pilot)
Milford (AEO)
Bright (NAV)

"Speedy Johnson," he said looking at Rob, "one of Kilton's gang."

"Gentlemen. What a privilege. Time to let an old fart in on the big secret." Johnson had appeared next to them, out of nowhere.

Millie turned to look across at Kilton's office. The TFU commanding officer stood in the doorway, watching.

————

KILTON RETREATED into his office and closed the door behind him. He picked up the green telephone on his desk and dialled the operator.

"Ewan Stafford, please. DF Blackton in Cambridge."

He doodled on his blotting pad while he waited to be put through.

He'd been a fighter pilot long enough to know that he had to take care of all the angles.

It was the one you never saw that got you.

"Good morning, Mark." Stafford sounded chipper.

"What do I need to know about Guiding Light that you haven't told me?"

The briefest of hesitations.

"What do you mean?" said Stafford.

"One of my crews is complaining that it nearly killed them yester-day. Are they overreacting?" Another hesitation. "Christ, Stafford. What do you know about this?"

"What happened?" the Blackton MD asked in a low voice.

"It tried to descend them into the ground in Wales, apparently, and now a couple of the girls have got their knickers in a twist. Something we could do without. What are you keeping from me?"

"I don't know, Mark. Can we look at the data?"

"Apparently not. Christopher Milford failed to record it. Which is the only good news."

"Good news?"

"Stafford, do you understand what's going on here? We stall the project now, we lose it. Every bloody day we get one step closer to the Soviets finding out. Too many people already know about it on our side and I don't trust half of them. Plus, I'm not sure you should trust the Americans, at least until they've paid for it. They're already trying to build their own version, you can bet on it."

"I'd like to see them try."

"Don't be naive. They would save themselves a fortune. And if they get close before the deal goes through, they'll drop the purchase in a flash. Downing Street is counting on that investment and they're counting on me to deliver it. The clock's ticking, Stafford, so no more bollocks from you please. Is there something I need to know?"

Stafford paused and then spoke so quietly, Kilton had to press the receiver to his ear to hear him.

"We haven't seen anything like this since early testing."

"Like what?"

"In the early days we got short bursts of incoherent data from the laser, but that was months ago and on our test rig. The problem went away."

"Apparently, it's back. What do we do to eliminate it, without stopping the project? We've got nearly two hundred hours of tapes here. Can you take a look to see if this has happened before? Millie thinks there may be something buried in the existing readings."

"He's right. The answer will be in there somewhere. Send them over and we'll take a look at them this week."

"This week? I'll send them in a car now and you'll bloody well look at them today."

"OK. And Mark, probably best to take some precautions, you know. Look after the men."

Kilton glanced into the planning room and saw May and Johnson hunched over a desk. "Leave that with me." He hung up. "Bloody sergeant pilots."

For a moment he tapped his pen on his desk, then got up and headed into the planning room and spoke quietly to May and Johnson.

"You can keep it above one thousand feet today if you want."

He started to turn back to his office.

"So, there is something wrong?" Millie said, just loud enough that Kilton couldn't ignore him.

Kilton turned on his heels and walked up to Millie. "No, but if you're scared, keep her above one thousand. And this time, try not to run out of tapes. It is, after all, your only job on board, Millie."

————

MILLIE STARED at the orange numbers. They updated rhythmically, clicking between one thousand, and one thousand one hundred. The descent into low-level had been tense, but at least they had a safety margin. Seven hundred feet higher than yesterday. Should be enough time to catch any sudden plunges.

He switched the dial and checked the other readings; everything looked normal.

He glanced at his stopwatch. Sixteen minutes since he'd loaded the first tape. Nearly time for a change.

Mustn't miss anything this time.

He felt the aircraft pitch nose down and his eyes flashed to the height reading. One thousand three hundred and twelve feet. He didn't blink until they levelled out just above one thousand.

It was just doing its job.

"Did we just go over a ridge?" he called up to the pilots.

"Affirm," Speedy Johnson replied.

They rocked in their seats as the jet banked, descended again, and levelled out. It was a bumpy ride even at one thousand feet, as Guiding Light still followed the contours of the ground below.

"The valley's coming up," Rob called over the intercom.

So they were nearly there, the place where it happened yesterday. It was a deliberate move to fly the same route, agreed by the entire crew, but at a safer height. If it happened again, this time Millie would have the evidence.

He looked at Steve Bright, who was unusually quiet. Bright looked back at him and Millie unlatched his oxygen mask, gave him a reassuring smile and mouthed, "It'll be alright".

He latched his mask again and when Brighty turned back to his screen, Millie stole a look at the hatch. Was it clear of obstacles? Would they get it open in time from one thousand feet?

Almost certainly not.

He went back to the Guiding Light panel and stared at the numbers.

The Vulcan was banked again by the system and Millie steadied himself.

"Here we go," called Rob.

Millie had a copy of the route on a chart clamped to his desk. The valley was relatively flat, which was another puzzling aspect to the laser's failure to read it accurately.

The numbers stayed steady, hovering between one thousand and ten, and one thousand and thirty. The system treated one thousand as a 'not below' mark and it was working well.

"We're through," Rob called. The aircraft rolled onto a new track and into another valley.

"There you go, fellas," said Speedy. "Nothing to worry about."

A few moments later Millie felt a jolt as Speedy disconnected the autopilot and took manual control, climbing them out of low-level.

Millie smiled to himself as Rob relayed instructions to his co-pilot.

The Vulcan climbed to nine thousand feet for the transit home. Rob switched off the oxygen and all four of them broke out the cigarettes.

As they swept into the circuit at West Porton, Speedy spoke over the intercom.

"Hello? We have visitors."

"What?" Millie asked, from their dark rear bay. They had a couple of small porthole windows but they were inconveniently high and pretty useless for looking out.

"You won't believe it, but some campers have set up in a field at the end of the runway."

"Inside the wire?" Bright asked.

"No, just outside."

Brighty laughed. "A nice quiet spot with four engine jets climbing out, fifteen inches outside your tent."

On the ground, after the shutdown, Millie again waited for Rob. He watched as Johnson hauled himself out of his seat and disappeared down the ladder.

Rob appeared and Millie extricated himself from the Vulcan.

As they walked back to TFU, Millie gave Rob a little pat on the back.

"Look at you, giving instructions to the famous Speedy Johnson."

Rob couldn't hide his smile. "Can't quite believe it."

"Well, believe it, Rob. You've earned it. Time to start believing what it says on your job description. Test pilot."

Rob smiled and they arrived back at TFU, the door wide open in an attempt to get some circulating air inside.

Millie climbed out of his suffocating flying coveralls.

By the time he looked up, Speedy and Rob were talking to Kilton in the doorway to his office.

Millie started to walk over, not wishing to miss another important conversation, but as he approached, Kilton gave Rob a pat on the back and the ad hoc meeting broke up.

———

MILLIE ATE a sandwich at his desk rather than join the others in the mess. He found a hot meal on a hot day too soporific.

At 2PM, the typist he'd ordered from the admin pool appeared. She was a smartly dressed middle-aged woman, in a floral pattern dress that reminded him of Georgina's wardrobe.

With no project material allowed out of TFU, they went into a side room. Millie watched while she typed up his handwritten account of yesterday's incident. He clarified the odd word in between the rhythmic clicks of the typewriter.

"Finished!" the woman announced, pulling the last sheet from the machine.

"Thank you." Millie scanned the final page. "Very good."

As she headed out, he made his way over toward the group of pilots. Rob was trying on Brunson's mirrored visor USAF flying helmet with others laughing at him.

Millie coughed to get his attention. "Can I have a quick chat?"

Rob leaned forward and wrestled the helmet from his head.

"Erm, about to go flying actually. Can it wait?"

"It'll be brief, I promise."

Rob followed him to a quiet corner.

Millie tapped his sheaf of papers. "Don't forget your report of what happened yesterday."

Rob nodded but said nothing.

"Try to make it as convincing as possible. Look, I've used the Board of Inquiry format."

"We should include everything?"

"Yes, absolutely."

"All possibilities?"

"Yes, I suppose so. But just make sure you describe what happened and what you saw. OK?"

"Sure."

"I know you're busy, but it is important to me. To all of us."

"Sure. I'll do it."

Rob headed off to the equipment hatch; a few minutes later Millie saw him walk out to a waiting aircraft with Brunson.

He headed over to the admin hatch.

The flight lieutenant smiled. "How can we help you, Millie?"

"I've got some extra Guiding Light paperwork for tomorrow's meeting. It needs to go into the secure cabinet, please."

"No problem." The junior officer unhooked a set of keys from a large board on the inside of the admin area. He appeared out of the office and led Millie to a row of green metal cabinets, each adorned with a padlock.

He handed Millie a clipboard. "Paw print, please, Millie."

Millie retrieved his pen and signed for the keys. As he did so, the previous signature caught his eye. Corporal Ratcliffe. A name he didn't know.

Beneath him, on his knees, the flight lieutenant opened the cabinet.

Millie stared.

It was empty, apart from a few folders of paperwork.

Not one of the dozens of recorded reels of tape was present.

He looked closer, in case he was missing something.

Not a single tape.

"Where are they?" he asked, turning toward the admin officer.

The man consulted the clipboard. "Corporal Ratcliffe removed the tapes this morning."

"Why?"

"Can't say, Millie, but it was all above board. Wing Commander Kilton signed the release form."

"But you don't know where the tapes went?"

"Not sure. Best ask the boss."

Millie placed his report in the cabinet.

"Everything alright, Millie?"

"Yes. Just lost in thought."

Millie walked over to Kilton's office and peered in. It was empty. He opened the door of the neighbouring office, where Kilton's secretary was typing with a cigarette hanging from her mouth, peering through half-moon spectacles.

"Jean, is the boss around?"

She looked up and removed the cigarette.

"Millie, darling, how lovely to see you. How's that gorgeous Georgina of yours?"

Millie smiled. "She's very well. I'll send her your best."

"You do that, Millie. Now, the good wing commander is over in station HQ. Is it urgent?"

"No, it's fine. Will he be back today?"

"I don't think so."

"OK. Thank you, my dear. Most helpful as always."

"Anything for you, Millie." She re-inserted the cigarette and resumed her typing.

Back at his desk, Millie sat before a pile of unrelated project work. He looked across at Secure Cabinet 3.

All those hours of recorded data.

Gone.

———

KILTON DID NOT RETURN, as predicted by Jean. Rob bustled in around 4PM, all smiles after a trip in the TFU Lightning with Brunson.

"There aren't many places where you can fly a bomber in the morning and supersonic fighter in the afternoon," Rob said as he passed.

The pilots walked off to the mess bar and Millie headed to his car.

The seats were almost too hot to sit on, and he had to grab the steering wheel on and off until it cooled under his touch.

Outside the main gate, he paused as a group of barely dressed youngsters sauntered by. A woman with a flower behind her ear stared at him for a moment. She broke off her gaze and the group retreated down the road.

"Odd lot," he said to the guard.

"More than odd, sir." The sergeant handed back his ID form.

As he drove out of the station, Millie recalled the chatter from the Vulcan cockpit. Were the youngsters part of the camping party at the end of the runway?

Georgina was in the back garden when he arrived home.

She kissed him. "I'll get us a drink."

Millie plonked himself in a garden chair and closed his eyes.

Distant guitar playing arrived on the light breeze. Incongruous, in a married quarter patch. But he found it soothing.

He tried to put aside his growing anxiety about Guiding Light. Work needed to stay at work for many reasons at RAF West Porton.

Georgina arrived back, two G&Ts in hand.

"Lovely," Millie said, taking one. "Oh, and ice. What a treat." He took a long draw on the cold drink.

"Sarah Brunson insists," said Georgina. "And I'm all for it."

"Agreed. How was your day, dear?"

"Well," she started and Millie immediately knew there was a story coming, "we had some excitement. The young people have arrived."

"Ah yes, I think I saw some. Who are they?"

"CND," Georgina replied, emphasising each letter.

"CND? As in the Campaign for Nuclear Disarmament?"

"The same. Lots of them. All in a field, camping."

"Huh." Millie turned to look in the direction of the airfield, but a row of tall conifers that ran the length of the back gardens blocked their view. Probably planted in a futile attempt to keep the sound of jet engines at bay.

"Is that the guitar music I can hear?"

"I think so. Come on, let's look."

They pushed their way through the firs. Millie closed his eyes and hoped not to get slapped in the face by a branch released ahead of him by Georgina.

As they emerged, Millie looked across to the airfield. The security fence around the western end of the runway was about three quarters of a mile away. Just this side of the barbed wire, a group of tents and a wigwam had sprung up. The wigwam drew the eye with its central position and a prominent fallen cross symbol on one side.

"Well, well. I've seen pictures of those Aldermaston marches, but never actually seen a peace protest," said Millie.

"Amazing, isn't it?"

"Looks harmless enough, I suppose."

Georgina laughed. "Kilton will have kittens, won't he?"

"Probably, but what's new? Must have been where he was this afternoon, locked in with the station commander."

"So what is it you lot do inside there that's got CND snapping at your heels?" Georgina said and nudged her husband.

"Lord knows. I can't think of anything." Both of them knew it was an area he couldn't go into.

Guiding Light wasn't a nuclear weapon, but it was its delivery system.

"They couldn't possibly know…" he mumbled, then shuddered at the thought.

"Know what?" Georgina asked.

"Oh, nothing. They can't know what goes on inside. The place is like Fort Knox."

They had dinner indoors and as the light faded, they took their drinks back out through the firs to spy on their new neighbours some more.

The sun was setting and the clouds to the west were a deep red, casting a warm glow over the camp and the airfield beyond.

"It looks like a scene from a western," said Millie.

Georgina slipped her arm through her husband's. "Does that make you my cowboy?"

Later that evening, Millie lay awake with the windows wide open, allowing the cooler air in and the hot stuffiness out.

The guitar started up, this time with the sound of singing. It was a woman's voice, a sweet sound.

He turned over and hoped to drift off to sleep, but the thought of the project meeting in the morning occupied him. He closed his eyes and did his best to push Mark Kilton out of his mind.

———

THE CLOCK on the wall in Ewan Stafford's office read 2AM.

Outside, he heard a bicycle bell and a couple of men laughing. Did Cambridge students ever go to bed?

The mainframe had taken nine hours to ingest all the tapes and run what the technicians called an analysis on the data.

The print-out phase was ongoing.

Earlier in the day, Stafford himself had set the parameters of what they were looking for. It was a task he couldn't leave to anyone else.

He hid away in his office for two hours, surrounded by the Avro Vulcan pilots' notes and technical specifications. Later he returned and told them what he was looking for: sudden changes in number ranges. He handed them a sheet containing the actual parameters.

"What are they?" one of the men had asked.

"Don't you worry about that, sonny."

It didn't take a genius to work out they represented changes in height.

Changes that were impossible for a Vulcan to have actually flown.

Changes imagined by a computer that fed an autopilot.

Once the processing was over, he sent all but the youngest technician home.

The computer room was fifty feet away, but Stafford could still hear the monotonous drone of the dot matrix printer drifting through the deserted building.

He smoked through a packet of Woodbines as he waited, contemplating the unthinkable.

It was no secret in the company that the Board had risked the house on this new technology. The computer itself was cripplingly expensive.

It was also no secret that he was the one who had persuaded his fellow directors to part with Blackton's hard-earned cash.

He promised to resurrect the company's fortunes with a groundbreaking system. Years ahead of the British competition still relying on drawing boards and old men who designed World War Two bombers.

On his desk, under the packet of Woodbines, was the first

contract for the American government. The numbers were big. Big enough to call Guiding Light an instant success and secure Blackton's future for years to come.

He knew from his days flying Hurricanes, you rarely got to a kill without taking a few risks. And he'd risked the house on Guiding Light.

He moved the cigarettes and opened the contract, staring at the final figure for the initial seven hundred and fifty units. With more promised, DF Blackton's deals would positively affect the UK's balance of payments. An incredible thing.

This was that moment, when you rolled out of your high-risk manoeuvre to find the Luftwaffe Me.109 in front and just below. Time to squeeze the trigger.

The printer noise stopped.

Stafford listened as the paper was collated.

By the time he got to the dimly lit computer room, the young technician was bent over a huge stack of perforated, green-lined sheets.

He had a desk lamp just above the pile, and scanned the columns, making the occasional mark with a pencil.

"Found anything?" Stafford asked as he stood in the doorway.

"Two, but I've only just started."

"Damn it," Stafford said and pushed the man out of the way.

His eyes needed to adjust to the harsh light from the angle-poise light reflecting off the paper. He blinked, and eventually saw the marks the technician had made.

Lines that met his parameters included a small star at one end.

A small star that said a lot.

Stafford ran his finger along the first starred line.

1,261, 1,261, 1,262, 1,278, 1,277, 1,298, 1,301, 1,265, 1,252, 1,998, 2,010, 2,618, 2,911, 2,871, 2,850, 2,799, 2,811, 1,261, 1,277, 1,279.

He circled 1,252 and 1,998. A jump of seven hundred and forty-six feet.

Unless the aircraft had flown over an unlikely hole in the ground, the equipment had suffered an aberration.

He counted the number of height readings that appeared wrong. Eight. He stood up and winced at a spike of lower back pain.

"The laser records, what is it, forty-seven readings a second? So, this was just a fraction of a second?"

The technician shook his head.

"No. The laser records twenty-seven readings a second, and the computer makes forty-seven decisions a second. But..." He tapped the sheets. "These are samples. The tapes only capture three height readings a second, and we limit the system to how much it can record."

Stafford looked back at the numbers.

"So, it was wrong for three seconds?"

"More like two and a half."

"And you've found two so far?

"Yes, sir."

"Carry on. It's essential we find them all. I'll need to know exact details. Leave the results on my desk. I'll be in very early, so be smart about it."

He walked to the door. "And have the day off tomorrow."

3

THURSDAY 9TH JUNE

A Handley-Page Victor emerged from the dark recesses of the TFU hangar, towed into the bright morning light. The TFU pan was filling up.

Men in green coveralls hurried about the aircraft, some with chocks in their hands carried by the rope that held them together, others on small tractors.

Millie watched them for a while from a bench, his incident report in hand.

He was in early to prepare, sensing a battle was coming.

Millie lifted himself from the wooden bench and headed inside, taking a seat in the empty meeting room. He re-read his notes one more time.

He went to the admin cabinets and pulled out a folder of memorandums from last year about the formation of TFU. Standing alone in the room, he read Mark Kilton's missives about the purpose and function of the newly established Royal Air Force Test Flying Unit.

It would be an aircrew led unit, Kilton stated. Industry to be kept at arm's length. Unlike their neighbours at Boscombe Down who rubbed shoulders with company pilots every day, TFU would be RAF only.

A place where they could assess aircraft and systems unencumbered by the usual politics that surrounded government contracts.

And yet Kilton was the most political animal he'd come across in his thirty-seven years in the RAF.

But the principles were helpful, so he tucked a copy of the paper in his folder and went back to the meeting room.

Just after 8AM the door swung open and in swept Kilton, Rob May, Speedy Johnson, a corporal note-taker and Ewan Stafford.

The Blackton MD's appearance was a surprise, but not unprecedented. Stafford took his seat, looking tired.

Rob sat next to Millie and looked as if he was about to say something, but Kilton began the meeting still on his feet, rattling at speed through the agenda.

"The equipment's now installed on one Canberra, one Vulcan and soon to be fitted to a second Vulcan when Blackton can get a new set to Woodford."

"It's already there," said Stafford. "We've sent a team up to carry out the installation."

"Excellent. We're through the high level, medium-level and now into the low-level phases of the trial. More than half the required hours are logged." He consulted his notes. "The evaluation is progressing satisfactorily. We must decide how to tackle the remaining hours for the project but I think we can all agree, these are the final stages. The icing on the cake."

"I'm sorry, boss, can we talk about Tuesday?" said Millie.

Kilton didn't look up from his notes, but paused long enough for Millie to continue.

"Unfortunately, we experienced a serious failure that almost resulted in the loss of an aircraft and crew." He looked directly at Stafford; surprisingly the civilian was expressionless.

He already knows.

Millie pressed on. "I've completed an initial report. It describes how the system tried to descend a Vulcan into the ground at two hundred and sixty knots. It was only the intervention of Mr May here that saved us." He paused. "And I'm afraid the only option open to us now is to suspend the trial pending a full investigation."

Kilton sighed. "Millie, while I appreciate your diligence in this matter, the fact remains, this is anecdotal."

Millie shifted in his chair. "It's true that I wasn't able to capture the data from the incident, but that doesn't deflect from the fact that it happened and was witnessed."

"And yet, without evidence, we are left with the possibility that it could have been anything that caused the temporary loss of height. One option I've been told of is that a pilot may have inadvertently put pressure on the control column while changing position in his seat."

Millie laughed at the ludicrous suggestion, before realising that the rest of the room was quiet.

"You're not serious, Mark?" he asked.

"Unless you have some evidence to the contrary, I must consider testimony from one of my pilots the likely explanation."

Millie sat back in his chair. "I'm sorry, Mark, but that's just not credible. Brian Hill said nothing to me whatsoever and he's no longer here to provide any such testimony—"

"Who said anything about Hill? The pilot who touched the control column is sitting next to you."

Millie took a moment to register what Kilton had said. He slowly turned his head to see Rob staring down at the table.

"Rob?"

"It's possible," Rob said quietly.

Kilton continued, in a chipper voice.

"Speedy, you're an experienced V-Bomber pilot, is it possible in the Vulcan to move the stick without meaning to?"

"Under normal flight operations I'd say it's unlikely, but in this scenario, with the pilot covering the controls, while they move independently, I would say it's an increased risk, certainly. An unintended consequence of this level of automation."

Millie kept his eyes on Rob. "Either you knocked the stick, or you did not knock the stick."

"That's enough, Millie," said Kilton. "The point is, we don't know for sure what happened and no-one is going to ground a critically important system without firm evidence."

Millie looked up at the men around the table. No-one else spoke.

"What if it wasn't? And what if we have a serious, potentially fatal problem?" He didn't wait for Kilton to reply before adding, "In which case, we need to look at all the flying data we have with a matter of urgency. As you note, boss, we've gathered many hours and the tapes are in the cabinet..." He stopped, suddenly remembering the empty shelves.

Kilton gave a dismissive wave. "The tapes have already been analysed by the mainframe computer in Cambridge. It took place overnight. Mr Stafford, would you care to illuminate us?"

Stafford cleared his throat. "Certainly, Mark. We asked the computer to search for any anomalies in the height data. Such things as sudden changes in the numbers, which if translated into aircraft movement would result in an aircraft loss. Specifically, we were looking for periods of erroneous data, enough to affect flying for a sustained time. We found no such occurrences, I'm pleased to report. So I have to concur with the meeting that whatever you experienced, it wasn't as a result of Guiding Light."

"That's not a conclusion you can draw, Ewan," said Millie. "You weren't there."

Kilton shot him a warning look. "Millie, don't be foolish. Ewan and his team have had full access to the data, and it showed no issues. That's it."

"I don't believe it," said Millie.

Kilton sat back in his chair. "You don't?"

A heavy silence hung in the room.

"What I mean is, I am very surprised. That's all. Can we have it analysed elsewhere? A second opinion, if you like? With all due respect to Mr Stafford and his team, boss, you set up TFU to be independent of industry."

"There's no chance," Stafford piped up. "We simply don't have access to another mainframe computer. We have one of the few in the country. Plus, I'm not sure why you would need a second opinion."

"Because DF Blackton have a vested interest in failing to find a fault."

Stafford harrumphed, with his shoulders twitching. "What are you suggesting, Mr Milford?"

"I'm not suggesting anything, but let's be clear. Blackton is playing both gamekeeper and poacher in this scenario, and—"

"I said that's enough." Kilton looked straight at him. "No-one respects you around here more than me, Chris, but this has to stop. I'll remind you that DF Blackton is a distinguished firm and subject to the Official Secrets Act. The very suggestion you are making is slanderous. I'll also remind you that at TFU we make decisions based on the evidence." Millie opened his mouth to speak but Kilton held up the palm of his hand. "Actual evidence, not stories. That's why we carry the data recording unit, Millie, and I might say it is your responsibility to operate that system to the standards required."

Millie removed his reading glasses and rubbed his eyes.

He placed his specs on the table and sat in silence.

Kilton picked up the pace again. "Now we have fewer than a hundred hours left to fly. We can split that between the Canberra and Vulcans, so I'll think about bringing in additional crew."

He turned to Millie. "And we can stay above one thousand feet if you'd recommend it, Millie. You are after all the project leader."

Millie shook his head in disbelief.

"Am I?"

"You've done good work on this project, Millie. Don't let us down at the final hurdle. I want you and Rob to get up to Woodford to check on the next installation. It needs to be identical so we can move crews between the Vulcans. OK?"

Millie glared at Kilton, who stared back. Eventually Millie shrugged.

Kilton sighed. "Good. Well, that's sorted. Finally, security. You've no doubt noticed that we have unwanted visitors at the zero-eight threshold. A so-called peace camp filled with those who would undermine national security. Our own military security police are working with the courts to take eviction action, but in the meantime, it goes without saying that Guiding Light is the British crown jewels. The power of any new weapon or system is reliant on it remaining secret. If any aspect of the project gets out of the confines of TFU, I would expect arrests, criminal charges and prison for the culprits. It doesn't matter if you are an air commodore or a junior technician, you will be prosecuted. There-fore, you will remain exceptionally vigilant. There will be no discus-sion with anyone outside of those directly involved with the system's evaluation. And, of course, no paperwork or items relating to the project are to go past the front door without express clear-ance and police escort."

The meeting murmured its agreement and broke up.

Kilton, Stafford, Johnson and the clerk stood up and headed out. Kilton trailed the group. Pausing at the door, he looked back.

"Millie, you're months from retirement. Don't do anything stupid. You need that pension, don't you? Why risk everything you've promised Georgina? You've made your case, but it's over."

"You're threatening me, Mark?"

"Just tow the bloody line, Millie. Now's not the time for one of your displays of petulance."

He left the room.

As the door swung closed, Rob looked up and made eye contact with Millie for the first time.

"I'm sorry. It happened in the bar. I'd had a few drinks and he cornered me. I felt like he wanted to explore all scenarios and I agreed it was a theoretical possibility."

Millie looked at his friend. "I'm trying to work out whether you are naive or stupid. Do you understand what's happening? This is where it starts, Rob. Meetings like this can save or cost lives, for god's sake. Think about all those rear crews in the V-Bombers, lost because they sent the aircraft into low-level without a proper escape system. What we do here matters." He banged the table.

Rob looked hurt, pitiful even, like a puppy who needed comfort. "Please understand my position, Millie. I had no choice. Let's not fall out."

Millie stood up and gathered his papers. "There's more at stake here than our friendship, Rob."

————

KILTON DROPPED into the seat behind his desk and studied the small square of paper handed to him by Stafford.

"I've bought us some time. Now tell me what all this means," he said, laying the piece of paper face up on the desk.

Stafford shifted in place. "We looked at nearly two hundred hours of flying records. The problem is definitely there. On that piece of paper are the extrapolated results. The frequency and magnitude."

"What does that mean in plain English? You said on the phone that in most cases, crews won't even notice?"

"In most cases, the burst of incorrect height readings will be too brief for the autopilot to react in any meaningful way."

"In most cases?"

"It's possible, on very rare occasions, that the flutter could last long enough to affect the actual flight. But they'd have to be very unlucky for it to cause a serious problem. Typically, even if it did happen, they'd observe the deviation and intervene, just like they did two days ago."

"Typically? What do you mean by that?"

"With a lot of bad luck, they might be in just the wrong position as the error occurs. At night, for instance, very low, fast, in a tight bank or maybe they're not monitoring the flight at the time, but..."

"But what?"

Stafford took a seat on the other side of Kilton's desk. "I don't think we have a choice here, Mark. As I told you yesterday, we saw this in the lab, early on. The laser itself fluctuated briefly, but minutely. They called it a flutter. As we designed and built the full scale versions, the magnitude of the flutter stayed the same and so became insignificant. And we thought it had just gone, refined away by a better build. But apparently not. The problem, Mark, is that we don't know what causes it. Our best option is to redesign the programme that sits between the laser and the autopilot to tell false readings from real ones. At the moment, how to do that is beyond us. And even if we did redesign it, that would mean starting again on the flying trials. High altitude, not connected to the autopilot while we build up the readings. All those hours flown again. To get back to where we are now, from my experience of how long it took to get here, I'd say we'll need six to nine months in the workshop, and another six to nine of early airborne trials."

"A year and a half? Out of the question."

"Then, you carry on." Stafford lowered his voice. "Nothing's without risk, Mark."

Kilton propped his elbows on the desk and interlocked his fingers.

"We pause now, Stafford, we lose it. The Yanks will have their breakthrough soon enough, and when they do, they'll drop the order."

"That would finish us. We've sunk too much into this."

"That's not my problem, Stafford. You made your decisions."

"Wouldn't it finish TFU, too? You don't exactly bask in the support of your superiors. I think a lot of them would love to topple this secret empire you're building. On the other hand, you deliver a multi-million pound contract for the government…"

Kilton picked up the piece of paper and looked at the handwritten numbers. He turned it over in his hand for a few moments.

"The point is, Guiding Light gives us an advantage over the Soviets. You heard Leivers. It could end the Cold War, and then how many lives are saved? Millions." He stood up. "Let's not get bogged down by the risk to a few unlucky crews." He screwed the square of paper into a tight ball and pushed it deep into his trouser pocket. "How many people know about this… flutter?"

"The team are aware it exists, but they believe it's insignificant. Only me and a junior technician know the truth, and he won't be a problem. We'll incinerate the printouts and demagnetise the tapes. There's hardly anyone working at Cambridge, anyway. I've moved the annual shutdown forward to accommodate the production. The mainframe goes into maintenance tomorrow." Stafford got to his feet and picked up his briefcase. "Of course, Mark, there's your crew here. Not much gets past Millie."

"Leave him to me."

"Just like the old days at Tangmere, the troops always feared you. I feared you, come to that."

Kilton smiled. "Just like Tangmere, Stafford, we're at war. The only people who need to be scared are the enemy. And those who get in the way."

———

Millie sat down at his favourite admin desk underneath the clock. Staring at the wall, he allowed the adrenaline from the meeting to subside.

After a few minutes, the admin officer appeared.

"Audit?"

Millie nodded and followed him over to the secure cabinets for the weekly check.

"Shouldn't take long," Millie said, looking at the bare shelves.

He noted the two tapes from yesterday's flight and checked the paperwork against the list. Everything had to be accounted for.

The only contents of the cabinet they didn't count were the number of blank tapes.

He crouched down to check the bottom shelf. Only about twenty left. They would need more.

The junior officer locked the cabinets and Millie called the department at DF Blackton from his desk.

As the call connected, he had a thought and quickly glanced around the office. No-one was nearby.

"Yes, hello, it's Squadron Leader Milford. RAF West Porton."

"Hello."

"Yes, ah, a quick one. We sent over about one hundred and seventy hours of records on magnetic tape yesterday, I believe?"

"Yes, that's right. We ran them through the computer until the small hours."

"So I understand. I haven't actually seen the results, and as the project leader I would like to study them if possible. Would you be able to send them over?"

The man at the other end laughed.

"The results are about two yards high. Not sure we could easily send them anywhere."

"I see. But were there any conclusions?"

"Let me check, one of my junior colleagues stayed late. Hold on a mo."

The phone handset clunked down onto a hard surface.

Ewan Stafford appeared out of Kilton's office.

Millie placed a hand over the receiver and watched as Stafford headed to the door, his path taking him just behind his desk.

Jean came running out of the office.

"Mr Stafford, can I get your travel receipts?"

Just two yards behind him, Stafford and the secretary got involved in a discussion about petrol prices.

"Squadron Leader Milford?"

"Hello, yes?" Millie turned toward the wall in front of him and leaned over the desk, desperately trying to put some distance between him and the Blackton MD.

"It's David Richards here. I'm the manager of the computer room. I understand your enquiry, but you will have to speak directly to Mr Stafford."

"Oh, I don't want to bother him. I was just after the results from last night."

"Mr Stafford has them and I understand he reported to you this morning. If there's anything else, you will have to take it up with Mr Stafford directly. I'm sorry I cannot be of any more help."

The phone line went dead.

To his left, Stafford disappeared through the swing doors toward the car park.

Slowly, Millie replaced the receiver.

For two full minutes he barely moved, one finger lightly tapping the desk.

The admin officer interrupted him again. "When are they coming?"

"Pardon?"

"The blanks? You ordered them?"

"Oh, no. Sorry, Peter. I'll do it now." Peter shot him a quizzical look. "That was another call I was on. I'll phone Blackton straight away."

He jotted down some numbers. The last hundred hours covered just over three hundred and twenty-one tapes, about twenty minutes per reel.

They had another hundred hours to go.

Another three hundred and thirty tapes should cover it. He underlined the number.

"But then, what's the point?" he muttered quietly to himself.

He looked across to Mark Kilton's office in time to see Rob and Speedy going in. Scanning the rest of the office he saw Jock MacLeish, Red Brunson and others, all in flying gear, ready to go.

Millie looked back down at his notes.

One hundred hours.

Three hundred and thirty reels.

He called up the Blackton computer department again, and ordered four hundred and fifty blank reels.

————

THE AFTERNOON MEETINGS WERE A DISTRACTION, as he and a small team went through future projects: a stronger braking parachute for the Vulcan, rough landing trials for the Argosy, a larger fin for the Blue Steel missile.

He made sure he paid attention to the important bits but as the clock approached 4.45PM he became anxious to get back to the planning room.

By the time he returned, Rob had left for the day.

"*Damn*." He picked up his case and checked it for any documents that shouldn't leave the building, then drove straight to the Mays' small married quarter.

"Millie! Come in." Mary beamed at him.

"Thank you, Mary. Is Rob home?"

"Not yet."

"Oh? I was told he might be."

"Well, the mess has become a bit of a habit for him."

"Fair enough. But I would like to have a quick word. Would you mind sending him around when he turns up, as long as it's not an inconvenience to you, of course?"

"I'll send him over after dinner if he's back in time."

Millie drove the short distance to his own quarter, agitated that a conversation he wasn't looking forward to would have to wait even longer.

Georgina was in the garden, table and chairs arranged for another *al fresco* dinner.

She smiled at her husband. "Make hay while the sun shines, Millington."

———

By 7PM HE was into his single-malt scotch. He was savouring it on his tongue as a cough came from behind. "I'm sorry, I couldn't get a response at the front door," Rob said, after emerging from the side passage.

"Robert!" Millie smiled at him. "How the devil are you? Whisky or gin, dear chap? Please say whisky."

"Not one of your more adventurous ones, please. I need my stomach lining intact."

"As you wish!" Millie went into the house and poured a second scotch, fishing a mixer out of the dresser cupboard.

When he returned, Rob and Georgina were laughing.

"I was begging Rob to bring over that gorgeous wife of his. It's the weekend."

"It's Thursday, dear," said Millie.

"That's what I told her," Rob said, "but she says Thursday is now officially the start of the weekend." He winked at Georgina. "And I'd like to agree. Why do we fly on Fridays, Millie?"

"Something to do with serving Her Majesty and preparing for war, I believe, Robert. Here you are. Glenfiddich mixed with ginger ale. Sacrilege in some parts of Scotland, but perfectly acceptable in Wiltshire."

As he handed over the drink, he nodded for Georgina to leave them alone.

She took the hint. "Right, well, the dishes won't do themselves. I guess my weekend is on hold. Shout if you need anything, boys." She disappeared into the house.

They sat quietly for a moment. In the distance, the sound of laughter floated through the air along with the now familiar sound of music.

Rob cocked his head.

"The peace camp," said Millie, and gestured toward the trees at the back of the garden.

"Oh. Yes, I've seen them on approach. Kilton's not happy."

"When is he, Rob? When is he?"

Rob put his drink down. "I'm sorry about this morning, Millie. Kilton got the better of me when I was worse for wear in the mess. But I also think he's right."

"You do?"

"It doesn't really matter whether I did or didn't nudge the stick—"

"Can we both agree that you didn't?"

"The point I'm making is that we don't have any firm evidence and it's a bit much grounding the project so quickly. We can't give in at the first bump in the road. We need Guiding Light, Millie. There are countries relying on us to deliver it. NATO needs us. You have to keep going. In any case, it's Kilton's orders, so we have no choice now. Unless you're planning on doing something silly?"

"Has he sent you here on an intelligence gathering mission, Rob?"

Rob put down his drink. "You asked me here."

"I did. And I wanted to talk to you because, well, I suppose you're right. We have no choice but to press on, despite the evidence we witnessed with our own eyes. But I intend to do my job, to examine Guiding Light thoroughly and pass it fit for production. Or not."

"Of course."

"What we need," Millie continued, "is to ensure we get as much data onto the tapes as possible." Rob looked confused. "I want to maximise our flight times. And bring some good old TFU independence to the project. Test crews putting Guiding Light through its paces without fear or favour."

"Right," said Rob slowly, "that's what we're doing, isn't it?"

"I don't know, Rob. I'm not sure the project is being examined completely without fear or favour, but we're the men with our hands on the equipment. And we should not be afraid of doing what's necessary."

Rob furrowed his brow. "I don't know about this, Millie. It sounds like you're trying to work outside of the parameters of the project."

"If that's what it takes to do our job properly, should we not adapt?"

Rob put his glass down and shook his head. "Adaptation's one thing, but it sounds to me like you're thinking of something completely different. Working behind the boss's back? I'm sorry, I really think it's best to leave it be. I certainly can't be a part of it. What would Kilton do if he found out? Seriously, Millie. He can be vindictive!"

"Which is why we need to put him aside, Rob, and work without fear or favour. If that's what we need to do to save lives. And I believe it is."

"You should stop saying 'we', Millie. This is your idea, not mine. Look, I know you're getting cynical in your old age, but I still believe in the system. And that's how it should be. It will fall apart if we go off on our own tangents. Really, you should take it from me. Whatever you're thinking of, it's a terrible idea." Rob sat up and leaned toward Millie. "Why mess everything up over a whim? You're months away from your cottage by the sea. Seriously, Millie, what are you thinking?"

"I'm not thinking about me, Rob. It's not me losing anything that worries me. It's the crews. Other men like us, who follow us. Our duty is to them."

Rob stood up, drained his whisky and ginger. "Thank you for the drink, Millie." He started to walk toward the side gate.

"Rob, please sit down."

"I think not. I'm actually scared you might tell me something I'll regret. Sorry Millie, it's a no-go. Time to let it go. Leave the politics to Kilton. It's for the best."

"Whose best, Rob?"

His friend stood for a moment, looking unsure of himself, before disappearing down the side of the house.

———

MILLIE STEWED in his own thoughts for five minutes. Georgina appeared from the house with a whisky bottle in one hand and a cigarette in the other.

"You look like a tramp on a night out," Millie observed.

She laughed. "Thanks. Rob gone?"

"Yes."

She sat down next to him.

"Everything alright between you two?"

"Not exactly."

"If it's work stuff, I know you can't talk about it, but... Maybe Rob's changing. He's not the green-around-the-gills pilot you took under your wing anymore." She leant in toward him. "Is it time to let him fly the nest?"

"Can I have some more whisky?"

She passed the bottle over.

He poured an inch more scotch. "You might be right, dear, but it's bloody inconvenient timing."

"Why?"

"I really wanted his help, but he's not playing ball."

"There are other pilots at TFU. I'm sure someone will help you?"

Millie sipped the whisky, again enjoying the dulling of the senses that came with alcohol. "Not for this particular task. I need a close friend."

Georgina narrowed her eyes. "Mr Millington, you're not getting yourself into trouble, are you?"

"Absolutely I am." He laughed.

She shook her head. "I'm serious, Millie. We have weeks left. Don't do anything stupid. Especially don't cheese off Mark Kilton. You know what that man's like."

"I have to do this."

"Jesus, Millie, it sounds ominous."

He smiled and patted her thigh. "Absolutely nothing to worry about. Really. It's just boring old work stuff."

———

LATER THAT EVENING, Millie sat at the bureau in the lounge and doodled some figures. He wanted to calculate how many height readings he'd end up with after recording one hundred reels.

From his memory, he understood the tapes recorded three moments in time every second, so just one twenty-minute tape would produce more than three thousand five hundred lines of records. More than a quarter of a million lines over one hundred tapes.

He stared at the result. It would take forever to look through them all. Even if he could get the numbers off the tapes.

Georgina appeared over his shoulder.

"I assume that's not our savings?"

Millie laughed. "Sorry, no. Work. Just lots of numbers."

"Oh, count me out. I don't do maths. Your son inherited that talent from you." She slumped down on the sofa and opened a copy of *Woman* magazine. Millie studied the front cover: a model with a brown bob of hair which, according to the headline, was a 'go anywhere hairstyle'.

Georgina's eyes appeared over the magazine. "Maybe Charlie could help with his bombe?"

"Bomb? Whatever are you talking about?"

She laughed. "Don't you remember at Christmas? We found it hilarious that he was going on about the bombe they used for calculations?"

"Oh, yes. A bombe. With an e. He told us it came from a wartime deciphering operation, didn't he?"

"God knows. Something like that."

A bombe. Millie turned the unusual word over in his mind. He imagined a large mechanical machine with rotating dials, tearing through calculations faster than a human could read them.

"I can't talk to Charlie about this."

He looked back at the figure. This felt like an insurmountable problem. What was the point of gathering data he couldn't read?

4

FRIDAY 10TH JUNE

Susie Attenborough sat naked in a tent. Legs crossed, in her unzipped sleeping bag.

She stretched before fumbling through a pile of clothes to find her wristwatch.

5.45AM.

The sun had been up for forty minutes; the thin canvas did little to keep the light out.

She wound the watch for a new day. Outside in the nearby hedgerow and copse, the dawn chorus was underway. She savoured the gentle birdsong, knowing it would soon be replaced by howling jet engines.

Susie yawned, climbed over the detritus of her clothes out into the daylight.

Her bare feet felt cold on the dewy grass. Rabbits hopped around the taxiway on the other side of the high security fence, their lower portions disappearing into a sliver of mist.

The peace camp was still. Her eyes swept over the other tents, scattered around the central wigwam. Silently she counted them, checking for new arrivals, until she caught sight of a man: tall with a beard, bare chested in cut-off shorts. He smiled back at her.

Susie recognised him from an introduction when she'd first arrived. David?

As it wasn't normal behaviour to stand around stark naked in the UK countryside, even at a peace commune, she put one arm over her breasts and the other between her legs and awkwardly backed into the tent.

She took her time in pulling on her clothes: a short skirt and a white blouse.

When she re-emerged, David was gone, but a few more campaigners had emerged from their burrows. She exchanged smiles before heads turned at the sound of a deep rumble reverberating from the airfield.

She checked her watch; barely 6AM.

She wandered over to the fence and looked toward the three large green hangars at the other end of the runway. A few aircraft were out already and one, with propellers turning, was the source of the noise.

A movement caught her eye: a Land Rover with a canvas hood over its back, speeding around the peritrack, heading their way. She stood her ground as the vehicle passed her, just a few feet the other side of the wire.

The driver and passenger glanced in her direction. She noted the green lining on their caps but couldn't place the uniform.

Since her arrival, all the talk had been about when they would come for them, armed with an eviction notice.

So far they'd been left alone.

She knew that would change once the direct action began.

———

MILLIE ARRIVED at TFU with a plan. A vague, not-thought-through plan. But at least it was a plan.

The map tables were empty as the pilots and some navs were at the morning weather brief.

He walked over to the admin office and ensured the Vulcan they were allocated was not needed too soon after they were due to return.

Rob appeared along with other aircrew as the met brief broke up.

Millie fixed an amiable look on his face. Rob looked nervous, but he greeted him loudly and asked if he wanted a tea.

He accepted the offer and his face brightened. They moved to the tea bar together and Millie kept up the conviviality, chatting about the cricket.

"Sobers was magnificent at Lord's apparently. One hundred and sixty-three not out."

Rob looked a little uncertain, as if he wasn't sure what was going on. But he joined in.

"It'll be hard for us to win the match from here."

"Indeed," said Millie. He paused and put a hand on Rob's back. "It's better to be on good terms, isn't it?"

"It is."

Speedy Johnson announced himself in the room and Millie took them over to a planning table. He spread out a chart that covered most of Northern England with the dramatic brown relief of the Lake District prominent in the top-left corner.

He pointed at the middle of the hills. "The Lakes. We need some big dips below us."

Speedy peered at where Millie's finger had landed.

"Wales has dips, famous for it. And it's a lot closer."

Millie nodded. "It does, but we need to cover as much different terrain as possible. We've done Wales a lot recently. Time for a change of scenery."

Speedy shrugged. "All good with me. It'll give Brighty something new to plan."

Rob kept quiet.

The group broke up and Millie found Steve Bright to brief him before moving to the admin office. While the flight lieutenant stood over him, he withdrew eight blank tapes from the secure cabinet, placing the cardboard sleeves into his flight case.

———

AN HOUR LATER, Millie stood on the edge of the TFU apron in his flying coveralls, helmet on, his oxygen mask hanging loosely by his chin.

He realised he was pacing and made an effort to keep his feet planted, concentrating on the ballet of manoeuvring aircraft in front of him.

A roar caught his attention and he watched an English Electric Lightning thunder along the runway. Its silver wings glinted in the sunshine as the pilot pulled it into a vertical climb and rolled around three hundred and sixty degrees. He smiled as the aircraft became a small silver dart and disappeared into a layer of cloud.

A moment later, Steve, Speedy and Rob appeared by his side and they walked toward the white, delta-winged Vulcan. Speedy climbed in while Rob set off around the aircraft, peering into the undercarriage recesses and checking various nooks and crannies.

Millie followed Steve Bright into the rear bay and settled in.

After agreeing that Bright would carry out the post hatch checks, he strapped himself in and set about organising the tapes.

He removed one from its sleeve and pre-loaded it, glancing across at the navigator as he did so. It wasn't so unusual, but ordinarily he loaded the reels only when needed during the flight.

Steve Bright was busy with his own preparation; a longer trip to a less visited part of the country for the young navigator.

Rob's head appeared in the hatchway.

"Ready to go?"

"Yep!" the navigator replied.

Rob climbed the next few steps into the cockpit and Bright checked the hatch was closed and latched.

They brought the Vulcan to life. The pilots weren't on the intercom yet, but he could hear them proceeding through the various checklists.

Ticking sounds and various mechanical whirrings preceded the familiar spooling up of the engines.

A few minutes later, they bounced along the runway before the aircraft pitched up and Millie and Bright were pressed forward against their straps.

Millie moved a hand forward and flipped the master switch on the Guiding Light panel.

It was unusual to power the system up so early. He knew the smaller repeater panels in the cockpit would also come to life; he could only hope neither Speedy or Rob would pay any attention to them at this stage in the flight.

He started the tape running.

After twenty minutes, an orange indicator blinked out and it was time to switch to a fresh tape.

Millie opened the metal flap over the reels; his hand was trembling.

He removed the full take-up reel, then switched the empty reel onto the take-up spindle. He reached down and retrieved a new blank reel from his flight bag.

In his peripheral vision, it seemed like Steve Bright was looking at him.

He glanced across, but in fact Bright was staring at his chart with his finger poised on the next waypoint.

Millie quickly dropped the new tape onto the spindle, closed the flap and restarted the data recorder.

He sat back, relieved.

The change took ten seconds; it had felt like ten minutes.

He put a white sticky label on the reel and marked it, simply BLANK 'A'.

A nonsense label that meant something only to him.

He retrieved a brand new pocket-sized notepad and opened it, noting down the date, time and location for the recording. He paused for a moment; even this note could be used against him at some point. After hesitating, he completed the entry anyway. There was no way around it.

He looked at his watch and checked the navigation plan. He had time for two reels more before they reached the entry gate.

Sitting back, he let the static whine from the intercom wash over him. It was warm inside from the time the aircraft had sat on the ground. He closed his eyes.

"You still with us, Millie?" called Steve Bright.

Millie woke.

"Falling asleep in a nuclear bomber? And we're only going to Keswick, chap. Not Vladivostok."

Millie looked at his stopwatch. Eighteen and a half minutes gone. Time to change reels again.

As he removed the second tape, Steve Bright turned to him again.

"We're not there yet, Millie."

He felt a spike of adrenaline in his stomach.

He looked up and smiled. "I know, just making sure we're ready."

Bright gave him a thumbs up.

Had Rob heard the exchange on the intercom?

Fourteen minutes later, they began their descent, and Millie swapped out the second reel, taking advantage as Steve Bright's attention switched to the nav-radar.

He quickly marked up his second tape and loaded the first of the official reels for today's run.

The Vulcan settled at one thousand feet straight and level. Millie glanced at his copy of the route. They should be about twenty miles north of Bassenthwaite Lake. He felt a jolt as Guiding Light engaged. The ride became bumpy as the computer, with none of the finesse of a human, mirrored the contours of the ground beneath them.

"Tape running, Millie?" Rob called over the intercom.

"Roger," Millie confirmed.

The ride became more undulating as they continued deeper into the valleys and hills of the Lake District. In the dark confines of the rear crew area, Millie started to feel nauseous.

After nineteen minutes of being heaved around, he was able to occupy himself briefly, changing another reel. As they passed the thirty-minute mark and began to climb out, he changed once more.

He had two official tapes to enter into the system, and he was onto his third unofficial tape.

On the transit home, he recorded one more reel, labelling the four sleeves *BLANK 'A', 'B', 'C' and 'D'*.

Ten minutes out, as they descended into the West Porton circuit, he powered down the Guiding Light panel, loosened his straps and tried to stretch in the limited space.

————

SUSIE WATCHED the white jet sweep directly overhead, her eyes following its wide arc around the airfield. The plane's landing gear unfolded as it travelled south before banking again, lining up to land.

It arrived over the fence and she watched it descend toward the runway, where it seemed to loiter in the air for a while before finally settling on its wheels with a screech and a puff of smoke.

David and his bushy beard appeared next to her.

"They take off heading that way and land coming back," he said.

"Wind. It must have changed during the day."

"Ah, I see. And that's a Victor, I think."

"Avro Vulcan," she corrected him.

He raised his eyebrows. "No, I think the Vulcan looks different, has a high tail at the back."

"The Victor is the one with the high tail, David. The white aircraft that's just landed is an Avro Vulcan. It's distinguished by its delta-shaped wing. Unique in bombers, I believe."

"Are you sure?"

"Yes, I'm sure, David. It's a bloody Vulcan." She smiled at him.

"Hmm."

She laughed. "Sorry. Don't mean to sound bossy. I grew up with three brothers and a father in the Navy. I can identify most cars, ships and planes. I could probably name you the England team for the World Cup as well."

"A tomboy? Fair enough."

They headed back toward the tents.

"So, David, what are we doing here? I mean, I know we're a protest camp, but what are we actually going to do?"

He reached into the back pocket of his shorts, produced a small packet of tobacco and began rolling a cigarette.

"Keen, aren't you?"

"Just don't want to waste my time."

He studied her. "Well, we're alerting the world to a new technology that's doing god knows what with aircraft capable of dropping nuclear bombs."

"OK, but that sounds rather... passive."

He smiled at her.

"Maybe, but it's important. We're also disrupting the military as they prepare for an unthinkable and unwinnable war."

"How?"

"What do you mean, 'how'?"

"How are we disrupting the military? I mean, we haven't exactly shut down anything or stopped anything happening, as far as I can see."

The smell of burning paraffin drifted over, and a noise rose from their left. They looked to see a dark grey Canberra taxiing. Inside the cockpit, the pilot looked directly at them, and Susie could have sworn he was laughing under his mask. She waited for the noise to dissipate, but as the aircraft turned onto the runway, the engines wound up into a scream. The Canberra rolled forward, disappearing behind trees.

Susie shrugged. "As I say, we don't appear to be disrupting very much."

He lit his cigarette.

"Well, we don't know that for sure. For a start, our very presence here is bringing attention—"

"We've got to do more than that, surely?"

"Let me finish. We're bringing attention to an installation the government seems desperate to keep out of the public's eye. Plus, they may have modified their behaviour. Do you think they would parade anything secret in front of us? We have no idea how much activity they have curtailed because we're here." He sucked on his cigarette. "You seem impatient, I hope you're not thinking of leaving us?"

She shook her head. "No. Well, I can't stay forever. It's just that if there's something going on that needs to be stopped, I think we should stop it. I didn't come here to watch planes."

He smiled at her before looking around.

"Not everything worthwhile involves a set of bolt croppers, Susie. Some things require a little more subtlety." He moved off toward the wigwam. "Patience is a virtue."

————

BACK IN THE PLANNING ROOM, Millie sat at his desk, flight case by his feet.

He had already logged the two official reels into the project cabinet, leaving six in his bag, each filled with height readings from Guiding Light.

He tried to concentrate on some paperwork, but he found it hard. His eyes kept drifting down to the case containing the illicit reels.

He wanted to go to the loo, but was reluctant to leave it unattended.

"This is silly," he muttered to himself.

Kilton emerged from his office, in blue coveralls and orange Mae West life jacket, holding his gloves and flying helmet.

"Ready?" he called over to a group of pilots at the tea bar. Rob left the group, also dressed to fly. The pair of them disappeared through the airfield door.

"Appraisal trip with the boss, apparently."

Millie looked up to find Jock MacLeish standing over him.

"Oh. Unusual, isn't it? For Kilton to take a junior pilot."

"Yes. But then Mark Kilton works in mysterious ways, Millie."

He helped MacLeish with his own project paperwork, instructing him on what could safely remain in his locker or case and what had to be placed in the secure cabinets.

"What would we do without you, Millie?" MacLeish said, and headed off to deposit his trial reports.

After lunch, Millie spent the afternoon on more admin, tea drinking and wondering how the hell he was going to smuggle Top Secret tapes out of the country's most secure Royal Air Force station.

———

ROB AND KILTON arrived back at 2.30PM, a long time after they left for a simple check of a pilot's flying proficiency.

Rob was all smiles on his return; clearly it had gone well.

Millie kept an eye on the clock, trying to judge the best time to leave and avoid a random search.

Best when it's busy? Quiet? He couldn't recall many car searches after leaving the mess in the evening. They were generally carried out during the morning and evening rushes.

Jock MacLeish worked at a desk nearby.

"Hey, Jock. Are you heading to the mess tonight?"

"It's Friday, Millie. Need you ask?"

"Ah, of course. Happy Hour."

As soon after 4PM as they could get away with, a group left TFU heading to the mess.

Millie stood up, lifted his case, and walked to the door. The case suddenly felt heavy in his hand and he was conscious of every step he took.

He left the planning room and walked the few yards toward the door that opened out into the car park. As he got closer, it swung open and the commanding officer of the RAF West Porton security police walked in.

The man, in smart light blue uniform with green stripes on his sleeves and cap, walked directly toward him.

Millie held his breath, but the officer brushed past him without making eye contact.

He exhaled and headed to his car, placing his flight bag in the passenger footwell.

At the mess, he carefully locked every door before heading inside to the bar.

He spotted MacLeish sitting with the old men of the Maintenance Unit. The Scot waved and held up a pint for him.

Millie took his seat and clinked glasses.

JR, one of the MU pilots, looked as old as the aircraft they flew. His dark, sunken eyes seemed to swallow light. But there was a twinkle in his eye and Millie always enjoyed the old boys' company.

The beer tasted good.

The room filled with smoke and chatter. Millie spied Rob at the bar, surrounded by the senior test pilots.

Jock informed him that Rob and the boss had landed away at Daedalus, a Navy base near Portsmouth. Had lunch together in the mess, apparently.

Around 8PM, several hours after he'd started drinking, Millie said his goodbyes and headed toward his car. He was a bit wobbly and realised he was not in the best state to cope with his first attempt to smuggle out a tape. Maybe the alcohol would provide Dutch courage.

After two attempts, he persuaded the Rover's engine to start. He steered through the full car park, peering across the playing-field toward the lights of the main gate.

There was one man on the barrier, maybe a corporal. In the hut next to him, a sergeant with a clipboard.

He got to the main road that ran through the middle of the domestic side of the station and turned left.

Slowing down, he willed the barrier to rise.

Nothing.

The sergeant, complete with clipboard, appeared by the side of his car.

Millie wound down the window.

The sergeant leant down to bring his head level.

"Good evening."

"Hello," Millie managed.

"Just a word of caution, sir. We've spotted protestors out and about tonight. Best not to stop on the way home."

"I wasn't planning to, Sergeant, but thank you for the tip."

The sergeant nodded, then appeared to scrutinise Millie, before he glanced at his car.

"You haven't had too much to drink, have you, sir?"

"Certainly not. Just one or two, Sergeant."

The man nodded again, but didn't change his expression. He raised himself back up and moved to the front of the hut.

After an age, the barrier slowly lifted.

Millie put the car into first gear, pushed the accelerator with his foot, released the clutch. The car lurched forward and stalled.

His heart pounded.

He waited for the sergeant to reappear, probably convinced that he was drunk.

Before he tried to restart the engine, he forced himself to pause. He put the car in neutral, left his foot on the clutch and turned the key.

It started.

This time, Millie made sure he pulled away with no further issues. He glanced into his wing mirror to see the sergeant staring, his image growing smaller.

5

SATURDAY 11TH JUNE

Susie woke next to David. She lay still on her back for a while as the tent grew lighter.

Friday evening had taken an unexpected turn; they had shared a long conversation away from the throng around the camp-fire, and at some point he had leant in and kissed her. The sudden feel of his bushy beard around her mouth took her by surprise. But the conversation was excellent, and she felt she'd made progress.

She allowed his advance to unfold.

The sex was predictably disappointing. *Perfunctory*, was the word she would use if she was back at Cambridge reporting to her girl-friends. But that was neither here nor there.

She quietly pulled on a pair of shorts and a thin jumper, and crawled out of the tent. She glanced back; David was awake and looking at her. She flashed him a smile and left.

The camp was quiet.

She made her way out of the field, onto the main road. The dawn air was cool on her lightly covered body, yet she felt the odd pocket of warmth as the sun began another day of heating England beyond its wildest expectations.

The hot days felt alien to an Englishwoman, reminding her of a childhood camping holiday deep in the south of France where the climate felt as exotic as the foreign language.

A memory floated in. She played cricket with her brothers on the sand, to the bemusement of the locals. Later, she became annoyed with her mother, always pushing her to make friends with the other girls in the campsite.

She entered the village, casually glancing around to ensure she was alone before pulling on the heavy, cast-iron door of the bright red phone box.

———

MILLIE ROLLED out of bed and made his way to the spare bedroom, shutting the door behind him.

He slowly drew open the curtains, trying not to make any more noise.

The sun was climbing; he guessed it was about 6AM. A movement outside caught his eye: a figure wandering along the road from the direction of the peace camp. A slip of a girl. Somebody's daughter. How would he feel if, instead of studying maths at Oxford, Charlie was living in a field?

He moved away from the window to a wonky filing cabinet that sat in the corner of the room. An untidy pile of paperwork, to be filed, lay on top.

He opened the top drawer and winced as the rollers complained at the lack of lubrication.

The file he wanted was nestled at the back.

CHARLIE – OXFORD.

Along with Charlie's formal letter of acceptance from the college, were a series of introductory leaflets for the new student.

He scanned the first few, but saw only notes about college rooms with a heavy accent on the rules they must obey. *NO FEMALE VISITORS* seemed to be a recurring theme.

On the fourth sheet of paper, he found details of Charlie's tutor.

Professor Leonard Belkin FRS, CBE.

It was too early to call.

Back in the bedroom, he placed the folded contact sheet under his Alistair MacLean novel and got back into bed.

He re-awoke to the sound of Georgina on the phone downstairs. Squinting at the alarm clock, he was surprised to see it was after 9AM.

Georgina's conversation reverberated through the house. Some mention of a new department store in Salisbury.

"We'll go together. What larks!"

He wondered what plans were being hatched, fearing they would involve him.

A few minutes later, he emerged from the bathroom with a towel wrapped around his waist. Georgina was climbing the stairs; she poked Millie's spare tyre as she passed.

"Ow!"

"We're going to have to get you a bigger towel."

He put his hand on his tummy. "It's all paid for."

"Well, let's get back into our Sunday walks."

She disappeared back into the bedroom.

Millie followed. "Been making plans?"

Georgina adjusted her make-up in front of the dressing-table mirror. "We're going into Salisbury with the Mays." She spoke through contorted lips as she applied a red coat of lipstick. "There's a brand new department store. Turner's."

"Oh."

"Don't be too excited, Millie. You and Rob can always disappear off to the pub early."

She closed the lipstick with a flourish.

"Right, well, I'm going to get milk." Georgina danced down the stairs. "Be ready by the time I'm back."

Millie heard the door open and shut.

He retrieved the letter from under *The Guns of Navarone*. He shuffled down the carpeted stairs, holding the towel in place, leaving damp footprints in his wake.

He lifted the green telephone receiver and dialled.

The phone rang four times; Millie tapped his foot.

Finally, a woman answered. She spoke slowly in an ancient, shaky voice.

"Oxford, five-four-four-one. Professor Belkin's residence."

"Oh, hello. I was hoping to speak to the professor, please."

"May I ask who is calling?" said the woman, enunciating every word.

"My name is Milford."

She set down the receiver.

"A Mr Milford for you, Professor."

Another age went by.

"Hello, young Charles. How can I help you on a Saturday?"

"Actually, it's not Charlie. It's his father here."

"Oh. Hello, Mr Milford. What can I do for you? I hope everything is well?"

"Yes, it's all fine. This is all rather unusual, but I wonder if I could speak to you about a matter of some urgency to me and one which is, I'm afraid, rather sensitive."

"Is this to do with Charles? Is everything normal at home?"

"No, I mean yes, everything is normal but no, this is not about Charlie. It's about me. I need your help."

"My help? Goodness, this sounds exciting. Please ask away." The professor had a warm, whimsical quality to his voice.

"As I say, it's rather sensitive, but in simple terms I need to do a lot of repetitive mathematics. Rather too much for the human mind. I don't think it's too complicated, just beyond the normal powers of a human. At least it would take an inordinate period of time. And I recall you have a bombe. Is that what it's called?"

"We used to have, as you say, a bombe, but I'm afraid it has recently completed its last calculation. It's currently dismantled and I believe in a skip behind the mathematics department. Such a shame. The old girl had a hand in winning the war, you know."

"Oh dear. I'm sorry to hear that." Millie sat down on the small bench next to the telephone table.

"I'm sorry about that," said Belkin. "But it's all about the computer now and we needed the space."

"You have a computer?"

"Yes, we do."

"That might be even better."

"Might it? It's an IBM mainframe. It uses different methods of inputting the numbers from the bombe. I'm afraid it's all rather specialised. Punch cards and magnetic tape."

"I have magnetic tapes."

"You do?"

"Yes, but they're for a different computer. Will yours be able to decipher them do you think?"

"Honestly? I have no idea. I have a small army of technicians who do all that stuff. I have a vague notion of how the numbers are laid out. Something called ASCII. But beyond that I can't really say."

"I see."

"Perhaps we could try it. If you would find that helpful?"

"That would be wonderful. Maybe I could drop the tape off for you today?"

"Today? You are in a hurry, aren't you, Mr Milford?" The professor paused. "Am I right in thinking you are an officer in the Royal Air Force?"

Millie heard the car pulling back into the drive.

"I am, Professor, and I am very much in need of some help. I must ask for your absolute discretion, and that you don't mention this conversation to anyone, including my son. Can I visit you today?"

"Why not? Rhodes Cottage, in Merton Street. It should be easy to find."

Millie scribbled down the address and directions next to the telephone number, just as the door opened and Georgina breezed into the room.

"Goodbye." He hung up.

Georgina stared at him. "Millie, you're not even dressed, for goodness sake! And who on Earth was that on the telephone?"

"Charlie."

"Our Charlie?"

"Yes. Look, I feel bad that I missed dropping him off at the beginning of term and he called to ask about my cricket bat. I thought I would deliver it to him. Give me a chance to see his new rooms."

Georgina put down the car keys on the sideboard in the hallway.

"You're going to deliver your cricket bat to Charlie?" She tilted her head at him.

"Yes."

"In Oxford?"

"Yes. He has an end-of-term match, and he wanted to borrow it."

"But Charlie gave up cricket at school."

Fishing rod. I should have said fishing rod.

"I know. But they've invited him to play and he wants to and I said yes."

She pulled a silk headscarf from a coat hook and draped it over her hair. "I see. So you won't be coming to Salisbury with Mary and Rob? And you'll need the car."

"Please don't make a thing of it to Rob. Tell him I'm very sorry to miss it and that we'll see each other at the cocktail party tonight. Tell him I'll drive."

"OK," she said, and finished tying the scarf under her chin. "Well, give him my love. Of course, we'll see him in three weeks."

————

In his college cottage, Professor Leonard Belkin sat at the kitchen table with a copy of *The Times*, folded to reveal the cryptic crossword.

After solving one clue, his mind wandered to the unusual telephone call.

"Mrs Lazenby," he called out.

A small woman in her eighties appeared at the kitchen doorway.

"We are expecting a guest, Mrs Lazenby."

"Tomorrow?" she asked, looking at the kitchen clock.

"Today."

"*Today?*"

"Today," he confirmed.

He watched as she turned this news over in her mind.

"What time are we expecting this guest?"

"This very afternoon, would you believe?"

"Shall I fetch some tea from Danbury's?"

"I think a selection of cakes from Danbury's would be most excellent." He thought for a moment. "I think it best not to mention this visit to anyone."

"Anyone?"

"No-one, perhaps I should say."

"I would never—"

"Mrs Lazenby, I know you would not. I'm just being cautious."

She nodded to the man whose house she had kept for thirty-seven years. "Of course, Professor."

As she left the room, Belkin picked up his pen to continue with the crossword.

He read the clue—*An amble in Provence (4)*—and entered the letters r-o-v-e into the empty boxes.

Too easy. He tapped his ballpoint pen on the newspaper.

An RAF officer requiring statistical enquiries in absolute secrecy. A little more tricky.

———

As HE PASSED the turn to Abingdon, Millie spotted a lay-by ahead and pulled the car over.

He took out the instructions again and checked the AA road map.

He pulled away again, having memorised the route.

Twenty-five minutes later, he drove along Oxford High Street, slowing for distracted shoppers as they stepped into the road. He thought of Georgina, Mary and Rob, doing the same in Salisbury, although he had no doubt that they had probably found themselves in The Haunch of Venison for a little pick-me-up and a sandwich by now.

He turned into King Edward Street and drove to the end before turning onto a narrow, cobbled lane, passing an ancient sign announcing Merton Street.

Small cottages hugged either side of the road as he slowed to a crawl and read the names. He stopped the car outside a set of closed wooden double gates marked *RHODES COTTAGE.*

He was suddenly aware that Charlie's college rooms were nearby. Hopefully, his son had found his way into a pub for lunch.

He got out and approached the faded green front door. There was no immediate response to his knock, but eventually, the door opened, and an elderly woman stood in the shadows.

"Do come in, Mr Milford. I'm Mrs Lazenby."

Millie glanced at his car. He imagined Charlie cycling past and stopping in surprise at the sight of his father's distinctive red Rover.

"Do you think it would be possible to open the gates such that I might park there?"

Mrs Lazenby slowly closed the front door. Millie stepped back and looked up at the low building. It was a sweet little place, but on closer inspection, the window frames were rotting and the paint was peeling from the door.

He heard a noise to his left and saw the brown gates opening inwards.

Moving them back was a short man, with wisps of grey hair, baggy beige trousers, a white shirt and, despite the heat, a cardigan and tie.

"It's best to reverse in and drive forwards out," said the professor. "You are statistically less likely to kill a student on a bike that way, although I have never run the actual numbers on that."

Millie got back into the Rover and pulled forward before loudly crunching the gears in search of reverse. As he backed in, he was glad to see the professor close the gates in front of him.

He picked up one of the reels of tape and secreted the remaining five under the passenger seat.

As he climbed out of the car, the professor beckoned him toward a side entrance. Although only five feet ten, he had to lower his head to pass under a wonky beam with more peeling paint.

The cottage was cool. The ancient wattle and daub walls were crumbling, and it smelled of damp. A grandmother clock ticked in the hallway.

He squinted at a souvenir plate on the wall. *His Majesty's Silver Jubilee 1910 – 1935.*

The place was a time capsule; a world away from the bustling, modern environment of TFU.

Mrs Lazenby, complete with flowery pinny, showed Millie into the kitchen where he and Belkin sat opposite each other around a small square table.

She poured the tea with great care.

The professor regarded him. "How was the drive, Mr Milford?"

"Fine. I got a little lost at Abingdon, but soon found my way back."

Millie's hand shook as he raised the teacup to his mouth.

Mrs Lazenby left the room and closed the door behind her.

"So, Mr Milford, what branch of the Royal Air Force benefits from your service?"

"I'm an engineer by trade. I used to keep various fighters and bombers in the air, but about ten years ago I found myself working on the electrical and now electronic side of things."

"Interesting. Do you work with innovations like Autoland?"

"I'm impressed you know the proper name. In fact I did some work for the Blind Landing Experimental Unit just after the war and then worked with Philips to develop autopilot technology. Quite satis-fying to see it in civil airliners today."

"I'm sure it is. I see where young Milford gets his prowess from."

Millie laughed. "I'm no match for Charlie when it comes to maths, I'm afraid. I'm much more of a practical type."

The professor smiled. "And that is why you need some help with the numbers from us?"

"I'm not sure even Charlie could decipher these figures. It's the sheer volume of sums needed. I think only a large computer will do."

"Well, that's what they're best for. It's frightening, actually, how quickly they can rattle through calculations. They can perform in an hour what a human would take many weeks to complete. Maybe months, actually." Belkin clasped his hands together on the table. "So, Mr Milford. Exactly how can we help you?"

The professor spoke with a soft Scottish burr, possibly Edinburgh. Much clearer in person than on the telephone. He looked kindly and had a gentle manner.

Millie replaced the teacup on its saucer, knowing he was about to gamble with his own freedom and possibly much more.

"I need to be very careful about what I tell you. Do you think it is possible for you to treat this as an academic exercise, unrelated to anything physical, as such?"

"I see. I think so. Academic exercises are what we do best at Oxford."

Millie delved into his sports jacket pocket and retrieved the tape. He placed it on the table between them.

"On this tape are numbers. The numbers represent distance, in feet, I think. I'd like to know if you can read it, and whether your computer could look through the readings and spot any imperfections."

"Imperfections?"

"What I mean is, anything that makes little sense. A sudden jump in the numbers that seems implausible."

The professor appeared to think about this and finally removed his half-moon glasses, waving them in his hand as he spoke. "You're talking about variance, I think. A mathematical term for deviation from a datum. With the right parameters, then yes, as long as we can extract the data, we can create a routine to trawl through and highlight any sets of data that deviate outside of parameters we set. Something like a percentile scale. Do you see?"

"I think so. Basically, what I'm looking for is a pattern unlikely to exist in reality. So, for instance, you might get ten minutes of height readings in a range of say three hundred to four hundred, followed by a second or so of height readings that show one thousand two hundred, then it goes back to the original range. Do you think that's possible?"

"I think so, yes. How many height readings are we talking about?"

Millie thought for a moment. "The tape records twenty-seven every second, and each tape runs for fifteen to twenty minutes."

"Twenty-five thousand numbers on the tape," said the professor. "It sounds like a lot to you and me, but to the machine, it's just a few hours of whirring."

"If you can read this tape, I am hoping to deliver one hundred more."

The professor put down his tea and clasped his hands together on the table.

"Mr Milford, may I ask whether this is an official visit from an RAF officer? Or are you doing some freelance work?"

Millie looked around at the kitchen. Faded cupboards and yellowed ceiling. One door to a lower hung off its solo hinge.

"It's not official," he said, watching Belkin, "but it is Royal Air Force business."

"I see. And yet I don't. Which, I suspect, is your intention?"

"Professor Belkin, I do very much appreciate the delicate position I am placing you in. I think I can only appeal to your good nature to help an RAF engineer who needs a dose of modernity in, shall I say, a neutral environment."

The professor seemed to consider this before giving a brief nod. "Very well. I do not operate the computer myself, I'm sure you appreciate that, but I do set the tasks for the boys in white coats and I believe I can enlist some help from the team."

Millie exhaled.

"Wonderful."

"Our first task is to read the tape. And I make no promises about the success of this. Lord knows if this tape will even align with our computer, but there's only one way to find out. "

A clock in the hall struck midday.

"If I can get you some more tapes in, say, ten days' time, would you be able to read them before the end of term?"

"It depends on how long the processing takes, but in principle, yes."

"When will you be able to let me know if you can read this tape?"

"I'm not sure. They are a keen lot, your son's cohort, and the department is open on a Saturday. I may wander over later today and try my luck. But it might have to wait until Monday. Would you like me to call you at your work?"

"No," Millie snapped back, more harshly than he intended.

The professor laughed. "Silly me, of course not. We are to move in the shadows, are we not? Perhaps you would leave a suitable contact?" He finished his tea as Millie wrote his home telephone number.

"You're nervous," Belkin said as he took the note.

There was a quiet tap at the kitchen door.

"I am. This is rather out of the ordinary for me and not without risk. But needs must, I'm afraid."

Belkin studied him for a moment before calling to Mrs Lazenby.

"Do come in."

The old woman appeared with two brown paper bags. She fussed about with plates on the kitchen top before placing a generous pile of cakes and sweets between Belkin and Millie.

"The chocolate eclairs from Danbury's are nothing short of sensational." Belkin pushed a plate toward Millie.

Mrs Lazenby left the room and closed the door.

The professor gave Millie a wink. "I suspect clandestine operations will take it out of both of us. Best to stock up on energy, Mr Milford." He pushed a long eclair into his mouth.

––––––

EARLY AFTERNOON HAD BECOME siesta time at the peace camp.

Susie rather liked it.

But something stirred her from her sleep.

The earth trembled. She raised her head to see her fellow campers walking toward the airfield fence. The sound grew louder.

They were used to the noise of aircraft, both propeller and jet engines, but this was different. A more familiar, prosaic sound.

Lorries.

She stood up.

In a cloud of dust on the southern taxiway, a stream of large, double-axle vehicles trundled toward them. Tarpaulin covered their loads.

"This can't be good," she said to herself.

She joined the others as they stood in a row up against the wire fence that separated them from the military world beyond.

The first lorries came to a stop, a few yards in front of them.

She counted at least twenty vehicles, with more coming.

Teams of camouflage-clad soldiers emerged and got busy pulling the covers back, revealing stacks of metal posts, and large rolls of what looked like knotted silver wire.

A man with a clipboard climbed out of the lead vehicle. He counted the lorries as they arrived.

David and a woman called Megan arrived by her side.

"Here to evict us?" David said.

"They're on the wrong side of the fence for that," replied Susie.

She stared at the silver wire, wound like hay bales. Narrowing her eyes, she could just make out the jagged surface of the material.

"Razor wire."

The first men marked out the ground a few yards inside the existing fence, and a team appeared with a pneumatic drill. They pushed a generator into place.

"If you want proof we're in the right place, here it is," said Megan. "This is all for us. They're frightened."

"Maybe we've missed our chance?" said David.

"No. We haven't." Megan wandered off.

Susie thought about the exchange for a moment.

"So, Megan's in charge?" She looked at David.

He smiled. "Of course she is."

The military men worked with military precision. The existing fence looked weedy and pathetic compared to the new menace.

Some protestors shouted at the men in uniform. They got no response, not even a glance.

"This is a well-planned operation," said Susie.

"We're organised as well. Don't worry about that. It takes a lot to defeat Megan."

A clanging rang out behind them and they turned to see Megan standing outside the wigwam banging a wooden spoon on a saucepan.

They joined the others converging on the central meeting tent.

As they assembled inside, Susie noted the hierarchical structure, with Megan and David at the front, preparing to address the throng. Someone she didn't recognise stood near the entrance. Tall, with a full blond beard.

It was hot and people set about pulling up the tent sides to let some air in.

Megan began her address.

"Our information was right. There's something secret at this base. Something nasty they are hiding from the world and they're going to great lengths to keep it that way. It's time for us to act."

The group murmured its approval. Susie exchanged looks with those around her. Some looked scared, others eager.

She turned back to the front; the bearded man was gone.

David spoke up, looking at his notes. "For a while we thought that an old Maintenance Unit, number 207, was a cover for something else. But now we know that most of the aircraft we see belong to a different squadron. A squadron that has no name and does not officially exist. We may be the first people outside the RAF to notice it."

"That will be our target," Megan said. "You won't all be involved. I will keep the details secret to protect the raiding group. But everyone can play their part. The preparation begins today."

The watchers applauded, and some pushed out into the cooler air.

Susie loitered back in the tent, edging her way through to David and Megan.

"I want to volunteer," she said as she got to the front.

"So does everyone," David replied.

Megan looked across at her. "Who are you? I don't know you."

"This is Susie," said David. "She's alright."

"I'm small. I can fit through small windows."

Megan appraised her again and nodded before going back to the keen volunteers in front of her.

Susie put her hand on David's arm. "This is the only reason I'm here. I think I've made that clear."

"I know."

———

MILLIE FUMBLED with the buttons on his suit shirt. He looked at himself in the mirror and practised holding in his stomach. It was the best way to avoid Georgina proposing a new fitness regime.

Georgina called from downstairs. *"Come on!"*

He was grateful it was a cocktail party, for which civilian suits were the dress order; it would have taken him even longer to squeeze into his mess kit.

He brushed the shoulders of his jacket and paused in front of the mirror. Since leaving Oxford, he'd been asking himself if he was doing the right thing. Wondering if there was another way, an official way, that would circumvent Mark Kilton, ensure the safety of future aircrew and not land him in prison.

The reflection staring back at him had no answers.

"Millie!"

He headed downstairs.

Georgina stood in front of the door, car keys in hand.

"Well?" she said.

"Well, what?"

"Millie! My frock."

He looked at her dress. It was black velvet with transparent sleeves. New. She must have bought it in Salisbury.

"It's lovely, dear."

———

AT THE MAYS', Millie got out so he could greet them properly. Mary emerged first; she looked beautiful in her red dress, but Millie thought better of mentioning it.

Mary galloped up and kissed Millie on the cheek, with Rob just behind her, grinning.

"Roberto! How was the shopping expedition?"

They shook hands.

"Delightful, naturally. You must let me know your secret for getting out of it."

They climbed into the car. Millie glanced across at Rob in the passenger seat. "Sorry I wasn't there to help you through what must have been a difficult afternoon."

Rob laughed. "I won't say you weren't missed. Anyway, how is Charlie?"

"He's very well, very well."

He heaved the heavy vehicle around the final bend, onto the straight that ran up to the main gate, and immediately had to brake hard.

A line of stationary cars ran along the main road.

Millie craned his neck to try and get a better view of what was happening. A car door was open at the front of the line. Had there been an accident?

He spotted two uniformed security officers, one of them leaning into a vehicle. The driver—an RAF colleague in his suit—was out, standing on the grass next to the road.

The officers appeared to be searching his car.

The tapes were still under the passenger seat.

A prickly heat rose up Millie's body and his hands tightened on the steering wheel.

"Is this about the new fence?" Mary asked.

"Looks like it," said Rob. "Security chaps have upped their game."

He turned to the women on the back seat.

"This gives me time to debrief you on your dress selection procedure."

They laughed.

"It's a very inefficient process, if I may observe."

"Oh, is it, Mr Dress Expert?" said Mary.

"Yes. You see, I watched you put on that dress, Mary. I made a note of the time. 11.02AM. I think it was the second dress you tried on. Do you know what you said when you tried it?"

The car crawled further forward. Millie could see more clearly now; the officers were opening boots and back doors. One man had a torch.

He could grab the cardboard sleeves containing the tapes and throw them into the bushes. But how could he? How would he explain it?

"I didn't know you paid that much attention, husband," said Mary.

Millie glanced at his rear-view mirror: smiles and laughing faces on the back seat.

"I was paying very close attention," said Rob, "mainly because I didn't have my partner in crime here to distract me."

Millie tried to smile, but his heart was pounding.

They crept forward again. The security men were now three cars ahead.

Millie's eyes urgently scanned the scene. How hard were they looking?

If they found the reels, they would arrest him.

In front of everyone.

He cursed his stupidity at leaving them under the seat. He'd simply forgotten.

"You said..." Rob waved his finger at the two women, who seemed to be enjoying the inquisition. "You said, 'this is perfect'." He shouted the word again. "*Perfect.*"

A gap appeared as the car in front moved forward.

He could pull out and drive home.

He could claim he'd forgotten something.

"And yet... you then tried on five more dresses. *Five.* Before, guess what? You bought the one you had tried on at 11.02. Two hours earlier. Because, and I quote, it was 'perfect'."

The car in front stopped; the gap wasn't big enough to get out cleanly. Millie willed it to move on, to give him space.

"Of course," said Georgina. "She tried on five more dresses. It's an essential part of the process."

"Is it?" said Rob, with more than a hint of doubt in his voice.

The vehicle in front was on the move again, but just as Millie prepared to pull out, a security man appeared and walked directly toward them.

He felt his hands become slippery with sweat on the steering wheel.

Rob settled down from his goading of the women and put on a more serious expression.

"Here comes the plod. I do hope you two paid for those dresses."

The officer leaned down and motioned for Millie to open the window.

"Good evening. We need to search the car, please. Can you open the boot?"

The women stifled giggles in the back.

Millie could barely breathe. He nodded, afraid to talk in case it came out as a croak.

He opened the door and stepped out, glancing back at the bottom of the passenger seat, where Rob sat inches away from stolen Top Secret information.

As Millie got to the boot, he realised he didn't have the keys and went back to the driver's door.

His hand shook as he reached in to the ignition.

"You OK, Millie?" asked Rob.

"Yes," he replied, his voice just about holding.

He opened the boot and the security man looked in at the spare tyre, jack and rusty foot-pump, before walking around to the far side of the Rover.

The man arrived at Millie's open driver's door, glancing back at the long queue of traffic caused by the delays. He leant in to the car, where the women were still giggling.

Millie took a step closer as the officer reached in and retrieved something from between the two seats.

Millie froze as the officer backed out and turned the object over in his hands.

It was Millie's tatty AA road atlas.

"There you are, sir. Sorry for the delay." He handed the map book to Millie and moved quickly on to the car behind.

After he'd climbed back in, Millie made deliberately slow movements to start the engine again, put it into gear and drive off.

He could feel Rob watching him.

"You look like you've seen a ghost."

"No. Just annoyed at all this palaver."

Rob nodded and turned back to face the road. "Yes, it's silly. They're getting their knickers in a twist about this peace camp. Paranoid that one of the hippies is going to get smuggled in, I suppose."

"Well, they're just doing their jobs," said Millie.

"I think the peace bunnies add a touch of glamour to the place," announced Mary in the back.

"For god's sake, don't let Kilton hear you say that," said Rob.

Millie turned into the main gate and wound down the window; he had his identification form ready and handed it over for inspection.

His hand was still shaking.

The corporal glanced at the paper and lifted the barrier.

———

THEY JOINED the throng in the large mess ante room. The furniture was pushed back against the walls with suited men and gowned women filling the space.

A waiter arrived with a tray of glasses containing room temperature white wine.

Millie enjoyed a long glug; he needed some fortification for the moment later when he would have to exit the RAF station.

The women headed over to an open window; Millie and Rob followed.

Red Brunson and his wife joined them.

"Howdy folks! Anyone else enjoying the warm wine?" Brunson said.

The group laughed. Georgina straightened her back; Millie realised she'd never been introduced.

"Red, can I introduce my wife, Georgina? Georgina, this is Red and Sarah Brunson. Red's on an exchange with us from Edwards Air Force base in California."

"California? Gosh, how glamorous," she said while shaking both their hands.

"Don't get carried away," Sarah Brunson said, "this ain't the California The Beach Boys sing about. We're a hundred miles from the coast in Nowhere USA. Salt flats and shacks. That's Edwards."

"Well, it still sounds more glamorous than Salisbury."

"Honey, I could not wait to get out." She looped her arm through Red's. "Just had to buy the right ticket."

Millie wanted to enjoy himself, but he had a task to carry out first.

As the group got into conversation, he removed his wristwatch and dropped it into his jacket pocket.

Noticing the glasses were getting low, he tapped Rob on the shoulder.

"Sortie to the bar?"

Rob nodded and followed Millie through the crowd to replenish the drinks. Once at the bar, Millie pulled his sleeve up, revealing his bare wrist.

"Feel naked without it."

"Your watch?"

"Silly thing. I left it in the office. Would you mind if I fetched it?"

Rob shrugged. "Fine. I'll see you back with the girls."

Millie marched out of the mess, climbed into his car and drove toward the main guardroom. He parked a short distance away—not so close that it would attract any further attention from the police—and got out, locking it behind him.

In the guardroom, he signed out the keys to TFU.

The sergeant asked to see his identification, which Millie couldn't remember happening before, but then he was in his civilian suit.

With the keys secured, he got back into the Rover and drove through the centre of the station to the airfield fence.

A security officer stood outside the open gate to the TFU car park. *Christ, they're everywhere.*

He drove in, with the security man watching him but making no attempt to stop the vehicle.

For the second time that evening, Millie found himself sweating. He quickly retrieved the five cardboard sleeves containing the reels and climbed out of the car.

He didn't look back, carrying the tapes in front of him as he marched up to the TFU front door.

Inside, he went straight to his locker and placed the tapes under his day jumper. Moments later, he drove back down to the mess and rejoined the group, feeling significantly more relaxed.

Georgina shot him a quizzical look.

"Rob says you've been off to fetch your watch."

"Yes, dear. Left it in the office."

"Do be careful. It was your father's." She pulled up his left sleeve; it was bare.

"Where is it, then?"

He retrieved it from his pocket. "Here."

"Really. You are odd sometimes, Millington."

He found his wine and topped up the alcohol buzz.

The Mays smiled and laughed with the Brunsons. Millie felt Georgina watching him.

"What?"

"Will you miss it?" she asked.

"I don't think so."

"Just think, we've stood in the corner at these events in Hong Kong, Nairobi, Singapore—"

"Church Fenton."

"Ah, yes. Yorkshire. Not quite as exciting, but we've had some fun, haven't we?"

"Yes, we have. I'll not forget the cannon battle in Tengah."

Georgina laughed out loud. "Oh, god. That was something. Didn't one of them explode and hurt someone?"

Millie laughed at the memory. "Rusty Brown. Set fire to his hair, as I recall. Quite exciting."

"Dear old Rusty. Where's he now?"

"Dead. Meteor ploughed in. Cyprus, I think."

They stood quietly for a moment.

The Brunsons and Mays burst out laughing.

"Getting on great guns," Georgina said. "It's their turn to have all that fun now."

"Lucky things."

Across the room, Mark Kilton stood next to Gilbert Periwinkle the station commander, chatting to a man with a gold chain around his neck and a small, plump wife. He supposed it was the mayor and mayoress, invited to keep the peace with the locals.

Periwinkle looked uncomfortable, as he usually did. The man lacked charisma and authority. Probably the qualities Kilton looked for in his own commanding officer.

The evening wore on. The Brunsons, Milfords and Mays stayed together, getting progressively more tipsy.

"Now here's a conspiratorial little group, if ever I saw one."

Kilton.

"Hello, Mark. How are you?" Georgina leant over to kiss him on the cheek.

"Now, Georgina, I need your help. Who do you think we should appoint as the new mess secretary?"

"Well, someone you trust, as I assume you're still president of the mess committee?"

"Indeed I am. But I need a number two to do all the work."

"Well, don't look at Millie, for goodness sake. He falls asleep in the evenings as it is."

"Yes, well, I believe this is beneath his dignity. How about you, May?"

Rob straightened his back.

"You think my husband's undignified enough to do the job?" Mary asked, and the group laughed.

"Yes," Kilton replied and drained his wine.

"I'd be honoured," Rob said.

"Well, I haven't made my mind up yet, May. Just keep your powder dry and you might just make it."

Kilton moved off. Georgina raised her eyebrows at Millie and leaned over.

"That man doesn't do anything by accident. Looks like young Rob has caught his eye."

6

SUNDAY 12TH JUNE

The phone rang three times before Millie was properly awake.

Georgina groaned.

"What time is it?"

Millie clambered out of bed.

"Eight-thirty."

"*Ugh.*" Georgina rolled over and pulled a pillow over her head.

Millie hurried downstairs and took the call.

"Mr Milford, Leonard Belkin. I hope I haven't called too early for you?"

"No, no, that's fine. I was getting up, anyway."

"Right, well I thought I might not catch you tomorrow. Would now be a good time to report?"

"You've looked at the tape already?"

"You'll be pleased to know the tape has been read successfully."

"That's marvellous, thank you."

"They had to transcribe it from binary, which took a while, but it's something we can create a routine for in the future. However, we will need your help to identify what we found."

"Just height readings, I assumed?"

"Not quite. Do you have a pen and paper? It's rather a long list, I'm afraid."

Millie hurried upstairs and retrieved a large jotter pad from the spare bedroom. He paused before heading back down and looked at the open door to the main bedroom. He eased it shut.

Back on the phone, he took down a long stream of numbers, none of which made any sense to him at first glance.

Belkin passed on his notes from the computer technician. "We see twenty-nine separate groups of digits. They call them fields, for reasons I'm not clear about. The first field is made up of ten digits, the second field is fourteen digits, and the following twenty-seven are all smaller, just five digits."

"The'll be the twenty-seven height readings."

"I thought as much. What about the first two sets of numbers? Young Strangways, the technician, insists we'll need to understand their role if we are to find what you are looking for."

Millie looked at the numbers he'd scrawled across the pad. He'd only taken down one line of data so far. The ten-digit number was *0000127344*, the fourteen-digit one was *15105550114922*.

He asked Belkin for more rows and wrote down nine more lines of the first two mysterious fields.

The first field increased with each line, but the second number changed in what appeared to be a random order.

"I'm afraid I just don't know what the first two sets represent."

"Well, there's no immediate rush, as we don't have the rest of your tapes yet, but if you could have a think... I believe the routine we will create for you will take a day or two, so try to let us know what these mean a week before you deliver the remaining tapes. How does that sound?"

"It sounds very good indeed. I'll do my best, and thank you, Professor. Honestly, this is more than I could have hoped for."

"Very good, Mr Milford. I will await your next communication."

The professor hung up. It would look odd if he went into work on a Sunday, but he was desperate to get to the Guiding Light files and make a start on identifying the fields.

He sat on the small bench by the phone, in his striped pyjamas.

It would have to wait; he'd displayed enough unusual behaviour for one weekend.

———

MILLIE AND GEORGINA meandered through the married quarter patch into the village.

Sunday church was more a habit than a rite, although Millie enjoyed the quiet moments of reflection the service offered.

As they sang their way through hymn 233, *Oh thou who camest from above*, Millie cast his eyes around the busy congregation. Mary stood a few rows in front, in a blue cloche hat, with Rob presumably just beyond her, although a pillar obscured his view.

He smiled at his women's hat identification skills.

Outside in the bright sunshine, Millie and Georgina waited for the Mays to appear. Eventually, the younger couple emerged, surrounded by a group of RAF colleagues. All smiles and handshakes.

"They look like minor royalty," Georgina said.

At that moment, Mary caught his eye, and she and Rob walked toward them.

"Who would like some lunch?" Millie asked.

Rob grinned. "We were hoping you'd say that. We have dresses and hats in the house, but no food, apparently."

"Just the essentials then," Georgina said.

———

BACK AT THE MILFORDS' quarter, the women got busy in the kitchen while Millie took Rob through the firs to spy on the peace camp.

"What do you think of the new fence?" asked Rob.

The new structure was unmissable: four or five feet higher than the existing fence and topped with angry looking razor wire.

"Appropriately nasty," said Millie. "Do you think it's there to keep them out or has Kilton installed it to keep us in?"

"He's not that bad, Millie. Just doing his job in the face of a serious threat to us all."

"Well, maybe the fence is there to keep you in and me out," Millie said, and watched for a reaction.

Rob didn't respond.

They walked back into the garden and Millie enlisted Rob's help in carrying the dining room table and chairs out onto the patio.

The more sherry Millie drank, the more he convinced himself that Rob was now a lost cause, sucked into Mark Kilton's gravity well.

During dinner, the sound of singing drifted over from the camp, accompanied by guitar and tambourine.

Rob tilted his head and tutted.

"I'm afraid Rob is becoming grumpy about our new neighbours," Mary said.

Georgina smiled at her. "I think it sounds rather gay. Brightens the place up. They don't do any harm, do they?"

"Ah! I'm afraid my husband thinks quite the opposite."

Rob looked grave. "It's what's underneath the gaiety that we should be concerned about, Georgina. They may look like a ragtag group of misfits who've failed to get a decent job, but believe me, they're dangerous."

"Dangerous?" Georgina raised her eyebrows.

"Yes, dangerous. And frankly, it's a little disrespectful to the work we do to think otherwise."

A short silence fell, broken only by cutlery scraping on plates.

Millie piped up. "It's odd though, isn't it? I watch them from a distance sometimes and wonder. I saw a pretty young thing—"

Georgina gasped. "Millie!"

"Don't worry. It wasn't in that way. I'm old enough to be her grandfather. But I can't help thinking that people like her just want to rid the world of weapons that can destroy entire cities. I find it hard to see her as a secret Soviet agent."

"Why then, does she only want us to disarm and not Russia?" Rob asked.

"I suppose she also wants the Russians to get rid of their weapons, but she doesn't have any influence over them, does she?"

"If she was in Russia," snapped Rob, "she'd be shot, or sent off to the gulags. They don't think about that, do they? The peace they enjoy is created by us being strong, not weak. They abuse it and undermine it."

"Gosh, it's like having lunch with Mark Kilton," said Georgina.

Millie held up his hands. "Well, we're all on the same side. Let's remember that."

"I hope we are. West Porton's now a large station. A lot of people work there. Can we be sure about everyone?" Rob looked up at Millie.

Millie stared back at him, their eyes unflinching until Rob eventually looked back down at his plate.

Millie picked up his glass and sipped his wine.

After lunch, the girls disappeared into the house with the crockery.

"You OK, Rob?" Millie asked. "You seem a little pent up."

Rob lit a cigarette.

"There's so much at stake for us, Millie. Don't you feel that pressure?"

"The pressure to stop communism in its tracks? No, not really. Of course it's a terrible tyranny, it really is, where life is not valued and no-one is free. But we, you and I, can only do our bit. We can't walk around with that sort of weight on our shoulders."

"But these people..." He waved his cigarette vaguely in the direction of the singing. "It's the way they hang their banners on the fence and tell the world they are the ones fighting for peace, when they're doing quite the opposite. They put us in danger."

"Give some allowance, Rob. They're young, idealistic. Naive, if you like. But the world needs a little naive optimism, doesn't it?"

Rob didn't respond.

"Come on, where's the old Rob? My carefree friend. Is he in there somewhere?"

He got the merest hint of a smile, but nothing more.

7

MONDAY 13TH JUNE

Even at 6.45AM, the new gate security measures made it a slow plod into the station.

Logic told Millie he had nothing to be concerned about, but he still felt his heart thumping as the guard peered into his car.

Inside, the TFU planning room was quiet, and he headed straight for the admin office.

Standing in front of a large board with magnetic strips, he scanned the list of unit aircraft, checking the allocations for the various trial flights.

He and Rob were due to fly to Warton to inspect the next Guiding Light Vulcan. They were down for an old De Havilland Devon; a 1940s propeller driven workhorse.

But there was no experimental Guiding Light on the Devon, and he didn't want to waste a flight opportunity.

Of the two aircraft fitted with Guiding Light, the Vulcan was a non-starter for such a menial trip. But the Canberra wouldn't be out of place.

He scanned the board. The Canberra was allocated to a different crew in the afternoon.

"*Damn.*"

He was about to leave when he spotted one of the unit's other Canberras listed under 'spare', at the bottom of the board.

He looked around and found the young flight lieutenant who ran the admin office.

"Morning, Pete."

"Good morning, Squadron Leader Milford," the young man replied, while sorting a pile of papers.

Millie pointed at the board. "I wanted to check something about the aircraft allocations."

"Oh, yes?" Pete put down the papers and looked at the wall.

"This PR.3 is serviceable?"

"Should be."

Millie nodded, as if he was having a thought for the first time. "I'd prefer if Rob May and I had a Canberra rather than the slow boat to China we've been given." He pointed up to the Devon with *Flt Lt May (Warton)* written next to it. "Any chance we could swap for the PR.3? In fact, ideally, we'd like that PR.3." He placed his finger on the Guiding Light Canberra, allocated to a different trial.

The flight lieutenant scratched his chin for a moment. "So, you want me to swap the spare Canberra for the ADF trial, release their jet for you, and move the Devon to spare?" He said it slowly, as if testing the viability of the suggestion.

"If it's not too much trouble?"

Pete looked at his papers, which Millie now realised were the tasking sheets for the day. No doubt he would have some unwanted new paperwork.

After a moment, he shrugged and said brightly, "I don't see why not."

"Marvellous. Thank you, Pete. Very kind."

Millie left the room, avoiding any further questions.

He walked to his locker. Having the tapes hidden within was dangerous. He'd openly raised concerns about the project; if the material was discovered, out of place in his possession, Kilton would probably jump to the correct conclusion.

A fast-track to retirement would the very best he could hope for.

Millie pulled his car keys out of his pocket and opened the wooden door. He felt inside, checking the reels remained in place.

"Millie?"

He slammed the locker shut, spinning around to see a surprised-looking Pete.

"Sorry to startle you. Just wanted to know how late you can depart."

"We need to be in a meeting at Warton for 14.30 local, so sometime after 13.00? Rob will come up with a more precise time."

Pete nodded and looked pleased. "OK, good. We need both Canberras this morning, but it should be no problem to get one refuelled for you in time for 13.00."

"Thank you, Pete. And make sure it's Oscar Mike, please." The whole exercise would be futile if Pete gave him the wrong aircraft.

Back in the main planning room, Millie sat down at one of the side desks. The room was filling up fast. Loud complaints about the gate security filled the air.

The pilots and navs disappeared off to the met brief.

Millie pulled a sheet of paper from his pocket. He placed it on his desk and stared at the ten lines of numbers he'd taken down from Belkin.

He had the secure cabinet unlocked, and retrieved the Guiding Light manuals. A normal enough exercise for the project leader.

The manual contained schematics of the equipment itself, detailed descriptions of the inner workings.

It was one of the most valuable documents in the world.

But after ten minutes of leafing through, he was no closer to explaining what the first two fields were.

Before handing the file back, Millie had a thought. He wondered if he would need the basic schematics to submit as part of his evidence? The file was rarely looked at now. They used it in the early days, but it was likely he was the first to pull it out in months.

There was a danger it would get moved to a secure archive soon.

He removed four key pages.

With the room still quiet, he handed the file back before slipping the folded schematics alongside the reels in his locker.

Back at the desk, he stared at the two fields, hoping for some moment of inspiration.

Again, he noticed how the first column of numbers appeared to go up sequentially, and evenly, with each line, but the second number went both up and down.

The first column might be the time, but not in a form he recognised.

The room filled up again; the met brief had obviously concluded.

An idea struck Millie, as he recalled a TV documentary he'd seen recently on the Apollo project. Casting around the room, he saw Red Brunson, friend of the astronauts, standing at the tea bar.

As he stood up, Rob appeared next to him.

"Morning. Thank you for lunch, and sorry if I was a little overbearing. Mary told me off when we got home."

Millie smiled. "No apology necessary. Living under the shadow of the bomb does that to man." Rob laughed. "Anyway, how's the weather?"

"Ah, well you can look out of the window, or I can tell you what the met man just said. I doubt the two are related. But we should be fine. Anything I need to prepare for this afternoon?"

"I don't think so. You just need to ensure the Guiding Light panels are identical at your end in the cockpit and I'll do the same down below. The boss wants crews to swap between the jets easily. And I think it's all being done in a bit of a rush, so the drawings might not be reliable."

"OK, fine. I'm up with Red in the Victor this morning. Simple radio trial. Should be done by eleven."

"Sounds like fun." Rob loitered for a moment, looking down at the sheet of paper on Millie's desk.

"Picked up some young ladies' telephone numbers?"

Millie's hand covered the handwritten lines of data.

"Oh, no. It's nothing."

"Ha. It's OK, Millie, I didn't really think you'd pulled." He moved off.

Millie slipped the sheet back in his pocket and went for a cup of tea.

The American stood over a planning desk. Millie poured himself a cup from the urn and joined him.

"Red, quick question. You once said something about the computer on the Apollo project?"

"Yeah, pretty neat. The guys at Edwards told me it runs the show. They do everything from the ground, more or less. The pilots—sorry, astronauts—they're only there to flick the odd switch. Strange."

"And I recall you said something about the clock."

"The mission clock, yeah. What about it?"

"Is it important to know the time?"

"It's not the time, it's the mission clock. A different thing. It's absolutely vital. Same as the Gemini and Mercury projects before Apollo, the computer does everything according to the clock. That famous countdown to launch? That's not just for the television. That's the mission clock, counting down. Then it starts counting up. T-minus something before launch and T-plus something after. Mission elapsed time."

"I see, so it's not the actual time? Zulu, Greenwich Mean Time, for instance?"

Red put his hand on Millie's shoulder. "I know you Brits think you're the centre of the world, but it ain't Zulu. It's just seconds, man. Seconds, minutes, hours, days."

"Interesting."

"Sure is, skip."

Back at his desk, Millie quietly opened up the sheet.

He did some maths on the first field, subtracting the second line from the first.

0000127681 - 0000127344

The difference was three hundred and thirty-seven. He furrowed his brow. Far too many seconds.

According to the file, the laser fed the computer three reports of height data every second.

He looked back at the numbers:

"Bingo," he whispered.

The fourth digit along must be whole seconds, followed by hundredths. So the first height came at 127.344 seconds, the next at 127.681, and the third at 128.001. Gaps of roughly one third of a second.

He could see it clearly now.

On the pad where he had written the numbers, he added column headers for the first set:

s s s s s s h h h
0 0 0 1 2 7 3 4 4

He thought back to the flight where these readings were created. Why did it all start at 127.344 seconds?

Millie had switched on Guiding Light as they rolled down the runway, but hadn't started the tape until they were established on their route. He'd checked it was working, first by dialling through the eleven data feeds, then switching the tape recorder to *RUN*.

127.344 seconds. Two minutes of fiddling. That was about right.

It all made sense.

One field down, one to go.

———

THEY GOT airborne in the Canberra at 13.40, for a meeting at 14.30 local in Lancashire. Flight time was a miserly forty minutes, but enough for two tapes of Guiding Light height data.

Rob flew using visual flight rules, avoiding the various air traffic zones.

As they climbed out of West Porton, Millie, strapped into the ejection seat usually occupied by a navigator, set the data recorder running. He'd quietly armed the laser and powered up the computer as Rob went through his checks.

They had chosen the Canberra as the first recipient of the Guiding Light because of the space, once the recon camera and equipment were removed. But it was a test-bed and nothing more. The system operated in isolation, with no autopilot, and no indication to the pilot that the system was installed, let alone actually running. An advantage for Millie on this occasion.

He had already decided he couldn't risk changing reels mid-flight. It was something Rob was likely to notice.

As the flight progressed and the reel came to its end, he considered it again, but then the Canberra's nose dipped and they began a descent into Warton. Too late.

As the jet engines wound down on the ground, Millie removed the full reel and slipped it into a loose pocket. Once out of the jet, he saw Rob removing his coveralls, in preparation for the meeting, and had to follow suit.

As he folded his coveralls, he paused. An unintended consequence of a land-away in a Guiding Light aircraft was the security implication. They would leave the equipment alone in the Canberra, including a full reel of data that could easily be accessed.

If something went wrong, there would be an enquiry to end all enquiries. Why was the Canberra used for such a journey? Who allowed the equipment change?

His name would be the answer to all the questions.

More than that, he was genuinely risking the secrecy of the project.

Rob appeared next to him.

He shut the Canberra up and cursed the lack of key and lock.

As they walked across the apron toward the factory offices, he realised it was a gaping hole that no-one had much thought about. It was all very well searching cars on the way in and out of West Porton, but nothing stopped them flying out with all manner of sensitive material. In fact, it was part of their routine.

No-one checked, no-one asked, no-one searched.

Inside the factory, they were given a quick tour of the Lightning production line. At the back of the cavernous hall, a section had been screened off by enormous black hanging material. Poking out of one end was the distinctive tail of an Avro Vulcan.

Millie pointed. "Are you already fitting it?"

The man nodded.

The Vulcan was literally shrouded in secrecy.

A man in a suit and tie showed them to a makeshift security barrier. Millie and Rob signed in, and moments later, they were inside the aircraft inspecting the installation work.

It didn't take long to confirm the panels would be identical to those they were already familiar with, and they headed back to the management offices and signed a few forms to say the work was proceeding as agreed.

They decided on a delivery date, and, twenty-five minutes later, walked out onto the apron.

The Canberra sat alone, and unregarded.

"I do enjoy a little day trip with our own private jet," said Rob.

Millie laughed. "We should take days out more often. Perhaps not Manchester, though."

"I'm sure we could find a reason to go to Cyprus." Rob disappeared around the Canberra to kick the tyres.

Millie dressed for the journey back, reassured by the weight of the reel in his coveralls pocket. Before he donned his life jacket, he slipped in the next blank tape.

Rob's hands moved across the Canberra's controls. He soon had them rolling down the long runway, then gently banking right as they climbed out.

He continued to fly them west to the Irish Sea, before turning south, heading for Wales.

It was a cloudless afternoon and Rob was clearly enjoying himself.

Millie's thoughts turned to the pressing issue of how to remove the growing number of tapes from highly secure West Porton.

There was no point in continuing to gather the height readings on a growing collection of tapes if he couldn't get them out of a locker inside the base.

Could he hide them in his car? Under the mats in the footwells? Inside the spare tyre?

Even then, how would he move them from his locker to the car park without risking everything?

He sighed and rested his head on the top of the ejection seat.

The roar of air across the airframe washed over him, and he closed his eyes.

————

BACK IN TFU, most of the men were in the mess or on their way home.

Millie was mildly embarrassed that Rob had to wake him up in the jet. He moved straight to his locker and added two more reels to his pile.

Rob breezed past, coveralls in hand with his helmet, oxygen mask and life jacket ready for a quick deposit.

Millie gathered his own things and walked toward the door.

"Milford. A word if you please."

Millie walked into Kilton's office and closed the door behind him.

"I'm adding Jock MacLeish and Red Brunson to the Guiding Light crew," said Kilton. "We need to speed this up."

"Why? We're working well together and it's a small team. You said yourself you didn't want to involve anyone else."

Kilton snorted. "I'm not asking for your opinion, Millie. Just make sure they're trained up as quickly as possible."

Millie stood, trying to think of a better objection.

"Goodbye, Millie." Kilton dismissed him with a wave of his hand, as if he was a schoolboy in the headmaster's office.

8

TUESDAY 14TH JUNE

A flash of red streaked across the junction ahead. Millie recognised Rob's Austin Healey, with the top down. He was also heading in early.

By the time Millie had negotiated the vehicle search and arrived at the tea bar, Rob was in animated conversation with Red Brunson.

Millie took his mug to his desk and sat down by himself.

An admin corporal arrived next to him and handed him a document.

As usual, it was marked *TOP SECRET*. Inside the front page was a reorganised Guiding Light trials schedule. By the following week, when the second Vulcan was in service, they would double the hours flown.

He tried to do the maths in his head, working out how little time he had left. Once TFU signed the project off, it would swing into production and quickly roll out to the waiting aircraft, both here and in the US.

And buried deep within the circuits, a mistake. A calculation that came out wrong, or maybe just a fluctuating current between tiny electronic components that should be steady. Either way, something had sent a four engine bomber plunging to the ground and no-one except him seemed to care why.

"Heard the news."

He looked up to see Rob smiling at him.

"Hmm?"

"Red and Jock are joining us."

"Yes, I heard. Is that exciting to you?"

Rob grabbed a chair and sat down alongside Millie's desk.

"Come on, Millie. Of course it is. I've been dying to share this with Red. Just think, we'll be flying with someone who rubs shoulders with the men selected to walk on the Moon."

"Just because he wears that fancy helmet doesn't make him an astronaut." Rob grimaced. "I'm sorry, Rob. Of course it's exciting, especially for you. Keep close to Red. He's a good man. And he likes you."

"You think?"

"I do. For the same reason I like you. You're very likeable."

"Don't make me blush."

A shout came across the room. Rob stood up to join the other pilots in the weather brief.

"When you get back, can you bring Red and Jock into the meeting room?" said Millie. "We need to start the induction."

Rob nodded and disappeared with a spring in his step.

After they re-emerged, Millie gathered the new crew around the meeting table, with Rob, Speedy and Steve Bright, before closing the door.

"Firstly, as the boss has no doubt explained, this project falls under 'Top Secret' and is subject to his philosophy of 'Need to Know', which is why a lot of this will be new to you.

"Alongside the more public development of Terrain-Following Radar, we're flying with a technology that does the same job, but uses light."

"Light? What do you mean?" Jock asked.

"Laser," Millie said, and looked up to enjoy the facial expressions he knew this would provoke.

"Laser beams? Are you serious?" Red's eyes widened.

"Absolutely serious. The boffins at DF Blackton in Cambridge have created what may be the world's smallest laser. It sits under the Vulcan's nose, carefully hidden in the usual casing. Mirrors and a gimbal allow it to sweep the terrain ahead. It works not only as a range finder, but it also deduces the ground speed."

"Phew-wee..." Red whistled.

"They've also designed a computer, running on microelectronics, that sits between the laser and the autopilot. We tell the computer where we want to be, using waypoints. It then uses the information from the laser to fly the aircraft at a pre-set height, as efficiently as possible."

"Just, wow," Jock said.

Red Brunson whistled again. "Incredible. I thought only NASA did stuff like this. I don't even think they're this advanced."

"They're not. Your lot have signed a memorandum of understanding. They're ready to hand the UK one of its biggest export orders in history, when it's ready."

Millie glanced at Rob and Steve. "But, we're not out of the woods on this one. We had a hairy moment a couple of weeks back and we're currently no lower than a thousand feet above ground level."

Brunson frowned. "What sort of 'hairy moment'?"

Before Millie could answer, Rob stepped in.

"Maybe something, maybe nothing, we're not sure. The jet descended briefly and we switched Guiding Light off. But everything checked out afterwards. The thousand-foot AGL is just a precaution."

MacLeish leaned back in his chair.

"Am I to assume that was the cause of the row in the mess and poor old Brian Hill's disappearance?"

"Yes—"

"He overreacted," said Rob, interrupting Millie. "The equipment was double-checked at Cambridge and the boss is on top of things. I think we should probably let sleeping dogs lie when it comes to Brian. We've moved on."

"Fine," said Jock. "What would test flying be if there wasn't the outside chance of plunging into the ground, anyway?"

Rob turned to the two new trial pilots. "When was the last low flying you did?"

Brunson shrugged. "When we practised for today's gas bomb drop. What was that? A month ago, in a slow Argosy. I haven't done much, to be frank."

"I'm definitely out of practice," said MacLeish.

"No problem," said Rob. "I'll arrange a couple of Vulcan training flights to get you into the swing of things. You can have your first experience of letting the computer take over." He glanced at Millie. "I have to warn you, though. Flying hands-off at low-level takes some getting used to. Jock, you can fly with Speedy, Millie and Steve today, while Red and I get the gas bomb drop out of the way."

Millie sat back. The pilot side of things was not his area of expertise, but he was taken aback at Rob's assertiveness. This was a sharp contrast to the timid young man who joined TFU the previous year.

An hour and a half later the same group of men stepped out onto the TFU apron.

"Man, I can't get over how ugly that thing is," Red Brunson said, looking across at the Argosy.

Millie watched, curious, as two men in white coats and gas masks fussed around a crate being loaded into the cargo aircraft's belly.

"Those your gas bombs?"

"Yep," Brunson replied. "The real things today. Dropping them on a mock village at Porton Down."

"What's actually in them?"

"*Chlorobenzalmalononitrile*," Brunson said with a flourish. "Took me a while to learn to say that."

"What the hell is it?" Millie asked as the last crate entered the Argosy.

"Just makes your eyes sting. We've been told it won't kill anyone unless we drop the crate directly onto their heads. In any case the village is populated by dummies."

"Just like this place then," Jock said.

The two crews set off for their separate aircraft. Rob and Red Brunson carried gas masks along with their helmets.

TFU's ageing resident loadmaster, Nigel Woodward, stood at the Argosy, in conversation with the Porton Down scientists. Millie smiled at the generational clash.

They arrived at the Vulcan. Millie made sure he was the last to board, after Jock and Speedy completed their walkaround together.

As Speedy instructed Jock on the differences in the cockpit from the standard production Vulcan, Millie loaded a reel of tape.

Steve Bright stowed the yellow ladder and closed the hatch.

Minutes later, the Vulcan came to life and the crew entered the closed world of the intercom.

As they climbed out of West Porton, Millie powered up Guiding Light and began a tape.

Over the intercom, Speedy thanked him and explained to Jock why the panel was now displaying height information.

They headed west to their usual playground in Wales.

————

THE VULCAN SHOOK the ground as it clambered into the air over the western threshold. Susie sat ten yards inside the double fence; she blocked her ears but could still feel the noise as it vibrated through her.

The sound became more manageable as the white aircraft banked right and headed toward the clouds.

Megan sat alongside her, looking anxious. She pulled her knees up to her chin.

"Are you OK?"

"Yes."

They sat in silence for a little longer, watching a slower propeller aircraft lumber off the runway. After the Vulcan, it was like watching a tractor.

"Argosy, I think," Susie said. "Quite a new one."

"David said you're a plane spotter," said Megan.

"It's hard to ignore them. They can be quite impressive."

Megan flashed an angry look at her. "What's that got to with anything? We're here to end all this, not bloody celebrate it. I hate them." Megan lay on her back and closed her eyes.

Susie left it a moment before carrying on. "Anyway, the plan sounds good. I definitely want to help if I can."

Megan opened one eye and gave her a sideways glance.

"You really want to be with us? It's no picnic you know." She closed her eye again.

"It's why I'm here."

"I wondered that."

"Wondered what? Why I'm here? Why are any of us here?"

"Different reasons."

Susie paused. "Well, I'm not sure about others, but I've had enough of marching and waving banners. I'm here because it's up to our generation to do something."

"Even if that 'something' lands you in prison?" Megan asked, still on her back with her eyes closed.

"It wouldn't be the first time."

"Really?" Megan propped herself up on her elbows.

"Not a big deal. A few of us took matters into our own hands in Trafalgar Square last year."

"And you went to prison? Actual prison?"

"I was arrested, held in a police station for one night, transferred to Holloway for a second night. Then they paraded us into magistrates' court, fined us, and that was it. As I say, no big deal."

Megan lay back down.

A moment later, a shadow flashed across them, followed by a roar as the Argosy swooped across the camp.

Susie followed it around as it drew a wide arc in the sky, just above the trees. An object fell from its open rear cargo doors.

"Blimey."

"What?" Megan asked without looking.

"That aircraft just dropped something. Is that Porton Down?" She could make out a series of low buildings in a field that backed onto the UK's chemical weapons centre.

"They gas animals in that place," Megan said, sitting up. "Perhaps they bomb them now as well."

The aircraft carried out two more runs over Porton Down, releasing one more object. It took a wider arc south and descended, turning back toward West Porton. As it levelled out on the far side of the airfield, it pointed directly at them.

Susie squinted, studying the flight path as the Argosy descended even lower.

"What's happening now?" Megan said.

"It's OK."

The aircraft travelled straight across the runway threshold and directly over the peace camp.

The engines sent powerful reverberations through the ground, and both women flinched as it tore overhead and pitched up into a steep climb.

The rear doors were still open and Susie could see a figure inside. From behind him, an object moved and the man leapt out of the way. A pallet, with what looked like a black barrel strapped to it, fell out of the opening.

She watched in horror, looking below the falling object to see who was in danger.

"*Watch out!*" she screamed, leaping to her feet.

The pallet hit the ground and smashed into several pieces; the barrel split in two or three parts.

As far as she could see it hadn't hit anyone.

But as the aircraft noise dimmed, a hissing sound emanated from the barrel, along with a plume of white smoke.

"Get away from it!" Susie screamed.

A stinging sensation in her eyes. It started as an annoying tickle, but soon became a powerful irritant. Susie closed her eyes tight as the gas caught in her throat and she doubled over, coughing. Screams sounded across the camp, then moaning and coughing.

Susie gripped Megan and walked as fast as she could while virtually blinded.

She tried to open her eyes as they hurried away, alongside the fence, but another blast of irritant hit her, and water streamed down her face.

"*Jesus Christ.*"

She forced her eyes open.

Megan's hand went limp. She dropped to the ground, hands over her face.

She looked in a bad way; incoherent and wailing.

Around them, people ran in different directions. Most campers escaped the field through the main gate.

Susie dropped next to Megan

"We have to get out of the field."

"No! Leave me." She curled up and began rocking.

Susie hauled Megan to her feet and set off with her under her arm.

As they neared the gate, Susie tasted fresh air again. The gas was dispersing.

They joined the others, spilling on the road.

A police siren wailed in the distance.

Someone had brought a bucket of water over, and the group splashed the cool liquid over their faces.

Susie looked at their puffy red eyes. Men and women, crying and wailing.

Her throat stung, and the acrid gas in her lungs triggered a coughing fit.

She squatted down and spat onto the road, desperate to clear the metallic taste from her mouth. "*Christ alive.*"

Eventually she regained control over her breathing and stood up.

A green military Land Rover with a blue flashing light arrived and two soldiers jumped out.

"Is everyone alright?" one of them shouted.

He got a chorus of anger from the protestors in return.

"*What do you bloody think?*"

"What the hell was that?"

"Are you bombing us, for Christ's sake?"

The men didn't answer. They scanned the crowd, then jumped back into their vehicle and drove onto the field. More sirens in the distance. A white ambulance rolled up, followed by another.

Susie walked to the field entrance and watched the two soldiers. They put on gas masks and slowly approached the remains of the crate and barrel, turning the debris over with their feet. They picked up the bigger pieces and loaded them into the back of their wagon.

The ambulance crews began to inspect the injured.

The Land Rover appeared at the gate and eased through the crowd onto the road before driving off.

"That's the evidence gone," Susie said. She looked at Megan, who didn't seem capable of speech.

Susie got down on her knees next to her.

"I think it was just tear gas. It's gone now."

Megan didn't respond.

She encouraged her to her feet. Slowly, they made their way back into the field where Susie sat Megan in the entrance to her tent and went off to fetch her water.

David was already at the plastic water barrel.

"Megan's taken it badly. I'm worried about her."

"Not surprising with her background."

"What do you mean?"

He moved away from the crowd around the barrel and beckoned her to follow. "She was orphaned in the war. House bombed in London. She and her brother lived, but both parents died."

"Christ."

"Like I say, she rarely talks about it. Keeps it all inside."

Susie took Megan fresh water and sat with her for a while, but she was unresponsive. Eventually she left her to sleep it off.

———

MILLIE WAS PLEASED WITH HIMSELF. The flight was purely a familiarisation for the new pilot, Jock MacLeish, and so no official tapes were due back. That gave him ample time to build up his stock. He was onto his fourth reel as they descended toward the circuit at West Porton.

"Something's happening down there," MacLeish said over the intercom from his right hand seat in the cockpit.

Millie and Bright, with no usable windows, just looked at each other.

"What?" Bright said.

"Loads of blue flashing lights at the peace camp. Looks like they're being evicted."

After taxi, Millie let Steve Bright open the hatch and attach the ladder. He followed him out, holding onto his flight case, replete with his haul of fresh reels.

As he walked into TFU, it was clear something was up. Loud laughter emanated from corners of the room. Broad smiles on faces.

Millie walked straight to his locker. First things first.

The pile of reels was getting large, but there was nothing he could do about it for now.

He closed the locker just as Speedy Johnson walked past him toward the equipment hatch.

"What's going on? Do you know?"

"Apparently Red and Rob accidentally gassed the hippies."

"What?"

Speedy continued to the hatch as Rob walked back into the main planning room. One of the pilots slapped Red on the back, laughing.

Millie walked over to Rob. "What happened?"

"Silly old Nigel Woodward removed all the safety pins from the spare bomb, just before we flew over the camp, and it rolled out."

"How exactly did it roll out? Did he launch it?"

"Red may have performed a rather steep pull-up, you know, just to wake them up. Unfortunate timing."

"I see. Was anyone hurt?"

"Apparently not. But the gas escaped and set off a bit of coughing."

Millie looked around at the pilots hugging the tea bar. A few more slaps on Red's back.

"And this is apparently a cause for celebration? You could have killed someone."

"Steady on, Millie. It was an accident. No-one was hurt. Well, not seriously."

Millie was still in full flying gear, holding his helmet and oxygen mask. It was too warm in the room and he headed off to the equipment hatch.

Jock was there when he arrived.

"Heard the news?" Jock asked.

"Yes. Not sure I can join the celebrations though. Unprofessional, if you ask me."

Jock nodded. "I agree. Doesn't seem the right response, does it?"

"It wasn't like this at Boscombe Down. We took it seriously, someone dropping a clanger like that would be for the high jump."

"Aye. But this is the empire of Mark Kilton and if he finds it funny, so do we." Jock gave him a friendly slap on the shoulder and wandered off.

———

BEFORE HE DROVE off the station, Millie called in at the sergeant's mess. He stood in the entrance, not wanting to overstep his welcome without a proper invite. But after a quick search it was clear Nigel Woodward wasn't there. As he drove out, he took a detour to the Non-Commissioned Officers' married quarter.

Mrs Woodward opened the door.

"Is he in trouble?" She looked terrified.

"I'm not here in an official capacity, Mrs Woodward. In fact, I just want to check he's OK?"

She led him in. Nigel was in the kitchen, drinking a beer. Mrs

Woodward offered Millie a drink; he declined. She shut the door, leaving them alone.

"What happened, Nigel?"

He looked confused.

"Today, in the Argosy? The gas bomb?"

Slowly, the loadmaster nodded.

"Ah, yes. It went well."

"Nigel. You released a canister over the peace camp. It wasn't supposed to go there."

Again, a slow nodding as if he was hearing this for the first time. "That's right. They told me that."

"Who did?"

"Oh, you know. Wing Commander Kilton."

"Nigel, is everything OK?"

"I think maybe I pulled the pins out and then Mr Brunson flew us up quickly."

Millie watched him for a moment; he was in a world of his own.

"Maybe go see the doc tomorrow, hey, Nigel?"

"Thank you, sir."

"Just call me Millie, at least here." Millie patted his arm and stood up.

As he left, Mrs Woodward stopped him at the door. She lowered her voice. "He's not been right for a while, if truth be told." She glanced back.

"What do you mean?"

"It's his memory. He forgets things. He goes through phases. Good days, bad days. This is a really bad one."

"Forgets things? What sort of things?"

"My name."

Millie stared at her.

"He doesn't want to tell anyone, in case it's the end of his career. He's worried about the money, you know, if he can't work."

"Of course he is. But he needs to see a doctor."

Mrs Woodward studied the ground for a moment. "The only person he sees is the landlord at The Black Horse. Goes most nights."

"That doesn't sound like a good idea."

"He says it helps to talk to strangers, but he won't talk to me." Tears formed in her eyes.

"Strangers?"

"I don't know. He's found some new friend. Anything but face the facts. He's not right, Mr Milford." She bowed her head. "Something like this was bound to happen."

Nigel appeared behind his wife.

"Nigel, you've got to go to the medic," said Millie. "You understand?"

"Oh, I expect I will tomorrow." He disappeared upstairs.

Millie turned back to the loadmaster's wife. "Leave it with me. I'll see what I can do."

9

WEDNESDAY 15TH JUNE

The buzz from the previous day's mishap was still tangible. The pilots, used to existing in a vacuum of secrecy, seemed to enjoy announcing TFU's presence to the outside world, albeit via an avoidable accident.

"Everyone in the meeting."

A voice from behind. Rob.

"Sorry?"

"Kilton wants everyone in the morning meeting. Think we might be about to get a rocket for yesterday."

"I doubt that," Millie said as he lifted his frame out of the chair.

By the time they arrived in the briefing room, it was standing room only. Steve Bright stood up from one of the soft chairs and offered it to Millie.

He laughed. "Am I that old now?"

"No offence intended," Bright replied, and Millie took the seat.

Loud chatter bounced off the walls as the assembled officers of TFU awaited their boss. Millie could just see Kilton's bald head at the front, deep in conversation with someone or other.

As they waited, Millie pulled out his handwritten copy of the tape readings. He'd had the numbers since Sunday morning and although he was sure the first field was the clock, he was nowhere near deciphering the second, longer field.

15105550114922

15105550114810

The magic moment of realisation once again failed to arrive.

He heard a voice over his shoulder.

"Is that for today?" Steve Bright nodded at the worn piece of paper.

Millie folded it up and cursed himself for exposing the numbers in such a public place.

"No, it's nothing."

Kilton called the room to order and handed over to the weatherman.

A tall, thin bespectacled man switched on the overhead projector. It showed a loosely packed series of isobars over the west of the country with a second system to the north-east.

"This chappie is the cause of the current stability in our weather," the man said, pointing at the system in the north. "It's preventing anything moving in from the Atlantic. That said, it will be a little cooler for the next few days. Seventy-five Fahrenheit, rather than eighty. But again, precipitation is unlikely. Locally today, light winds at surface level, but check winds aloft carefully, as they will be up to sixty-five knots above twenty thousand feet. For those of you venturing further north, expect a strong sou'westerly at surface level above Carlisle, all the way to Orkney.

"The copied bulletin will be in the admin office before 9AM."

Millie watched as the pilots and navigators made notes.

The weatherman shuffled out with his wad of papers. Kilton stood before them again.

"The station commander has asked me to read out the following notice."

There were a few titters as the boss theatrically rolled his eyes.

"*The standards to which we must aspire were not present in TFU yesterday. The inadvertent release of a container of irritant was a serious error. It places us in an embarrassing position with our neighbours and it has exacerbated an already fractious relationship with the peaceful campaigners, currently exercising their democratic right."* More titters around the room. *"While we have avoided the need for a full Board of Inquiry, I expect those responsible to be left in no doubt that we expect and demand more from the officers and men stationed at RAF West Porton."*

Kilton looked up from the wooden rostrum.

"So that's us told. Please don't bomb the peace campaigners."

The men laughed.

"In all seriousness, we do not wish to draw unwanted attention to ourselves, so no more slip-ups, however hilarious they may be. Now, while we've avoided a drawn out and pointless inquiry, we are suffering some consequences. We need to step up vehicle searches." The room groaned and Kilton put his hands up "I know, I know, but they are there to protect our secrets. I don't need to remind you that many of our projects lose what value they have if exposed. So let's be patient with the men at the gate who are doing a good job. In addition, the station commander has ordered each unit to carry out a review into their own security arrangements. So, execs, I need you round the table with me tomorrow morning at 8AM. This takes priority, so rearrange flying around it."

The four squadron leaders in the room, including Millie, grumbled at the unwanted invitation.

Not only was there no conceivable way to get the reels in his locker out of West Porton, but he was now part of the committee ensuring his options would be even more limited.

The meeting broke up, and he trudged back to the planning room.

Glancing at the flying programme, he saw, for the first time since its inception, two Guiding Light flights were scheduled for the same day: one in the morning with him, Speedy Johnson and Red Brunson and a new young navigator, followed in the afternoon by Rob, Jock and Steve Bright.

Frustratingly, Bright would be in charge of the reel changes in the afternoon.

He lingered on Steve Bright's name, recalling his comment about Millie's piece of paper.

"Is that for today?"

He looked around, trying to see if Bright was somewhere he might speak to him alone. As his eyes swept the room, Red Brunson appeared and announced their own pre-flight brief.

———

IT TOOK them an hour to plan the trial and another thirty minutes to dress and prepare for the flight. Millie was happy to let the new young navigator look after the hatch.

As soon as the wheels tucked up into the belly of the Vulcan, he flicked the master switch on the Guiding Light panel and started a tape.

By the time he was required to gather height readings, after their descent into the Welsh hills, he had two more reels for his own collection.

During the official stretch at one thousand feet, Millie watched the orange digits as carefully as possible, waiting for a stream of numbers that made no sense. Several times, he'd seen moments of what looked like anomalous readings, but they were too fleeting to be sure.

The aircraft buffeted along the contour of the ground below. It was impossible for him to tell whether they were exactly tracing the ground level or occasionally deviating. The pilots would have a better idea, but only if they were looking.

He glanced across to the new nav. An eerie green light projected onto his earnest face from the radar hood in front of him.

In the dark of the Vulcan's rear bay, Millie went back to his task of monitoring a system he was certain hid a fatal flaw.

He drummed his fingers on the black top below the panel. The engine noise grew and he felt the nose pitch up as they climbed out of low-level.

He stopped the recorder, labelled the official reels and set it going once more with an unofficial tape.

Millie daydreamed about the moment he could march into the station commander's office with proof, in black-and-white, that Guiding Light was unfit.

He tightened his straps and locked his chair in place as they joined the West Porton circuit. They were back on time, ready for the Vulcan to be fuelled and prepared for a second trial.

Time was no longer on his side.

The nose gear unfolded with loud clanks, just a few feet below his seat.

The main gear met the runway with a squeal and they taxied in.

Two tasks ahead. Get the tapes to Belkin and decipher that second field.

———

INSIDE TFU, Steve Bright was nowhere to be seen.

Millie rid himself of his flying clothes and equipment, and stowed the tapes.

At his desk, he ate the sandwich Georgina had made for him and got on with his paperwork.

At 2.30PM, he finally heard Steve Bright across the room, but he was already with Rob and the others, planning the afternoon trip.

Two hours ticked by before they returned, from Scotland. It would have been a perfect opportunity for him to gather more data.

He watched Bright as the crew arrived back into the planning room, hair matted with sweat. The group stayed together as they changed and headed out to the mess bar.

Millie packed his bag, checking it for secret project papers before following them.

The mess was busy, and his eyes stung from the amount of smoke in the air. He made his way to the fire exit and pushed it open, before searching the growing crowd of officers.

Steve Bright was there, in the centre of the room, laughing and talking with a small group.

Millie ordered a drink and joined them.

He sipped his beer and bided his time.

Just before 7PM, the group broke up and Millie followed Bright out into the lobby. Checking no-one was too close by, he called out.

"Steve, can I have a quick word?"

The nav stopped by a portrait of the Duke of Edinburgh in full RAF flying clothing, standing in front of an Avro Anson.

"What is it, Millie?"

"What did you say when you stood over me earlier?"

Bright looked perplexed.

"When?"

"In the met brief."

Bright shook his head. "No, sorry, can't remember."

Millie looked around again before retrieving the piece of paper from his pocket.

"Oh, that. Yes, I just wondered if that's where we were going today, but clearly not."

"I don't understand. What did you mean?"

Bright looked at the paper again. He pushed Millie's hand further away as if to try and focus on it.

"Coordinates, aren't they? Lat and long."

Millie looked back at the digits.

15105550114922

15105550114810

"Really? I don't recognise them."

Bright shrugged. "Well, maybe not. At least I'm not sure what the '1' at the beginning is. But '51 05 55'... What's that?" He tilted his head up toward the ceiling. "Somewhere north of here? Midlands? And... He studied the paper again. "'1 49 22'. That's west. Maybe Cheltenham? Trust me, Millie, I'm a navigator and I know latitude and longitude when I see it."

Millie stared at the figures.

"I see. But like you say, there are too many digits."

"It's your note, Millie. Can't you ask whoever gave it to you?"

He wasn't sure what to say, and so said nothing. Bright smiled and took the sheet from his hand, scrutinising it.

"Look, there's a 'I' at the start and a 'I' in the middle before the long. No idea what that means, sorry chap."

He handed the paper back to Millie, leaving him alone, staring at the numbers.

More people arrived from the bar and he pocketed the sheet before heading to his car.

As he drove up to the central road that ran through the station, another car pulled alongside him.

Steve Bright motioned for Millie to wind his window down. He leant across and wound down his own passenger side window.

"Probably the hemisphere!" he shouted.

"What?"

"The 'I's on your sheet. Probably represents north, south, east or west. Maybe 'o' would be south and the opposite east or west?"

"Right."

Bright laughed. "Normally there would be letters to show the hemisphere. North, south, east, west. But maybe your example uses numerical labels. Where did it come from, anyway?"

There was a beep behind them as someone else pulled out of the mess car park.

"Never mind," Bright finished and wound up his window before pulling ahead.

———

BY THE TIME Millie arrived home, even Georgina seemed to notice his raised mood.

"Good day at the office, dear?"

"Something like that. Don't look so surprised. They do still happen, occasionally."

He took her hand and pulled her close.

She laughed. "Millie, whatever's got into you?"

He kissed her and tilted his head. "Shall we go down to the Railway Hotel for dinner tonight?"

This time she raised both eyebrows. "Well, I had a pie out, but it'll keep."

"Excellent. Saves on washing up."

"Are you going to let me know what we're celebrating?"

"As you note, my dear, just a good day at the office."

10

THURSDAY 16TH JUNE

Each time he approached the main gate, Millie studied the security officers as they busied themselves with the car in front. The routine involved a cursory look into the boot, but occasionally he saw a man lean in and give a more thorough search.

The same went for the interior of the vehicle itself.

He simply couldn't risk transferring the tapes through the checks. There had to be another way.

At TFU, he took his seat at the meeting to help tighten security even further.

"We need to be certain our system is watertight," Kilton began. "No papers going astray, everything accounted for. The cabinets, for instance. How secure are they?"

"They've got padlocks," Speedy Johnson offered.

"They look weak. Beef them up."

Speedy added a line to his to-do list, and Millie made a mental note not to answer questions in case he got lumbered with an impossible task.

But Kilton looked directly at him. "And what about the lockers?"

"What about them?"

"Are they secure, Millie? What do people keep in them? We need to do an audit."

"An audit?" His heart thumped.

"Yes. Search them all. Make sure there's nothing compromising and remind people they're for unclassified jumpers and hats, not secret project paperwork."

A familiar prickly heat crept up his neck.

Kilton stared at him.

"Well?"

"Well what, sir?"

"Wake up, Millie! Can you carry out the audit?"

"You want *me* to? To search people's lockers?"

"If it's not an inconvenience. Yes, please."

"Yes, boss. No problem at all."

"Right, have I missed anything?"

"What about when we fly out?" Millie said.

"What do you mean?"

"Land-aways for instance? We carry secret equipment and its paperwork all the time. What do we do at another airfield? I mean, it's unlikely, I know, but one of us might accidentally carry classified documents to another station, leave them in a meeting room, or even on the aircraft while we brief or..."

Suddenly, he saw it: the only way to get the reels out of West Porton and avoid the security forces at every gate.

He could fly them out.

Except, like the world's most colossal idiot, he had just alerted Mark Kilton to the option. The only loophole he could conceivably have exploited was about to be closed.

Kilton looked impatient. "You OK, Milford?"

"Yes, sir."

"Well, you're absolutely right. We need a procedure in place. From now on, all land-aways must be authorised by me personally. A security officer can sign classified material out of the building and back in again. Excellent idea."

"Won't the chaps resent this, boss?" Speedy asked. "They might feel like they're being spied on?"

"I don't care what they think. This is for their own protection. To ensure they don't make a mistake that could cost us, and them, dear." Kilton stood. "Right, well, let's be getting on with it."

The meeting broke up; Millie stayed in his seat.

He thought back to the recent land-aways. He'd been to Oakington for a meeting with Red Brunson and Wyton a few weeks earlier. He and Rob flew to Warton in the Canberra. On any of those trips, he could so easily have carried an extra bag.

He could have packaged the tapes into a parcel and posted them to his own home address, or directly to Belkin.

But that door was closed now.

And he had closed it.

———

SUSIE LISTENED INTENTLY. She needed to remember every detail.

Since the gas bomb had dropped, the camp felt galvanised and ready for action.

And she was part of the raiding party. A team of just six.

Megan paced the wigwam.

"We now know what they're hiding."

The room went quiet. David stood up.

"Sampson has extracted vital information for us."

So, the mysterious blond man had a name. But how could he have extracted the information?

"The secret squadron occupies the large green hangar on this side of the airfield," David continued. "The collection of old aircraft on the other side is a maintenance facility. Much less interesting."

Megan spoke again. "Sampson has befriended a serving member of the squadron. This man has unwittingly passed on some very interesting information. There's something fitted to a white Vulcan. A Top Secret project. He believes the project is called Guiding Light. He claims not to know any more than that. He's probably telling the truth. That's how secret Guiding Light is. Even people inside TFU aren't aware of the details. So, we're going to blow it wide open"

David picked up a camera. "We have two tasks once inside. Take close-up photographs of whatever is on the aircraft, and retrieve any paperwork relating to Guiding Light. For that purpose, we'll split into two teams.

"We will arm the aircraft team with this camera and a light. The paperwork team will have a rucksack and some tools to open filing cabinets and drawers."

"We have an extensive set of keys accumulated over the years," said Megan. "Most hangar doors use the same locks and we're confident we'll find a match. But it may take a while to go through them, which means we won't have long on the inside. Do not restrict yourselves to just Guiding Light. Pick up anything relating to nuclear, biological and chemical weapons."

"Right, let's get down to the detail," David said. He led the group to a trestle table with a hand-drawn map of the airfield and lists of times. Susie was impressed. It turned out all the lying around by the fence had a purpose. They had meticulously noted the times and nature of the security patrols for weeks.

"We've identified our best chance," Megan said. "Overnight on Friday through to Saturday."

"They call it Happy Hour," David continued, "but as far as we can see, it starts mid-afternoon and finishes in the small hours of the morning.

"The men are drunk and behaviour around the gate becomes erratic. The guards congregate around the entrance, leaving the rest of the airfield unpatrolled. 2.15AM is our chance.

"The two wire cutters will remain at the fence, so if you'd prefer not to be part of the team that goes all the way in?" He looked expectantly at the group.

Susie raised her hand. But Megan intervened.

"No. She's small. We need her with us."

A range of implements were laid out on an adjoining table, from heavy jemmies to tiny Allen keys. David placed an Olympus camera in the centre of the tools.

————

MILLIE SEARCHED the lockers as requested.

He found a couple of items that shouldn't be there, including a flight plan annotated 'G/L' in Speedy Johnson's own cubby hole.

Nothing too sinister, but Millie dealt with it quietly, directly with Johnson.

After finishing the lockers, he went out of the airfield door and stood in the June sunshine. Leaning back against the red brick extension that nestled at the base of the large hangar, he took out a packet of cigarettes.

A long draw on his John Player Number 6 went some way to calming him down.

On the apron in front of him stood the Guiding Light Vulcan, ready for its afternoon trip. He looked at his watch and realised he had only forty minutes to prepare.

He dropped his cigarette and stamped it out.

A noise caught his attention. He looked across the runway to see a lumbering Valetta taxiing up toward the eastern threshold.

The Maintenance Unit. The Graveyard.

In that moment he envied them, recovering withdrawn aircraft from around the country and ferrying them to final resting places.

No secrets, no pressure, no paranoid security.

He watched the Valetta lining up on the main runway.

No-one searches their lockers.

And no-one checks their aircraft.

The old men of 206 MU. Those wonderful old men and their eccentric flying machines.

No-one pays them any attention. Kilton would have got rid of them if he'd had his way, but for once he hadn't had his way.

He went back into TFU, eager to get the afternoon's flight out of the way before he could head to the bar and seek a quiet corner with some old friends.

———

THE FLIGHT WENT BETTER than expected. Not only did Millie capture two tapes on the way out and way back, but at Jock MacLeish's request they carried out part of the low-level run a second time, allowing Millie to load and record two more extra reels.

He stood in front of his locker, waiting for two of the chaps to walk past before he opened it. He now had two stacks of reels up against the rear wall, with his jumper barely covering them. It was time to get rid of them.

He'd been lucky today, extremely lucky. But that wouldn't last.

He closed the locker and dropped off his flying clothing.

By the time he got back to the planning room and entered the official tapes into the system, it was 5.20PM. He headed to the mess.

Just inside the front door was a notice informing all that the bar would be closed tomorrow night in preparation for the Summer Ball on Saturday.

"No Happy Hour?" said Speedy as he passed the notice with Rob. "It's a disgrace."

"Well, it's the VIP reception," Rob replied as Millie caught up with them.

Speedy frowned. "What VIP reception?"

Rob looked taken aback, as if he'd said something he shouldn't have.

"The local dignitaries. Just a few drinks. I believe it's instead of inviting them to the ball which got rowdy last year. Station Commander's idea."

"Really, and who's invited?" the senior pilot said.

"I'm only going because I'm mess secretary now."

"You kept that quiet." Speedy gave Rob a slap on the shoulder as they arrived in the bar. "So you are a high flyer. Remember us won't you?"

"Well done, chap," Millie said and shook his hand.

"Thanks, Millie." Rob beamed back. He and Johnson continued over to a group of pilots at the far end of the bar, leaving Millie on his own.

He looked around the room.

The MU boys usually occupied a circular table in the far corner, but it was empty.

He ordered a scotch and drank it by himself. The nearby group of test pilots laughed loudly at their own jokes.

By 6.30PM it was clear the Graveyard men were not showing up.

Millie cursed under his breath, remembering there was no bar tomorrow night.

His locker was full of incriminating evidence, and he still had no way to safely transfer it to Belkin.

11

FRIDAY 17TH JUNE

The cold woke Susie up. That was a first. She'd arrived during the heatwave but now the nights carried a chill.

Her watch said 6.10AM. She wound it for the new day and dressed.

As the village church bells struck 7AM, she was back at the village phone box, dialling a familiar London number.

A man's clipped voice answered. "Yes."

"It's Susie."

"Ah, Twiggy. How the devil are you?"

"What did you call me?"

"We're calling you Twiggy now. She's a model, was on the front page of the Express yesterday. Looks like a boy, curious isn't it? Anyway, you fit the bill."

"You think I look like a boy, Roger?"

"Well, you have short hair."

"Right, well, how about shutting up and taking down some notes?"

"Keep your short hair on. Let me get a pen."

She tapped her foot.

"Go ahead, Twigs."

She sighed. "They're planning a raid on RAF West Porton. This secret squadron I mentioned, it's the target. Apparently it's called Test Flying Unit, and there's a project called Guiding Light. They seem to know what they're doing. TFU may have a leak."

"It sounds like you know more about West Porton than we do."

"I thought we knew everything?"

"It's time to stop believing what they told us in training, dear. Even Her Majesty's Security Service hits a brick wall sometimes. We do know something about TFU. It's independent of the squadron structure. Set up last year to handle the sensitive stuff. But, and this is odd, we know very little more. The unit has a direct line of command to Whitehall, so our usual sources aren't much help. What we do know is one of their projects has Downing Street's attention."

"Guiding Light?"

"That, we don't know. But you might be right. We do however know the identity of your mysterious blond gentleman."

"Sampson?"

"Yes, well, that confirms it if you've heard that name as well. Sampson Parker. A dangerous sort. Got a bunch of ne'er-do-wells all the way into Faslane last year."

"The Polaris subs?"

"Indeed. They ended up doing some damage a few feet away from Britain's independent nuclear deterrent. He was clever enough to stay outside the wire, so they couldn't pin anything on him. But you say he'll be on the raid tonight? That could be useful."

"No. He's not part of the raid itself. Just seems to be the brains behind it."

"Same MO as Faslane. Disappointing. The plan was to let the raid go ahead and nab him red-handed."

"That might still be possible. He's due to receive what we find and take it off site in the small hours."

"I see. Well, I'll pass that up the line and they can decide what should happen. Good work. You'll need to check in later. Let's say 4PM, unless something changes significantly at your end."

———

A LAND ROVER lurked in the shadows, in the corner of the TFU hangar. It was used by the engineers and mechanics to ferry parts and people around. The junior engineering officer was happy to let Millie borrow it for a run across the airfield.

He climbed in and found the key was already in the ignition, next to a note telling drivers to inform air traffic control before they drove on the active taxiways.

Millie cursed but then noticed a large radio built into the underside of the dashboard.

He followed instructions pinned next to the ignition switch to pre-heat the coil for thirty seconds, glancing around the hangar, hoping no other officers noticed him.

The vehicle spluttered into life and he edged out onto the apron.

A Victor taxied nearby, and he was suddenly aware of the small vehicle's vulnerability.

Switching on the radio, he heard the end of a sign-off from the Victor crew. He waited for them to finish and keyed the press-to-transmit button.

"Tower, this is the TFU Land Rover. I need to cross the airfield to the Maintenance Unit."

Millie followed instructions to use the southern taxiway and wait at the western threshold. As he got closer to the end of the runway, he looked out of the right hand window at the peace camp.

A group of the protestors were gathered outside a white wigwam in the centre of the field. From this range, Millie could see their faces: young men and women. In other circumstances, he would describe them as fresh faced, but it looked as if rough living had taken its toll.

He pulled up in front of thick white lines that marked the boundary of the runway and called the tower again, as instructed. They told him to wait.

Millie opened the door and stood next to the vehicle. Looking back down the runway, just visible above an undulation that took it a few feet down, was a distinctive white tail.

Through the heat mirage, the shape of the Victor emerged, just as it lifted into the air.

Millie plugged his ears as the four jet engines climbed overhead.

The radio crackled into life with clearance to cross and five minutes later he found himself in the drab interior of 206 Maintenance Unit.

The walls were covered with faded photographs of ancient aircraft. Millie squinted at a black-and-white print of a biplane that had two machine guns mounted in front of an open cockpit.

"That's a B.E.2C, Millie." JR's voice over his shoulder. "And no, none of us are quite that old. We keep it up as a reminder."

"A reminder of what? The good old days?"

"Not exactly," JR said as he led him into what passed as a planning room, complete with old leather chairs that looked like they'd been thrown out of an officers' mess as unserviceable. "The B.E.2C was a death trap. Too slow and too difficult to manoeuvre. It should have stayed as a reconnaissance kite, but they kept sending the RFC pilots up to their inevitable deaths. Worth remembering the type of organisation we work for."

Millie sank into a red armchair.

"So, to what do we owe this rare privilege?"

"I need a lift. To Abingdon. Soon. Preferably Monday."

JR nodded. "You have about twenty aircraft over there, don't you? And more pilots than Pan Am. Any particular reason you need a lift from us?"

Millie looked around the room. There were five others in various corners, a couple of men in conversation by the kettle. No-one seemed to be listening in.

"I need to fly below the radar on this one."

"I see." JR studied him. After a moment's pause, he looked across to the couple at the kettle. "Beanie, how's the Anson behaving?"

"Purrs like a cat on heat."

"That sounds like a doubtful claim for that heap of rust, but I'll assume it will get to Oxford and back?"

"A very good chance of success."

JR turned back to Millie. "What time would sir like his carriage?"

"As easy as that? You don't need an authorisation?"

"We're masters of our own destiny here, sort of. We work for Support Command and our boss flies a desk in Brampton. As long as we don't start a war, he's happy not to be involved in day-to-day."

"Must be lovely."

"It was until TFU turned up. I suspect our days here are numbered."

Millie sighed. "It's all a little different over there."

"Indeed. Anyway, what time on Monday?"

"How about 9.30?"

"Fine. I'm sorry but we've lost our own airfield gate, since the security hysteria, so you must drive around the peritrack. If you're here before 8AM you don't need to clear it with ATC."

"Thank you, JR. I can't tell you how much I appreciate this."

"Think nothing of it, Millie." The old pilot stood up.

Millie raised himself from the depths of the armchair. JR stepped forward and offered him an arm. For all the age lines writ into his face, JR was nimble.

As they walked out, JR stopped at the front door. "You can always talk to me, Millie."

"Thank you. For now, I think it's best I keep you in the dark."

"Your decision, old chap."

Millie headed back across the airfield, careful to give a Twin Pioneer a wide berth as one of the MU team started her up.

Back in the planning room he retrieved a folder from a cabinet labelled *TFU GLOSTER JAVELIN ACQUISITION*.

At his desk he dialled the number for 1 Squadron at RAF Waterbeach.

"1 ops, Flight Lieutenant Digby."

"Hello, it's Squadron Leader Chris Milford from West Porton here. You're due to transfer one of your modified Hunters to us, I believe?"

"Are we? What squadron are you again?"

"Test Flying Unit."

"Ah! The unit that dare not speak its name. We were told not to discuss it." The man laughed.

"Yes, well, it's not a secret that we're having one of your aircraft and I just need to make sure we have an engineering plan in place. Can I pop over on Monday to chat with your senior engineering officer?"

"I'll have to check the SENGO's around. Stand by, please." The man went off the line briefly, before reporting back that the appointment had been accepted.

After the call, Millie made sure they marked him as out of TFU on Monday for a meeting in Cambridgeshire. They would expect him to take the train, so he went the extra mile and asked for a rail permit.

————

THERE WAS a problem with the raid plan.

Two more campers were dispatched to confirm the news a lanky young man had brought back from his patrol: the officers' mess car park was empty, save a few tradesmen's vans. There was no sign of the usual drinking jamboree.

It was now 6PM, and they had to face facts: the routine they had meticulously noted over previous weeks was not being followed.

Susie's 4PM call delivered some surprising news of its own. The fourth floor at Leconfield House was happy to let the raid go ahead. They wanted to catch Sampson Parker with incriminating evidence.

He would be a high profile success for the Service, if everything went to plan.

As Roger, her desk officer, had explained what would happen—or what was supposed to happen—she felt the weight of responsibility on her shoulders.

But along with the nerves came excitement.

She knew they had chosen her for this role purely on looks and sex, but here was a chance to gain a significant notch on her belt.

To complicate matters further, in the grand tradition of the Security Service, they were working alone. The RAF were not informed, partly because no-one was forthcoming to them about the secrets held at West Porton.

But as long as it went to plan, they would save the TFU's backside.

As long as it went to plan.

———

AT 7.30PM, two more campers who'd been sent out on patrol disguised as an evening ramble returned with more news. Susie was called over to the wigwam.

It was a still night. The cloud hung low, trapping in the heat of the day and softening the sounds of wildlife and chatter.

"According to Charlotte and Purdy," said Megan, "there's an event in the mess tomorrow, which is why it's shut tonight. They overheard a delivery man at the main gate. More pertinently for us, half the security men have been sent home. Presumably they'll be working long hours tomorrow."

"So we're on?" Susie asked.

"Yes."

She felt a rush of nerves in her stomach.

They went over the details once more.

Susie went for a lie down and woke at 11PM. She headed back to the wigwam and found the others searching through a pile of black clothes with a torch.

Megan threw her a pair of slacks and a thin polo neck. She winced at the fashion, but accepted them for the practical purpose.

The minutes ticked by. The wigwam was quiet, save the occasional report from the fence. Patrols were still taking place, but fewer than normal.

At 1.45AM, Purdy arrived to report a patrol had driven past and disappeared back into the main RAF station.

Megan stood up.

"It's time."

Outside, Susie heard a vehicle reversing toward them. Puzzled, she looked out of the flaps to see the blond man climbing out of a battered Morris van.

"Sampson Parker," she said, under her breath.

He opened the rear doors and lifted out a large glass container of liquid and a set of trays. He took the items into the tent without speaking to anyone.

David appeared next to her and whispered.

"He's setting up a darkroom. He wants to develop the pictures here before they leave the site, just in case."

They stashed the final tools into rucksacks. Susie noted the camera disappearing into Megan's shoulder bag.

At 2AM, they gathered behind the tent closest to the fence. David handed Susie a black rucksack. She heard the gentle clang of metal tools within it.

Megan led them. "No talking," she hissed, even though they were all silent.

The group began a fast jog toward the corner of the field, continuing around the airfield fence, following a pre-planned route. They passed a small collection of derelict-looking buildings and aircraft on the far side of the airfield, including a black silhouette of a large tail-dragging propeller aircraft.

Just beyond the buildings, they set to work with the wire cutters. Susie sat back in the bushes with the others, listening to the cracks and pops as the fence wires gave way. The first fence had been easy, but the second, newer fence was putting up more of a fight.

Eventually, the cutting team called softly to the waiting group.

Megan moved forward in a crouch. The cutting team held the wire up as the four of them crawled under. Susie had to remove the rucksack and push it through ahead of her.

Across the runway, orange lights flooded the bare aprons.

They ran.

No sooner had they crossed the peritrack, than Megan fell and cried out.

She had tripped on something; it looked like a light housing protruding from the ground.

"Airfield lights," said Susie, "they're everywhere."

Megan put some weight on her ankle and winced.

"You won't make it across. Give me the camera."

"No. I'm fine." She set off ahead, limping.

They came to the wide runway and scampered across. All the time, Susie and the others scanned the areas in front of them for any sign of movement.

Susie could hear David wheezing. He was clearly not fit enough for this run.

As they crossed the taxiway on the other side of the runway, they came closer to the boundary of the floodlighting.

Megan changed direction. The others followed as they headed for the eastern corner of the field. It was as far as possible from the domestic side of the station, and the darkest area close to the hangars.

They reached the internal fence that separated the airfield from the rest of West Porton, and moved along its line, approaching an enormous hangar from its rear, bathed in shadow.

At the bottom corner of the vast building was a door marked *TOILETS*.

"Rucksack," said Megan, clicking her fingers at Susie.

Megan rummaged around and produced a huge set of keys.

"Apparently there are only seven different keys for each hangar door across the entire RAF," David said.

"We're about to find out if that's a myth," Megan replied.

Susie watched as the first key refused to budge. The second was the same and the third.

The fourth key slipped in and easily turned with a satisfying clunk.

It was a large, cold space; clammy, even on a June evening. It stank of urine and toilet cleaner.

On the right hand wall were a row of urinals; on their left were three cubicles.

In front of them sat the two internal walls, but neither had a door.

Susie walked forward and ran her hand against them.

"They're pretty solid."

"No internal door," said David, pointing out the obvious. "What kind of arrangement is this?"

"Doesn't matter, we have more keys," said Megan, and she went back outside.

They followed her along the side of the hangar, hugging the building in the shade, but it was getting brighter. The car parks on the other side of the fence were lit by street lamps.

Susie was at the back and couldn't see where they were going.

Samantha halted in front. Susie bumped into her and whispered an apology. Ahead, she could see Megan looking back and holding her finger to her mouth.

Then Susie heard it.

Men talking.

No, not talking. Singing.

They pressed themselves against the hangar and silently shrunk to the ground.

The men appeared at the far side of the car park. Arms around each other, three of them.

With horror, Susie realised that two of the three cars directly opposite were facing them.

"We've got to move," she hissed at Samantha.

No reply.

"The lights. The car lights!"

Slowly, Samantha shuffled forward, stretching out on the ground, following Megan and David's lead.

She did the same, lying as flat as she could on her front, arms stretched out along her side.

The drunks were close now. The singing had been replaced by a chirpy discussion.

"I'll drive," announced a slurred voice.

"No way," replied the other two in chorus. "Americans can't hold their drink."

The first man protested, but appeared to give in.

The car started, followed by a grinding of gears. Susie raised her head. The car was facing them, but the headlights were off.

The car backed away, did a clumsy three-point manoeuvre and drove out of the car park, lights still off.

She let out a breath.

The others took off again, and she leapt up to follow.

The next door yielded to another key and once inside they found an unlocked internal door that opened into a corridor. They turned left, but this led only to another enclosed office. Turning around, Susie found herself at the front of the band of activists. As she moved forward, she came to an additional door, but this had a glass panel which revealed the inside of the actual hangar.

Her eyes stared at millions of pounds worth of modern military aircraft.

A Victor faced them with its sad eyes; beyond that, under its tail, a Hawker Hunter. Beyond both of them: a huge white Vulcan. Aircraft took up every inch of the hangar.

She tried the door; it was locked.

Megan appeared and ran through her collection of keys.

The fifth one she tried made another clunk as the lock sprung open.

The four of them entered.

"They're huge," Samantha said. "I hadn't realised."

"*Shhh!*" Megan hissed.

Susie watched as she retrieved the camera.

Megan turned to Susie and Samantha. "Find the offices. Remember, anything that looks secret."

They set off and walked past a yellow ladder hanging down from the underbelly of the Vulcan.

The internal door between the hangar and the offices that ran along the front of the building was unlocked.

After walking down a corridor lined with pictures of experimental aircraft, they came to a large room with high desks.

The orange light from the apron threw strange shapes on the walls.

Susie read the sign on the nearest office door.

CO 'TFU'.

And above a hatch at the far end of the room: *ROYAL AIR FORCE TEST FLYING UNIT.*

At the opposite end of the room was a bar, complete with tea urn and kettles. On the left side ran a wide corridor. Susie investigated.

It contained rows of lockers, each with a name. Bryan Dillain, Chris Milford, Frank Vansertima, Speedy Johnson.

Two of the wooden doors were unlocked and half open. She peered inside and saw only jumpers and odd items of clothing.

Susie moved on, monitoring Samantha across the room.

She walked between the map tables, back toward the hatch.

Alongside the internal wall that enclosed what appeared to be an admin area were a row of padlocked cabinets. Each was labelled *SECURE CABINET* with a number.

"Bingo," said Samantha.

Susie examined the flimsy padlock. None of the keys they had would fit it.

She retrieved the bolt croppers from her rucksack and handed them to Samantha. But the teeth were too big for the small metal loop.

Susie examined the lock again; it was held on by four screws that had been painted over.

She rummaged in the rucksack and produced a couple of screw-drivers.

It only took a couple of minutes before the fastening fell away and one side of the cabinet opened.

Inside, in the gloomy light, there were folders and a pile of cardboard sleeves. Samantha picked up a wad of folders and leafed through them. She held one up for Susie to see.

GUIDING LIGHT – TOP SECRET

Susie nodded, and Samantha stuffed it into the rucksack.

Susie picked up one of the cardboard sleeves.

Inside was a reel of magnetic tape.

"Do they make music here? Is that their secret?" She slung the tapes into the rucksack and moved to the next cabinet.

As they removed the first screw in the next lock, they heard an engine noise.

Both women froze.

A vehicle door slammed close by.

"Shit," Samantha said.

Susie looked back along the room to the tea bar. She pushed the cabinet doors shut, but had to leave the lock hanging off.

"Follow me." She ran in a crouch across the full length of the room, just as a door swung open on the airfield side.

The two women reached the bar as the beam of a torch swung over the surrounding desks.

They tucked themselves in. Susie was out of puff but desperately trying not to pant.

She clutched the rucksack, now full of stolen documents, and opened her mouth wide to breathe as quietly as possible.

Samantha, who was nearest the edge of the bar, leant out.

"I think he's gone into the hangar," she whispered.

"Nothing we can do."

They waited.

After what seemed an age, they heard footsteps back in the room. The torchlight swung about again.

The footsteps grew louder.

The women's hearts thudded in their chests.

The man shuffled up to the tea bar; Susie could hear his breathing.

She rolled her eyes up, without moving her head. If he stepped behind the bar, they were caught.

A hand appeared. She almost let out a whimper.

The hand settled on the tea urn, followed by a disappointed grunt, and the footsteps receded.

A minute later, they heard the vehicle start up and drive off.

Susie and Samantha rose to their feet.

The room was empty; the open cabinet hadn't been spotted.

Megan and David appeared at the door.

"Over here," said Susie.

They walked over, Megan with a pronounced limp.

"He didn't see you?" asked Samantha.

"No, we were inside the Vulcan but we switched the light off in time."

"Are you OK?" Susie asked, nodding at Megan's foot. "Do you want me to carry your stuff?"

"I'll be fine." She waved a hand.

Susie glanced down. Megan held the camera.

"I think this is the quickest way out," Samantha said, pointing at the door the security guard had used.

It had a Yale key they could open from the inside. The group spilled out onto the brightly lit apron.

They stood still for a moment, and Susie strained her ears. She could just about hear the guard's vehicle retreating.

This time they didn't avoid the shadows; instead they ran across the apron. After thirty seconds they found themselves back in cover on the grass.

They eventually reached the fence, adrenaline flowing, but couldn't locate the cut wire.

Megan whimpered with pain.

"You did a good job disguising the entry point," Susie said to David.

"It's here somewhere..." He ran his hand along the lower part of the wire.

Behind them: the distant sound of an engine. Susie spun around to see a pair of headlights heading across the apron.

"Quickly, for Christ's sake!" Megan shouted, no longer worried about being overheard.

"Over here!"

They ran in the shout's direction, a hundred yards further along.

Susie held back and helped Megan through, keeping an eye on the patrol vehicle. It hadn't spotted them.

She was the last to crawl out. As they made their way around, she kept her eyes fixed on the camera while she carried the documents.

Back at the peace camp, they hurried to the wigwam.

Sampson was waiting. He emptied the contents of the rucksack on a trestle table and shone a light at the documents.

Susie caught sight of some headings.

'Laser Function Parameters' was one.

A laser? She whistled to herself.

She picked up a tape. "What are these?" she asked Sampson.

He shrugged and said nothing.

Megan placed the camera on the table.

"You got something?" he asked.

"Yes."

"Right. Give me five minutes."

Sampson disappeared behind a screen into his makeshift darkroom.

Samantha took Megan off to her tent to inspect her ankle, leaving David and Susie alone.

"We need to hide the rucksacks and tools in the woods," said David. "Sampson will take the keys."

Susie glanced at the camera. "Would you mind doing that? I'm shattered."

"Of course."

He checked the rucksacks to make sure they had retrieved everything bar the tools, and headed out.

Susie figured she had a few seconds before Sampson would reappear from the screens. She pointed the torch directly at the camera, turned its back toward the light and fiddled with the catch on its base until the back flipped open.

She held it in the light for as long as she dared.

Too long.

Sampson appeared next to her.

Shit.

She closed her eyes. There was nothing she could do. Caught red-handed.

Nothing happened.

Opening her eyes, she reached forward and as softly as possible pressed the camera shut.

"Move, please," he eventually said.

She looked to her left to find him crouching under the table, groping for something.

As he stood up, with a brown foolscap size envelope marked *ILFORD PHOTOGRAPHIC PAPER*, he nodded toward the torch. "Switch that off, please. Go outside and make sure no-one comes in. I'm about to open the camera. Where is it?"

She handed it to him.

"Susie," she said as he walked away. "I'm Susie."

"Thank you, Susie," he said without looking back.

She pulled the flaps of the wigwam closed and took her position guarding the entrance.

Megan reappeared in shorts with a neat bandage around her ankle.

"Samantha's done a good job," Susie said.

"It's fine."

Susie handed over guard duty and slipped off to her tent.

She sat cross-legged in the opening, pulling a sleeping blanket around her to keep off the overnight chill.

And waited.

Her watch said 4.10AM. They were just a few days from the summer solstice, and the sun was about to come up.

It was deathly quiet.

After a few minutes, she saw Sampson appear at the wigwam opening.

A rising inflection in Megan's voice.

It sounded like panic.

"No! Impossible!"

Susie got up and walked over.

"Everything all right?"

Megan shot her a look like thunder.

"There's nothing on the bloody film. It was all for nothing."

"What do you mean, nothing on it?" Susie asked, looking wide-eyed and innocent.

Megan pulled out a packet of cigarettes and lit one. Sampson appeared through the flaps of the wigwam, his arms laden with the darkroom equipment.

"The film's exposed," he said, as he headed to the back of his van.

"Exposed? How did that happen?"

"It happens," Sampson said.

"Or someone sabotaged us," Megan said, exhaling a cloud of smoke.

Sampson didn't look up but he made a derisory snorting sound.

"Sabotage?" Susie said.

"Leaky camera," Sampson said. "I told you to test it." He disappeared back into the tent to retrieve the rest of his kit.

Susie turned to Megan and spoke with as much sympathy as she could muster.

"We still have the folder. Where is it?"

The lines of Megan's face looked deep in the grey first light. She didn't reply, and wandered off.

When Sampson came back out, he held a bulging rucksack.

She followed him, not taking her eyes off the bag.

"Can I help with anything?"

"No."

There was something in the way he looked at her. The first signs of suspicion, maybe?

She decided not to push her luck.

It was out of her hands, now.

As she walked back toward her tent, he drove past, the Morris van rocking as it trundled over the uneven grass. It turned onto the main road and disappeared from view on the other side of a hedge.

She bit her lip, listening to the receding engine noise.

The van came back into view in the distance, heading toward the S-bends south of the airfield.

After what seemed an age, a second set of headlights came on and a car swung out behind the van.

The two vehicles disappeared from sight.

12

SATURDAY 18TH JUNE

"Where are they?" said Kilton.

"On their way, boss," the adjutant replied.

Millie stood between the two, staring down at the broken door.

Secure Cabinet 3 had been cleared out. The small padlock discarded on the floor, along with the thin metal base plate.

The room was quiet.

They'd followed so much protocol to ensure it remained hidden from view. Not just from the public, but from the rest of the RAF and armed forces.

And yet someone had been inside TFU, forced open the cabinet and simply walked out with it.

Who was reading about Guiding Light now?

Kilton's breathing grew heavier.

He kicked the cabinet; it rocked against the wall, flakes of paint fluttering to the ground.

The adjutant flinched.

Rob May and Red Brunson crashed through the doors.

Kilton set off toward his office.

"Follow me."

He sat down as the men shuffled in behind him.

"It was targeted. They must have known about Guiding Light."

Brunson and May looked at each other.

"We had a break-in last night," Millie said. "One cabinet was accessed. Guiding Light material is missing. Tapes and project files."

"Christ," spluttered Rob. "Do we know who it was?"

"Who do you think it was?" Kilton said. "It was obviously those bloody fairies at the end of the bloody runway." He paused. "But they must have had help. There's someone in here leaking. Someone on the inside. We have a traitor in our midst."

"Or they just broke in to do some damage and got lucky?" Millie suggested.

"Don't be so bloody naive, Millie. They knew what they were looking for. Nothing else is gone. The hatch to the Vulcan was open. Engineers are certain it was left closed."

Millie had seen Vulcan hatches left open overnight before, but said nothing.

"They've stolen Guiding Light from the Vulcan?" Rob said.

"No. Everything's still there. But they know it exists and that could be the end of the project."

Millie could contact JR to stand down the flight to Abingdon. The peace protestors may have just done him a favour.

But Kilton continued. "We can't let that happen, can we? We've come too far. There's too much at stake."

Kilton looked galvanised, eyes wide.

"We need to move quickly and surely. First, we find out who the traitor is. I need a list of everyone who has had any dealings with the project. Anyone who knew what it was, where the paperwork was, and which aircraft it was fitted to. And I want the list now."

Rob looked at Millie.

"That'll have to be you, Millie. I wouldn't know where to start."

"That's a lot of people, boss," Millie said. "Only a few of us properly know about it, but others know *of* it."

"Just draw up the bloody list, Milford."

"May, Brunson, you can start by rounding up everything to do with the project now. This place is no longer secure. From now on, everything stays in the safe in the HQ building."

The men stayed where they were for a moment, not sure if Kilton was finished. He looked at them, exasperated. "Go! Get on with it!"

―――――

THE CELL WAS DAMP. Condensation clung to the thick stone walls. Susie pulled her arms tightly around herself and tried to settle on the hard wooden bed.

The police had come for them just after 6AM.

A shout went up, and some of the girls shrieked as the men jumped out of their vehicles and marched toward the tents, truncheons drawn.

A few put up a token struggle, but most went quietly.

They knew it was coming, of course.

Susie expected Megan to brief them on how to say nothing and wait to learn what, if any, evidence they had against them. But that was not part of the plan. Quite the opposite, in fact. Megan wanted a fuss. Court appearances would be maximised as an opportunity to shout at the press.

Initially, Susie was in a cell with Samantha and two other girls, but shortly after names were taken, they came for the other three and moved them elsewhere, leaving her alone.

"Stay strong," Samantha had said as a constable led her away.

It was 10AM.

A bolt clunked on the other side of the door.

A spindly police sergeant appeared. He said nothing, but beckoned her with his finger.

Susie lifted herself from the bed and walked behind him past two other closed cell doors and out through a rear exit into the daylight.

She shielded her eyes from the bright sun.

In front of her was a small car park filled with police panda cars and a black Vauxhall saloon with dark windows.

The rear door was open, and the sergeant gestured her toward it.

She climbed into the back seat alongside a middle-aged man, clean-shaven and wearing a suit and tie.

The camera and rucksack sat on the seat next to him.

"Where are we going?" she asked.

"You're going back in there." He picked up the rucksack and opened it, removing a thick wad of papers, including three brown paper files.

"Is this everything?" he said.

Susie looked at the folders and camera.

"Yes."

"Are you sure? There was only one film and no prints."

"That's right, one film. I exposed it before he could develop it. There should have been some over-exposed prints?"

The man opened a cardboard box of photographic paper. She picked up the top three sheets, noticing the others were below a thin layer of brown paper.

"I think these are the attempts at developing the film."

The man held them close to his face. "OK."

Susie's eyes went to the paperwork. Red 'Top Secret' stamps and the carefully written project name: *GUIDING LIGHT*.

The man produced a strange leather satchel with twisted metal wire running through a black clasp.

He inserted the folders, camera, film and the three over-exposed prints.

He showed her a box of cardboard sleeves containing the reels of magnetic tape.

"Is this all of them?"

"Looks about right."

"You didn't count them?"

"No. But I'm sure that's it. Sampson took them all. None were left in the tent and they couldn't be anywhere else."

The man nodded. "The tents were searched. The plod found a bag of tools in the woods, but that was it. Still, if you didn't count them, we can't be a hundred per cent."

"Where else would they be?"

"OK. But next time be more observant."

"You have Sampson?"

"Yes."

"What happens to everyone else? What happens to me?"

"It's up to West Porton. I suspect they won't want to press charges. They seem a little shy when it comes to publicity." He paused. "But for now, you can go back to your cell."

"Thanks. What next? I'm done here."

He looked at her and shrugged. "Not my call, I'm afraid. Speak to your desk officer." He looked her up and down. "I must say this is a first for me. And it's true what they said, you are quite pretty."

"Right."

He fed the tapes into the pouch. It bulged, but he managed to seal it using the wires.

"Off you go. *Shoo!*" He motioned toward the door.

"Thanks. I'm not a cat. And no 'well done'?" She climbed out.

"If you want to be told 'well done', become a nurse."

The police sergeant looked expectantly at her.

"I need to go back to my cell. The same as everyone else, please."

"Oh. OK." He looked uncertain. "So, are we to be told what this is all about?"

Before Susie could answer, the man in the car called out, "In here please, sergeant. I need you to make a delivery."

———

"MARK, this is extremely serious. They will soon take it out of our hands."

Group Captain Gilbert Periwinkle's office was spacious. He spoke from behind his desk, leaving Kilton to pace the room. "We need to tell people what's missing. Group for a start."

"No," Kilton snapped. "They don't need to know. They don't have the full picture, anyway."

"What about the Ministry? And Blackton? At least let's tell Ewan."

"I'll talk to Ewan. But we'll lose the project if we lose confidence."

"How can we be confident? You heard the police. They've found nothing at the site. Just some wire cutters. None of the material. For all we know it's sitting on a newspaper editor's desk, or halfway to Moscow by now."

Periwinkle looked stern. "I'm just trying to be realistic here, Mark. I think you're hoping for a miracle that won't come. We've lost the material and we need to alert the proper authorities. We haven't even told the police we're missing anything. We can't just pretend."

Kilton slumped down at a chair against the back wall.

"The flimsy bloody cabinets. I told Johnson to beef them up. What about a D-Notice?" he asked. "We need one. If the documents are in the hands of the press, we need to stop publication."

"D-Notices are extremely hard to get, Mark. Telling newspapers they may not cover stories is not the politicians' favourite pastime. I think this government in particular will be reluctant. Having said that, it would be a first step to inform the Ministry."

"Not yet." Kilton softened his tone. "Let's be sure of what's missing. I've got the men going through everything."

"If we sit on this, it will only get worse for us."

"Worse? How?"

The phone on Periwinkle's desk rang.

The station commander picked it up and listened for a moment. "Yes. I see. Please escort him straight to my office."

He hung up and looked at Kilton. "The police are here."

Kilton stood up. "Remember, we tell them nothing."

The door opened. A corporal ushered in a short police inspector. His hat was under one arm and in the other he clutched a large leather satchel.

"Officer, how can we help you?"

"Regards to the break-in you've had at the fence. You believe nothing was stolen?"

Periwinkle glanced at Kilton. "Well we can't be a hundred per cent certain..."

"Right, only this has been passed to us, to pass to you."

He put the satchel on the desk.

It had an elaborate seal with two loops of metal wire.

The station commander stood up and peered over his half-moon glasses.

"Looks like the old diplomatic pouches we used to take through civil airports. Do you know what's in it?" he asked, looking up at the policeman.

"For your eyes only, was the instruction."

"Who gave the instruction?" asked Kilton.

The policeman shuffled on his feet. "The gentleman worked for the government, is about all I can tell you."

"Excuse me, inspector," Kilton said, "if this is our property I think we deserve to know where it came from."

"That's the thing, sir, I don't actually know. All I can tell you is that he worked for Her Majesty's government. And he returned stolen material, which, he informed us, belongs to you."

Periwinkle smiled. "Security Service, Mark. Don't expect a calling card."

Kilton stared down at the satchel, clearly itching to open it.

He looked back at the policeman. "And you have no idea what's in here?"

"No, sir. It's sealed."

"Thank you then, officer. Is that everything?"

The policeman looked disappointed, but said his goodbyes and left.

Kilton picked up the satchel, but Periwinkle emerged from behind his desk and took it from him. He snapped the black seal on the table and the metal wires sprung out.

He emptied the contents onto his desk: the secret Guiding Light files, a collection of magnetic tapes, a box marked *ILFORD PHOTO-GRAPHIC PAPER* and an Olympus camera.

Kilton stared.

"It's everything, plus this camera."

The station commander sat back down behind his desk. "Don't expect an explanation, Mark. My experience with these types is that they rarely tell you anything. But it looks like you have a guardian angel."

He looked up to Periwinkle. "This was a warning. The longer Guiding Light's held at the trial stage, the greater the risk of it being blown wide open."

"It's time to bring things to a conclusion."

The station commander stood up to see him out. "Well, let's not rush anything, but yes, I agree. I'll be rather pleased when it moves on.

"See you at the ball tonight, Mark? I think we've earned a stiff drink."

"We're still going ahead with the ball? After all this?"

"Of course. The show must go on."

———

THE OFFICERS' mess dining room was adorned with orange ejection seat parachutes and packed with loud chatter and laughter. The RAF West Porton Summer Ball was in full swing.

Millie sipped his gin & tonic, venturing away from his usual tipples on this special occasion.

It had been a strange day. Seeing Kilton go from a state of fury to light-hearted banter was quite something.

But there was a look on his face Millie didn't much like. A new determination seemed to fuel him.

He looked around the room. Catching JR's eye, he raised his glass across the sea of heads.

As usual for West Porton, very few people knew the truth of what was happening. The break-in was public knowledge, but that was about it.

The gong sounded; people cheered. Millie couldn't see him, but he imagined Rob with the hammer in his hand.

He found Georgina, and they walked arm in arm through to the dining room.

After the meal, they stood for the loyal toast, and the cigarettes and cigars came out.

Mark Kilton rose to his feet.

The TFU commanding officer launched into a lecture on national security and loyalty.

He began with the debt they owed their grandfathers, who fought in the trenches, moving on to their duty to protect their loved ones.

"But foul play of the worst kind will undermine all our efforts. Make no mistake, gentleman, we are under attack."

Georgina whispered in Millie's ear. "This doesn't apply to the ladies present, then."

Everyone listened politely, but this was not the time or place for a Churchillian rant.

Kilton, though, was oblivious to mood. "I will meet treachery with swift and vicious justice. Changes are already in place to ensure our work continues uninterrupted."

People shifted in their seats.

He came to a loud conclusion. "We will not allow our freedom to be lost in the name of naivety or deliberate treachery. We *will* do what is required, however unpleasant that may seem to the outsiders, such that those same people can sleep peacefully at night."

A few men greeted the speech with rapturous applause, while others put their hands together politely.

Millie glanced over to see Speedy Johnson start a standing ovation; others joined in, including Rob.

"Is he feeling alright?" Georgina asked.

Millie shook his head.

"No. He's getting worse. The man has too much power."

"He's a bit manic, that's for sure."

"And that's a dangerous combination, my dear."

Kilton sat down, having had the last word. There were no more speeches. It was a ball, not a dining-in night.

Millie drained his glass. He and Georgina walked out to the ante-room while they cleared the tables for the dancing.

They found their place by a window. Millie looked out at the darkening skies.

He recalled the moment that morning when it looked like the project had been brought to a premature end. Then later being told the items had been recovered.

He assumed it was some kids maybe, looking for cash or something valuable, and imagined them cursing the drab papers and reels.

So there was no need to cancel his trip to RAF Abingdon and onto Oxford on Monday.

———

THREE MORE DRINKS and one hour later, he was dancing with Georgina, followed by Sarah Brunson, then with Diana Johnson.

And then with Mary May.

Anxiety ebbed away with the alcohol.

Mary was tipsy and fun. The band played 'In the Mood'. They laughed together as Millie struggled to bring any kind of coordination to his movements.

When the tune finished, he thanked Mary for her charity and they fell down into nearby seats. Rob and Georgina joined them and they ordered a fresh bottle of wine.

They danced more and drank on until the first grey notes of dawn filtered through the mess windows.

A rumour went around: an expedition to Stonehenge was planned.

"It's your last RAF ball," said Georgina to Millie. "Let's make it memorable."

Millie and Rob followed as the women linked arms and skipped out to the cars.

A few minutes later, Millie pulled on the handbrake, on the side of the A303, and they stepped out into the orange dawn light.

The four of them walked across the grass toward the giant Neolithic slabs.

They weren't alone. A crowd of youngsters occupied the place: the early twenties set. Despite the warning notices, they climbed over the stones, laughing and hooting.

The four of them stood in the cool air, the men in black tie and the women in ball gowns and furs. They looked like they'd just walked off the set of a David Niven film.

Georgina nodded to the youngsters. "Do you think these are the traitors Mark was warning us about?"

"*Treachery will be met by swift and vicious justice!*" Mary said in a mock deep voice. More laughter.

Millie stole a glimpse of Rob, pleased to see him joining in with the smiles.

He hugged himself and watched the youngsters on the stones. They didn't seem to have a care in the world.

"I wonder what they think of us?" Mary asked.

"We're the squares, no doubt," Georgina said.

The sun climbed above the eastern horizon. A perfect disc diffused by a thin layer of clouds.

Millie smiled to himself at the glorious vision of a star, ninety-three million miles away, rising to give life to their planet.

He felt the first radiated warmth on his face and linked arms with Georgina.

He smiled at her.

"What are you grinning at, Milford?" she said, with a smile of her own.

"Just noticing how absolutely beautiful you are."

"Oh, Millie, don't. You'll make me cry."

He leant forward and kissed her.

"Come on," Rob said from over Millie's shoulder, "let's get these lovebirds home."

As they drove slowly along the country road, Millie pondered his plans to expose the Guiding Light flaws. He had become more resolute during the day, but time was no longer on his side. The logistics were going to be more difficult than ever.

Had Kilton's angry, panicked speech been inspired by genuine fear for the security of the country? Or out of fear that his own secret might still be insecure?

The bluster was bearable for one reason.

He had a plan.

On Monday it would take a giant step forward.

13

SUNDAY 19TH JUNE

Just after 7AM. Susie heard a noise in the corridor outside. Doors clanged, and she heard the familiar voices of her campmates.

Finally, her own door swung open. A young police constable stood in the frame.

"Out to the front desk, please. Queue for your personal effects."

She emerged and saw her earnest peace colleagues, looking worse for wear, shuffling to the front of the police station.

She joined the queue to retrieve personal effects.

At the front, Megan was arguing.

"You're supposed to charge us. What about the trial?"

"You're being released without charge, miss. Be grateful."

Two constables ushered them out onto the street. The group trudged back to the camp; a walk of three miles.

The field was a mess. Tents collapsed, clothes strewn around the entrances. They had combed the place.

It didn't take them long to discover the rucksack of tools was missing.

But the wigwam still stood. Susie wandered over.

"How long do you think they'll let us stay here?" she asked David.

"We've paid the farmer enough to make it worth his while. They won't get us out without a court order."

"Do we need to stay now?" Susie asked, glancing toward Megan, who was bent over a stack of boxes. She straightened her back.

"As long as they're there, we're here. But you're free to leave any time, Susie. This isn't the police station."

She went back to her boxes, which appeared to be filled with old clothes.

David gave Susie a sympathetic smile as she backed out of the wigwam.

Many were folding up their tents, preparing to leave. It was clear only a hardcore would remain.

With Megan preoccupied, Susie wandered out onto the main road and walked back to the village phone box.

After waiting an age for a teenage girl to finish her call, she entered and paused before dialling, waiting for the girl to leave the immediate area.

Roger answered.

"In on a Sunday, Roger? Don't you ever take a day off?"

"Not when there's such excitement in the West Country. Well done, my dear. Plaudits all round. The hairy blond one is in custody. Caught, as planned, red-handed."

"What will happen?"

"He'll be held long enough for us to thoroughly drain him of anything useful. After that, it's up to the plod and West Porton."

"And what about me?"

"I said well done. What else do you want? A bit soon for a medal."

"I mean, shall I pull out?"

"Maybe. What's the situation? Have they gone home?"

"Some have. But the leaders are still here."

"Then I suggest you stay put. Sorry, love. You must miss a soft bed. How was the police cell, anyway?"

"All part of being on active field service. You should try it sometime."

"My time will come. Hopefully in a four-star hotel rather than a field."

She ended the call, too low on energy for another back and forth.

14

MONDAY 20TH JUNE

A call from Jock MacLeish marred Millie's Sunday afternoon, informing him an all-personnel meeting would take place in TFU at 7.45AM the next day.

As he set off from home he had to hope whatever Kilton had planned would be over quickly. He needed to be on his way to the far side of the airfield before 8AM. After that, it got tricky. He would have to be in touch with ATC en route. The engineering Land Rover had a built-in radio, but he couldn't very well take that and abandon it all day.

The planning room was packed out. From the most junior aircraft marshaller to executive officers like himself, they had summoned the entirety of TFU.

Millie looked across to the admin hatch, where he could just see reference to his trip to Wyton on a list pinned to the wall. It looked innocuous enough. Above the hatch was a clock displaying the local time. It was already 7.49AM.

Kilton emerged from his office and pushed his way into the centre of the room.

Back against the wall, Millie couldn't see him, save the occasional glimpse of his bald head.

But he certainly heard him.

"One of you has given the enemy an advantage that could cost lives and freedom. One of you is heading to prison. You *do not* under any circumstances *ever* discuss *any* aspect of your work outside of these walls. *IS THAT CLEAR?*"

General mutters.

"PARDON?"

A louder "YES, SIR!" resonated from all quarters.

Kilton droned on about serving Queen and Country before eventually getting into announcements of new procedures, although he was vague on details.

Millie kept one eye on the clock and another on Nigel Woodward.

The forlorn-looking loadmaster was standing close to the airfield door with his head bowed, shuffling from foot to foot.

Writing off the chance of making it across the airfield in his own car, Millie had to get to Woodward before he said something.

By the time the boss had finished and stormed back into his office, it was 7.58AM.

Definitely too late.

He hurried to a phone on one of the aircrew admin desks.

"JR, it's Millie. Look, I hate to ask, but is there any chance you could pick me up in one of your wagons, discreetly?"

They agreed to meet at the NAAFI shop at 8.45AM.

Millie headed to the airfield door and made his way to the cramped office used by some of the sergeants, close to the hangar entrance.

Woodward was sitting at a table on his own; Millie closed the door behind him. The loadmaster looked pale and frightened.

"It was you, wasn't it Nigel?"

He didn't respond.

"Your wife told me you've been drinking your troubles away at The Black Horse. And talking to strangers. In your state that's not a good idea."

Finally he looked up.

"Will I go to prison?"

Millie tapped the table while he thought quickly. He pulled out a chair and sat opposite Woodward.

"No-one needs to know. We didn't lose anything. I can't see any good coming from it." Millie shuffled his chair close and looked Woodward directly in the eyes. "But you have to promise me you'll go to the doctor. Get a full medical."

Woodward nodded.

"You agreed before Nigel, but you haven't been. Say it. You've got to promise me. I'll book the appointment myself if needed."

He shook his head. "I'll go today."

"Good. In the meantime, tell no-one you spoke to a stranger about TFU. Do you understand?"

"Yes."

"It'll blow over. But you've got to get yourself sorted."

"What will happen to me?"

"I don't know, Nigel. But you can't keep flying and putting yourself and others in danger, can you?"

Woodward bowed his head. Millie glanced at his watch. "I've got to go."

BACK IN THE PLANNING ROOM, he tapped on Kilton's door.

"Come."

Millie went in but didn't wait for Kilton to look up.

"I think Nigel Woodward is unwell."

"Unwell?"

"Some sort of dementia, I think."

"Is that why he removed four pins from a payload that was supposed to remain in the aircraft?"

"I think so."

Kilton leaned back on his chair. "Makes sense. He couldn't explain himself to me."

"He's a couple of years from retirement. I suspect the docs will sign him off flying. Can we keep him on ground duties? Or give him his pension early?"

Kilton dropped his pen on the desk. "We haven't got space for people who can't do their jobs."

"Then let him retire. He's scared."

Kilton appraised Millie for a moment. "I haven't had a medical report yet."

"You'll get one soon."

Kilton nodded. "We'll see."

"Thank you."

As Millie left, Kilton resumed his work. "The trouble with you, Millie, is you're too soft."

————

THE CORRIDOR with the lockers was disappointingly busy.

Just when Millie thought it might be clear, more men appeared, walking back from the equipment counter with helmets, oxygen masks, and other flying paraphernalia in hand.

The clock ticked on.

For the second time in quick succession, he found himself up against a stressful deadline.

He cursed himself for not having a better plan. The locker was too exposed.

It was now 8.38AM. A large group of aircrew pushed open the door to the airfield and disappeared toward their aircraft.

He looked around the planning room at those who remained, either at the tea bar or hunched over charts, drawing lines.

For the moment at least no-one needed flying clothing. The corridor was clear.

He picked up an empty black holdall brought in from home and marched to his locker, dropping it at his feet as he unlocked the wooden door.

One more check to ensure the corridor was clear.

He quickly raised the bag to the open locker and scooped in the bulk of the reels.

He also withdrew his annotation of the fields.

The holdall was nearly full. He could have squeezed in his day jumper as well, to cover the contents. But he couldn't risk leaving anything behind. This was his one chance to clear his locker of incriminating evidence.

Just as Millie reached in for the final items, someone appeared in his peripheral vision.

He grabbed his jumper and slammed the locker shut, leaving behind a couple of tapes and the Guiding Light schematics.

Dropping the holdall to the ground, he crouched, fumbling with the straps.

Polished shoes appeared next to the bag.

Slowly, reluctantly, he looked up.

Mark Kilton stared down at him.

Millie raised himself upright, clutching the bag to his stomach, as if this would somehow protect his secret.

"There's something else. Follow me."

Kilton turned on his heels and walked back to the planning room.

Millie was stunned and for a moment failed to move.

Kilton turned back. *"Come on."*

He followed, unable to dispose of the holdall. Kilton loitered at his office door and beckoned him in.

Millie's eyes were wide with fear. As he moved to the middle of the room, he slowly set the bag down at his feet.

Kilton sat back down behind his desk and peered over it to look at the holdall.

"You flying today?"

"Maybe," Millie croaked, then cleared his throat.

"What does that mean?"

The phone rang; Kilton thumped on the frosted window behind him and shouted "Not now!"

He turned back. He looked agitated, even more than usual.

"Right," Kilton began, apparently having forgotten Millie's stupid answer to his question, "we need to improve our security and everything about this project. We've been amateurs, outwitted by hippies.

"We should have expected an attack, Millie. We've been wasting time, drawing things out and leaving the project exposed."

The TFU boss picked up a pen and turned it over in his fingers.

"I want all Guiding Light material to live in the safe in the station commander's office. Most of it's been moved, but there's a pile of reels in Cabinet Two. I assume they're blank tapes?"

"Yes, boss."

"Right. Well, there's forty-eight of them. I want you to move them as well. And be careful not to mix them with the used reels."

"That will make it time consuming, sir, if we have to trawl over to the HQ building just for blank reels before every flight."

"So? Get into work ten minutes earlier. Even the blanks will be signed out. We can't take any more chances, Millie. We've been lackadaisical."

Millie glanced to his left. He could just see the admin clock. It was 8.50AM.

"And second..." Kilton continued to talk but Millie's mind was elsewhere. If Kilton had them count the blanks out, and full reels in, how would he generate more height data for Belkin?

"...half the time."

"I'm sorry, sir. What?"

Kilton looked impatient. "Just make sure the reels and anything else project-related are moved out by the end of the day. You don't need to concern yourself with the timetable."

"The timetable?"

Kilton shook his head in despair and stood up. "Get on with it, Millie, for god's sake."

Millie picked up the holdall and walked out, heading straight to his car.

———

THE AVRO ANSON was battered on the outside and worn on the inside.

Millie sat alone in what passed as the passenger compartment, although only three tatty leather seats remained. JR had invited him to sit in the cockpit, but he couldn't risk a TFU crew member spotting him as they taxied past the buildings.

He looked around and wondered how many troops the old bird had conveyed around the world. It looked like a ghost plane now. The fact it was with the MU meant its prospects were not good.

JR quickly had them in the air and turning north, and in what seemed like no time at all they were descending into the circuit at Abingdon.

After landing, they taxied to the visiting aircraft apron.

JR shut the engines down and opened the door, lowering the steps for Millie.

"Is this what it's like being an Air Marshal?" Millie joked as he stepped out.

JR followed him onto the Tarmac as two marshallers appeared and placed chocks in front of the wheels.

Millie surveyed the airfield. Typical 1930s hangars with ridged rooves, a red brick control tower and a busy pan of mainly transport aircraft.

A noise erupted to their right and Millie looked across to see a giant Blackburn Beverly burst into life. A cloud of black smoke drifted from each engine in turn as it was fired up.

"Come on," JR said and led him away. He pointed to the base of the nearest hangar. "47 Squadron. They handle visitors for the airfield. We need to book in. So what are you going to tell them?"

"Hopefully, they're expecting me. I've booked a car from MT."

"Clever."

As they arrived at the hangar, JR pushed open the door and strolled into the squadron.

After looking around, he turned to Millie.

"Why don't you wait here? I'll book us in and tell them you've arrived."

Millie stayed back, close to the door.

He watched JR arrive at the ops desk and fall into conversation with a sergeant. JR made an entry in a hardback logbook and shared a joke with the sergeant before wandering back over.

"They've telephoned MT, Millie. Someone will pick you up from here shortly." JR studied him. "You OK?"

"Yes. A little nervous I suppose."

JR gave his arm a quick pat. "It's all fine. No-one's batting an eyelid. You'll be one of dozens of officers ferried somewhere or other by Military Transport this month. Try to relax."

"Thank you, JR."

"Good. Well, I'll find a comfy seat in the ante room of the mess. Don't want to get in anyone's way here. How long do you think you'll be?"

Millie shrugged. "I can't be certain. Two hours max, I hope."

"Fine. I'll wander back to the aircraft and make sure we're ready to depart in an hour and a half or so." He paused before leaving. "Good luck."

"Thank you."

After a few minutes, a corporal appeared in front of him.

"Squadron Leader Milford? Your chariot awaits, sir."

––––––

MILLIE WAS DRIVEN through the Abingdon main gate. It was decidedly more relaxed than West Porton's.

The driver had noted the professor's address in his vehicle logbook and Millie again realised he had not thought this through. Everything he was doing was traceable.

Save for a hundred bicycles, the traffic in Oxford was light. The driver dropped him in front of the cottage and Millie confirmed he would arrange his own taxi back.

As soon as the corporal's black saloon disappeared back onto the main road, Millie knocked and waited.

The door creaked open, and Mrs Lazenby ushered him in.

The professor, his saviour in an increasingly fraught and

dangerous endeavour, wore a green cardigan with a pair of silver-rimmed spectacles hanging from a chain around his neck.

Millie piled the tapes on the kitchen table. Each sleeve was labelled meticulously to reflect the order in which he had gathered the readings.

Next to the tapes, he set down a piece of paper with the annotated fields as requested.

"It took me a while to work it out, but I am fairly certain that what we have here is the time in seconds, which counts up from the moment the laser is switched from standby to on. That happens before I record, so you'll never see zero on the reels. Does that make sense to you?"

"It does. And I see the next field is the position in latitude and longitude."

"That's correct, with a '1' or a '0' replacing the hemisphere letter. '1' in front of the latitude for north, '0' for south. Not that we've been south of the equator, of course. And '1' in front of the longitude for west, '0' for east. I believe we drifted across the Greenwich meridian on at least one flight."

"Excellent work, Mr Milford."

With that, the professor sat down and Mrs Lazenby tapped at the door.

"Yes?"

She popped her head into the room.

"Would you like me to make a cup of tea, Professor?"

Millie glanced at the pile of secret tapes and material on the table.

Belkin shot him a reassuring look. "Yes please, Mrs Lazenby."

They sat in silence for a moment.

After the kettle reached screaming point, Mrs Lazenby poured the water into the teapot and set it down on a tray on the table, along with four Rich Tea biscuits.

She left the room. The door closed with a clunk.

"So," said the professor, "I have a young man ready to cut his teeth on the routining effort required to interrogate this data. Excuse the word 'routining'. It is apparently correct in this circumstance."

"Thank you."

"However, I think we need to know a little more about what we are looking for."

"I've been careful not to say too much for a variety of good reasons—"

"If it helps, I believe you may already have let the cat out of the bag."

"I have?"

"Just a moment ago, you referred to switching on the 'laser'. I'm sure it was inadvertent, but am I to gather that you are testing a laser range-finding device?"

"Oh, dear me. Yes. I didn't even notice." Millie sighed and toyed with a biscuit. "The atmosphere where I work is now at fever pitch and here I am spilling our deepest secrets."

"I think it's something we cannot avoid, I'm afraid."

Millie took a breath.

"I suppose you *need to know*," he said and laughed.

"I do, I think. Is that funny?"

"Just a private joke, sorry. Well, if I explain the system to you, perhaps we can then devise a way of you explaining it to your student without giving the game away?"

The professor nodded. "It sounds like a starting point."

Millie pointed at the data sheet.

"So, as I've already given away, this all comes from a laser beam. The laser is mounted in the front underside of the aircraft. A rather beautifully engineered mirror on a small gimbal directs the beam in an oval pattern. Quickly, repeatedly. The laser measures the distance to the ground at twenty-seven pre-set positions during each scan. And it does this around three times a second."

"Gosh," said the professor, clearly impressed.

"This is the clever bit, though. A box of microelectronics sits between the laser and a new flight control system which in turn talks to the rather older autopilot. The result is that the computer flies the aircraft at low-level, avoiding the ground while moving the aircraft in as straight a line as possible to the next waypoint."

The professor nodded. "I see. So, an aircraft can fly automatically at low-level to its target. But what is the advantage over a human performing this task?"

Millie sat back. "Humans are frail and make mistakes. At least that's the theory. The boffins are doing everything they can to write the crews out of the equation when it comes to flying these days. The real question is, why use a laser instead of a radar? Terrain-following radar is already developed and was to be deployed in the TSR-2. But it has a drawback. It makes a noise."

The professor raised an eyebrow. "Radar makes a noise?"

"Not an audible noise, but it gives off energy. The exact type of energy the enemy's aircraft defence system is looking for. Initially, we believed it would be too weak to be picked up. But it turns out the Soviets are rather good at this aspect of modern warfare."

"So, this laser system solves a rather big problem for the RAF?"

Millie took a sip of tea. "Not just the RAF. If it works, this system will go into virtually every United States attack aircraft as well."

"I see. And why do you need my help?"

"It's flawed. We suffered a sudden height drop a couple of weeks back."

"The sort of thing you're testing it for? Why hasn't it gone through the usual channels at Boscombe Down?"

"If this project was at Boscombe Down, I'm convinced it would have been grounded. But I now work at a new unit, cloaked in secrecy, somewhat autonomous from the rest of the RAF and it's... not the same, shall we say. It's almost as if it's gone too far to fail. There's so much riding on it. A massive export order for the UK, for one. And I have a boss who places human life further down the list of priorities when it comes to fighting the Soviets. So he's prepared to press on."

"Even so, won't it be noticed if it goes into production? What happens when an aircraft crashes?"

"I might be wrong but my hunch is, they know it's flawed. I think they would find a way of covering it up. The manufacturer is the sole expert on the system and will likely be consulted by any Board of

Inquiry. As I found out, only they can analyse the height readings."
He looked at the pile of cardboard sleeves. "Until now."

The professor sat up, grabbed a pen and started writing.

"Righty-ho. Let us sketch what we're looking for. Firstly, height readings that vary significantly, and implausibly, from the previous and subsequent readings. Secondly, we should look at these... events and extrapolate the frequency. Of course, that depends on whether we see more than two or three events. We can't extrapolate from fewer than three and, even then, the reliability of the extrapolation will be down to the sample size."

"The more data, the more reliable the conclusion?"

"Indeed."

Millie toyed with his moustache. "I'm working on that, but I may be about to run out of time."

"Well, we can make a start, I suppose."

Millie propped his elbows on the table and tried to read the professor's notes, which appeared upside down to him. "There's something else."

"Go on."

"This data was gathered at a safe height, a minimum of one thousand feet. Sometimes without the autopilot even engaged. In reality, this system will be used at low-level, very low and very fast. I need to be able to show what the effect would be from one of these 'events', as you call them, occurring at various phases of flight."

The grandmother clock struck midday on the other side of the kitchen door; Millie glanced at his watch.

"Well," said the professor, "once we know the frequency of the events, and the percentage variance, we should be able to apply that to different flying circumstances. In fact, this is precisely the type of exercise we set the boys. Usually it involves the weather for some reason. The chance of a certain type of weather event based on historic data which is then used to decide where to build houses, for instance."

Millie frowned in confusion.

The professor smiled. "I'm sorry, I'm rambling. I'll set this as a theoretical task for a couple of the boys. Leave it with me."

"Thank you, Professor. When do you think you might have a result for me?"

Belkin stood up slowly. "It will take a few days, but I head to Devon for a fortnight on Friday, so it will have to be before then, otherwise you'll be waiting rather a long time. Why don't you call me on Thursday evening?"

"That sounds wonderful, thank you." Millie nodded at the pile of Top Secret material on the professor's kitchen table. "Can you destroy this after you've got what you need? Is that possible?"

Belkin scratched his chin. "Well, we do have a rather large and fearsome boiler in the department's basement. I dare say we could make use of the firebox. Unless you would need the physical evidence?"

Millie pondered. "I can't be sure, but it's probably better not to hold on to any of this material a second longer than needed."

Belkin nodded. "The furnace it is, then."

As they got to the front door, the old professor turned to Millie. "What exactly do you intend to do with the results, Squadron Leader Milford?"

"I think I'll start with the station commander. If he buckles to my boss, I'll go above both their heads to the government minister."

———

MILLIE WAS DROPPED BACK at 47 Squadron. He didn't go inside, but instead walked out to the Anson. JR peered into the radial engines, appearing to brush away some dirt.

"He returns! All go well?"

"Yes. Thank you so much, JR. You've no idea how grateful I am to have you with me."

JR wiped his hands on a rag. "Think nothing of it. Whatever it is you're doing, I can see it's important to you. Which makes it important to us."

Millie followed him back on board and took his seat in the body of the aircraft.

He watched the experienced pilot's hands glide over the controls. After pausing for the engine to warm, JR advanced the throttles to taxi.

A couple of minutes later, they accelerated down the main runway.

Millie stared down at the countryside through the small window. Largely brown after the heatwave, with occasional tractors and a combine harvester busy at work; an early harvest for the wheat.

The journey took a few minutes. JR taxied down the western perimeter and paused for Millie to leave the aircraft just beyond the TFU hangar; out of sight of the offices, but close enough to walk back inside.

No-one paid him any attention as he arrived in the planning room.

He checked his locker. Not much left. A few pages of schematics, two of the early test tapes. He might need the schematics, but it was too risky to keep the tapes.

Then there was the material still at his house.

He could have a bonfire this weekend. A nervous chat over the fence with Jock MacLeish as Top Secret papers went up in smoke behind him.

He shut the locker and checked his notebook for the day's tasks.

Reluctantly, he transferred the remaining blank tapes to the safe in the headquarters building.

He watched, dispirited, as a corporal carefully counted and noted the exact number.

As the corporal pushed the heavy safe door shut and double-locked it, the opportunity to record any more secret data disappeared.

Everything now relied on Belkin.

15

TUESDAY 21ST JUNE

"We're off to get the second Vulcan," Rob said to the growing group of men who made up the Guiding Light project. They all stood around a map table in their own secret huddle, away from the crowd. "Red and I will fetch her tomorrow. From the afternoon, the boss wants both birds in the air twice a day. We should be able to knock off the remaining hours in no time, maybe less than a week."

"What?" said Millie. "No, no. He's not said anything to me about this."

Rob looked surprised. "The boss said he briefed you yesterday?"

Millie looked across at Kilton's office. It must have been part of the half-heard ramblings about the project timetable. Millie hadn't been paying attention, distracted by the trauma of getting the tapes out of the building.

"A week? How's that even possible?"

"Well, we have forty-eight tapes left to fill, and with two Vulcans available every day, he thinks we could get through them. He wants to invite Ewan Stafford up next week for the handover. Apparently we're going to demo it to him and that will be that. A good job all round."

"Christ," Millie said, more to himself than anyone else.

They moved into planning mode. Another trip to Wales. A long winding route at one thousand feet from Shrewsbury down to Swansea.

"Plenty of time for recording, Millington," Speedy said, smiling at him.

Millie stared at him. Unwanted thoughts cascaded into his mind. *Did they know?*

———

AN HOUR before they were due to get airborne, Millie walked over to the squadron HQ building where the door to the station commander's outer office was open. Two secretaries sat at typewriters, tapping away. He coughed and one of them looked up.

"I need to access some files." Without replying, the woman picked up a phone and dialled.

"John, you have your first customer."

Moments later, a corporal arrived and led Millie to the safe. As he opened it, Millie exchanged a nod with Periwinkle, who was behind his desk working.

"Take what you need," the corporal said.

Millie withdrew six reels from the pile. The corporal made a careful note of each item. Millie checked the dwindling stack of cardboard sleeves. Forty-two left.

Last week he needed to get extra blanks into the aircraft and run the machine as much as possible. Today, it was the opposite.

He needed time.

———

THEY BROUGHT the Vulcan to life. Millie locked his seat and tested his straps.

The pilots went through the checklists and spoke to air traffic control.

Millie loaded the first tape out of habit. They all contributed to the completion of the project now. Fewer, not more, was the new order of battle.

He waited until they were established at one thousand feet, held on for another minute, then started the recorder.

The run was bumpy.

Around eighteen minutes in, Millie lifted the plastic cover from the two rotating reels.

He studied the tape's intricate journey through the mechanism. It wound through two rubber rollers which stretched it over two metal heads, which he assumed contained the magnetising process. He pulled a pencil from his coveralls and gently pressed the left side rubber rollers together. Immediately the tape curled up and out of the machine. He stabbed at the stop button, dimly recalling instruction on how to deal with a jam. He began to wind the tape back onto the right-side reel, then stopped the process, leaving the tape loose and hanging out of the recorder.

To his right, Steve Bright looked bored.

Millie unclipped one of the reels and lifted it up, with the magnetic tape trailing back into the recorder.

"Something's jammed," he said, and Bright looked across. The navigator leaned closer and squinted.

"Do you know how to un-jam it?"

"I think so. Will take a while, though."

Millie fiddled with the mechanism for as long as he felt he could get away with it, before eventually appearing to free the tape from the clutches of the machine. He slowly loaded a second reel, just as they turned toward the final waypoint of their low-level run.

———

As they emerged from the Vulcan, Millie reported the tape jam to Rob, to add to the list of aircraft defects.

"What does this mean?" Rob asked him. "Can we still use it?"

Millie removed his helmet and ran his hand over his sweaty head, enjoying the cool air. "No, I'd rather they looked into it. We don't want to waste precious time in the air. I only got two tapes done this time."

Rob sighed. "Fine. Can you speak to engineering?"

"I am still the project leader, Rob. It's my responsibility to ensure we get the hours flown as well."

"Yes. Of course, Millie. Sorry, old boy. It's just you know how Kilton is about this. He's worried."

"He's always worried."

Millie headed off to engineering. He looked at his watch and stopped.

He would report the defect later in the day. That should take the aircraft out of action tomorrow morning.

16

WEDNESDAY 22ND JUNE

Millie smiled when he saw the annotation *U/S* appear next to *Vulcan XH441* on the admin board. The jet was unserviceable while they looked at the tape recorder.

It wasn't much, especially as Rob and Red were headed up north to ferry back the new Vulcan. But it all helped to stall the project's completion while Belkin ran the comparison figures.

Millie busied himself with unrelated paperwork. Kilton appeared by his side.

"Shouldn't you be flying?"

"Jet's on the blink. Engineering are looking at her now."

Kilton grunted but didn't pursue the issue.

———

AFTER LUNCH, a gleaming white Vulcan sat on the apron.

"Are any of these left on the squadrons?" asked a passing pilot. "Or has TFU commandeered them all?"

Millie shrugged. Adding a second Vulcan to the TFU fleet was a sign of the project's importance. And Kilton's growing influence.

Rob appeared from Kilton's office, still in flying coveralls. He marched directly up to Millie.

"What happened with the tape recorder? Why wasn't it fixed yesterday?"

"I'm not sure, Rob. I guess they're busy."

"Didn't you tell them this is top priority?"

"I'm sorry, Rob, are you running this project now?"

"No, you're supposed to be."

"What the hell does that mean?"

Rob didn't reply but moved off to the tea bar. Millie thought about following him, but Red appeared by his side.

"He's just had to tell Kilton the new Vulcan needs a hundred-hour service before we can use her. So Kilton kicked him and he kicked you. Sorry, pal."

"How long will the service take?"

"Tomorrow, apparently. They would do it this afternoon, but they've got to reinstall your tape recorder first."

"Rob's never spoken to me like that before."

Red nodded. "He's moving up the ladder now. Things getting more serious for him. He'll adapt. Not everyone's a cool cucumber like you, Millie."

"I don't feel cool, I can assure you. This whole thing, it just worries me."

"What does?" Red asked.

Millie turned back to look at the American, and wondered how far he could go.

"What's the bloody rush? When did we go from being careful and thorough to moving at such an indecent speed?"

Red patted him on the back. "I guess when anti-nuclear campaigners learn about the existence of our secret new system."

17

THURSDAY 23RD JUNE

By Thursday afternoon, both Vulcans were serviceable. Kilton watched from the apron as the men charged with Guiding Light trial flights walked out in two groups.

Millie strapped into the back of the older aircraft. In the rear bay of the new jet was Steve Bright. There was only one rear crew member in each; it was Kilton's way of recreating the likely crewing situation in the next generation of military aircraft, now that the computer was doing most of the work.

It also allowed him to operate both at the same time.

They got airborne within a few minutes of each other. Millie's aircraft, flown by Rob and Speedy, headed north to the Peak District. Red Brunson and Jock MacLeish headed west to the Brecon Beacons.

All Millie could think about was the sheer number of blank reels they would get through between them.

He had at least seen off the possibility of the final flight, with Stafford on board, taking place tomorrow.

But it had only been pushed to next week.

If Belkin came back with news of a serious flaw buried deep in the data, Millie would have just hours to make his move.

The Vulcan slammed into a pocket of air as they descended to low-level.

Reluctantly, Millie powered up the system and engaged the laser.

He began the first reel recording the height data.

The aircraft levelled out around one thousand feet and Millie felt a familiar jolt as the autopilot took over.

He scanned the orange numbers, rotating the dial to check all angles before bringing the readout back to the '1' position, below and just ahead of the nose.

1,011 flickered over to 1,023 followed by a stream of numbers all within a few feet of each other.

After fifteen minutes, the ride became rougher. The land rose and dropped below them and the Vulcan fell in unison, causing Millie's stomach to turn.

"Working perfectly!" Rob called over the intercom.

"Wonderful," said Millie. "It's all perfect. That must be why we're not allowed below one thousand feet."

Millie concentrated on not throwing up. Air-sickness had crept up on him in recent years, exacerbated by flying at low-level.

After ten more miles over the hills, Rob piped up again.

"How we doing? On to the second tape yet?"

"When reel one's full, I'll switch over. Not before, thank you."

"OK, OK. Keep your hair on. I was just asking."

"Just concentrate on your job and I'll do mine."

Rob didn't reply.

Millie was well into the third tape before they climbed out of low-level and headed north of Manchester, giving the city a wide berth before turning south.

He poked the reels into the sleeves and marked them up. At least six more would have been consumed in the two flights.

―――――

As they shut down, Millie heard some low whispers between Speedy and Rob.

The pilots appeared down the ladder and Millie let Rob undo the hatch and lower the ladder down, all in silence.

Speedy and Rob walked off toward TFU, leaving Millie to follow twenty yards behind. Once in the planning room, Millie piled the freshly recorded tapes on his desk, along with the one extra blank he hadn't used.

Rob appeared by his side.

"What was that about?"

"What?"

"You know very well what."

Millie fixed him with a gaze. "And you very well know what I think—"

"No, Millie, I don't know what you think. The system's working flawlessly. It's embarrassing in front of Speedy, who's seen nothing but a brilliant new system working without fault. There's no reason to keep batting on about it, and most of all no reason to take out your grievances on the rest of us. It's unprofessional."

Millie looked over Rob's shoulder. Speedy and a couple of others watched from afar.

"That's what you all think? It's flawless?"

"Yes. I'm afraid you're alone in thinking otherwise. Don't make this difficult for me, Millie—"

"Difficult for you?"

"Yes. Everyone knows you and I are friends—"

"Are we, Rob? Still friends?"

Rob looked disappointed. "I thought we were."

The two men stared at each other for a moment before Rob walked back to the tea bar.

Millie stood by himself, next to the little corner of the planning room he'd made his own.

The pilots and aircrew on the far side were in good cheer, with laughter bouncing off the low ceiling.

He removed his flying coveralls and checked in his equipment before picking up the tapes and walking slowly over to the station commander's office.

Periwinkle was behind his desk again, ignoring the comings and goings to the safe. Just as Millie was signing in his tapes, Steve Bright appeared.

"How many complete reels?" the corporal asked.

"Four," Bright replied.

"Four?" Millie said.

"Yep." Bright handed his tapes to the corporal, complete with annotations on the sleeves.

Bright and the corporal left the room.

Millie gazed at the dwindling pile of blanks as the safe door closed, then checked he'd passed everything from his case.

As he walked to the door, he turned back to Periwinkle and hesitated.

Should he say something now?

TFU was quiet, with most of the men in their respective mess bars.

Millie looked at his watch. He was due to call Belkin in an hour.

———

Susie watched as two Vulcans screamed out of West Porton. So much for their disruption.

"They appear to be expanding."

"What?" David asked, lying on the ground next to her.

"That's the first time I've seen two Vulcans."

David didn't bother looking.

"Are we done here now, David? I mean, what are we doing? It just feels like the energy has gone, along with half the people."

"Megan's waiting to hear from Sampson. He's obviously working on how to get the information out."

"Right."

"Meanwhile, she wants to march again. If they're not going to charge us, we may as well make the most of our freedom."

"Won't that provoke them?"

"I think that's the point."

Susie sighed. "I see."

––––––

LATER IN THE AFTERNOON, she made her daily call.

"Nothing's happening or going to happen," she told Roger. "They've done as much as they can, and it did nothing. They're talking about bloody marching around the airfield now, as if that will suddenly force Britain into giving up her nuclear deterrent."

"They want you there a little longer. Number Ten got back to us rather late in the day. Apparently that project you stumbled across is rather high value. They're keen we protect it from any further interruptions."

"That's not our job, is it? Don't they have their special branch for that?"

"Not sure they covered themselves in glory when you and your friends walked under their noses and into the heart of a secret test flying unit. Anyway, won't be long. The project is due to end next week and move into production."

"Fine. What is it, by the way?"

"Guiding Light. Some sort of guidance system for the delivery of nukes. Don't know any more, I'm afraid, and probably won't find out. But they are all jolly keen on it at the top of the tree. Something about a big export order to our American friends."

"So we really stumbled across something."

"Well, it's done us no harm. The PM is personally grateful for our work—"

"My work."

"I thought we were a team, my dear?"

"When it suits you, Roger."

––––––

AT 7PM, Millie checked Georgina was safely in the garden with a drink, before he went into the house through the French doors. He closed the living room door behind him and stood over the telephone.

He dialled the Oxford number with a shaking hand.

"Ah, Squadron Leader Milford. Good evening. Are you well?"

"Quite well, yes, thank you, Professor Belkin." His legs were jelly.

"Good. Well, I expect you'd like to hear the results of our digging?"

"Yes, please."

"Well, let me tell you, we had quite a week of it." The professor spoke slowly and deliberately.

"Did you find anything?"

"No."

The response hit Millie like a knife in his chest. His shoulders hunched forward.

"Not at first."

"Not at first?"

"It was a case of adjusting the parameters. Initially, my erstwhile undergraduate set the computer a task of finding a variation in height readings that moved two thousand feet or more in two seconds. Something he considered would be a clear sign of an error."

"That's quite a dramatic change."

"Well, yes. I thought so, too. And it provided a negative return. However, I then instructed young Strangways to look for a more moderate difference, and we settled on seven hundred and fifty feet or more in three seconds or less."

"And?"

"And, Mr Milford, I think I can safely say there is a problem with your new equipment."

Millie sat down on the small bench by the telephone desk.

"Tell me more."

"We found seven instances initially. When we looked at the surrounding data, three of them were normal. The aircraft appeared to be descending or ascending as part of a planned manoeuvre, although the numbers may have exaggerated the rate of climb or descent."

"Right, but the other four instances?"

"Yes, well, they point to anomalies. The sudden change in height didn't fit with readings around it. A definite issue for you to resolve. Something we would call a systemic problem."

"Incredible work. I can hardly believe it."

"Interestingly, when we narrowed the parameters further, we kept finding anomalies."

"How many?"

"Many. The narrower the parameters, the more we found. Small deviations, I should say. But a clear sign that there is a recurring issue with the data received by the computer from whatever is feeding it."

"I want to say I'm relieved, but it doesn't feel like the right reaction. In fact, as I think about it, I'm becoming angry."

"Well, I must remind you, this is a very small sample size. We measured less than thirteen hours of data according to the time field."

Millie toyed with his pen.

"I understand, but from what you've seen, you believe this is enough to predict actual losses?"

"Well, that brings me on to the more complex side of the equation."

"More complex? I'm only just keeping up as it is."

"Then I'll try and be gentle with you. Now, you may wish to make some notes. We've done what we can to be as accurate as possible on the limited information. One of the students found a Parliamentary Written Answer on Royal Air Force establishment numbers with predictions for the next five years. From there we made an estimate of flying hours and within those hours, an estimate of low-level flying.

"After that, we applied the occurrence frequency we found on your tapes. That produced a startlingly high number of incidents."

"Really? How high?"

"I can't recall the actual rate, but too high. So high that you would have experienced mishaps every week, just during this trial."

"So the data is wrong? Or your calculations are wrong?"

"Neither, I'm happy to report. We went back to the detail of the incidents and realised that in the vast majority of cases, the incorrect readings would go unnoticed."

"Unnoticed? Can you explain that? How would a crew not notice a sudden change in height?"

"Because the erroneous height information would be just a quick burst, in many cases less than a second. So the aircraft would either not have time to react, or would only just start to change velocity, before the correct readings flowed through, cancelling any required change."

"I see."

"We refined the search parameters and asked the mainframe to search for those large variations. This is where it gets interesting."

"Go on," Millie said, pen poised over the back of one of the data sheets.

"While far rarer, longer bursts of incorrect data that could affect flight do occur. Although, again, in many cases we estimate this would be inconsequential."

"How so?"

"Firstly, the higher the aircraft is from the ground, the less likely that even three seconds of deviation could cause an actual accident. Secondly, even at low-level, when straight and level, the aircraft would often recover itself, even without pilot interference, as the wrong height readings would run out and be replaced by the actual distance to the surface. But..."

"But?"

"Well, that leaves us those occasions when an aircraft is low, fast and banked, when even two to three seconds worth of incorrect height information could be catastrophic. Add into that scenario a flight at night or with restricted visibility and you have an unwelcome circumstance. Albeit rare."

"How rare?"

"We estimate 0.014% of the time."

"Small enough to be inconsequential?" Millie asked.

"Not when you apply that frequency to the overall hours. Now, the number I'm going to give you is based on our predictions and it involves a good deal of extrapolation on a limited data supply. So, fair warning of its accuracy. We estimate the RAF will operate around two hundred and sixty-two hours of training flights at low-level, around the world, per day, over the next couple of years.

"If we guess that fewer than half will employ your new system, that still leaves twenty-five thousand hours over the course of a year.

"Even at just 0.014%, that points to 3.5 aircraft caught in the very worst of scenarios.

"Now, you told me the system will be fitted to a range of aircraft from those with two seats to those with a crew of four or even five?"

"That's correct."

"So, another guess is the average number of crew members per aircraft. We rounded that to 2.5."

Millie quickly did a calculation.

"8.75?"

"Indeed. 8.75 is the number we reached. In our view, based on limited data and much guesswork, the Royal Air Force would expect to lose 3.5 aircraft on average each year, risking the lives of 8.75 crewmen."

Millie stared at the figure at the base of his scribbled notes.

"8.75. And you're sure?"

"No, we're not sure. But with more data, a refined figure will be more certain." The professor paused. "However, the important point here is that the true number will not be zero."

There was a long silence on the phone.

Eventually, the professor spoke again. "Mr Milford, may I ask you something?"

"Of course."

"You told me you would speak to the station commander at West Porton, correct?"

"Yes, that's still my plan."

"You also told me the man in charge of the project wields a lot of influence?"

"Yes."

"May I ask, is the station commander trustworthy and able to support you in what you ask for?"

Periwinkle had never come across as a strong character; Kilton got the better of him most of the time.

"I can't be sure."

"Well, if you don't mind me making this observation, I think you may place yourself in a challenging position if, for instance, the conversation with the station commander does not go as you would like."

"I know what you're saying, Professor, but I can't see a less risky option. My alternative is to contact the government, and I wouldn't know where to start."

"Well, permit me to make a suggestion."

"By all means."

"I will give you a telephone number. You should call it, I suggest sooner, rather than later."

Millie noted the number and a name on the bottom corner of his sheet.

Leconfield Ho. Ger. 6672
Ask for 'A W Strutthers'

"And who is this?"

"That will be a matter for them to tell you, should they wish. But I promise you, the fact you have this number and name means you will be taken seriously and given a hearing at least. You may know the Oxford Maths Department has rather useful connections with some of the less well-lit areas of government. I have never given this number out to anyone who I didn't consider a candidate for employment in such a place. But in your case, I believe this is warranted. I wish you good luck."

Georgina opened the living room door and walked past Millie as he finished the conversation.

"Boring work thing," he said and disappeared upstairs.

Next to the old filing cabinet in the spare room, he pulled out a cardboard box labelled *VEGETABLES*. Under his old log books were the Guiding Light materials he had initially smuggled out of West Porton. He added his precious page of notes to the box, hiding them in the middle of the pile. He could study the statistical conclusions later.

He stayed on his knees with the box in front of him for a moment, before digging the sheet out again, and tearing off the corner containing the number and name Belkin had given him.

Millie left the house and headed down the hill toward the village.

He entered the red telephone box, dialled 100.

"Operator, how may I help you?"

"Ah, yes. Could you connect me to the following number, please? Ger. 6672."

"That's a London code. Hold the line, please."

After a few whirrs, the ring tone sounded, followed by the pips demanding money. He inserted a threepenny coin.

"Hello. Can I help you?"

"May I speak to AW Strutthers, please?"

There was a pause and the sound of rustling papers.

"Please hold."

The phone clicked.

"Hello? May I help you?"

"Hello. Mr Strutthers?"

"Yes. Can I help you?"

"My name is Squadron Leader Christopher Milford and I think I need to report something."

"I see. A serving officer or retired?"

"Serving."

"Where are you?"

"I'm stationed at RAF West Porton in Wiltshire."

"I see. And are you calling us from a public telephone box?"

"Yes."

"Can I call you back in one hour?"

Millie looked at his watch; it was 6.17PM. He didn't think he could get away with being out that long.

"Would it be OK to call me on my home number?"

"As long as you are not overheard. Please have a pen and paper ready when we ring."

Millie gave the man his number and he hung up almost immediately.

He walked back home, calmed by the assertiveness he had heard at the other end of the mysterious line.

At home, he sat down in the living room, unsure of what to do with himself.

Georgina breezed in.

"Oh, hello. What are you up to?"

"Nothing," Millie snapped back.

"Oh. It's OK, Millie. I wasn't accusing you of anything. Just wondered..."

"I'm sorry. Have you had a nice day, dear?"

Georgina dropped into an armchair. "Fine. A little boring. It has made me wonder what we'll fill our days with, come retirement."

Millie studied his fingernails.

"Millie? Are you listening to me?"

"Sorry, yes. What were you saying?"

Georgina rolled her eyes. "Really, Millie, sometimes you are off with the fairies. I was just saying, I don't know how we'll fill our days when we retire. I mean, you want to sail, but what will I do?"

"I'm sure you'll find something. You enjoy shopping."

"But with whom? We're moving to the south coast. Mary will be up here, busy being an officer's wife. Everyone we know who's retired is scattered to the four winds. They don't think about that when they post us all over the place, do they?"

"I'm sorry, who's being posted?"

Georgina threw her hands in the air. "For goodness sake, Millie. I might as well be talking to the bloody wall."

The phone rang. Millie leapt up.

Georgina stared at him.

"Whatever's got into you?"

He looked at his watch.

7.17PM exactly.

"It will be for me." He left the room and closed the door behind him.

The caller spoke first.

"Squadron Leader Milford?"

"Yes."

"Someone will meet you. Will that do?"

"Yes."

"Do you know St Mary and St Melor Church in Amesbury?"

"Yes, I do."

"8AM on Saturday morning. You will meet one of our staff members who is located close by. She will be instructed to wear blue and sit toward the rear of the church. A young woman with short dark hair. Please come alone and do not discuss this or any aspect of your concerns with anyone else."

"Yes, of course."

"Actually, I can't be certain she has something blue to wear, so don't be put off if she's wearing something different."

Millie had no sooner agreed than the man hung up.

The living room door opened and Georgina stood, one hand on the frame, with a bemused look on her face.

"If I didn't know better, I'd say you're hiding something from me, Christopher Milford."

18

FRIDAY 24TH JUNE

Rob woke early.

The sun streamed through a gap in the curtain, illuminating a swirl of house dust. He watched the slow rotation for a while.

The sound of an early morning engine run drifted into the room.

He still found it hard to believe that he was a part of it all. West Porton, TFU. Secret projects the outside world would be amazed to learn about.

And not just a part of it, but an important part.

Mary was in the kitchen in her nightie when he came down the stairs.

"Will I see you tonight?" she asked.

"Happy Hour on a Friday. I'm expected to be there."

"But it's not a formal do, is it? Do they need the mess secretary to help them drink?"

"We've been over this, Mary. The boss will probably be there and at the moment, yes, I think I should, too."

He decided against a bowl of cereal and made for the door.

"We can do something tomorrow," he said as he left.

"With Millie and Georgina?" Mary called after him, following him out.

Rob pulled back the canvas top of his Austin Healey.

"What is it, Rob? Why are we suddenly not friends with Millie and Georgina? You and Millie were so close."

"It's complicated." He climbed into the car and drove away before Mary had a chance to reply.

———

IN THE PLANNING ROOM, Rob spotted Speedy Johnson at a desk. As he went over, he also checked for Millie. No sign.

"Speedy. Now might be a good time to see the boss about our suggestion?"

They headed over to Kilton's office.

The boss was head down in paperwork as usual.

"Yes?" he said, without looking up.

Rob cleared his throat. "Speedy and I think it might be a good idea to take Guiding Light back down to three hundred feet."

Kilton stopped writing and looked up. He tapped the pen on the table and leant back.

"Obviously, you'll want to clear it with the station commander," Johnson said, "but from our point of view it's behaved impeccably and there's no reason for the safety margin."

"No abnormalities?" Kilton asked.

Both men shook their heads.

"We've only got a few flights left, boss," said Rob. "I think it would be a display of our confidence in the system."

Kilton smiled. "Good. I agree."

"And the station commander?" Johnson asked.

"It's my decision, Speedy. I run TFU."

"Very good." Johnson grinned. He and Rob headed out.

"Boys," Kilton said as they reached the door. "Keep your wits about you."

———

THE SKY WAS blue with dusty white streams of high cirrus clouds. Millie sat on the bench in front of the TFU offices, in full flying clothing. The planned departure had been delayed because of some mysterious admin task handed to Speedy and Rob.

His mind was on tomorrow's clandestine meeting.

He watched as a Shackleton with lethal whirring propellers taxied onto the edge of the apron. A marshaller walked toward it, chocks in hand.

The flight-line was busy. Kilton had always ensured Friday was a normal flying day at TFU.

Millie lifted his face to the warm sun and raised his life vest to generate a breeze around his face. Then closed his eyes.

He saw a vision of a young woman in blue, kneeling in an empty church. He didn't yet know her name, but it was as if he suddenly had a friend, someone to help him. Someone on his side.

Rob and Speedy bustled out of the building, helmets in hand. Steve Bright joined them.

"Let's go," Rob said and Millie followed them out to the waiting jet.

"Joining us today, Brighty?" Millie said. "An almost full size Vulcan crew."

"Yeah, I think they're playing it safe, just for this one."

"Really?"

"Just this one, I think."

Minutes later, panel lights flickered on as the Vulcan woke from its slumber. A growing whine outside signalled the engine start.

They held for a while as a queue formed at the threshold. It was approaching lunchtime and Millie realised he should have brought something to eat.

Eventually the acceleration force pushed him forward in his rear-facing seat as they thundered along the runway and up into the summer sky.

THIRTY MINUTES LATER, they descended to the entry gate for the low-level run west of Shrewsbury.

Rob pointed the nose at a distinctive oxbow loop on the River Severn. He levelled the Vulcan at one thousand feet.

Carefully managing the thrust and attitude, he settled them at two hundred and seventy-five knots.

"Ready."

He could see from the modified panel to his left that Millie had activated Guiding Light some time back, as he always did, so it was just a case of Speedy connecting it to the autopilot.

"I don't think I'll ever get used to that sensation," Speedy said over the intercom as the control column moved independently.

Rob lifted his fingers from the stick.

"All yours, Speedy."

Rob watched as the more experienced pilot's hands loosely covered the throttle and stick as he took control. Or what passed for control while a laser, a computer and a mechanical autopilot did the actual flying.

After thirty seconds, Speedy seemed to relax and rested his hands on his thighs.

"Shall we take her down?" Rob asked.

Speedy gave a thumbs up. Rob reached down to his left.

The aircraft descended until it plateaued at five hundred feet.

The ride was stiffer, the large jet reacting more quickly to changes in the terrain beneath. They rolled right, then gently left; nothing too dramatic, but a distinctly busier sensation. With the ground closer, everything felt faster.

Rob enjoyed the sensation, grateful for the return to proper low-level.

"Let's take her all the way," Rob said. A moment later, the aircraft sunk to three hundred feet above the grassy plains as they approached the first set of hills.

"Hey! Height!" Millie's voice sounded over the intercom.

Speedy and Rob exchanged a look.

"Oh, did I forget to mention it, Millie?" Rob said. "We're cleared back to three hundred."

"What? No. No. That's ridiculous. Who cleared us? No-one spoke to me."

"We met with the boss this morning. Sorry, I should have told you."

"The staish signed it off, Millie," Speedy said. "We need to get back down. It's no good loitering at one thousand feet. We need to test this thing properly."

"What the hell? You spoke to Kilton about this, but forgot to talk to me? And no brief for the flight? We're supposed to be a project team, for god's sake, Rob! And I'm supposed to be project leader."

"Sorry, it was a genuine error," Rob lied. "But we do need to trial Guiding Light properly. We haven't got it for much longer and we all need to have faith in the system."

"Faith? Jesus, Rob, you were on board when it failed last time, and don't give me that blarney about hitting the stick accidentally. Neither of us believe that."

"That's enough." Speedy's voice came over the intercom. He had his head turned, glaring back at Millie below. "We're airborne. Save it for the ground." He turned back to face front.

Rob concentrated on the picture in front of him; it was relatively flat for the moment and the ride was smooth, but it was about to get interesting. Should he concede and move them back to one thousand feet?

He adjusted the intercom to cut Millie and Bright out of the loop. "Maybe it wasn't such a good idea to spring this on him?"

"It's done. Let's just concentrate on the flight," Speedy said, staring forward.

Rob opened the intercom to the rear bay again. "We're watching everything, Millie. Worry not."

"Rob..." Millie's tone had changed; he spoke quietly. "I'm begging you. Now's not the time to put your trust in this system. There's something wrong with it."

Rob looked across at Speedy, but Speedy shook his head.

"Sorry, Millie. I promised the boss we'd carry this one out at three hundred. Tell you what, let's run in at three hundred for the first fifteen minutes, and we'll go back to one thousand as the hills steepen. How about that?"

"Promise me you won't take your eyes off the view outside? First sign of anything and you cancel?"

"Of course."

They crossed a hatched pattern of arable fields that stretched over the Welsh border, with rising ground ahead.

Forty-five seconds later, the aircraft made its first steep bank and positioned them for a run down the northern side of a wide valley.

Rob imagined the laser flashing across the approaching terrain. This was where the system came alive, down with the trees.

Under the enemy's nose.

———

STRAPPED into his dark cave with no windows, Millie grimaced.

"Come on, Mills," said Brighty. "It's not that bad. At least we're not on our way to Tbilisi to drop the bomb. Imagine low-level for four hours."

"The aircraft wasn't designed for this," Millie said.

"Well, as ever, ours not to reason why, eh?"

The Vulcan dipped sharply and rose again; Millie scanned the height readings. He rotated the black dial to get an idea of the terrain around them. Two thousand and thirty-four feet to their left, three hundred and sixty-one feet to their right. As usual the system was taking the Vulcan down one side of a valley.

According to Belkin, the error would occur down in the one hundredths of a per cent. And even less frequently, it would occur in a situation that would cause an irrecoverable situation. He'd added up over a year of RAF flying, but the chances on an individual flight were extremely low.

As far as they knew.

Millie looked over his shoulder. The curtain separating the rear bay from the cockpit was tied to one side. He could see Rob, thankfully looking forward.

When had he let his friend down? When did their relationship become so bad, he'd cut him out of important conversations?

Another sudden plunge, and Millie snapped his head back. But the aircraft levelled off. He switched the dial to the first position, looking directly down. Three hundred and sixteen feet. He took another deep breath and checked his watch.

Eight more minutes of this.

———

MARY MAY KNOCKED ON THE MILFORDS' front door. It flew open.

"Mar! My favourite gorgeous person in the whole wide world." Georgina beamed at her.

Mary burst into tears.

"Oh, blimey. Mar, whatever is wrong? Come here." Georgina stepped out of the house and enveloped Mary in her arms.

"Nothing. It's nothing, really. Just silly marriage stuff." She wiped away her tears, delving into her cardie for a tissue. "I didn't mean to cry. I feel embarrassed."

"Nonsense. Get in here, my lovely."

Mary stepped into the married quarter.

"What you need, young lady, is gin. What do you say that we set up a couple of chairs in the garden, get ourselves G&Ts and you can tell me all about it?"

———

THE VULCAN WORKED HARD. They entered a steep valley complex, and the huge delta wings rolled with strong rudder and throttle input to negotiate the tight turns.

Rob tried not to fight it, allowing his body to ebb and flow with the movements.

He learned in the single seats to roll with the aircraft and resist the temptation to lean upright.

He kept half an eye outside and half an eye on Speedy, who looked relaxed, with his hands on his thighs.

But it all looked good. Guiding Light, back in its natural habitat, was performing well, as expected.

They rolled level and went over a small ridge, the aircraft rising and dipping before sweeping over a long reservoir.

Four minutes until the end of the fifteen-minute stretch he promised Millie would be the extent of their run at three hundred feet.

The aircraft flew across a flattish area of plain between two sets of hills. They were about to enter Snowdonia.

He retrieved the chart from the side of his seat and checked the route. The computer had taken them slightly away from the intended path, but that was part of its method; it would choose the best route and get them to the fixed waypoints.

A large wood passed underneath; the ground became more undulating. The aircraft rocked and bumped as the autopilot responded to the instructions from the computer.

Three more minutes.

He thought about where he would command the system to go back to one thousand feet. He wanted to be level and avoid asking for height changes while banked.

He turned the chart over in his hands. His eyes searched ahead of the aircraft's track, looking for a feature he could use to initiate the climb.

Typically, they were flying toward a fold in the paper. He opened the map up, orientating it to show a good thirty miles ahead, then refolded it.

"Something up?" Speedy asked, leaning across, peering at the chart.

"No, I just—"

There was a loud bang. Rob smashed down into his seat. The chart fell from his hands as a violent, crushing weight forced his body ever lower. His helmet struck something hard, and his sight began to turn grey. He felt woozy.

The aircraft creaked around him. He struggled to get upright, to see clearly, to urgently assess the situation.

The g-force subsided. He pushed himself back up in his seat.

Looking out, all he could see was sky.

"What's happening?"

As he regained full vision, his eyes darted to the artificial horizon; they were seventy degrees nose up, and rolling.

Shit.

Speedy shouted something at him.

Was he injured?

They must have hit something.

No hesitation, Rob.

He grabbed the stick and hit the cancel button.

Nothing changed.

"Groundstrike!"

He finally resolved what Speedy was yelling.

The sky outside was replaced by green and yellow hills as the aircraft rolled all the way over.

They were upside down, and still rolling.

Another loud bang behind them; it sounded like the main spar.

The aircraft was about to break up.

He and Speedy were hanging in their straps, with the Welsh hills above them. They couldn't even eject now.

Shit. SHIT.

But they had some height on their side.

Rob stared at the Guiding Light panel; it showed all nines. It was useless now, with the laser pointed into the sky. The altimeter needle seemed to be around two thousand five hundred feet.

But they were coming back down.

He tried the stick again, and the rudder pedals.

"Nothing's working!"

He looked at the engine gauges; both the port side engines had wound down. They only had thrust on the starboard side.

He closed all four throttles, hoping to restore balance.

Keep working, he said to himself.

But there was no emergency drill to cover this.

He could shut down the broken engines, but that would take time and wouldn't achieve anything.

They needed to roll upright.

He snapped the braking parachute handle to *STREAM.*

There was a jolt, and the rolling seemed to slow.

"Damn!" He switched the lever to *RELEASE,* praying the roll rate would pick up again.

The green grass and rocks grew larger as the Vulcan hurtled downwards.

The stick still moved in his hands, but had no noticeable effect on the aircraft.

THINK!

He stabbed the *ABANDON AIRCRAFT* button to light up the notice in the back for Bright and Millie.

"*GET OUT! GET OUT!*" he shouted over the intercom.

An enormous bang.

Light filled the cockpit.

It took Rob a beat to register what had happened.

The canopy was gone.

"*Speedy! No!*" he shouted, but it was too late.

He shielded his face against a burst of orange flame as Speedy's seat fired out of the aircraft.

The roll rate had increased.

Finally, they were coming through ninety degrees back to upright.

It was his only chance to live: to eject while the aircraft was the correct way up.

He wrenched his head around and looked back.

"*GET OUT! GET OUT!*" he screamed again.

Steve Bright stood over the hatch, but Millie was on the ground, trying to get back up.

Rob glanced forward. He estimated they were at six hundred feet.

This was it.

A terrible, awful dread filled him.

There was nothing he could do, unless he chose to die with them.

It was an option.

He looked back a final time.

"Get up, Millie!"

Rob's voice was weak and broken.

They were now too low.

Millie stared at him, terrified eyes wide above his oxygen mask.

Blood leaked from a gash on his forehead.

"Please, Millie." His voice croaked. "Please get out. *Please.*"

He broke eye contact, turned around, and saw the last two seconds of his life as a collection of grey rocks and yellow flowers raced towards them.

Yellow life amid grey death.

I have to live.

His hand went down to the ejection handle.

Did he even have the strength to pull it?

He felt the kick as the seat erupted upwards.

He blacked out.

———

EMILY TRIGGS TAPPED a pencil on the desk and considered her options.

She cross-checked the flying programme.

Evergreen-four-two was now twenty-five minutes overdue.

Up in the glass-house at the top of the control tower, she had an unobstructed view of the airfield and a few miles around. She scanned the skies, but there was no white Vulcan.

She reported it to the senior air traffic controller, who reached for his binoculars and confirmed they were not in sight.

The SATCO leaned over her shoulder to check the record of aircraft movements.

"It definitely took off, sir. I remember it. Vulcan XH441, four persons on board."

"It may have diverted, can you call TFU, see if they've heard anything from the crew? It would, of course, be typical of them to keep us in the dark."

She picked up one of three telephones and dialled the operations desk at the Test Flying Unit.

———

A FLAPPING NOISE, like sheets being shaken out of a bedroom window.

Rob was on a hard surface, his eyes closed.

Birdsong. Cheery whistles filled the air, along with the strange flapping.

An orange glow formed through his eyelids. He tried to open them, but the sunlight was too much.

His head was heavy. He reached up, and with his eyes still shut, pulled his flying helmet off.

Rolling onto his side, he felt a sharp pain in his lower back.

He inched open his eyes, allowing his pupils to adjust.

His head pounded.

He had no idea how much time had passed.

The flapping sound came from above. He craned his head to see his parachute rippling in the breeze.

The straps tugged at him. He rolled onto his back and fumbled with the five-point harness, twisting until it released with a clunk. The pressure on his legs disappeared.

He lay still, facing up, watching the thin clouds gently rove across the sky.

Images formed in his mind. Unwanted, intrusive images.

The final few seconds of the flight.

Chaotic and violent.

He shut his eyes tight and waited for the moment to pass.

To distract him from the visions, he focused on practicalities.

He pushed himself up onto his elbows.

He was in a relatively flat field on the bottom of a slope. There was no sign of the jet or Speedy Johnson.

Twisting around, he saw a plume of black smoke rising beyond the hill.

Another image entered his mind.

Millie, wide-eyed, staring at him.

He searched the memory for a sign of forgiveness in those brown eyes. But he saw only terror.

An abject, appalling terror; the type only a condemned man knows.

He lay back down, not wanting to leave this place, not wanting to face reality.

The parachute continued to flap, drifting across the craggy land.

The birds continued their song.

Eventually, the sound of a vehicle engine carried across the field.

Reality was coming for him.

The vehicle stopped. A door slammed. A dog barked.

Rob remained on the ground. A black-and-white collie appeared over him and licked his face.

"Meg!" a voice said.

A man leaned over him.

"You're alive then?"

Rob stared at him.

"Broken anything?"

"I don't know."

He propped himself up and again felt a pain in his lower back. He brought his knees up.

Both legs appeared to be in one piece.

His ribs ached, but nothing felt broken. With help from the farmer, he got up.

"Luckier than your friend, I'm afraid." The farmer put an arm around Rob and walked him toward the Land Rover.

"I'm sorry?" Rob asked weakly.

"He's over yonder." The farmer pointed to the winding narrow road that ran along the bottom of the hill. "Still in his seat. Not a pretty sight, I'm afraid. All bent up. Hit the ground hard. Very nasty."

"He's dead?" Rob asked weakly.

"'fraid so."

They got to the vehicle and Rob climbed in gingerly.

Meg jumped up and sat next to him. Rob put his hand on her neck. Soft and warm. She looked up at him, panting, with her tongue hanging out. It looked like she was smiling.

He gently stroked her, as she curled up on the bench seat.

The farmer drove slowly down the hill, speeding up when they got to a Tarmac road.

As they rounded the bend at the end of the valley, Rob saw the white and orange of Speedy's parachute. A tractor was parked nearby and two men stood to one side. They had stretched the silk over the scene and weighted it down with stones.

Rob stared at the lifeless bulge.

He thought back to Speedy's ejection. They were rolling, still inverted. His eagerness to abandon the aircraft had killed him.

He looked around for the black smoke.

"Can you take me to the aircraft, please?"

The farmer looked surprised. "Don't you want to go to the doctor?"

"Please, I need to see."

They reached a T-junction. The farmer turned right and they headed toward the black smoke.

The road wound around the hill. The crash scene was somewhere over the next slope.

From a distance, it looked like the Vulcan hit the ground flat, as the distinctive triangle shape was still recognisable.

But as they got closer, he could see the aircraft was ripped down its centre, fire consuming what was left of the wings, the white paint giving way to the unruly metal framework.

Scattered fragments sat further up the hill, including what looked like a fan assembly from an engine.

"This is as close as we can get," the farmer said, pushing the Land Rover's front two wheels onto the base of the steep slope.

Rob opened the door and climbed out, followed by the dog. The farmer called to her and she stopped and sat by the vehicle.

As Rob walked, he winced at the back pain, but pushed on, picking his way over loose rock, tufts of grass and occasional yellow flowers.

Soon, he felt the heat of the fire on his face.

As he approached, he began a methodical scan of the twisted remains.

The nose section was recognisable. He gave the debris a wide berth, walking around the right hand side. Behind the nose, the missing canopy revealed the inside of the cockpit and behind that, a tear in the frame of the fuselage gave him glimpses of the rear crew bay.

He moved further around, his eyes tracking along the blackened, distorted outline. Jagged metal protruded at untidy angles. The painstakingly constructed modern bomber, torn into thousands of barely recognisable pieces in an instant.

He continued to search, moving slowly, ensuring he could see into every area of the downed jet.

He needed to know. He had to be sure.

Finally, his eyes settled on a shape.

Two legs. Twisted, charred.

He moved further around.

Just visible in the dark recesses: a helmet. Wisps of smoke partially obscured the blackened face within.

He wobbled, his legs in danger of giving way.

He crouched, steadying, then forced himself back up.

The farmer had made his way a few yards up the hill.

"Come on, now," he shouted. "This is no good for you."

Rob moved further around the far side of the wreck, continuing to search with his eyes.

Beyond the central rise of collapsed metal, he saw an outstretched, lifeless arm.

He followed it back and stared at the torso.

A moment later, he emerged from the smoke.

"We can go now."

———

THE PLANNING ROOM at TFU was filling up. Even with the full flying programme, the chaps usually found a way to be done a little earlier and head off to Happy Hour on a Friday.

When the call came in from the tower, a couple of pilots near the hatch overheard the sergeant take down the details of the overdue aircraft.

They exchanged looks, but nothing was said.

The missing crew could have diverted with a technical problem.

They could have extended the trial in the air.

They could be carrying out a touch and go at Boscombe.

But sometimes, they could just sense it: none of the above would be the case.

In the thirty minutes that followed, the mood grew sombre, although still no-one speculated out loud.

They delegated Red to let the boss know.

"No need to panic, Brunson," said Kilton, carrying on with his paperwork.

But as Brunson backed out of the office, there was a rise in volume in the planning room.

Jock MacLeish arrived, looking pale.

"Rob May has just called in from a farmhouse in Wales. They crashed."

"Did everyone get out?" Kilton asked.

MacLeish shook his head. "Just Rob."

"Just Rob?" Red said.

MacLeish nodded.

Kilton dropped his head. "Names?"

"Speedy, Steve Bright and..." MacLeish hesitated and looked directly at Kilton.

"And Millie."

The men waited in silence, watching their boss.

Eventually Kilton's head came back up. Slowly, he got to his feet.

MacLeish moved out of his way as he walked into the middle of the planning room.

"No phone calls out. Someone order me a car."

———

Somewhere in the hedgerow, a blackbird sounded its alarm call. Such an urgent sound on a peaceful day.

A cat?

Probably.

Georgina closed her eyes and let the sun warm her face.

"Thank you, darling." Mary finished her drink.

"Think nothing of it, Mar. We all go through this. God knows I hardly saw Millie during the bloody war. Mind you I was digging for victory in Norfolk and he was at Tangmere most of the time."

Mary laughed. "I'd loved to have seen you in your land girl dungarees."

"Ha! I can't remember if I ever wore them, but it was certainly muddy." She sighed at the memories of those strange days. "Bloody hard work, but good fun in the evenings. Back then, every day felt like it could be your last. Maybe that's why we enjoyed ourselves so much at night." She stood up and gathered the two glasses. "Perhaps that's a tale for another time. One more?"

"One more."

Georgina smiled and headed into the house.

In the kitchen she noticed an insect of some sort had found its way onto the lemon in her glass. She tipped it into the bin, put the glass in the bowl and took Millie's whisky tumbler from the draining board.

"That'll do."

As she headed to the fridge, a movement caught her eye.

A car turning slowly into Trenchard Close.

A black staff car.

She froze.

A staff car in the middle of the day, in a married quarter patch, brought only one type of message.

Her hand tightened around the tumbler.

The vehicle passed Sarah Brunson's house, then Louise Richardson's, in a macabre game of widow roulette.

It drew to a halt, precisely and unmistakably at the end of the short path that led to her front door.

Mark Kilton emerged, looking grave.

The whisky tumbler fell from Georgina's hand and smashed on the hard kitchen floor.

"Please, god, no..."

She blinked back the first of the tears, before straightening her top and opening the front door.

Kilton stood, stiff back, hat tucked under his arm.

Silence.

He lowered his head.

"One hundred and twelve days, Mark," said Georgina. "The old bugger only had another one hundred and twelve days to retirement."

He looked up and stared deep into her eyes.

"I'm so sorry, Georgina. I'm so sorry."

She tried to hold it off, but the collapse was coming.

She bent forward and clutched her head. Tears flowed between her fingers.

Kilton held her shoulders.

"He was a fine man, Georgina," he whispered. "A fine man. Let us be proud."

Kilton guided her inside the house.

She looked back at him. "Rob?"

"Alive. Shaken, but alive."

"He was with him?"

"Yes."

Mary was in the kitchen, staring at the broken glass. She looked up and put a hand to her mouth.

"Georgina. *No!*"

"Rob's OK. Isn't that wonderful news?"

Mary's arms stretched out and they fell into a tight embrace.

————

Rob sat at a worn kitchen table in a dark farmhouse kitchen, nursing a lukewarm cup of tea.

Someone would have to move the bodies off the hillside. They would secure the crash site, throw a cordon around the secret military equipment, whatever was left of it.

The farmer appeared in the doorway.

"So what happened?"

Rob shook his head. "I'm not sure. We struck the ground, I think, and bounced back up, but it disabled us."

Again, a vision: Millie and Bright scrambling to evacuate.

The terror in their eyes.

They knew they were going to die.

He didn't expand on his answer, and the farmer didn't pursue the conversation.

A distant beating in the air.

Rob rose from his seat.

"I think that's my helicopter."

Immediately beyond the house was a small cottage garden, and beyond that, a paddock with two horses.

"Is it possible to move the horses?"

The farmer bustled out, pushing past Rob, and waddled up to the paddock. The horses, perhaps sensing food, came to greet him. He unlatched a five-bar gate and let them through to a narrow garden that ran down the side of the house.

Rob scanned the sky. A yellow dot, growing larger; an RAF Wessex, with the word *RESCUE* emblazoned on the side. It came to a loud hover just short of the paddock, dust and soil swirling in the downwash. The machine inched forward before settling down on its vast wheels.

Rob gathered his helmet and harness and thanked the farmer,

who handed him his bundled parachute, tied with a cord.

As he left the kitchen and made his way to the open gate, a small contingent of soldiers jumped out of the Wessex. A sergeant with a moustache met him as he approached the paddock.

"Flight Lieutenant May?" he shouted over the noise of the whirring blades.

Rob nodded.

"Where's the crash site?"

He pointed at the farmer.

"A few miles away. He'll tell you."

"OK. Thank you." The sergeant then looked him up and down. "Rescue 3 has instructions to take you back to West Porton, unless you need urgent medical treatment?"

Rob shook his head. "I'm fine."

As the helicopter sped above the Welsh borders, Rob stared out of the only window, blind to the rolling countryside.

He saw only the wreckage, the outstretched arm.

The winchman shouted over the intercom.

"About forty minutes."

———

SUSIE SAT on a bench opposite the phone box, waiting for a quiet time to make her daily call.

After a procession of pram pushers, she got her chance.

"Any news?" Roger asked in his sing-song voice.

"Nope. I really don't see the point of being here."

"You're protecting England's precious military assets, my dear. One more week, they think. So be a good girl and sit tight."

"Fine."

"There is one more thing. A minor task for you."

"Oh, yes?"

"You're to meet an RAF chappie, a squadron leader. He has something for us. Listen to him and report in afterwards."

"Oh. That's odd, isn't it?"

"It happens from time to time. Might be nothing, but he had the wherewithal to find the right number to call us, so they want him heard. Tomorrow morning 8AM, St Mary and St Melor Church, Amesbury. Choose a rear pew and wear something blue."

"Something blue?"

"Yes, so he knows it's you. He's five feet nine, balding, and described himself as 'podgy'. And be discreet, for god's sake."

————

THE HELICOPTER SETTLED onto the taxiway across from TFU. Rob removed his helmet, thanked the winchman and climbed out. Two NCOs appeared next to him and carried his parachute, harness and helmet.

Mark Kilton stood at the door, waiting. He held out a hand; Rob shook it.

"How are you?"

"Fine."

Kilton led the way into the planning room. Rob tried not to catch anyone's eye, but Red intercepted him, placing a firm hand on his shoulder.

"Buddy, tough situation. Come and see me when you want."

Rob nodded and followed Kilton into his office.

Kilton shut the door.

"What happened?"

"I don't know. We were at three hundred, as planned. It was all fine. I looked at the chart just for a few seconds and we struck the ground. It must have been a glancing blow, as we went back up. But the port side was wrecked and we rolled. Speedy ejected when we were banked over. Millie and Brighty got themselves out of their seats, but not much more..." He tailed off.

"Speedy had control?"

"Yes."

Kilton made a note.

"Millie didn't want us to go down to three hundred. In fact, he—"

"Of course he didn't. We knew he was against it. But it's what we agreed. You were right."

Rob furrowed his brow. "But we didn't listen to him—"

"Robert." Kilton held up a hand. "We did. Look, there's a procedure to follow. We will recover the wreckage and find out what happened. Do not, and I repeat, do not speculate to anyone about the cause, is that clear? Be especially careful what you tell Georgina. She doesn't need an unpleasant situation made worse with ill-informed speculation."

Kilton opened his office door and motioned Rob to leave.

"Can I go home?"

"We drink tonight for the men. You need to be there. So, come back. Understood?"

"I don't want to."

"You need to. I'll see you later."

————

CARS LITTERED the street around Millie and Georgina's married quarter. Rob approached and paused for a moment, listening to the sounds of tea and sympathy within.

He pushed open the door.

Mary appeared in the hallway and rushed up to him. She hugged him tightly, and he screwed his face up, willing the tears to stay away.

He wrapped his arms around her, gripping her shoulders. He didn't want to be anywhere else in the world but in her arms.

She pulled back and kissed him.

"Are you OK? Mark says you ejected."

He nodded.

"What happened?"

"What did he tell you?"

Her arms slipped down his body and she held on to his hands.

"Only that it was routine. There was some sort of problem and that the others didn't make it out."

She let go of one hand.

"He also phoned a few moments ago and told us that you should go to the mess tonight. He says it's important you're all together. I honestly don't mind and I think he's right. You need your friends tonight."

Rob stared at her and saw something terrible in her eyes: relief.

She had the winning ticket. Her husband had come home.

She led him into the living room. "Come and see Georgina first."

The new widow sat on the sofa, eyes puffy, a hanky in her hand.

He couldn't bear it. He shouldn't be there.

She spotted him and let out a little yelp.

"Darling, darling, Robert."

She held out her arms, beckoning him in. He knelt down. They locked together in another tight hug. He inhaled, trying to smell Millie on her clothes.

Rob felt dizzy. The room was warm. He pulled back from the hug but remained on his knees. Someone put a small glass of whisky in his hands. The smell brought a smiling Millie to mind.

He downed it in one gulp. The smoky scotch tasted sweet.

"Are you OK?" Georgina asked.

He stared at her; the room was spinning.

"Rob?"

Mary eased him back into a soft chair. The room settled down.

He leant back and closed his eyes, listening as they talked about Charlie.

He was still at Oxford, helping with the summer school. The college bursar had relayed the news and he was on his way back home.

Mary appeared in front of him.

"Are you OK? You went very pale."

He nodded.

"I think Kilton's right. I should go."

———

OFFICERS from every quarter of West Porton crowded into the mess bar; men and women from Boscombe Down, too.

Everyone knew Millie.

Everyone loved Millie.

As Rob stumbled into the room, a few heads turned.

Red led him to the bar. On the way, he received several pats on the shoulder and a few muttered words of sympathy.

Red pushed his way through the throng and held up a hand to attract a white-coated steward.

He turned back to Rob to check what he wanted and ordered a couple of beers.

As the pints appeared, the TFU boys gathered around them.

"Put this on Squadron Leader Christopher Milford's tab," Red told the barman, following the tradition to drink on the dead man's bill, knowing it would never be settled.

The boys raised their glasses in unison.

"To Speedy, Brighty and Millie," someone said. They all muttered their own personal toasts.

Rob downed half a pint in a single go.

There was an awkward silence. Rob stared at the rising bubbles in his Skol.

Red broke the moment by putting a hand on his shoulder. "You wanna talk about it, buddy?"

He desperately wanted to talk to him. He wanted to tell him everything.

"No, it's fine."

"Listen, man, you need to get this off your chest. If you want to talk over the weekend, just holler. Remember, we all have to go flying again on Monday."

"I can't imagine ever flying again."

Red squeezed his shoulder. "You will, buddy, and you'll make Millie proud. Y'know, I think you always were the son he really want-ed." He picked up the empty glasses. "I'll get a refill."

The other pilots talked among themselves: tales of Millie, and the many comical moments he had presented them with over the four-teen months of TFU's existence.

"He was clumsy, but no-one knew the electronics like him," one said.

Rob stood on the edge of the group. Someone tapped him on the shoulder and he turned to see one of the oldest officers at West Porton: JR from the Maintenance Unit, and two of his colleagues.

Rob stepped away from the TFU set.

"We wanted to pay our respects, Robert. Millie was a fine man. More one of us than one of you, I think." He smiled, nodding toward the gaggle of TFU pilots. "And I know you two were close, so we just want to say how sorry we are. If there's anything we can do, Rob... If you need to finish anything Millie started, you know where we are."

"Here you go, buddy." Red appeared next to them and handed him his second drink. JR smiled a greeting at Red and then looked back at Rob.

"As I say, you know where we are." He and the other MU men headed back to their corner of the bar.

Red laughed. "Living fossils. Quite something to see."

"Yes. Indeed."

He rejoined the TFU men and downed his next pint.

The crash had left him aching, particularly his lower back. His head was slowly spinning. If it was the beer, why wasn't it helping with his emotional pain?

He found the drinking ritual distasteful. He looked around at the sea of laughing and smiling heads in the bar, but he couldn't bring himself to join in.

This was the RAF way. To tell stories of the fallen, to drink. And to forget.

Perhaps it was OK for everyone else, but not him.

The thick fog of cigarette smoke and stench of booze was a comfort blanket for them, but Rob was surrounded by jagged edges. He was still in the centre of the broken remains.

Another vision: Millie's cold, dead arm in the dark on the Welsh hillside.

In the centre of the room, his eyes rested on Mark Kilton. The boss stood by a pillar with two junior pilots.

Something told him his only salvation was through the boss. The man in charge, whose orders he followed.

The two men with Kilton made their excuses as he approached.

"May," Kilton said in greeting, before sipping his pint.

"What happens now?" Rob asked.

"There'll be a Board of Inquiry, but because of the nature of the project we'll have some control over it, purely to protect the secrecy." He appraised Rob for a moment. "Why? Are you worried?"

"So, Millie was right. There was a problem with the laser. And we didn't listen to him."

Kilton put down his glass and leant closer. "They will comb the wreckage for clues. You're free to describe what happened, but you will not second-guess the outcome of the inquiry. Understood?"

"Yes, sir."

Kilton smiled, a look that didn't suit his face. "You're part of my team, Rob, don't forget it. Come in tomorrow and write everything down before the memory fades, and leave the rest to me." Kilton looked over Rob's head toward the bar. "You do not discuss this with anyone. If you do, I won't be able to protect you and you'll land yourself in deep water, quickly."

Rob felt confused, as if he was missing something, but Kilton walked off, leaving him standing alone by the pillar.

For the first time in weeks, he wanted to talk to Millie properly. To talk to him about Guiding Light.

Red Brunson appeared with fresh drinks.

"There you are!"

Rob took another long drink of soothing beer.

He felt dizzy again, but finally the beer was taking the edge away, dulling his heightened senses.

Jock MacLeish joined them and told a story of the time Millie rode in his sidecar with an open-faced helmet on backwards. They all laughed at the vision.

"He was adept at many things," Jock said. "But borderline incompetent at the menial tasks. Like putting on a crash helmet."

Toward the end of the evening, Rob was very drunk, pushed into a corner of the room with Jock and Red keeping watch over him.

He wanted to go home. To climb into bed next to Mary. And to cry without being seen.

19

SATURDAY 25TH JUNE

An elderly woman pushed an upright shopping trolley as she headed toward the newsagents. A tradesman drove by in a Morris Minor van. Two men passed each other walking their dogs.

Susie noted that both men had military haircuts.

Amesbury was busier than she expected for an early Saturday morning. Not ideal.

She glanced at the two military men again. Both slim. Neither matched the description of Squadron Leader Christopher Milford.

The church clock bells tolled 7.45AM. Susie kept close to the stone wall that ran around the elevated graveyard and dipped into the path that ran to the porch. Lifting the heavy metal latch, she slipped inside the Norman building, taking a pew immediately to her left.

She lowered herself into a praying position and monitored the entrance.

It was cool in the church. After a few minutes, her knees hurt, and she shifted back onto the wooden bench.

Another glance at her watch. 7.55AM.

Milford might arrive early.

She imagined a nervous man unaccustomed to stepping outside strict military protocols.

A copy of *The Book of Common Prayer* sat on a wooden ledge on the back of the pew in front. She browsed it, keeping the doorway in her peripheral vision.

Most of her field training anticipated the briefest of exchanges with other agents, or distanced observation of a mark. This was different; she'd been authorised to speak to an outsider.

An informant.

The CND sting had given her a taste for field work.

As the seconds ticked toward the appointed time, she went through her pre-contact checklist a final time.

Had the contact been followed? Would they be overheard? How reliable is he?

The bells tolled for 8AM.

The church stayed silent.

She frowned. She didn't expect him to be late.

The standard operating procedure was to abandon a meeting the moment the mark failed to show, but she gave Milford some allowance. After all, he wasn't an intelligence professional.

A bird flapped high up in the rafters.

After a few minutes, the door latch made a sharp metallic scrape which echoed around the empty church.

She startled as a man in a dog collar and long black cassock swept in.

He walked straight to the centre of the church and headed up the aisle, without glancing. She had chosen her position well.

Once his flowing frock disappeared into a room by the organ, she slipped out.

8.12AM.

Susie cursed her luck at the failed meeting, already anticipating the grief from Roger.

She crossed the road outside the church. More Amesbury folk were up and going about their Saturday morning. She walked over to the newsagent, picking up a copy of *The Daily Telegraph* from a rack outside before entering.

A man with a labrador was chatting to the ancient shop owner. She stood in line, occasionally glancing toward the church, just in case she saw a balding, slightly plump man who looked as if he was running late for a meeting.

"Not good. Not good."

The man in front shook his head, gossiping with the owner.

He tapped the newspaper on the counter. "Happened in Wales, apparently, but they were all from around here."

Susie ignored them. She might go home and snuggle down in an actual bed tonight. The thought made her feel warm.

"See you later, Peter."

She set her paper down on the counter and pulled the change out of her pocket. As she did so, she noticed the picture on the bottom half of the front page: a grainy shot of twisted metal and the smoky remains of an RAF jet. The headline sat beneath the photograph.

RAF BOMBER CRASHES – THREE DEAD.

"Thruppence please, love."

She held out the money as her eyes continued to scan the article. Below a brief paragraph describing the barest details were three pictures, each one an RAF officer in his peaked cap, looking proudly into the middle distance.

She read the names of the dead.

"Oh, shit".

"I beg your pardon?" The shopkeeper looked shocked.

"I'm sorry."

"Well, it's thruppence, love."

She stared at the man.

"Thruppence. That's tuppence." He pointed at Susie's open hand containing two one penny coins. She dug into her pocket and pulled out a twelve-sided thruppence coin, dropped it onto the counter and hurried out of the shop.

Breaking into a fast walk, she headed back past the church, to the bench.

She unfolded the paper and stared at the face of Squadron Leader Christopher Milford.

Deceased.

He was more than just late for their meeting.

The article had almost no information.

A routine flight ... the cause under investigation.

"Christ alive."

The clock tolled for half past the hour.

Susie entered the phone box outside the newsagent and called Roger.

"My dear, how are the flower people?"

"We have a situation."

"Oh, yes?"

"Christopher Milford, the RAF officer I was due to meet?"

"Due to meet? Don't tell me you missed it. Did you oversleep in your tent?"

"Roger, he's dead."

There was a moment's pause.

"How so?"

"He's been named in the *Telegraph* as one of the crew killed in a crash, yesterday."

"The Vulcan in Wales?"

"Yes."

She heard shuffling and rustling on the other end of the line.

"Well, well. That's interesting. Of course, it could be a coincidence."

"Roger, we spent three years in training being taught the Service doesn't believe in coincidences."

"True. On the other hand, it could actually be a coincidence."

She rolled her eyes.

"I obviously need to follow this up," said Susie. "Who brought him in?"

"Stand by."

She waited while he disappeared, presumably to dig out the file. Outside the phone box, a young woman with a pram had appeared.

Susie smiled at her and made a motion with her hand to indicate that the call had some time to go. The woman pushed the pram off toward the newsagents.

Roger's voice came back on the line. "He called us."

"Really? No-one brought him in? That's unusual, isn't it? It's not like we're in the Yellow Pages. Someone must have given him a number and codename."

"Well, whoever received the call didn't ask him, unfortunately. I have the transcript. It was brief."

"Damn."

More rustling at the other end of the line.

"There is something here, though," Roger said. "Have you read the report in the *Express*?"

"No. What does it say?"

"Check out the last line. It's not much but might be a start. Meanwhile, I'll send this up the pole. Give me an hour or two to find out what I can and call back."

She replaced the handset and pushed the door open.

In the shop, she tapped the young mother on the shoulder.

"I'm all done."

The woman gave her a wan smile. It looked like she might have been crying.

It was a small community and three people were dead.

She picked up a copy of the *Express* and took it to the counter.

"Ah, it's sweary Mary," the shop owner said when he saw her. "Can't get enough of the news today, dear?" Susie passed over another threepenny coin.

As she walked out, she scanned the report, which was on page two. Again, it had little detail, but Roger was right. The last line was of interest.

There was one survivor.

———

ROB AWOKE.

He entered a twilight between sleep and consciousness, where yesterday's events were neither real nor unreal. As if it was a story he'd been told in the mess the night before.

As he fully awoke, the reality set in and the weight of grief settled on him again.

He lay still, facing the open window.

The birds tweeted merrily, reminding him of the few minutes spent on the Welsh hillside.

He closed his eyes and saw Millie in his kitchen eating breakfast with Georgina.

Planning their Saturday, looking forward to dinner with the Brunsons.

Millie faded from view. Now he saw Georgina, sitting alone.

Robbed of the love of her life.

"Are you awake?"

Mary's hand appeared on his shoulder. He turned over but kept his eyes closed, curling up against her.

"It's OK. It's OK." He felt her breath as she spoke.

"It's not OK."

"We'll get through this and we'll help Georgina get through it."

———

It was breezy on the small dock, as it was every year.

Professor Belkin inhaled a lungful of air and let it out slowly.

He looked across the Bristol Channel to the faint outline of his destination.

Ahead, the small Lundy ferry approached, the bow rising and falling in the gentle swell.

"Leonard!"

He turned around to the sound of a familiar voice.

"Callum! How the heavens are you?"

"Aye, still alive. And you, I see."

Belkin smiled and held out his hand. "The Lord has spared me for at least one more Lundy fortnight."

"Aye, well, here's your ham and a few other provisions."

The bearded Scotsman, exiled in Devon, handed him a brown bag. Belkin opened it and sniffed.

"Smells excellent."

"And there's a wee present from Mrs MacPherson and me when you get to the cottage."

"Really, Callum, you shouldn't have." Belkin thought for a moment. "Is it Ruth's sloe gin?"

"Indeed. Careful, though. It's a strong one. If you don't like it, take it home as paint stripper."

Belkin laughed. "I'm sure it will be quite delicious. I also have a couple of bottles liberated from the college cellar, so I think I'll survive."

The ferry gingerly approached the dockside. Callum held out a set of keys.

"It's not locked, but just in case you want them. I'm afraid we still have no telephone and the electricity is very patchy. Best light a candle in the evening before it goes off. There's plenty of firewood."

A young man in a thick sweater jumped from the ferry onto the dock and caught a rope as it was thrown from the boat. The diesel engine chugged and spewed black smoke that wafted across, causing Belkin to cough.

The Scot took a step closer and put a hand on Belkin's arm. "How long's it been now?"

Belkin smiled. "Twenty-four years."

"Aye, well, we remember Winifred like it was yesterday. I hope you have a pleasant fortnight, Leonard."

He helped Belkin down the steps toward the small passenger craft. "Oh, I've put the paper in there as well, in case you fancy a read."

Belkin peered into the bag to see a copy of *The Daily Telegraph* wedged between the side of ham and a large loaf of bread.

"Now, that would spoil my splendid isolation. But I might use it to light the fire."

Callum laughed. "So be it, Leonard, so be it."

A couple of families with day bags traipsed past them.

The ferry tooted its horn.

"Thank you again, Callum. I'll see you in a couple of weeks."

Belkin turned and made his way along the short boardwalk until the young man in the sweater took him by his arm and helped him onto the ferry.

Minutes later, he sat at the front of the open deck, the wind in his face, headed across the twelve miles of water for two perfect weeks of solitude.

———

ROB HELD Mary's hand as they walked the short distance to Georgina's.

Inside, Georgina took Rob's hands and gazed into his eyes.

"Was it the same for you, waking up this morning and hoping it was all a nightmare?"

He nodded.

"He adored you, Robert. I know you had your difficulties recently, but that doesn't matter."

She looked around the room, apparently to make sure their son Charlie was out of earshot. "He loved Charlie, of course, but he would have loved to see him join the Air Force. I think that's why he liked you so much."

Rob screwed up his eyes and willed the tears to stop.

"I'm sorry, Georgina."

Georgina hugged him. "It's OK to cry, whatever they tell you." She kissed him tenderly on his forehead.

Rob sat on the sofa. He took some deep breaths and regained his composure.

A strong shaft of sunlight streamed through the front window; again, he found himself mesmerised by the swirling particles of dust.

He was once told that dust in a house is discarded skin cells.

So, in a way, Millie was with them in the room.

The image of the outstretched arm pushed its way back into his mind.

Why had he gone to look?

He wondered if the fire had consumed the bodies after he'd left.

Mary sat down next to him.

"You alright?"

He shook his head.

Across the room, Georgina laughed.

"How does she do it? She's stronger than me."

"Nonsense, she's just better at putting on a show. Plus, it's different for her, isn't it? You were there. It must have been awful, Rob."

He turned to her and whispered. "It's worse than anything you imagine. And there's something else. Something truly awful about it all."

"What?" Mary asked, her face etched with anxiety.

He bowed his head and whispered. "I've got this awful feeling, like I've been handed a life sentence to carry out in secret."

"What do you mean?"

"Everyone else is dead, but I know the truth."

"What are you talking about?"

"Mr May?"

A wiry, ginger haired twenty-year-old stood over them.

"Charlie." Rob stood up and offered his hand to Millie's son. "I'm so sorry, Charlie. You must be devastated."

"Thank you, Mr May. Yes, it was a terrible shock. If you don't mind, I'd like to know what happened. My mother has warned me not to ask." He glanced over nervously toward Georgina.

Rob smiled. "Let's go somewhere quiet."

In the small dining room, they sat close to each other at one corner of the polished oak table.

"We were at low-level. A routine trial flight, I suppose, but in our business, your father's business, there really is no such thing as routine.

"We were about ten minutes into a run through central Wales, the hills higher than us both sides." Charlie looked alarmed. "I'm making it sound more daredevil than it really is. Much of the RAF's flying is at low-level now, even lower than the three hundred feet we go down to in the Vulcan.

"Anyway, something went wrong. A glancing blow from an outcrop, we think. It damaged the left side of the aircraft, left us with no ability to control it." He paused, picking his way through the most delicate part. "It happened quickly. The aircraft dived. We had no option, we had to eject or stay with the aircraft."

"And father?"

Rob looked down at his shoes.

"The Vulcan. The emergency egress for the rear crew was designed by men who believed it would be used at high level. If something went wrong at thirty thousand feet, they would have minutes to release the hatch and bale out. But at low-level... I'm sorry, Charlie. Your father and Steve Bright, they had no chance. No chance at all. At least it would have been instant."

Charlie screwed his eyes closed, then opened them again.

Rob held out his hand, clasping his shoulder.

"Why did they fly at low-level if the men in the back couldn't get out?"

Rob had no answer.

"I'm sorry, Charlie."

They sat in silence for a while as Charlie dabbed his eyes with a blue handkerchief.

"I am so pleased you got to see your father a couple of weeks ago."

Charlie looked confused. "But I haven't seen him since Easter."

Rob furrowed his brow. "I thought he visited you in Oxford the Saturday before last?"

Charlie shook his head. "No."

"Ah, there you are!" Georgina appeared in the doorway. "Charlie, darling, there are people here who want to remark on how much you've grown since you were four years old."

"Thank you, Mr May." Charlie followed his mother into the living room.

Rob rose to rejoin the group just as Georgina popped her head back into the room.

"Rob, I think you should take Millie's work bits, don't you?"

"Yes, of course, I can come back with the car later."

He and Mary left the house as more of Georgina's relatives and old friends turned up.

"You accumulate a lot of friends in the RAF," said Mary, as they walked back toward their own quarter.

"Yes," replied Rob, "and you lose a lot as well."

———

IT WAS A WARM DAY, and Rob fastened back the soft canvas top of his Healey.

He ached from the ejection, and he wasn't sure he had the strength for meetings with anyone, let alone Kilton.

The low car barely skimmed over the surface of the single-track road that led to the main gate.

He slowed for a group of walkers ahead. They held banners, and tatty white sheeting painted with black CND symbols.

The group ambled toward him; clearly, they had no intention of letting him pass. He put two wheels on the verge and pulled on the handbrake.

They drifted past. He was conspicuous, sitting in his open-top car, in his Royal Air Force uniform. From the group of stragglers at the back, a young woman approached the car. She was pretty, with short, dark hair and wearing a thin top which was loose and open.

She walked up to the Healey and leant forward, placing her hands on the bonnet. His eyes automatically followed the line of her neck to her small breasts.

There were jeers from the others, laughing at his obvious discomfort.

He snapped his eyes up, mortified that she should have trapped him like that. The woman had a sweet smile; her eyes scanned the car, taking everything in.

She looked directly at him, held eye contact for a few moments, then straightened up and walked on.

Rob watched the group meander away in his wing mirror.

He put the car into first gear and pulled off toward the main gate.

The car search was tediously long. It was a quiet Saturday, so everyone received maximum attention from the security guards.

Rob got out of the car and waited. His eyes tracked back along the road, but the protestors had disappeared from sight.

"They give you any trouble?" the sergeant asked, following his gaze.

"No. No trouble." A corporal continued to comb his car. "Must be nice, though."

"What's that, sir?"

"To be so free and easy. They didn't look like they had a care in the world."

"They didn't look like they'd seen a bath recently, either. You can carry on now, sir." He stepped back and gave a smart salute.

At TFU, Rob was faced with a new barrier, manned by a group of West Porton Security Police.

He edged toward the temporary bollards, assuming the officers would pull them aside for him, but a security man stepped out, raising the palm of his hand.

"Sorry, sir. This unit is out of bounds. If you're after TFU staff, they're in the station headquarters building."

"Really? Are you sure?"

"Yes, sir."

———

THE HQ BUILDING WAS QUIET.

A corporal sat at a desk in the station commander's outer office.

"Mr May?"

Rob nodded.

"Wing Commander Kilton is expecting you. You can go in."

In the office Mark Kilton sat at a small conference table; Periwinkle was behind his desk.

"Sit down, May. I'm afraid I have some very serious news."

Rob took a seat.

"In clearing out Millie's locker, we have found something very disturbing."

"I'm sorry?"

"We found extensive evidence that Millie was stealing information about Guiding Light. Data tapes, records of previous trials, part of a manual with his own handwritten annotations. And that's just for starters." Kilton stared at him. "You look surprised, May, but I'm not."

"You're not, sir?"

"Millie was bad with money, May. We all know he lost his savings on that stupid investment. This project was worth millions. He was nearing retirement. I'm afraid it all adds up. And to think I charged him with the investigation into who leaked Guiding Light to the outside world."

Rob glanced at the station commander, who so far had said nothing.

"It was probably an oversight. I mean, they were still in TFU, weren't they? So he hadn't actually stolen anything?"

"We don't know that, May. The locker was probably just a staging post before he smuggled them out. We'll find out everything. Dead men have no secrets." Kilton stared at him. "Is there anything you need to tell me? It will be a lot better for you if you speak now."

The phone rang. The station commander answered it, said a few curt words and hung up.

"Well, May? Anything we need to know?"

"Millie worried about the system," said Rob. "I'm sure that's what this was all about."

Kilton didn't look convinced. "What does that mean, though, Rob? Did he tell you he was up to something?"

Rob shook his head.

"Of course, he might have used his supposed concerns as a cover for something else entirely."

Rob could only stare back at Kilton, who stood up.

"Fine. We'll know more once they carry out a full search. They'll turn his house and car upside down."

"But Georgina's at the house."

"So? This is simply too serious to delay."

Realising he was being dismissed, Rob got to his feet.

"Have you written your account of the crash yet? *May?*" Kilton had to raise his voice to get Rob's attention back.

"No, not yet."

"Well, find a table and chair and do that now."

Rob left the office and walked back down the corridor, out of the main doors and straight to his car.

Once through the main gate, he put his foot down and sped quickly along the lane. The protestors had moved on.

He came to a halt with a squeal of the tyres.

Georgina opened the door; he stepped toward her and put both hands on her shoulders.

"Are you alone?"

"They're all in the garden, apart from Charlie. Why?"

"No-one else has called? No-one official?"

Georgina shook her head. "No. Not since Mark yesterday. Should I be expecting someone?"

"You said earlier that you wanted me to come back? You had some things for me?"

She looked blank for a moment. "Oh, yes. Just some work stuff. What's going on, Rob?"

"Can you get it now?"

"If you like."

She headed upstairs.

Charlie was in the kitchen to his left, staring at him. Rob gave him a weak smile.

A moment later, Georgina tramped down the stairs in her slippers carrying an open vegetable box.

He glanced in, relieved to see Millie's flying logbooks and nothing more sinister. He picked them up and handed them to Georgina. "You can keep these. Maybe Charlie would like them?"

"Thank you," Charlie said from the kitchen.

Rob looked back in the box. A large brown envelope filled the bottom. It looked new.

He pulled open the top and peered inside.

Guiding Light – Data Output May 1966 – Page 12.

"Oh, Christ."

"What is it?" Georgina said, staring at him.

Underneath the envelope were two reels from the project.

"Oh, no."

He looked underneath the tape sleeves.

More and more. Each document stamped with a red *TOP SECRET*.

Outside, a car turned into the road. Rob pulled the front door shut.

"What's going on, Rob?" said Georgina, peering over his shoulder to see who was arriving at the house.

"Don't open the door."

"Why ever not?"

He pushed past her to the small porch window.

Two green RAF security police Land Rovers, complete with blue flashing lights.

One other car, unmarked.

Several serious looking men climbing out and heading toward the house.

He turned back to Georgina and, still holding the box in one hand, grabbed her wrist.

"Listen to me. These men, they will search the house. They think something's missing. Millie wasn't doing anything wrong. You have to believe me."

"Rob, you're scaring me. What are you talking about?"

"Do not mention this paperwork. Do you understand? Don't tell them you gave it to me."

Footsteps and voices.

"There's more upstairs."

"Christ! Georgina, get it quickly. *All* of it."

She ran upstairs.

Charlie looked panicked.

"It's going to be OK," Rob said.

He moved to the sitting room door, away from the porch window.

There was a knock at the front door.

Charlie moved as if to open it, but Rob shook his head.

Georgina appeared with a stack of papers in her hand. "I think this is everything."

"Let's hope so." Rob placed them in the box.

He spoke in a whisper, "Both of you. Please listen. Do not tell them you gave me this material."

They nodded.

"What has my father done?" Charlie said, his voice wavering.

Another sharp knock at the door.

"Nothing wrong, Charlie. Your father has done absolutely nothing wrong."

Rob hurried into the living room and out of the French windows into the garden.

Half a dozen women milled around with cups of tea. He walked through the middle of the lawn, nodding and smiling, before disappearing through the firs.

With clumps of greenery in his hair, he broke into a trot along the path that ran down the back of the married quarters, where he was shielded from the houses by the trees.

Ahead, the CND marchers continuing their circumnavigation of the station. He stopped running and tried as best as he could to look normal, avoiding any eye contact.

There were a few jeers as he pushed past them, but eventually the small group disappeared behind.

At the end of the row of houses, he made his way along the far side of a group of garages, and ran until he got home.

He burst through the kitchen door, staring at Mary, looking wild.

"What on earth?"

"Millie's in trouble."

"What? What are you talking about?"

"I can't tell you why, but I need to hide this stuff."

He brushed past her into the hallway and threw open the door to the understairs cupboard. He stashed the box inside.

"Rob, what are you doing?"

He backed out of the cupboard, closed it and stood up.

"Never look at the contents of that box, do you understand?"

"Is that an order, sir? Why would I?"

"Look... They think Millie may have stolen something."

"What?"

"Kilton's launched an investigation. Georgina could lose her pension. She might even be dragged into it. I mean, people could go to prison. I'm not exaggerating."

"But that's ridiculous. Millie wouldn't steal anything, would he?"

"No, of course not. But it's complicated."

Beads of sweat trickled down his forehead.

Her eyes went to the cupboard.

Mary stepped forward and put a hand on his chest. "Rob, are we in danger because you've brought this into the house?"

He shook his head and disappeared upstairs without replying.

———

"He brought nothing here that looked like this?"

The plain-clothes security man held up a cardboard sleeve in front of Georgina's eyes. He tipped the contents into his hand, revealing a reel of tape.

She shook her head. "No. We have a record player, but not a tape player."

He studied her.

"And no other papers that you know of in the house?"

"I've already told you, no. I'm sorry, officer, can you please tell me what this is all about?"

Next door, she could hear one of the man's uniformed colleagues moving furniture about. Charlie stood in the kitchen doorway looking agitated.

"As I explained, your husband was involved in highly sensitive projects and this is a routine operation to ensure the security of those projects is maintained throughout this incident."

"This doesn't feel very routine."

He ignored her and tapped his foot, apparently waiting for his searchers to find something.

Noises from upstairs suggested they were being thorough.

———

MARY SAT on the arm of a sitting room chair and waited for her husband to reappear.

Eventually, she heard his footsteps on the stairs; he had wet hair and carried a change of clothes.

He sat on the sofa, looking anxious.

Before she could ask him anything, he began to talk.

"Millie and I were both working on a project that was Top Secret. Officially 'Top Secret'. It's not just an expression."

"What does that mean?"

"What it sounds like. It's the highest level. It means that in theory, at least, we can't discuss it with anyone, even our own colleagues. Although many people at TFU knew of the project's existence, they cloaked everything about it in a security blanket. That's why they search cars going on and off, just in case someone has some paperwork they shouldn't have. Even if it's inadvertent, the consequences can be severe."

"OK," she said. "I assumed that's the sort of thing you did. But why the sudden panic?"

Rob's eyes searched the carpet.

"It looks like Millie was stealing it."

"What? Rob! That's ridiculous."

"Of course it's ridiculous and of course he wasn't, but it *looks* like he was."

"So, what was he doing?"

Rob exhaled, screwed up his eyes and covered his face with his hand. She got up and moved in close, wrapping an arm around him.

"I let him down. I should have been listening. I've been the worst friend and now he's dead."

"I don't understand, Rob. What should you have been listening to? What did he say?"

Rob took a few moments to recover himself. He wiped away his tears. "I can't tell you, I'm sorry. I can't involve you."

"But the box, Rob. It's in our house. You've already involved me."

"The less you know, the better. Please."

Behind Rob, something caught Mary's eye: a figure crossing the lawn. It was Jock MacLeish from next door.

Rob looked at her. "Say nothing about the box."

She went to the front door; MacLeish looked anxious.

"The police are at Georgina's. They're searching the house."

"Goodness me, what are they looking for?"

Jock gave her a quizzical look. "No idea, but I thought you should know. Georgina might need some support. Rob's car's outside the house. Is he over there?"

Rob emerged and stood behind her.

"Hello, Jock. No, I left it there earlier."

"Oh, right," Jock said. He looked at Rob. "Are you OK, friend?"

Rob nodded. "Yes, thank you, Jock. Just a bit of delayed reaction, I think. Look, we'll go over now."

MacLeish loitered for a moment, looking uncertain, as if he was going to say something before moving off. Mary closed the door and turned to her husband.

"Jesus, Rob, what exactly is in that bloody box?"

His eyes turned to the cupboard.

"It was an impulse. I need time to think." He turned back to her. "Can you go to Georgina's? But you don't know anything, OK?"

"Rob, it's true. I don't know anything."

———

ONCE MARY HAD LEFT, Rob skulked around for a while, until he was sure the coast was clear.

He retrieved the box and brought it into the kitchen.

After pulling down the window blind and switching on the single bulb lamp that hung from the ceiling, he spread the contents out on the table.

He recognised the data sheets; the mainframe computer produced them at DF Blackton. Lists of height readings from the laser. He had seen them earlier in the trial.

Each sheet was labelled *GUIDING LIGHT DATA FEED EXTRACTION.*

It was shocking to see the project name in black letters anywhere but inside the four walls of TFU.

As he leafed through the data, he could see hand-drawn rings around some of the figures.

At the bottom of the pile was a single sheet of data, separated from the rest and used as some sort of scratch pad. Millie's hand-written notes filled it and spilled onto the back.

He scanned the black ink scrawl. Numbers, percentages, and a few equations.

None of it meant anything to him.

Beneath the data sheets were two tapes.

Under those were two tasking sheets for the project.

He lifted them up, revealing the most incriminating document of them all: a schematic. It was a single sheet, straight from the blue-prints, showing the flow of electrical signals and data.

This is what terrified Kilton, and rightly so. It revealed the project, what it was, and more or less how it worked.

"Jesus Christ."

He put the schematic back at the bottom of the pile and turned to the sheet of Millie's handwriting.

Millie's ponderous voice floated into his mind, as his calculations shifted from disconnected numbers to an equation, and at the end, on the reverse side of the data sheet, what looked like a conclusion.

$2.5Cr/ = 8.75$

The phone rang.

He hurried into the hallway and snatched it off the cradle.

"Hello?"

"May. Mark Kilton. We have carried out an initial search at Milford's house."

"Yes, it was noticed."

"Well, we can't hide this. I just need you to know that the investigation is ongoing. I need you all to be careful with how much contact you have with Georgina."

"I'm sorry, sir?"

"May, we don't know how much she was involved. It's more important than ever that you do not share any information with her. We have no idea where it might end up."

"You don't seriously believe she and Millie were doing anything sinister? Surely there's a more logical explanation."

"At the moment, May, we have no alternative but to treat this as a most serious breach of project security."

"What about Mary? Can she still talk to her?"

"It's best to keep your distance. Things could get tricky and I don't want them to get tricky for you."

Kilton hung up.

Rob's feet felt heavy as he wandered back into the kitchen.

He shuffled the notes back into the box.

As he pushed the handwritten paper deep into the middle of the pile of papers, the black ink letters and numbers disappeared into the fold.

There was something pleading and urgent in the scrawls.

Kilton wanted him to stay away.

But Millie's notes said something else.

————

DESPITE THE STUFFY heat inside her tent, Susie pulled the entrance flaps together and sat cross-legged, out of sight from the dwindling group of protestors.

She pulled out a small notebook and annotated her observations, using a shorthand that couldn't easily be deciphered.

It had been an extremely interesting day.

Firstly, an encounter with the survivor, Robert May. She'd recognised his car from the information Roger had provided. He looked younger than his twenty-nine years, but was pale and drawn. Not surprising.

She noted the time of the sighting and added 'nothing out of the ordinary' following her cursory scan of the vehicle.

But the second sighting was altogether more strange.

The same man, an hour later, running, then walking fast, with a box in his arms, for all the world looking like a thief escaping from the scene of a crime.

She couldn't break off from the march around the perimeter fence without arousing suspicion, so she noted the exact location of the back garden from where she believed he'd emerged.

Later, on her own, she walked past the end of Lancaster Close and noted the address.

She folded the notebook, slipped it into her shorts pocket and headed into the village.

Roger was waiting for her call.

"My dear, we have some interesting news for you."

"I have some for you, too."

"Well, let me go first. Your initial contact, the now deceased Christopher David Milford, is posthumously under investigation."

"By who and for what?"

"That's the thing. The RAF Test Flying Unit is covered by a new branch of the military police, rather vaguely called the West Porton Security Police. It seems to have been created along with TFU and reports directly to the Ministry of Supply. So, we can get hold of the odd bulletin, but not much else. Now, what about the survivor?"

"Robert May. I've seen him, twice. On his way to the airfield this morning. And this afternoon he left the rear of a nearby house with a box under his arms. The address..." She pulled the notepad from her pocket. "8 Lancaster Way."

"That's Milford's house," Roger said.

"Bloody hell."

"All rather peculiar. But you are not to contact him."

"Why not?"

"They're jumpy about this upstairs. Too many eyes, including Number Ten's, on the project."

"So what am I supposed to do?"

"Operate in the shadows, of course. If you feel you need to approach him, you'll need authorisation from above. And you'll need very good cause if the director's to agree."

"The director's taking a personal interest in this?"

"Don't flatter yourself, darling. Maybe he thinks you need babysitting?"

Susie sighed. "Fine, but it won't be easy if I can't talk to anyone."

"If you wanted easy, you should have signed up for MI6. You'd be sipping a G&T in Raffles by now. Of course if you need help, I can always recommend we dispatch a more experienced officer—"

"No." She relaxed her tone. "No, that won't be necessary. Thank you."

"Well, don't get your hopes up, my dear. There's no actual evidence of wrongdoing and you yourself have said the CND thing has lost its threat. I suspect they'll pull you out any moment."

Susie left the phone box and walked past the church, cursing her luck at Milford dying the day before they were due to meet.

She could divert past Lancaster Way and Trenchard Close, but it was still light.

An image of May formed in her mind: hurrying down the path, cardboard box under his arm. Had it said *VEGETABLES* on the side of the box?

The road split into two: left to the West Porton main gate, right to the peace camp.

Susie looked up.

The sky was alight with fiery red colours as the sun set.
Operate in the shadows.

————

"KILTON WANTS US TO REMAIN 'DISTANT' from her," said Rob. Mary stood in the living room doorway, having just returned from Georgina's.

"This is all too much to take in, Rob."

He shrugged.

"Well, surely I'm not subject to your silly orders? I can still see her?"

Rob stood up and walked over to her. He placed his hands on her shoulders and gazed at her face, glowing in the soft, warm light. "Yes. And to hell with Kilton if he thinks otherwise." He kissed her forehead.

"I don't think I've ever heard you speak about anyone like that before."

"It's not right, is it? And I think it's all part of something else."

Mary's head turned to look at the understairs cupboard.

"Tread carefully, husband."

"I'm minded to go to the dinner party tonight and hope Georgina comes."

"The Brunsons'? It's still on?"

"Apparently."

"Yes, let's do that."

————

As THEY ENTERED THE BRUNSONS' lounge, Sarah walked up to Rob, put a hand on his chest and kissed him on the cheek. "You OK, honey?"

Rob nodded, but avoided her eyes.

She squeezed his shoulder. "I'm sorry, hun. I didn't mean to upset you. Come on, let's get a drink in you."

She found him a beer, Mary had a lemon and port.

They took their seats at dinner and talked about the warm weather, the protest camp, the new department store in Salisbury, and the evening's glorious sunset.

Rob finished his beer quickly, and moved on to red wine.

Sarah cleared the main course away, and there was a gap in the conversation.

"Aren't we going to talk about Millie?" Rob said. "And Steve and Speedy?"

Test pilot Rory Davies looked down at his lap. His wife smiled at him.

"Rob," Mary said, with a hint of admonishment in her voice.

"No, it's OK," said Red. "Of course we can. What do you want to say, Rob?"

"I don't know, but we can't just chit-chat like nothing happened." His words were slurred.

"Honey, it's just our way of coping," Sarah said. "God knows we've been here before, right? At Edwards we had some pretty bad days. It's awful. And hard. But, y'know, I'm not sure dwelling on it is the answer either."

"I don't want to dwell on it, but it's like it didn't happen." He drained another glass of wine. "I mean, where's Georgina?"

No-one answered; Rob sensed he was missing something.

Sarah Brunson was the first to answer. "It's not like it would have been appropriate, anyway. She lost her husband yesterday and she's got family over."

Rob looked at Red. "Don't tell me you uninvited her?"

Red put his hands up. "We had no choice, buddy. Orders from the top."

"What the hell? Why? Because Kilton's trying to pin something on Millie even after he's *dead*?" Rob raised his voice.

"Rob, we mustn't discuss it," said Red. "You know that."

"Of course we mustn't. We mustn't discuss anything, right? We can talk and talk and bloody talk, but for god's sake *DON'T SAY ANYTHING!*"

The guests shifted in their seats as Mary's hand reached across the table toward him. Rob glared at the guests, one by one.

"Will none of you stand up for Millie?"

"It's not a case of standing up for him, Rob," said Jock MacLeish. "We simply have to let officialdom take its course."

Rob continued to stare at Red.

"Do you agree with that? We sit back and do nothing?"

"We have no choice, Rob. We have to trust the system."

Rob stood up.

Sarah Brunson got to her feet and walked around the table. "Honey, you're still in shock. It must be so hard."

Hands appeared on his shoulders; he turned his head and was surprised to find they belonged to Red Brunson, not Mary.

He whispered, "Buddy, now's not the time, OK?"

"Then when will it be the time?"

"Why don't you sleep it off tonight, huh? Let's talk tomorrow, just the two of us."

He lowered his head. "I just want to talk to Millie."

Sarah produced a hanky and Rob dabbed his eyes.

Red patted his shoulders. "Come on, buddy. This is not good for you. Why don't you get some rest?"

Mary appeared by his side.

"I think we both need to rest."

"You know where we are, buddy." Red stood in the doorway as Rob and Mary made their way out.

Outside, it was dusky, with the first stars appearing overhead.

They walked along Trenchard Close, arms locked together.

Mary stopped. "What was that?"

"What was what?"

"Did you see a light in the house?"

Rob looked up at their semi-detached quarter. It was in darkness.

"No."

They carried on and up to the front door. As they did so, a distinct torch light flashed across the window and they heard a noise inside.

"Someone's in the house, Rob," Mary whispered.

He stiffened next to her and took the key from her hand. He inserted it into the lock as quietly as possible. He eased open the front door and paused, listening.

Another noise.

"Who's there?"

They waited for a response.

Another noise from the living room. Rob ran through in time to see a figure exiting through the back garden toward the firs and the fence at the end.

A slim woman with short hair.

"Hey!" he shouted and immediately set off after her.

He tripped on the door frame and went sprawling onto the patio.

"Rob!" Mary ran toward him, but he recovered and set off again.

Once through the fir, he ran along the path between the garden and a field of wheat. Beyond that, the orange sodium glow of RAF West Porton.

The girl was nowhere.

He stopped, panting at the sudden exertion.

She was gone, and he had no idea which way she'd turned down the track.

After getting to the end of the row of garages, he checked up and down the streets of neat lawns and brown fences.

Nothing.

The burst of adrenaline seemed to have sobered him up. He trudged back home, reappearing in the garden to see the house lights switched on and Mary opening the drawers to the Welsh dresser.

He entered the living room. She looked expectantly at him, but he walked straight past her to the understairs cupboard.

It took him a few seconds to confirm the worst.

He reappeared in the living room to see Mary scrutinising the fireplace, where a couple of silver candlesticks lived.

"She wasn't after the silver," said Rob. "She's got what she came for."

Mary stared at him. "The box?"

He nodded.

"It was a woman?"

"I'm sure of it. I recognised her."

"What?"

"I don't know her name, but she's one of them, from the camp."

————

IN THE GLOOM of her tent, Susie switched on a torch and shuffled through the contents of the open box.

She had given herself a few minutes to calm down; the couple had appeared home unexpectedly early.

Luckily it hadn't taken her long to find the box.

"I hope you're better at flying than you are at hiding things, Flight Lieutenant May," she whispered as she leafed through the contents.

She read the title on one of the sheets.

GUIDING LIGHT.

She flicked through quickly. Lots of numbers, some sort of hand-written calculations, and what looked like a wiring diagram.

None of it meant much to her, though there were repeated references to a Vulcan bomber.

Susie reached the end of the box and examined two cardboard sleeves containing reels of magnetic tape.

She retrieved her notebook and wrote a description of the contents.

The key thing was the *TOP SECRET* stamp on virtually every sheet.

Highly sensitive military documents, in the hands of a junior test pilot, apparently retrieved from the house of a recently deceased engineer, currently the subject of a security investigation.

A recently deceased engineer who had contacted the British Security Service shortly before his death.

It was getting late, and she was shattered. She piled the paperwork back into the box and covered it with some clothes.

She rested her pillow against the box and lay down.

Had May recognised her? Maybe it hadn't been such a good idea to leave a lasting impression on him with her loose fitting top. At the time, she thought it might be useful.

She used the few minutes before she was ready for sleep to allow her mind to flow freely. It was a technique learned from an eccentric former MI6 type in training. She'd sensed the other newbie agents, including Roger, had dismissed him as a lunatic, but Susie felt the logic in his thesis that our minds hold more than we can readily access, and some things only rise to the surface when our thoughts are elsewhere.

A few minutes later, Susie reached for her pad again and made a final note.

May=Milford.

20

SUNDAY 26TH JUNE

Rob rose at 7AM, feeling jaded.

He sat alone at the kitchen table, mulling a course of action he had settled on in the early hours.

Back upstairs, he pulled on an old pair of beige trousers relegated to gardening duty. He also found the scruffiest short-sleeved shirt he owned and headed out in the car.

Instead of turning left onto the road that ran up to the West Porton main gate, he turned right.

He parked the car on a verge and walked on until he came to an old five-bar gate, adorned with a large white bedsheet with a painted fallen cross CND symbol.

He entered the field and walked as confidently as he could toward the collection of tents.

Although it was early, the peace camp was alive with movement.

Slowly, the occupants of the field noticed their uninvited visitor.

Two men and two women, in a loose formation, moved toward him.

"What's up, mate?" called the hairiest of the men.

"One of your lot broke into my house last night."

"We're not thieves."

More protestors joined the initial four.

"It was one of you. I recognised her."

"Her?" said a woman next to the hairy man.

"Yes. And she has something of mine."

"What?" asked the woman.

"I can't tell you."

"Oh, right. So, you came here for our help but can't tell us who you need to speak to and you can't tell us what she's supposedly got. I think you need to leave, chap."

"Look, I'm not with the police—"

"We know who you are," the hairy man interrupted and Rob stared at him.

"No, you don't."

The woman who was behind the leader stepped forward.

"You're one of them." She gestured toward the airfield.

A movement behind the small group caught his eye.

A slim woman emerged from an orange tent, a few hundred yards away.

"Hey!" he shouted, and started to move forward. But the largest man blocked his path and put a hand on his chest.

The slim woman stared at him but stayed put.

"Wait here," a woman in the group said, before moving off.

Rob stood in an awkward silence as the protestors stared at him. More joined the back of the crowd.

"Nice haircut," said someone. Others laughed.

"So, what do you do?" one of the men asked. "You a pilot?"

"You the one who gassed us?" asked another.

He looked between the heads in time to see the slim woman disappear back into her tent.

The protestor who had spoken to her walked back, shaking her head. "She doesn't know what you're talking about, and she doesn't want to speak to you. It's time for you to leave."

"She would say that, wouldn't she? Please let me search her tent. It's important."

"Search her tent?" a woman in the crowd snapped. "I hope you're joking. If it's important, go to the police. Now, please leave, before we call them."

Rob took a step backwards, staring at the group. No-one budged.

He turned and walked back to the car.

———

MARY WAS UP and sitting at the kitchen table when he got home.

"Where have you been?"

"Futile attempt to recover the box."

"You went to the peace camp? Are you mad?"

"What choice did I have? I lost the secrets, I have to recover them."

He walked through the kitchen and headed upstairs to change. Mary followed.

"But it's so risky, Rob. What if they report you? You said yourself no-one can know the box was here, so no-one can link it to you. Unless you suddenly go around asking for it back."

He sat down on the bed; Mary stood in the doorway.

"What I don't understand is how she knew."

"The peace girl?"

"I mean, how on earth did she even know to come looking for it? And how did she know to come here and not Millie's?" He looked up at Mary. "She must be watching me."

"I don't understand any of this, Rob. Who is she? Why does she know anything about this? You don't think..." Mary trailed off and sat next to Rob on the bed.

"Think what?"

"You don't think she was working with Millie?"

"Impossible."

"There's no chance Millie was passing something to her? To the peace protestors? Was he angry at the gas bombing? Trying to make amends?"

Rob shook his head. "No, of course not."

"Then what's going on?"

"I don't know." He dropped his head and stared at his fingernails. Black dirt, probably from the five-bar gate to the field. "I'm missing something, Mary. Something important. God, I just want to talk to him."

Mary stroked his hair. "Why don't you speak to someone you trust? Someone like Red?"

"I can't. It's too late now. I have to protect you. If anyone finds out I had the box and then lost it, then... I don't know. It's the end of my career for a start. Maybe prison."

———

THE PADDOCK at Golygfa Fynyddig farm showed signs of its temporary role as a helicopter landing area. For the third time that day, a yellow Wessex settled into a hover twenty feet above the surface, before firmly dropping onto the worn grass.

A winchman slid open the side door. Mark Kilton emerged.

The TFU boss ducked under the rotor blades as the helicopter engine wound down.

The farm sat deep in a valley. Kilton's eyes searched the surrounding hillsides for signs of the crash, but there were only specks of yellow flowers and white dots of sheep.

An officer in the uniform of RAF West Porton security police was waiting at the farmhouse gate.

"Just so you know, sir. The farmer, Davies, is chuntering about compensation. Says he's had to move his horses into a nearby livery, which is, and I quote 'not cheap'."

"Naturally. He's hoping the Ministry of Supply will buy the farm. Where's the crash site?"

"You can't see it from here, sir. It's about a two-mile journey by Land Rover. Your guests are waiting in the farmhouse."

They continued through a small kitchen garden toward the ramshackle grey-tiled home.

The farmer appeared in the doorway. "You in charge?"

"Don't worry, Mr Davies. You'll be recompensed for your losses and inconvenience."

"I should hope so."

Kilton waited for a moment before Davies invited him in. Sitting at the table in the dimly lit kitchen was Ewan Stafford, one of his technicians, and a man with Group Captain stripes on his day uniform.

Stafford introduced them.

"Mark, this is Group Captain Gordon McClair from Bomber Command."

"Sir," Kilton said and extended his hand to the senior officer. "I assume you've been appointed to the Board of Inquiry?"

"I'm chairman. I'm expecting a pilot from Boscombe and an engineer from ETPS at Farnborough to join me from tomorrow. In the meantime, perhaps you'd like to tell me why I'm here?"

Kilton looked around and waited. It took a moment for the security officer to take the hint.

"Is it possible we may give the gentlemen some privacy?" he said to Davies.

The farmer did not look pleased at being asked to leave his own kitchen, but slowly withdrew and headed off toward the garden. The security man closed the door behind him.

Kilton turned back to the group. "The Vulcan was equipped with a highly secret system called Guiding Light. It's classified as 'Top Secret'. It's a matter of national security that knowledge of its existence is confined to as few people as possible."

"Yes, I'm aware of that already," the group captain said.

"It's also highly specialised. The panels require experience to install and remove correctly. Which is the subject of this meeting."

"This is Stephen," Stafford said, "he's one of our technicians."

The group captain nodded to the young man before turning back to Kilton. "You realise the bodies are still in the wreckage, Mark? Are you telling me that you want to pull out panels before recovering your fallen comrades?"

"Yes."

"Right, well I also have to think about the integrity of the Board of Inquiry. The wreckage is now evidence. There must be a clear separation between TFU and the BOI. I'm content to allow Mr Stafford's technician to help us identify what pertains to the system, provided the lead engineer at the site says it's safe to do so. But we'll keep all recoveries secure at Farnborough after that."

"I want one of our security officers to guard it," Kilton said.

"That won't be necessary. We'll organise the security. Don't worry, Mark, we're used to keeping things under lock and key at Farnborough."

"Then you could examine it as a priority and return it to us for disposal."

"Fine."

"Right. Well, let's get this over with." Kilton stood up. The group trudged through the garden toward a pair of Land Rovers with blue lights on top.

The journey took fifteen slow minutes as they inched up the rocky path toward the site.

Kilton got his first view of the downed Vulcan as they rounded a small rise. The blackened remains were scattered in an elongated triangle pattern. The heavier parts had continued higher up the hill, but the main fuselage seemed to be largely intact in the centre of the debris field.

They left the vehicles a hundred yards short of the first piece of aircraft. A squadron leader with an engineering badge on his camouflage fatigues greeted them.

"Good morning. As you can see the site is barely accessible. We can't get the low-loaders anywhere close, so recovery is going to take a while, I'm afraid. We've already recovered Squadron Leader Johnson's body and ejection seat, but they were way down the hill. Our priority now is the bodies in the fuselage, but it's not straightforward."

"You have a new priority for now, Squadron Leader," said Kilton. "We need to remove certain items from the aircraft this morning." He looked beyond the engineer to the wisps of smoke from the wreckage.

"The base of the wreck is still hot. I can't send my men in I'm afraid. Also, sir, with respect, I think we should remove the men before we move other parts of the wreckage. It's a matter of dignity."

"And this is a matter of national security. What's the state of the cockpit and rear bay?"

The engineer looked across at the group captain.

"It's OK, Michael," said McClair. "Mark here is overseeing an important project. They have instructed us to make it a priority."

"I see. You'd better follow me, then."

As they got closer to the wreck, Kilton stared into the twisted fragments. It took him a second to realise what he was seeing in the centre of the mess: human legs.

"Christ."

"We don't normally leave them in there this long," said the engineer. "But we also want to extract bodies as completely as possible, while disturbing little for the investigators. And that takes time. Now, the cockpit panels are roughly together there." He pointed toward the front section of the site. Rolled over on to one side was the back end of the nose section. Kilton could see where the canopy once was.

The group walked further around.

"Jesus!" the group captain said as they came across an outstretched arm.

"And the rear bay panels?" said Kilton.

"Indeed," said the engineer. "Just back from that arm, facing upward. I think that's one set of panels. However, the others—"

"That's them," Kilton said. Despite the charred and blackened metals, he recognised the distinctive Guiding Light switches and dials.

"Well," the engineer said, "they should be safe to access if they're clear of the centre section."

"Who will remove them?" McClair asked.

"We can have a go, as long as it's a standard fit."

The Blackton technician stepped forward.

"There's nothing standard about it. I installed these panels at Warton using specialised torque retainers. They're also on spring mechanisms to protect them in flight. I'll need to remove the retaining assembly before anything else."

The squadron leader looked across to the BOI chairman, who nodded.

Kilton watched carefully as the engineer led the technician, step by step, toward the remains of the rear bay.

When he arrived, just beyond the outstretched arm, he crouched down and began work on the fixings.

The men watched as he worked, carefully removing eight long bolts.

Kilton turned toward Stafford and made a small motioning movement with his head.

Stafford walked over to the group captain.

"Sir, you're going to need some information about Guiding Light. Perhaps now's the time for me to brief you?" He looked over his shoulder at the small group of engineers from the recovery team. "Perhaps over here?"

Stafford led him away from the wreckage and they stopped on the path fifty yards down the hill.

Kilton looked back to the technician; the squadron leader in charge of the recovery crew stood over him as he worked.

The young man released another of the bolts and handed it up to the officer, who looked across to his men and called out, "We'll need a stretcher to get this lot out."

As the man spoke, the technician's hands moved quickly over the panels before returning to the retaining bolts. After ten minutes, he announced he was done. "The panels will come out easily now."

As he stepped past Millie's arm, careful to tread only where he'd been told to, the young man looked up at Kilton and gave him the faintest of nods.

21

MONDAY 27TH JUNE

R ob dressed quietly that morning. Donning each item of uniform seemed like an effort. Each movement he made would lead him closer to TFU.

Mary kissed him on the lips at the door.

"I'll go to Georgina's. When do you think the funeral will be?"

Rob shook his head. "I don't even know where Millie is. Or Brighty. They might still be on the side of the mountain."

She smiled at her husband and brushed a tear from his cheek.

"Come on now, Rob. You'll need to keep that inside today."

———

THE MORNING BRIEFING began with Kilton addressing the aircrew at the tea bar.

"In the aftermath of Friday's crash, it has been discovered that our most important and Top Secret project has been compromised. Precautions are now being taken to recover materials. An investigation is underway. If you see anything, hear anything, you are to report it. Withholding information could cause serious difficulties for you.

As an additional precaution, I would like any contact with Millie's family to be carried out through my office."

Rob winced at the mention of his friend's name. He looked around; his colleagues' expressions didn't change.

"There are logistical difficulties with the crash site which I visited yesterday. Unfortunately, extracting the remains is going to be a slow process, so the funerals will have to wait. Please be sensitive. No-one outside TFU needs to know these details. Refer any enquiries from relatives directly to me."

Kilton paused.

"Friday was a difficult day for TFU. We're a young unit, but we practice a high-risk profession. We must remain operational and dedicated. It serves no-one to dwell on the past."

After the brief, Rob walked back into the planning office with the twenty other pilots.

Red Brunson appeared beside him. "How you holding up, buddy?"

"Look. I'm sorry about Saturday—"

"No apology necessary, friend. We know it's tough on you. Hell, it's tough on all of us. I thought you might come over yesterday."

"I wanted to stay with Mary. Sorry."

"That's fine, but anytime. OK?"

Rob looked across as Kilton disappeared back into his office. "The boss made it sound like we're done with it. Time to move on. What was it he said? 'It doesn't do to dwell on the past'? It was only bloody Friday, Red. Is that it now? We just move on?"

Red put a hand on his arm. "I don't know what to say, buddy. No-one's going to find this easy, but we pretend, don't we?"

"I'm not sure I can."

"Yes, you can."

Red's crew called him over for planning. Rob scanned the flying programme but couldn't see his name.

"Flight Lieutenant May?" It was Jean, Kilton's secretary.

"Hello, Jean."

"You're to report to medical for an examination. After that, the wing commander would like your written report of Friday's incident."

"I give my report to Wing Commander Kilton, not the Board of Inquiry?"

"I'm just relaying the request."

"OK. Thank you, Jean."

With his colleagues getting on with their morning routines, Rob wandered alone to the Station Medical Officer.

The thin, wrinkled doctor drew heavily on his cigarette and proffered the open packet toward Rob.

"No, thank you."

The doctor looked in his ears, eyes and throat before prodding him a few times and declaring him fit.

"Is that it?" Rob asked.

"That's the physical side. How are your nerves? Must have been quite a moment."

Rob looked down at the floor. He wanted to tell the SMO that he felt on the verge of tears at every waking moment.

"I'm fine."

The SMO smiled. "Well, cigarettes can help with nerves and of course a wee dram of the hard stuff if it all gets too much." He finished writing a brief report with a flourish of his fountain pen.

"That's it. You can go."

———

Back in TFU, Rob sat down at Millie's old desk with a pile of blank report pages, each one pre-marked *SECRET*.

He ran his fingers over the wooden surface, savouring the soft indentations that could well have been made by his old friend's pen.

He set about a longhand description of the flight.

When it came to the last few seconds, he composed every word with careful precision.

He had checked the chart, assessing the area ahead for a suitable place to disengage Guiding Light and climb out of low-level.

Speedy had said something to him, but he couldn't remember what. He just remembered Johnson, oxygen mask on, head turned, peering across at the chart.

Neither of them looking forward.

The initial jolt had dazed him, and he struggled to recall any immediate detail beyond the feeling of disorientation.

He described the moment Johnson ejected. He knew it was the wrong time, but his only concern was the rear crew.

After he noted the final traumatic seconds, he set the pen down.

Something small had lifted from his shoulders. He couldn't place what, exactly, but somehow describing the experience had helped.

————

IN THE AFTERNOON, he felt at a loose end. Officers and NCOs worked around him. The sense of normality grated.

At 4PM he tapped on Kilton's door.

"Come."

The boss looked at him, eyebrows raised. Opposite him was a security officer. The conversation stopped as he stood in the doorway.

"Sorry to interrupt. I thought I might go home to Mary, if that's alright with you, boss?"

"Yes, that's fine, May." Kilton picked up a piece of paper from his desk; Rob recognised the SMO's writing. "Check the flying programme in the morning."

"Thank you, sir," Rob said, backing out and closing the door.

Without saying goodbye to anyone else, he walked to his Healey and sat for a moment, hands on the steering wheel, thinking.

He drove off.

Staff at the gate checked his boot and carried out a search of the footwells before letting him go.

At the main road, he turned left.

The gate to the peace camp field was only a few hundred yards along the road. As he got closer, he slowed, finally pulling over about twenty yards short.

He put a hand on the door handle, but a green military Land Rover with a blue light on top appeared in his wing mirror. West Porton Security Police.

He waited as it passed, and then drove home.

22

TUESDAY 28TH JUNE

Next morning, the tea bar chatter was less subdued than the day before. Rob supposed it would take just one more day before everything was back to normal, with Millie, Brighty and Speedy consigned to the past.

Red Brunson found him sitting at Millie's old desk.

"Hey, you look like you need a distraction, and I've got one for you."

They walked over to the admin hatch.

The top line of the flying programme read:

Fl lt May. - HUNTER F.4 - XF940 - REFAMIL

Kilton had tasked him with a re-familiarisation flight in a single seat Hunter. The most basic of flying tasks.

"Now that will be fun," Red said.

"Or perhaps he thinks I might be a liability in a crew."

"Just enjoy it, buddy."

Back in the planning room, men gathered around charts and drew lines on maps. Rob walked through in his coveralls, carrying a yellow Mae West life jacket, silver flying helmet and oxygen mask.

On the apron, he inhaled the fresh air and got a nose full of burnt paraffin.

It took his mind back to the smoking wreck on the ground in Wales.

The twisted fragments of metal, the acrid smoke.

The outstretched arm.

He steadied himself on the wall of the building, then found a bench near the door and sat down.

A group of chaps emerged, laughing and heading out to a waiting Victor.

They glanced at him and he pulled out his local area chart and studied it.

The men piped down and carried on.

A couple of junior marshallers loitered by the Hunter. Rob climbed up a short red ladder attached to the side of the aircraft and placed his helmet on the seat before backing down to check the jet before flight.

Walking around, he occupied himself with the inspection: peering into the engine intakes to ensure they were clear, examining the underside for fluid leaks.

In the aircraft he settled in slowly, confirming his own ability to operate.

If he walked back in now, would they ever let him fly again?

Closing the canopy, he brought the jet to life.

The oxygen started to flow, and he gulped the air.

A teenage marshaller appeared in front of the aircraft. Rob signalled, completed his pre-taxi checks and got permission from the tower. After the chocks were held up by the teenager, Rob pushed the throttle forward and the aircraft lurched. He dabbed the wheel brakes to ensure they were working, then continued to the taxiway.

He felt brighter.

Away from TFU, alone in the single seat aircraft.

He busied himself with the checklists and procedures. It had been a few weeks since he'd last flown the TFU Hunter and he was low on hours.

With the flaps set at thirty-eight degrees and the trims set to neutral, he received his clearance and entered the active runway.

He advanced the throttle and watched the engine revolutions rise. At four thousand five hundred RPM he checked the power indicator; one of the no-go moments in a Hunter would be a lack of power to the flying controls.

Was he looking for an excuse to bin the flight?

The indicator remained black.

He quickly reached a hundred knots and a moment later, the Hunter seemed to take itself up into the air.

Rob looked down at the peace camp to his right.

In one of those tents: the ticking time bomb of the lost papers.

The airspeed crept up; the Hunter vibrated.

He brought his attention back to the cockpit and realised he'd failed to raise the gear or carry out the after take-off checks.

"Concentrate!"

He called the tower and set a heading of one hundred and sixty, allowing the jet to climb to ten thousand feet. Rob took an occasional glance at an air chart of southern England before pushing it back down the side of his ejection seat.

Ahead of him was the coast. The day was clear and he could see Bournemouth and the distinctive outline of the Isle of Wight.

He dropped the nose and settled a little lower at seven thousand feet. As he crossed the beaches below, he banked left and pulled back on the stick, entering a four-G turn.

The nervousness subsided.

Below and ahead, a fast sea vessel created a significant wake. Curious, he pushed the nose of the Hunter further down and brought the visual gun sight over the vehicle.

As the jet sped up, he reduced the thrust to hold the speed at around three hundred knots. About half a mile short of the target, he realised it was a military hovercraft. The grey vessel sat on a shiny black skirt, with white spray billowing in all directions.

He pushed the nose beyond the hovercraft and squeezed the trigger to simulate an attack, imagining the shells curving downward and striking the vessel below the gunsight.

The Hunter flashed over the BH.7 at three hundred feet.

He threw the Hunter into a steep, banking turn.

Rob smiled under his oxygen mask at the sensation.

He continued along the Solent. To his left, an aircraft carrier sat in dock at Portsmouth. Staying at low-level, he used the Napoleonic forts in the sea as aiming points.

A gunmetal grey warship edged out of the harbour as he banked back around, mindful of the controlled airspace around the Daedalus airfield.

The military was everywhere. Frigates, aircraft carriers, hovercraft. All these branches of Her Majesty's armed forces; and here he was, flying a Hawker Hunter as an RAF pilot.

For the first time in a while, he thought about Millie's mantra for test flying: that every person to follow them relied on their diligence. Every sailor on every ship, the pilot of the hovercraft, the Royal Marines below decks... they all relied on the men who came before and made sure their equipment was effective. And safe.

The aircraft bumped along in the thick air at five hundred feet. He lined up behind a container ship, presumably out of Southampton. He raised the nose and passed a thousand feet above it. Checking the chart, he saw that controlled airspace began at eighteen thousand feet, so he increased the power, accelerated to four hundred knots, and pulled back on the stick, making sure he was visually scanning the air above him as the Hunter fired upwards. He looped until upside down, facing in the opposite direction.

After rolling the wings, and righting the aircraft, he set the throttle to idle and let it drift back down.

Rob cleared the eastern side of the Isle of Wight, and banked around, wheeling through the air at five thousand feet.

He chose one more target for a practice strafe run before turning north, climbing, and pointing the nose at West Porton.

A hovercraft, two forts, and an oil tanker would now be in flames, had his attacks been real.

He found the idea ridiculous.

He was not a warrior.

But he could fly. He was good at flying, and following procedures, evaluating systems. He was a good test pilot.

Until recently.

Until the moment he stopped listening to his closest friend.

Rob flew mechanically and accurately as he positioned for his return to the airfield.

He swept into the circuit, talking to air traffic as he carried out the pre-landing checks. All completed with the consummate ease afforded to a skilled flyer.

As he descended on the dead side, he looked over at the peace camp. It was dwindling in size. Even since yesterday.

"Damn her."

On the final landing, he let the jet roll long, taxying past the camp at its closest point.

There was no doubt about it: they were leaving.

He had made up his mind.

––––––––

WITH THE PAPERS and tapes neatly folded into an old blanket, Susie placed them under the rubber mat and tool kit in the front of her VW Beetle.

She shut the bonnet and locked the car.

From her tent, she discarded most of her clothes and hoped the Service would approve some modest expenses for a shopping trip to Salisbury.

The tent itself looked weathered and old; it was a good job it hadn't rained. Another reason to remove the sensitive documents from such an unsuitable hiding place.

As she crawled out, David appeared in front of her.

"Looks like your friend's back. He must really like you."

––––––––

ROB MARCHED INTO THE FIELD.

A man and a woman approached him.

"I'm sorry, I'm not taking no for an answer," he said, as he changed direction to avoid them.

"Hey! Mate!" the man shouted. "She doesn't want to see you. I thought we made that clear?"

He ignored them and scanned the field.

"Damn. Where's she gone?"

A yellow VW Beetle trundled across the field, with a small, dark-haired woman at the wheel.

He broke into a run, choosing an interception angle ahead of the slow-moving vehicle.

The car sped up.

He knew enough about the angles to know he'd only just make it.

They converged on the entrance to the field, but the car was now ahead, bouncing on the uneven ground.

Just a few yards. He puffed and sweated.

Finally, Rob got close enough to reach out. He banged on the back window with his fist, just as the car put on a last burst of clanking engine noise and disappeared out onto the main road.

Rob collapsed on to the ground, panting. He looked up to see every remaining peace camper staring at him. One man shook his head in puzzlement and turned his back, walking off toward the last of the tents.

Rob looked down at the dried mud, took a deep breath, and got up and left.

He'd parked fifty yards away, as a precaution, so chasing the woman down in his car was a non-starter.

She was gone.

———

BACK AT THE HOUSE, he quickly changed, shaking his muddy uniform out of the window.

Mary served a lamb joint for dinner.

"I thought I'd do a roast. Something approaching normality." She stumbled on the last word. "I didn't mean that, I don't mean we should... return to normal."

He smiled at her. "It's OK. It looks delicious."

They ate quietly.

"Will you fly again next week?" Mary asked.

"I flew today, actually."

"Oh. Is that not a bit soon?"

Rob shuffled a piece of brown meat onto his fork. "The boss wanted me up. You know how it is."

"And how was it?"

Rob shrugged. "Fine. Just a short trip in a Hunter." He paused. "Actually, I quite enjoyed it."

Mary reached over and held his hand. "And that's OK. It's OK to enjoy things. It's what Millie would have wanted."

She released his hand and they finished the meal in silence.

After dinner, with a drying up cloth in his hand, he looked out into the street.

Mary passed him the dripping crockery.

A couple walked by, pushing a pram.

A large dog on a short lead pulled a teenager along the pavement.

The sun shone, the people looked happy.

"I'm sorry," Rob said. "I can't do this."

He put the plate on the top, left the kitchen, and hurried upstairs.

He curled up on the bed. Mary followed, and as he rolled over to look at her, it was clear she'd also been crying.

"I'm sorry," he said. "I just can't stop it sometimes."

She crawled onto the bed. They embraced.

"I want to help you, Rob."

"I can't explain it, but I feel I'm nowhere at the moment. I don't feel I'm back at TFU. Nothing feels the same, nothing feels normal."

"You miss Millie."

"It's more than that." He pressed his head onto the pillow.

"Then what, Rob? What is it? The box?"

"Yes. There's something going on, I can feel it, I just don't know what. I think my only chance to save Millie was somewhere in those papers."

"You're bound to feel guilty, being the only survivor. Maybe that's what it is?"

"Maybe."

She pushed her head toward him and they kissed. The embrace went on. He rolled over on top of her and she moaned softly.

Without closing the curtains or windows, they made love.

Mary giggled as she tried to keep her cries as quiet as possible, aware the neighbours may well be in the garden on a summer's evening.

"Mustn't scare the MacLeishes."

After, Rob rolled back onto his side, pushing his discarded trousers to the floor.

A warmth washed over him.

He stroked Mary's hair, bringing his hand down and letting it brush over her breasts.

"Not much feels right anymore, but this does."

"Good." She kissed him on the forehead. "I think it's time to let the box go."

———

A CHILL WOKE ROB. It was dark. He pulled on a pair of pyjama bottoms and covered Mary with a sheet.

He crept downstairs and poured a glass of water in the kitchen, drinking it by the orange glow of the street lamps.

The living room light was still on. He walked in and found the French doors open. Moths and insects busied themselves around the hot bulb. He switched it off and went to close the doors to the garden.

The lawn looked a pale grey colour as a full moon struggled to assert itself over the orange sodium of RAF West Porton's perimeter floodlights.

He stood for a moment looking out at the still night.

Straight into the eyes of the young woman.

He stumbled back and nearly cried out.

She put a finger to her lips and stepped into the dim light of the patio.

Framed in the doorway, she hissed at him.

"Robert May?"

"Yes."

"We need to talk. Thursday evening at this public house."

She handed him a slip of paper.

"Do not tell anyone. Act normally at work. Do you understand?"

He nodded.

"And stop turning up at the bloody peace camp."

23

WEDNESDAY 29TH JUNE

At the tea bar, Rob poured himself a mug and added two sugars.

Alone behind the wooden top, he removed the small slip of paper from his pocket and read it one more time.

The Bell Inn
Wyle
7.30PM SHARP

"How was the hop in the Hunter?"

Rob clenched his fist, holding the paper tight. He looked up to see Jock MacLeish.

"Very enjoyable, thank you."

MacLeish raised an eyebrow. "Oh? Feeling better?"

"Yes, well, it doesn't do to dwell on the past, does it?"

MacLeish didn't look convinced, but he gave Rob a pat on the shoulder.

Rory Davies announced his presence in the planning room.

"Bloody hippies all over the bloody road. I nearly killed one of them."

"You should have," someone replied.

"Seriously. Idiots holding tents and bags, taking up the whole bloody street, ambling off to god knows where. They deliberately ignored my horn."

"At least they're leaving," Jock said.

"About bloody time. Snivelling little pinko commies. A danger to society and menace to drivers. Good riddance."

Rob watched the exchange without joining in. He wandered over to the planning desk. After yesterday's return to flying status, they had handed him an unexciting trip in a Canberra, making polar diagrams with a newly fitted compass system. The trial would require nearly three hours of high level orbits over the same track north of Warrington.

The assigned navigator, a junior Flight Lieutenant called Watkins, joined him, and they planned the trip.

Rob looked up to see a group captain flanked by a pilot he recognised from Boscombe Down and another officer, without wings, striding past the desks.

Kilton emerged from his office, shook their hands, and ushered them inside.

As he closed the door, Kilton's eyes swept the room. Rob looked quickly down at his flight plan.

"Board of Inquiry, I suppose," Watkins said.

"I know who they are. Let's just plan this thing and get airborne."

After retrieving flying clothing and equipment, they walked out to the jet. Rob dropped his helmet and life vest by the open hatch before carrying out his walkaround checks.

As he rounded the nosecone, pressing the latch to ensure it was secure, Kilton walked out onto the apron with the group captain, and pointed at Rob.

The senior officer approached, leaving Kilton by the door.

"Flight Lieutenant May?"

"Yes, sir."

"I'm Group Captain Gordon McClair. They have appointed me as the Chairman of the Board of Inquiry into the loss of Vulcan XH441."

McClair had blue eyes and fair hair. He looked like he'd fit on the cover of a romantic novel, but the eyes were sharp and searching.

"Well, I don't want to disturb you. I can see you're about to fly, which is pleasing. I just wanted to hear how you are and whether you're ready to sit down and go through the events with us."

"I'm fine, thank you, sir. I had a sore back, but it cleared up over the weekend."

"Good. Your boss tells me you're an exemplary pilot and informally I thought you should know that we do have a very early indication of the cause. But of course I will need your version of events to corroborate. I don't want you to unduly worry, though. Now, I'm in Farnborough tomorrow and back here on Friday. Can I slot you in then?"

"Yes, sir."

"Good." McClair lingered for a moment. "Are you quite certain you're feeling OK?"

"Yes, sir."

"We want no more mishaps up there." He glanced at the Canberra.

"It's fine, sir. I went up yesterday and got it out of my system, so to speak."

"Good. We'll see you on Friday."

McClair turned and walked back to Kilton with the stiff-backed gait common in many senior officers.

"He seemed nice," the navigator said.

"Let's go." Rob donned his Mae West and climbed into the cockpit.

———

FIFTEEN MINUTES LATER, he signalled to the marshallers that he was about to perform a cartridge start. He pressed the button and looked over his shoulder as a stream of black smoke emanated from the top of the starboard engine. Back in the cockpit, he watched the revolutions climb, and the engine caught.

The flight was as uneventful as it appeared on paper.

During the slow, straight legs, it was hard to keep his thoughts only on the flying.

What if it was a trap? What if she was blackmailing him?

"You've missed it!" Watkins called over the intercom.

"What? Oh, sorry." Rob looked down at the needles they'd set for the orbit. He banked left, glancing ahead to check the airspace was clear.

"Want me to count you down to the next turn?" the navigator called.

"No. It's fine."

He shook the errant thoughts from his mind and concentrated on the flight.

After two hours and seventeen minutes they departed the orbit track and headed south.

As soon as they'd shut down, the navigator opened the hatch to let some cool air in.

Rob followed him into TFU where Kilton's secretary, Jean, was waiting for him.

"Wing Commander Kilton would like your logbook, please, Mr May."

"Oh, I haven't completed it yet."

Jean just stood there. Clearly, she wasn't about to leave without it.

He put his helmet down, and, still wearing the rest of his bulky flying gear, he leant over a desk and filled in the entry for the Canberra flight before handing it over.

"What's this about?"

"No need to be nervous. It's just part of the investigation." She headed back to Kilton's outer office.

————

As home time approached, MacLeish, Red and a few of the others headed to the bar for a couple of drinks. Rob joined them.

He downed his first pint and leant over to MacLeish.

"Jean took my logbook."

MacLeish shrugged. "For the BOI?"

"Maybe. But she used the word 'investigation', which I thought was odd."

"Ah. Then not the BOI. That'll be the other thing. Millie's locker and all that."

MacLeish drank his beer and turned away.

24

THURSDAY 30TH JUNE

The following evening, Rob drove the Healey cross-country through the Winterbournes, a cluster of small villages littered with army buildings.

The Bell Inn was ancient, with a small wooden door, forcing him to duck as he entered.

An old man with a white beard nursed a glass of dark ale at the bar. A golden retriever slept at his feet.

Behind the bar, a short, stout woman regarded Rob over her half-moon glasses.

"What will it be?"

Rob scanned the draught beers.

"A pint of Harp, please."

A stuffed fish sat in a glass case mounted on the wall above the bearded man. It looked like a pike: long, with nasty-looking teeth.

The landlady gave Rob a pleasant enough smile and lifted a glass down from a hook.

She poured the lager, while the man half-turned to take him in, before reaching down to pat his dog.

"Just you, is it?" the landlady asked.

"I'm expecting a friend."

"I can run a tab, if you like?"

"Thanks." He nodded, and she noted the drink on a pad next to the till.

Rob picked up the pint and made his way to a small, round table furthest from the bar. He tucked himself into a corner by the fireplace.

The place smelled of old wood. Brass horseshoes were tacked to the beams and ugly Toby jugs stared out at the empty chairs.

The door opened and the young woman walked in.

She'd undergone a transformation. The black bob of hair was now shoulder-length blonde. She looked smarter, too.

He stood up. She smiled at him, waved and called out.

"Hi!"

The landlady picked up a wine glass, in anticipation of a fresh order. "The gentleman has a bill running, so what would you like?"

"Half a Guinness," the woman said brightly. The landlady replaced the wine glass and poured the stout into a straight half-pint glass. There was a pause while she let the beer settle before topping it up. Rob remained standing, feeling awkward.

The young woman came over to the table. She looked friendly and confident, as if they met here every Thursday evening. Following years of behaviour training, he let her take her seat before resuming his.

She leant over and kissed him on the cheek.

"How are you?" she said, loud enough for the pub's other two occupants to hear.

"Fine, thank you."

Her new hair made a difference, but her clothes changed everything. Gone were the loose fitting tops and scruffy jeans. She now wore a smart, cream blouse and black slacks, and had a shiny new handbag. She looked as if she'd just come from an office job, not the peace camp.

She studied him with clear, green eyes. She had a turned down mouth, dimples in both cheeks.

She hung her handbag on the chair, before crossing her hands on the table.

"How was your day?"

"Fine, thank you."

She leant in close. "Let's wait for the background noise to rise a bit."

His eyes scanned the empty pub.

The door swung open again and three men bustled in wearing boots, wax jackets and ruddy complexions.

They laughed about something, and the landlady greeted them by name. The woman leant forward again.

"Why did you steal Top Secret documents from the military?"

"I don't know what you mean."

"You had them in your house."

"I didn't steal them."

"Then why did you have them?"

She kept her serene smile. At a glance, anyone would think they were having a cosy chat about holiday plans.

The three newcomers stood at the bar and tucked into their hard-earned pints, chatting loudly about some adventure with a bailer.

She spoke again. "Georgina Milford gave them to you to hide?"

"No."

"Then what was the arrangement, Robert?"

He shook his head. "Who are you?"

"Don't look so worried, it will attract attention."

"I can't look like anything else at the moment."

"Well, being caught with Guiding Light material means jail time. Why risk it?" She spoke with such casualness, but Rob winced at the project name.

"I wanted to return them, but... it's complicated."

She leant back and folded her arms, those green eyes constantly assessing him.

"Tell me. I can cope with complicated."

"Are you with CND?"

She reached to her handbag, unclipped the strap and pulled out a sheet of paper, placing it on the table between them. Rob looked down as she turned it around to face him. He didn't recognise the handwriting, but the pattern of numbers and equations was familiar.

"These are Millie's notes?"

"Millie?"

"Milford. Christopher Milford. Everyone called him Millie."

She nodded. "I copied them out."

"Where is the original?"

"Safe. Look, Robert—"

"Rob. And everyone calls me Rob."

She gave a little laugh. "Rob and Millie. You boys. Just like boarding school."

"I didn't go to boarding school."

"I know you didn't."

He stared at her. She laughed again. "You can call me Susie."

"Is that your real name?"

She raised an eyebrow. "What sort of person makes up names?" She tapped the sheet again. "What does it mean?"

Rob studied the notes.

$$262 \; ll/d$$
$$TFR \; 100$$
$$5 \; dys$$
$$250/y$$
$$= 25{,}000$$
$$0.014\% = 3.5$$
$$2.5 \; Cr/ = 8.75$$

"You don't know, do you?" she asked, sounding disappointed.

He put a hand on the piece of paper. "I might work something out, but I'll need to keep it."

She shook her head. "I don't know, Rob. You're a bit of a loose cannon. Pitching up at a peace camp, shouting off to anyone and everyone. I don't know if I can trust you."

"You can't trust *me?* I have no idea who you are." He spoke louder than he'd meant to; a few heads turned at the bar.

Susie looked around and turned back to him, laughing. "You're so funny." She leaned forward and kissed him on the lips before slouching back in her seat and taking a sip of her drink.

His heart pounded. She was young and beautiful. He hadn't kissed another woman since meeting Mary.

She sat up again.

"You see, Rob, I can't even trust you to keep your voice down. Let's try to look like a normal, run-of-the-mill couple, so no-one remembers us."

"Sorry."

"What's your next move?" she asked, again with that same smile, as if enquiring about his plans for Saturday night.

"I need the box back, please. That's why I'm here."

"And what will you do with it?"

"I don't know."

"Well, that sounds like a solid plan."

He shrugged.

"OK. So how about I tell you what I know? Your friend Millie found something, didn't he? Something that worried him. Something that needed reporting, but not through the usual channels. Am I getting warm?"

"Maybe."

"Is that why he's dead, Rob?"

"No."

"Are you sure?"

"He's dead because I wasn't paying attention."

"The crash was your fault?"

He took a breath. "I don't know. No, probably not. But I could have prevented it. I think."

"And you feel guilty?"

"I'm sorry, who did you say you were again?"

"Another drink, Flight Lieutenant?"

He looked down and saw he'd finished his first pint. Susie headed off to the bar.

As Rob watched her chatting with the landlady, he tried to reconcile this smart, confident woman with a peace girl living in a tent.

She arrived back at the table.

He opened his mouth to speak.

"So what did he find?" she asked before he got the first word out.

"I can't possibly discuss that with you."

"I understand." She nodded. "OK, let's try this. I am not, as you might have guessed, a member of the Campaign for Nuclear Disarmament. I was in fact under cover, keeping an eye on the subversive types from within. So. Now you know my secret and you could easily compromise me, isn't it fair we share some information? After all, I'm not going to hand the box back unless I'm sure the security of the country is not at risk from you."

"From me?"

She shrugged. "I don't really know what you were doing with it, Mr May. All I know is, you're desperate to get it back."

He looked around the pub again. The farmers had sat down. The man with the golden retriever was still at the bar, and two other couples sat at nearby tables.

"You work for the police?" he asked.

"Sort of. A little higher up the chain. I'm the sort of person who could have helped your friend, if events hadn't intervened."

"You would have helped him?"

"He asked for my help. In fact we were due to meet on Saturday morning. He trusted me, Rob. So I think you can."

"You were due to meet Millie?"

She nodded. "Yes. In St Mary and St Mellor church. I was ready to listen to whatever it was he had to say. But he died, hours before. And I'm finding it hard to see that as a coincidence."

Rob put a hand to his forehead and rested one elbow on the table. He gave a long, deep sigh.

"I just don't know. I don't know anymore."

"What don't you know?"

He shook his head. "The crash. It wasn't deliberate. But..."

"But?"

Rob sat upright and stared at her.

"I think I've been played."

He picked up the cryptic notes. "I can't decipher these notes exactly, but it's clear that Millie believed the system was flawed. I'm guessing that's what the numbers are about. The thing is..." He stared at Millie's handwriting. "The thing is, it doesn't matter anymore."

"It doesn't?"

Rob shook his head. "No. The crash proved his point and in one way it achieved his aim. It's put paid to the project. At the worst possible price."

"So, Guiding Light is dead?"

"Yes. The Chairman of the Board of Inquiry has as good as told me they know the cause and it can only be the laser."

"Laser?"

"Forget I said that, please."

"Sure. But what I don't get here, Rob, is how your place operates. Millie was a senior officer, right? If he had concerns, why were you still flying?"

Rob bowed his head. "I suspect that's what Millie was going to talk to you about. There was no hard evidence. Just one moment when it may have gone wrong. So his objection was overruled."

"Your boss overruled the concerns of his pilots?"

"Millie was an air electronics officer."

Rob studied the bubbles in his pint.

"Oh, I see," said Susie. "It was just Millie. So you didn't believe him, either?"

"I don't know."

"You don't know?"

"I mean... I sided with the boss because it felt like the right thing to do at the time."

Susie leant back, not taking her eyes off him. For once she said nothing.

"It was confusing. Kilton, he's the boss, he convinced me the system was working normally. I agreed for the sake of the project. I gave him an alternative explanation." He met Susie's eyes. "I did think it was the right thing, doing what experienced test pilots would do. They've seen everything and don't get fazed by the odd moment in the air.

"Plus, he's my boss. He gave me all this spiel about Millie being old and about to retire. He said that I was the future and when things happen quickly in jets, it needs fast acting decision makers like me. What else could I do?"

Again, Susie stayed quiet.

"Is Kilton in trouble now it turns out Milford was right?" she asked eventually.

Rob shook his head. "I doubt it. That's not the way it works. I don't even know if there's an official record of the first incident. But he's lost the project he was so devoted to. So I guess that's punishment enough."

She finished her drink and scooped up the piece of paper, clipping it back into her handbag.

"Right, well. That's that, then. It sounds like the crash did the job Milford wanted, only he paid a heavy price." She placed a hand on his. "Look, I doubt an intervention from you would have made any difference. If I know the military and men like Kilton, they don't have their minds changed easily and they get their own way."

"I didn't even try."

"Well, it's done now."

She stood up.

Rob stayed at his seat, her casually spoken words tearing into him.

"What about the box?" she asked.

Slowly, he got to his feet.

"Actually, I wouldn't know what to do with it. I can't imagine strolling into West Porton and handing it back. They'd want to know exactly why I had it. Plus, I think Kilton would use it to destroy Millie's reputation and try to get the project back."

"Want me to dispose of it?"

"Can you burn the documents? I think it's the only guaranteed way to ensure they don't fall into the wrong hands."

"I'm not sure Mrs Holleroid allows bonfires at the Prickwillow B&B, but I'm sure I can organise something. Leave it with me."

Rob paid the bill at the bar and they walked out together and stood near a VW Beetle in the gravel car park.

"It was nice meeting you, Mr May."

"And you. Goodbye, Susie."

She looked back at the inn, then gave him a goodbye kiss.

"Just for show, you understand?"

He watched her climb into the car before wandering off to his own.

She drove off quickly. He started the engine, suddenly feeling numb.

Her question had wounded him.

Oh, I see. It was just Millie. So you didn't believe him, either?

He found it hard to drive.

After a mile, he pulled into a lay-by, and cried.

25

FRIDAY 1ST JULY

The HQ building was quiet. Rob walked down the lime green corridor and peered into the offices.

The second to last door on the left was open. Group Captain Gordon McClair sat with his back to him.

"Ahem."

McClair whipped around.

"Flight Lieutenant May."

Rob saluted.

"Have a seat."

As Rob sat down, he spotted his handwritten accident report on the desk, with notes in blue ink added at various points.

"Thank you for your observations, May. Very thorough and very useful. And thank you for your honesty about the moments leading to the crash. You're in a rather unique position as the only survivor and I appreciate your candour. It will serve you well through this process."

"Yes, sir."

"So, let us start at the beginning."

For half an hour, Rob walked the chairman of the BOI through the Guiding Light project planning and execution. He explained the procedure of entering a low-level gate and how they handed over control to the system. For the moment of the crash, Rob slowed his explanation down, choosing his words carefully.

He explained how he had unfolded the chart, to ensure he could select a safe area for a climb back to one thousand feet.

"You were planning to ensure it would be a safe manoeuvre?"

"Yes, sir."

"And what were you looking for exactly? I mean, where would be an unsuitable place to ascend?"

"Well, you wouldn't want to interrupt the autopilot if it was manoeuvring hard, which it often is at low-level. So somewhere flat below, ideally where you're not climbing, descending or banking."

McClair made a few notes. "I see. And is that the same for disengaging the system?"

Rob thought for a moment. "Yes. We select level flight usually before switching back to manual control."

"What would be the result if you disengaged during a descent, for instance?"

"It's not necessarily a terrible thing, but the aircraft would continue to descend unless you manually intervened. Which of course you would. You'd only disengage with your hands on the stick and throttle, ready."

"Thank you, Flight Lieutenant. And just so I'm completely clear, squadron leader Johnson was the nominal handling pilot for this leg?"

"Yes. We still called it that, even though Guiding Light was actually handling the aircraft, it was your job to monitor and be ready to intervene."

"But as you note here, Johnson was looking over to you at the time of the ground strike?"

Rob took his time. The memory was foggy and further blurred by the horror.

"I think he was looking at the chart, maybe to brief himself ahead of the climb out. But I'm not really sure why. I was about to brief him and give him a landmark."

For the next twenty minutes, McClair pushed him on the final thirty seconds. Rob stuck to a flat monotone, treating the questions as an academic exercise, trying his best to distance his emotions.

But McClair's questions made it hard.

"You communicated with Milford and Bright as they tried to escape? You saw them?"

"Yes, sir. We usually left the divider to the cockpit open, so I could turn back and see them."

"Describe that to me, please."

Rob looked down at the pen marks and scratches on the table. How many men had been through this before? How many bomber pilots in the war headed back down the aircraft to bail out, passing dead and mortally injured colleagues?

"Bright was out of his seat. He had his hands on the side of the compartment. Remember, we were upside down but still rolling. He hadn't made any progress toward the hatch. He was pushed further away from it, as I looked. It was like a nightmare where you're running through treacle trying to escape from someone."

"And Squadron Leader Milford?"

Rob shook his head. "He looked paralysed. He just stared at me." His voice finally broke.

McClair put his pen down. "Take your time, Flight Lieutenant. I know this must be hard."

Rob took a few deep breaths.

"He was injured, a cut across his forehead. I think he was dazed. Even if the hatch was opened, Steve Bright would have had to manhandle him out."

McClair made notes.

"I have just one more area I need to ask about. The timing of Squadron Leader Johnson's ejection. Did you discuss it at all?"

Rob shook his head. "No. We barely said anything. It took me by surprise."

"So he acted unilaterally?"

Rob nodded.

"Thank you, May. You've been most helpful. Do you have questions for me?"

"When will the report be ready?"

McClair shrugged. "We've only just begun the examination of the main wreckage, and I've an eye witness to speak to in Wales. After that we'll put everything together, but it won't be for some time, I'm afraid. You know how it is." He shuffled his papers into a single pile. "But I don't expect our conclusions to change."

"I don't suppose there's anything else it could be."

McClair furrowed his brow. "Has Wing Commander Kilton already spoken to you?"

"No. It's just... It must have been Guiding Light."

McClair leant back in his chair. "We wouldn't normally discuss our early conclusions publicly, not that any of this will become public for some decades, of course, but Wing Commander Kilton is keen that I share our initial findings with you. I think he's worried about your sense of guilt, being the only survivor.

"What I'm about to tell you is preliminary, but as I say, I will be very surprised if the conclusions change. Because of the sensitive nature of the project, we were required to retrieve the Guiding Light panels and equipment from the wreckage first. All of that has been thoroughly examined by technical experts at Farnborough with assistance from Blackton technicians. We are now certain of one fact. Guiding Light was not operational at the moment of ground strike."

"I'm sorry, what?"

"Well, I'm not sure how familiar you are with the panel in the rear bay, but you might know there is a master switch. It was in the off position. So you see, you had a chart in front of you, not unreasonably planning ahead. Speedy took his eyes off the terrain, and at that moment, Guiding Light was disengaged. As you know, there's no audible alarm and so neither of you noticed. But the aircraft was already at three hundred feet and descending, gently, so you suffered a glancing blow off the ground, enough to severely damage the elevons on the port side and fill the engines with dirt."

Rob's mouth hung open.

"Wing Commander Kilton suggested the conclusion might surprise you, but I was hoping it would reassure you. You could not have predicted it, and you were certainly acting appropriately, carrying out in-flight planning. It's just a shame of course that Speedy Johnson chose that moment to become distracted from his task."

Rob shook his head. "I'm sorry, sir. I'm having difficulty with this. You say the master switch in the rear panel was off?"

"It was most definitely in the off position. There are several possible explanations and they'll be listed in the final report."

"Such as?"

"Well, Squadron Leader Milford may have become disorientated. He was, after all, quite old to be flying about at low-level in the back of a Vulcan." Rob shook his head, but McClair pressed on. "He may have inadvertently knocked it with something like the sleeve of a magnetic tape. Or, and I hesitate to suggest this is likely, but we have to consider the possibility that Milford did it deliberately."

Rob stared, stunned to silence.

"As I say," McClair continued, "I'm not a fan of that last possibility, but as I understand it, Milford had taken against the project and there's a school of thought that he may have benefitted from a repeat of an earlier incident in which he believed Guiding Light had briefly suffered an aberration. The theory goes that he aimed to momentarily disengage, long enough for you two to notice and claim back control of the Vulcan. Unfortunately, neither of you was looking out at that very moment. But as I say, it's far-fetched in my opinion and it may not even make it into the final report."

Rob leant forward. "But Guiding Light was flying us. It can't have been off. And Millie was right. There was something wrong. Something buried inside it that didn't work."

McClair shot him a look of sympathy. "I'm told you were close to Christopher Milford?"

"With respect, sir, why is that relevant?"

"Well, Wing Commander Kilton suggested you may find any blame put on Milford hard to digest. But I have to tell you what we found. The master switch, as you may know, is caged. I've inspected the other TFU Vulcan and seen it for myself. The investigators at Farnborough, who have a wide experience of such matters, are determined the crash forces could not have moved the switch. The metal cage guards are not damaged and like all such switches, it requires a specific force. No, it's an immutable fact of our investigation that the master switch was in the off position and therefore Guiding Light was not operational at the time of the ground strike. The good news for you is that the project continues. I believe you are to resume as early as next week. That is, as long as you wish to? No-one will blame you, Robert, if you ask to transfer to something different."

Rob's head swam. The room was unbearably hot and stuffy.

"Are you feeling alright, Flight Lieutenant?"

"I don't understand... It can't be..."

"I can see this has been a bit of a shock for you. If it's any consolation, I am strongly minded to leave the last possibility out of the final report. I doubt anyone will object and it just seems unlikely to me."

"But you find it likely that Millie, with decades of flying experience, accidentally switched off a critical piece of equipment? Endangering his and everyone else's life?"

"Accidentally? Yes. I'm afraid we've seen it all too often in the past. This is my third Board of Inquiry and I can tell you in all three cases the aircraft were perfectly serviceable but put into a configuration by the crew that led to a crash. It's far too common unfortunately. Of course, we will never know for sure, but as it stands we have no other conclusions we can draw." McClair stood up. "Look, I understand this has been upsetting for you. I should probably go now, but please do use this room for as long as you want. It's booked for the afternoon. It might be a nice place to recover yourself before heading back out."

Rob should have stood for a senior officer, but he stayed slumped in his seat.

McClair loitered for a second.

"Well, I'll be off then. Very best of luck, Flight Lieutenant May." He picked up his briefcase and pushed his chair under the table. "No need to salute." He headed out.

His heels clicked on the wooden floor as he departed.

An image filled Rob's mind.

A box of secret conclusions; pages of Millie's precious, scrawled handwriting.

Evidence that Guiding Light was fatally flawed, burning on a bonfire.

He leapt from his seat and walked as quickly as he could without running down the corridor and back to TFU.

———

IN THE PLANNING room he headed straight for his locker, picked out his car keys and turned to find Mark Kilton blocking his way.

"How did it go?"

"Fine."

"Just fine? Did he explain the BOI's theory to you?"

"Yes."

"Good. So you know the project resumes flying next week? I'd like to hit the ground running."

Rob winced at the clumsy metaphor.

"We'll carry out the remaining hours back at one thousand feet just as a precaution," Kilton continued. "It's good news for the unit and for you, May. I'd like you to take the lead. We'll need a signature on the project recommendation and I know I can rely on you."

"You want me to take Millie's place?"

"I can't think of a better man for the job. You've come a long way in a short time. Don't let this unfortunate incident put the brakes on a career that has so much promise."

"Can I think about it?"

Kilton looked surprised, then suspicious. "If you must."

"Thank you. Now, if you don't mind, boss. I'd like to go home to Mary. I found the interview rather upsetting."

Kilton moved aside.

In the car park, he started up the Healey and sped out, thankfully avoiding a car search.

On the way into the village he pulled over into a long lay-by with a phone box.

He dialled the operator. "Yes, I need a bed and breakfast called Prickwillow."

"In which area?"

"Try Amesbury."

A few seconds of pages turning.

"Nothing listed, I'm afraid. Would you like me to look further afield? How about Andover?"

"Yes, please. It's urgent."

Seconds ticked by. More pages turning. Other operators in the background.

"Sorry, sir. There's a Willows Surgery in Andover, but nothing like Prickwillow."

His heart sunk.

"I could try Salisbury?"

"Yes, please."

"Hold on."

The line went quiet. More seconds went by. He couldn't get the image out of his mind: Susie tipping the box onto a raging fire.

"Please... *hurry up,*" he said to the silence.

The line opened again. "Sorry about that. I had to get a different directory. Now, let's have a look. Porch Hall, Practice... Ah, Prickwillow Bed and Breakfast. It's Salisbury 2197. Would you like me to connect you?"

"Can you give me the address first?"

"Bell View Road. I'll connect you now."

He waited as the line clicked and whirred. The phone rang four times with agonising pauses between each tone. A woman answered, but the pips interrupted her.

He pulled out a handful of coins; several clattered to the floor. He fumbled a threepenny coin into the slot, pushing it hard against the clunky mechanism.

"Susie?"

"Do you mean Miss Attenborough?"

He didn't even know her surname. And what if she'd made up a first name?

"Susie Attenborough," said the woman. "Is that who you mean?"

"Yes. Yes, please."

"Please wait."

The phone went down, but was quickly picked up again. "Sorry, who shall I say is calling?"

"Rob," he said, immediately wondering if he was breaking all her rules.

The phone went down again. In the background he heard a tap on a door and a mumbled exchange.

A moment later, Susie's voice appeared on the line, bright and friendly.

"Hello?"

"Have you burned the stuff?"

"Oh, hello, Robert. How are you? Everything OK?"

"Have you burned the stuff? Please tell me you haven't."

"It's all fine here, thank you. No fires. Ha ha. How's your father?"

Rob was at a loss. How to take part in this conversation... Clearly the landlady was listening in.

"So you haven't burned the stuff?"

"No, no. Not yet. The weather's been lovely, hasn't it? How's it looking over there?"

"It's all changed. They're pressing on with the project. They've blamed Millie for the crash. I don't know what to do."

"Oh, that's so sweet of you, but really. You didn't have to. I'll tell you what. Why don't I buy the drinks next time? I've been going to a very nice place in Salisbury. Do you know The Haunch of Venison? It's quite famous."

"Yes, yes. I do. When?"

"Oh, you know. The usual. Same, same. Anyway, we mustn't chat on like this, it must be costing you a fortune. Do give my love to Sandra. Byeeee!"

She hung up.

His hand shook as he replaced the receiver.

Same, same.

7.30PM sharp?

He looked at his watch; it was nearly 5PM.

————

AT DINNER, he wrestled with the idea of telling Mary everything.

But he decided news of a secret meeting with a young, attractive woman might not go down well and he didn't need any more complications.

"I've got to head off to the mess. I promised the boys."

"OK," Mary replied and smiled at him.

He paced the garden, willing away the minutes. At one point he caught Mary staring at him from the dining room.

Susie's admonishing first words came to him.

Act normally.

————

THE HAUNCH of Venison was packed. It was a small pub and 7.20PM on a Friday was the middle of the overlap period, mixing office workers and Friday night revellers.

Smoke stung his eyes as he pushed his way to the bar.

The landlord, with reading glasses on a chain around his neck, poured a succession of pints before he caught Rob's eye.

"I'll be with you in a moment, sir."

"Thank you."

A voice piped up beside him. "Bloody Friday nights."

It was Susie. Still blonde. She flashed a smile.

"The usual?" he asked.

"Yes, please. Why not make it a pint? It'll take a while to get back to the bar."

"A pint?"

Rob couldn't remember ever seeing a woman with a whole pint.

A group of drinkers had spilled onto the pavement outside and they headed out with them. A couple of men were clearly taken by this slim blonde with a pint of Guinness.

They walked along the Tudor exterior of the pub and found themselves a quiet spot.

"So, what's changed?" she asked.

"I had my Board of Inquiry interview today."

"I see. And who runs that?"

"A group captain. They always appoint someone more senior than anyone on board. Anyway, it was all awful, going through it again. But at the end, he said it wasn't Guiding Light that caused the crash."

Susie didn't look surprised.

"Did he say what did cause it?"

"Millie."

"I'm sorry?"

"He's going to blame Millie. He says the master switch on Millie's Guiding Light panel was off."

"So who was flying the aircraft?"

"That's just it. No-one. If that was the case, and I'm bloody certain it wasn't. But if Millie had switched it off, the aircraft would have reverted to manual control. Unfortunately, on this version of the equipment, there's no alarm that goes off to alert us that the autopilot's been cancelled. So in theory, the Vulcan just drifts without any input from the crew. In our case, he's going to say it must have drifted lower until we glanced off the rocks, ripping the elevons off on one side."

Susie looked puzzled.

"So what's this group captain's theory? That Millie did it deliberately?"

"That's one option, although he says he's minded to leave it out. But someone, and by someone I mean Mark Kilton, must have suggested to him that Millie did it to trigger a manual intervention from us, which he'd then blame on Guiding Light to prove his point. It's a neat theory, I'll give him that."

"Rob, is there any chance Milford was that desperate? Maybe he was wrong about Guiding Light, but felt too committed to his theory. Could he have done something like this?"

"Absolutely not. No."

"He was your friend, Rob. Are you being honest with yourself?"

"I promise you, it's beyond any possibility that he would have done it deliberately. And frankly, I don't buy for one second he did it accidentally."

"But yet they found the switch in the off position. Do you have any reason to suspect this group captain of anything? You think he's working with Kilton?"

Rob thought for a moment. "It's possible, I suppose, but doesn't seem likely. Look, I can't explain it, but I'm certain of a few things. Millie didn't switch it off. The system failed. And someone is covering that up to keep the project going, despite everything we should know about it."

They stood in silence for a moment. The light was fading, and Salisbury's street lamps were starting to illuminate.

"Before we go any further," said Susie, "let's examine your options. Firstly, the earlier incident you mentioned. Why not use that to have the project grounded? Tell them you regret agreeing with Kilton and get everyone else on board. Go in as a team. Go straight to the station commander."

Rob shook his head. "The other people on that flight are dead or gone. Millie and Steve Bright are dead, Brian Hill was effectively sacked from TFU for insubordination. And..."

"And?"

"I'd have to say I lied, which doesn't make me a good witness. Plus, Kilton was right. We had no evidence, anyway. Millie wasn't running a tape. I just can't see Periwinkle overruling Kilton based on my say-so."

"Periwinkle's the station commander?"

"Yes."

"OK." Susie took a deep breath. "Let's say you're Millie, coming to me with ... what, exactly? That sheet of notes? Is that the evidence I need to take upstairs at my place? I can tell you the burden of proof for corruption is pretty high when you're dealing with a national security project that reports directly to Whitehall."

"The answer's in there somewhere, I'm sure of it. I just need to decode it. Where is the box now?"

"Back at the B&B, but they strictly forbid visitors of the opposite sex after 6PM. It's Saturday tomorrow. How about you come to me in the morning?"

He nodded.

"There's one more thing, Rob. I can't promise I'll be here next week. Even telling them the project's running again might not change their minds. As a matter of fact, I think they're scared of this one. It's a huge deal. We go in guns blazing, making serious accusations... We would need to have solid gold evidence."

"I can't let him down again."

"I know. But the focus is now on your black-and-white evidence. Nothing more, nothing less. It can't be about your remorse, Rob."

26

SATURDAY 2ND JULY

The B&B was a red brick Victorian semi. Rob found a parking space close by and walked the short distance, feeling self-conscious in his RAF uniform.

An elderly woman opened the door; she wore a pinny and had rollers in her hair. Her eyebrows raised as she took in the uniform.

"Mr Attenborough?"

Susie appeared behind her.

"Hello, Robert."

"You didn't tell me your brother was an RAF pilot, my dear," Mrs Holleroid said.

"Oh, did I not? He's the family hero."

Rob followed Susie upstairs to the first room on the left. She shut the door and then put her finger to her lips and whispered. "The old bat will listen for a bit."

Rob nodded.

"How was dad when you saw him?"

"Fine, yes. On excellent form."

"Right. So making a good recovery from the heart attack?"

Rob nodded. "Yes." He whispered. "I'm not very good at this."

She switched on a small transistor radio. A man was reading a tennis match report from Wimbledon.

Standing by the bed, Susie lifted the mattress and retrieved two black leather pouches. She spread the contents of Millie's box over the bed.

"Why the bloody uniform? It's Saturday."

"I had to tell Mary something. I told her I had to work."

Rob created separate piles for the papers.

The technical documents, the most damning to possess outside TFU, were straight from the project folders. But they contained no obvious clues.

The data sheets were more promising. Two large printouts containing lines of numbers, some of them were circled.

"I remember these. We saw them early in the project. They came back from DF Blackton."

"What do the numbers mean?" Susie asked.

"They're height readings from the laser. They're sent to some sort of magic box that sits between Guiding Light and the autopilot. If I remember rightly, just one reel of tape produced a foot-high pile of paper, so this is just a few seconds' worth."

"That's a lot of numbers for a few seconds."

"The only fact I really remember is that the laser reported half a million height readings every hour."

Susie picked up the sheet of Millie's handwriting and placed it between the two of them.

Rob stared at Millie's equations and notations.

Again, his eyes went to the bottom of the page and the underlined *8.75.*

"This looks like a conclusion. The summary of what he was looking for. I just don't know what kind of conclusion."

Susie walked around the room. The radio now played classical music.

"Explain something to me. These tapes…" She pointed at the two cardboard sleeves. "You mentioned Millie recording something yesterday, when you talked about the first incident."

"That's how we got all these height readings. Millie recorded the numbers on the reels. We sent them off to DF Blackton and they checked everything. But that was more at the start of the project. In the early days we didn't engage the autopilot. We just flew about with the laser running, collecting readings so the technicians could look at them."

"Look at them? What does that mean? Did they play them?"

"Sort of. They have a powerful computer which looks at them and makes sense of it all." Rob picked up one sleeve and tipped the reel onto his hand. "Millie definitely became more interested in these after the incident."

"Rob, is it possible Millie was creating tapes for his own assessment of Guiding Light? Is this them?" Susie held up the two reels from the box.

"It's possible, but those two tapes would hold a maximum of forty minutes' flying time. Doesn't seem like a lot."

"Could there be more tapes? Somewhere at West Porton?"

"I doubt it. Firstly, he'd have to have dozens for anything meaningful and secondly, what's the point of having them at West Porton? We can't read them. As far as I know, only the DF Blackton computer can do that."

"So, he must have had some help on the inside. That must be it. Someone at DF Blackton, outside the official channels." She picked up the sheet of handwritten notes. "And this was the result."

"You think that's possible?"

"I'll make inquiries at HQ, see who we have close to DF Blackton. There's usually someone on the inside for us when it comes to weapons manufacturers. Meanwhile, you sniff about inside TFU. We need to stay one step ahead of this Kilton person. It would be useful to know what he has on Millie." Susie moved to the bed and shuffled the papers together. "Are you ready for this next phase, Flight Lieutenant? It may run counter to everything you've been taught about following orders."

"I'm here, aren't I?"

"Yes, you are."

Susie slipped the first batch of sheets into the pouch.

"Still, something's not quite right, is it?" She turned over the next batch.

"What?"

"Why hasn't this mystery person helping Millie said anything? I mean, they must have heard the news, but they haven't come forward? They know something's wrong. They've seen men killed, but they haven't raised any alarms."

―――――

PROFESSOR LEONARD BELKIN looked out across the Atlantic Ocean. It was overcast and grey. In the distance, plumes of rain swept across the sea from the low cloud. For the first time since his arrival a week ago, the westerly breeze brought a distinct chill.

He would light a fire today.

Heading back toward the cottage, he used a stick to keep steady on the uneven ground.

He wore a pair of binoculars on a leather strap around his neck; they bumped on his chest as he ambled up the gentle slope. At the top of the plateau, he paused and caught his breath before heading to the cottage by the old lighthouse.

After removing his binoculars and outer layers, he looked around for kindling and spied a newspaper.

As he unfolded *The Daily Telegraph*, something caught his eye.

Lions Thrash Out of Sorts Australia.

He fished out his reading glasses and checked the date of the paper. 6th June 1966. He wasn't much of a newspaper reader anymore, but he couldn't resist the details of a successful Lions tour down under, even if it was nearly a month out of date. He left it on the kitchen table, and rummaged in the bag Callum had handed him on the mainland. Inside, he found Saturday's paper.

He picked it up and leafed through, sticking to his routine of avoiding the day-to-day ructions of politics and crime that seemed to pervade every page.

He moved to the open fire and scrunched up the large middle pages.

The travel section had a picture of a beach in Beirut. He stared at the image of the Bristol Hotel and wondered if twenty-four years in a row was enough for Lundy.

He screwed up the sheet and pressed it into the fireplace. Eventually he came to the last of the paper: the inside of the first and last pages.

Cricket scores on the right, news of a successful Gemini space rocket launch on the left.

He screwed the sheet up without turning it over to look at the front page.

The fire had a bed of old ash, which was perfect for building on. He pushed the scrunched up balls into a base layer.

Finally, he added a few twigs before fishing out a small log from the basket, placing it on top of the pile.

He rummaged in the wood basket for the packet of Swan Vestas matches.

Holding the lighted match against the newspaper, the flames took hold. The paper curled up quickly with the heat, revealing an RAF hat and a pair of eyes looking out at him, before the fire quickly consumed it.

Belkin paused for a moment, before using a stick to push the log further into the centre of the growing fire.

Standing up was an Olympian effort.

He put a hand out to the wall to help his balance, before sitting at the wooden dining table in the centre of the room. After balancing his strongest reading glasses on the end of his nose, he settled down to read of the Lions' heroics down under.

27

SUNDAY 3RD JULY

"You're not authorised to contact anyone at West Porton."

Susie sighed. Roger hadn't answered this time. Instead, she'd been connected with a more senior desk officer.

"I had to initiate contact. May saw me leave the house. He also turned up at the peace camp, twice. He nearly compromised me."

"I see. And he was working with Milford?"

"Sort of. They worked on the project together, but May didn't share his concerns. So we are drawing a bit of a blank at the moment. But the tapes that went to Blackton will hold the answer."

The man paused. "The Service has someone there who will spot anything out of the ordinary with the mainframe computer. It's a prized asset and under a great deal of scrutiny. Best keep your distance. They're twitchy about this one."

"So I understand."

"This is your first field case, isn't it?"

"Second, actually."

"Well, be careful."

He hung up.

Susie strolled around a quiet Sunday afternoon Salisbury, going over her training.

Pay attention to anything out of place, however insignificant. Try to picture what's considered normal, what routines people follow, then investigate anything out of the ordinary.

―――――

BACK AT THE B&B, a parcel was waiting for her.

She broke the seal on the pouch and pulled out a set of personnel records.

So, Mark Kilton had an MI5 file. A red flag.

It dated from the BAC TSR-2 project cancellation. They observed Kilton to have had contact with Number Ten through back channels. It was a brief note and nothing came of it.

Susie made her own notes.

Ambitious and prone to step outside protocols?

She read his official service record.

Fighter pilot in the war. Battle of Britain, North Africa, Malta. By D-Day, he was at Bentley Priory.

Early jet test pilot after the war, commanded one of the first squadrons to equip with Meteors. Went through the Empire Test Pilots' School. Promoted to squadron leader. And then...

Odd. His career faltered at that point. Desk jobs in London. Then, suddenly in 1965, he's promoted and handed the Royal Air Force Test Flying Unit as its founder commanding officer.

She checked the date on the MI5 note about TSR-2.

So that was his reward.

The personal side of the file was brief. Wife, two children. Son died aged eleven from sepsis, daughter married with a baby somewhere in Hampshire. Wife Margaret died in 1965. Last year.

Still raw?

But nothing else. No debt, no financial impropriety. None of the things she might expect to find in the circumstances.

She lay back on the bed and let the information wash over her, allowing her mind to roam.

A dead child, a dead wife. God knows how many dead pals from the war.

That's a lot of death to live with.

After completing her coded notes, Susie moved the papers to the floor and lay back on her bed. She closed her eyes and allowed the sounds from the garden to float through her mind.

She spent a few minutes shifting through her immediate thoughts, closing off the day-to-day until she was ready. In the quiet of a first floor room in a semi-detached B&B on the edge of Salisbury, she went through everything that had happened, moment by moment.

Her eyelids glowed yellowy-orange as the diffused sunlight filtered through the net curtains and fell on her face.

The answers lie in the shadows. Something that was said that was not quite right. Someone in a room who shouldn't have been there.

The 'recall' sessions in training had been marred by men giggling. An eccentric former MI6 tutor taught them a technique to pull memories from hidden parts of your brain. Most of the men dismissed it as hokey. But Susie liked the idea of something that could give her answers.

The tutor had described it as a cross between meditation and self-hypnosis, insisting that the subconscious memory held a vast amount of information hidden from conscious thought.

He had urged them to let their minds roam freely.

Don't force it.

Don't try to remember anything specific.

Let your mind think for itself.

Susie often practised alone in her tent. She always came away refreshed, even if she hadn't been searching for anything.

She learned the trick was to follow rather than push. The instructor likened it to picking out the faintest of stars in the night sky by looking just away from them, allowing them to register in peripheral vision.

Thinking about something else, when you were keen to learn more about a particular event, was counterintuitive, but it worked.

She steadied her breathing, becoming conscious of her chest rising and falling.

A van clattered in the distance, trundling over uneven cobbles.

Susie allowed the man-made noise to mix with the birdsong until it drifted beyond her hearing range.

Her mind felt cluttered and busy. She'd learned a lot in eight days.

The newspaper where she'd first read of the crash floated into view. She went forward to conversations with May, then backward to the peace camp visits he'd made.

That look on his face. Desperation? No, something else. Determination. Words, images, sounds, all floated by. She resisted the temptation to concentrate on any one thing, allowing the flow of thoughts to continue unfettered.

After several minutes, she sat up and made two notes.

Number. Who?

Tapes off West Porton. How?

She curled up, this time for a nap.

The image of Rob May's face was back in her mind.

Frightened and weighed down.

He was pinning much on her ability to help him. But she had so little to go on, and the man who knew everything was dead.

The only thing she could see clearly was the A33 back to London.

28

MONDAY 4TH JULY

"Friday? Is that possible?" Red Brunson asked.

Kilton turned over a piece of paper with a series of boxes. Each one represented a flight, concluding on Friday that week.

Rob's head spun.

"Two flights a day until Thursday morning," Kilton explained. "The final flight, Friday afternoon, with DF Blackton in attendance, will be ceremonial. Upon landing, we'll hand over the signed documents to the Ministry and it's done. Guiding Light can move into production."

"What about the required project hours?" Rob said.

"You look pale. May. Are you feeling alright?"

"Yes, it's just I thought we had nearly a hundred hours left?"

"That was before the break-in and before we discovered exactly what Millie was up to."

The room went quiet.

"What I'm about to tell you stays in this room." Kilton rose from his seat and closed the office door. "An audit of the blank tapes delivered from DF Blackton revealed more than sixty missing."

"Missing?" said Brunson.

"Missing. They haven't been returned to Cambridge. They're not in our cabinets or safe. Every square inch of West Porton has been searched, but we've found only two of them, despite widening the search to Milford's married quarter."

"Why would they be there?" Brunson asked. For the first time, there was a hint of confrontation in Red's question.

"Because the two we did find were hidden in Millie's locker." Kilton locked eyes with Brunson, as if challenging him to come back with another question. "The Blackton computer read one tape. It contained records that matched one of the project flights. And yet, the official reels for the flight are safely with the rest, signed in by Millie."

"I don't understand," said Brunson. "So, Millie forgot to log a couple of tapes? So what?"

"Not just the odd tape, Brunson. Sixty reels are missing. That's twenty hours of secret Guiding Light material that's now... god knows where. We have to assume the worst. We have to assume it's in the hands of an illegal third party. And so, with the project compromised, the Ministry has agreed to fast-track the remaining phase. We know the system was disconnected at the time of the crash, so there's no reason not to proceed. There's still a chance the UK can secure the export order to the United States before any of this becomes public."

"Why would Millie do something like that?" Red asked.

"Misguided intent, at best. Financial gain, at worst."

Red leant back in his chair and shook his head.

"Millie's funeral," Rob said quietly to himself.

Kilton frowned. "What?"

"Friday. The final flight and the handover. That's the day of Millie's funeral."

Kilton gathered his papers. "That's why it's scheduled for the afternoon, May. The funeral's at 11AM." He stood up and headed for the door. "One more thing," he said, turning back to the room, "we don't believe Millie was acting alone. Be alert. Anything out of the ordinary, any suspicions about anyone, you come straight to me."

Kilton walked out, closing the door behind him, leaving Red and Rob alone.

Rob didn't have to check the schedule; he knew he would be down to fly a Guiding Light trial. Possibly two.

"It's you and me, kid," said Brunson, studying the papers. "Back in a Vulcan. You ready for this?"

"What choice do I have?"

"Listen, if you don't want to do it, you need to say something."

Rob toyed with the tasking paper. "And then what happens? How do you think he would react?"

"I'm not sure, but he can't force you to fly."

"I'd be out of TFU by the end of the day."

"Probably."

Neither man said anything for a moment. Red leaned forward on his seat and folded his arms on the table. "You should be stronger from this. Not weaker," he said.

"I'm sorry?"

"I was like you, not that long ago."

"Like me?" Rob raised an eyebrow.

"Sort of. I was under-confident, worried I would be found out as not good enough."

Rob felt hurt.

"I can see it in your eyes. You were just growing out of it when the crash happened. But listen, something similar happened to me, back in the States."

"You had a crash?" Rob asked.

"No. Not exactly." Red looked away. "It was worse actually. A major blunder, and it was my fault." He snapped his head back. "Listen, you know the world we live in, I can't tell you any details, but afterwards, once I'd thought it all through, I became more confident, not less. These moments, these brushes with death, they test us and we pass or fail. If you've survived, which you have, you've passed. That makes you stronger. Honestly, you wouldn't have recognised me when I arrived at Edwards, but when I came here, I reinvented myself. Drew myself up to my full height, as it were." He nodded at

Rob. "You my friend, need to do the same. I can see that it's eating at you. Time to punch it away buddy."

Rob looked carefully at Red. His mind spinning. Red had got it all wrong. This wasn't about his flying confidence. But Red was trying to help him.

Could he say something?

Was it time to bring someone else in?

He leaned forward, opened his mouth to speak.

Then he heard Susie's voice in his head.

He gave a quick nod.

"You're right. Let's go flying."

"Attaboy."

They moved to a spare desk and planned the route.

After a couple of minutes, Kilton approached with Dave Berringer. Rob recognised the young air electronics officer from a few flights in the Shackleton earlier in the year, but they didn't know each other well.

"Dave's been in the Vulcan and instructed on the procedures, so should be up to speed." He turned to Rob. "Can I have a word?"

Rob put his chinagraph pencil down and followed the boss toward his office. They stopped just outside and stood next to the doorframe.

"I know Millie was a father figure to you, and I'm sorry. But sometimes our parents aren't right about everything. Sometimes they hide things from us. My advice? It's time to let him go. There's more at stake here. Something bigger than both of us."

"Yes, boss."

"We get these hours flown, no lower than one thousand feet. Blackton will scrutinise every moment of every flight. On Friday, we sign it off. *You* sign it off. It will be the biggest moment in TFU's short history and it won't be forgotten. You won't be forgotten."

THE FIRST OF the four Olympus engines wound up to deafening roar status.

Dave Berringer interrupted the static whine on the intercom, muttering to himself as he struggled with the magnetic tapes.

Rob isolated the rear bay, so they didn't have to listen.

He got a good start on all four engines.

The jet was on the edge of the apron, away from TFU. It had been overhauled prior to the Guiding Light installation; it smelled like a new car.

Rob called up ATC and requested taxi.

Brunson, in the left hand seat, exchanged hand signals with the marshallers before shifting the jet from its haunches and swinging her around to head out to the active runway.

Rob spotted Kilton in his day uniform standing on the apron watching them.

They lifted off into the mainly blue sky and banked immediately right. Rob glanced down at the remnants of the peace camp.

Forty minutes later, they let down over Northumberland.

Brunson held the aircraft steady at one thousand feet as they approached the Union Bridge. There was a familiar jolt as Guiding Light took over.

Rob grabbed the control column.

"Easy, buddy." Rob looked across; Red stared at him.

"I'm OK."

He stared ahead, watching every rise and fall of the nose.

Poised to hit the cancel button.

The flight continued across to Solway, where they climbed out.

Rob took over the flying and wondered why he wasn't receiving heading information, before realising he'd left the rear bay off the intercom loop. He opened it up.

"Finally," Berringer said. "I was about to climb up the ladder."

"Did you get the tapes done?" Brunson asked.

"No problem at all. Piece of piss."

It was easy to imagine Millie a few feet behind him. He wanted more than anything to chat over the intercom about whisky, card games and to promise that he and Mary would be over for both tonight.

––––––

AFTER SHUTTING DOWN, they walked back into the planning room together.

Rob queued at the equipment hatch along with the other returning crews.

Kilton's secretary Jean watched from her side office.

When he emerged back into the room and sat down to complete his logbook entry, she made her move.

"You're to report to Squadron Leader Hoskins in the chart room," she said.

Rob looked at the office next to Kilton's which contained shelves of charts covering the UK and the rest of the world. The security force had apparently commandeered it.

He stood up and closed his logbook.

"You'll need that," said Jean.

With his stomach in a tight knot, he walked toward the office, leaden-footed.

He knocked on the door and opened it.

Kilton was leaning over the desk, with the security force squadron leader studying documents.

Kilton looked up. "Come back in five minutes."

Rob's mouth was too dry to reply. He backed out and shut the door, wondering if this was all a psychological trick.

Five minutes took an eternity. Even then, no-one appeared for him.

He thought and walked back to the office, knocking and entering.

Kilton was still there, but he glanced at his watch and stood up, brushing past Rob on his way out.

"Please take a seat, Robert," Hoskins began, "this is part of the investigation into a security breach concerning the Guiding Light project."

Rob didn't respond.

"You have been a pilot, acting as commander and co-pilot for multiple flights, since the project's inception?"

"Yes."

"So you know Guiding Light inside and out?"

"I suppose so."

Hoskins made a note and looked up. "Tell me about your relationship with Chris Milford."

"We used to be close."

"It's a curious thing. Each tape of data generated by the equipment is meticulously logged. So, we have nearly two hundred and fifty already dispatched to Cambridge. Twenty-three have been logged since that last transfer and stored in the cabinet inside the station HQ. In addition, there are another thirty-nine blank tapes in the same cabinet."

Rob remained impassive.

"Which leaves sixty-four blank tapes delivered to West Porton, most of which are unaccounted for. They've simply vanished. Apart from these two."

He reached into a bag and placed two tape sleeves on the table. Rob peered down. One was marked 'Blank F1', the other 'Blank F2'. He recognised Millie's handwriting.

The man continued. "The tapes themselves are at DF Blackton in Cambridge. Their computer is not fully operational, but they've been able to read one of them and contrary to the word 'blank' on the sleeve here, it contains height readings from a recent flight. And yet it doesn't exist as a logged tape anywhere in the system."

"Yes, the boss explained all this."

Hoskins gave Rob an appraising look.

"I'm told there was simply no scope for a logging error. Would you agree with Wing Commander Kilton about that?"

"I suppose there isn't. It was a well organised process."

"You see, the lettering on the sleeves, 'F1' and 'F2', doesn't match the way the official tapes were logged. One theory is there was a parallel project going on. A separate set of tapes generated during the Guiding Light trial flights."

Rob put on a look of surprise. "How would that be possible?"

"Oh, it's quite possible," the man said, with a confident look, "with the right help."

Hoskins stayed quiet for a while, then continued. "And if these are 'F1' and 'F2', where are the A, B, C, D and E tapes, do you suppose?"

"You think there might be more?"

"I just told you, we've found just two of the sixty-four missing reels." He paused. "So you have no idea where they are?"

Rob shook his head. "Why would I?"

"Well, that brings me onto the flight information we were able to glean from one of the reels."

He turned some sheets over.

"You may not know, but the information captured by the reels includes the geographic position and time elapsed. So, with the help of Wing Commander Kilton, we have been cross-referencing with your logbook entries."

The investigator produced a chart of the north of England, with a route marked by a thick red line. Every so often along the legs between waypoints, a black cut had been drawn across, presumably where one tape ended and the next began. Rob recognised the track; it was the route they'd taken home after a low-level run that ended near Carlisle.

"The tapes produce a track that runs from a point in the Irish Sea just off the coast from Cockermouth, running south, coasting in at Rhyl and then a left turn east toward home." Hoskins placed a pen on the chart just above Shrewsbury. "This is where the tape change happened." He looked up to Rob. "Do you recognise this route?"

Rob screwed up his face in thought. "Maybe one of the northern low-level runs we did?"

The investigator nodded. "Spot on. Wednesday 22nd June. You and Speedy Johnson at the controls." He turned over a piece of paper that had all his Guiding Light flights noted.

"Well, yes, that makes sense, but the Guiding Light run ended at Carlisle." Rob leaned forward and pointed to the chart.

"I'm aware of that. So why do we have two additional tapes of data from that flight? And who decided that a simple exercise in running the Guiding Light equipment involved a long transit north and south when, according to Wing Commander Kilton, you could have flown straight from the airfield and run the trial locally?"

Rob glanced behind Hoskins at the frosted glass that marked Kilton's office. He could see a dark shadow, occasionally moving, and assumed it was the boss at his desk.

"Anything you know could help me, Robert."

"I didn't get involved in the planning. Millie ran the project. Speedy and I just flew the routes."

The officer made a note.

"Squadron Leader Johnson had a conversation with Captain Brunson later that day. Apparently, you quizzed Milford about exactly how many tapes he would produce. That seems like an odd conversation to have if your only job was to fly where he told you."

"I recall being a bit frustrated that we had such a long trip, when, as you say, we could have flown it locally. That's all."

"Anything else to add?"

"No."

Hoskins made further notes and Rob shifted in his seat.

"Finally, we have the conundrum of the missing reels. Part of that is discovering exactly how they were smuggled out of West Porton. I don't suppose you could shed any light on that aspect of this case? Did you for instance ever see Squadron Leader Milford making any unusual adaptations to his car? Perhaps creating a secret compartment that would fool the guards?"

Rob laughed.

"Something amusing about that concept?"

"Millie could barely operate the indicator in his Rover."

There was another pause. Hoskins closed the paper file and placed the tape sleeves back in his case.

"Right. Well, please continue to give it your thought."

Hoskins stood up; Rob quickly followed suit. The security officer held out his hand. As Rob shook it, Hoskins gripped it and stared at him again. Rob wondered if this was some ploy the man had seen in the movies.

"This is no time for misplaced loyalty. If anything transpires that reveals you haven't been completely forthcoming, you will be the man who takes the fall and, believe me, it will be a very, very big fall."

"I've told you everything I know."

After an uncomfortably long time, Hoskins released Rob's hand. He turned and made for the door.

"One thing occurs to me," Hoskins called after him.

Rob reluctantly turned back.

"You haven't attempted to defend Squadron Leader Milford, and you don't appear particularly surprised about these accusations. Did you suspect this was happening all along?"

"I think I'm still in shock, to be honest. But no, I don't think there is any way on god's earth that Christopher Milford was a traitor, if that's what you're asking."

Rob left the room, and loitered for a second, just outside the door. He needed to talk to Susie, but it wasn't even 2PM.

Five and a half hours until his next arranged meeting with his new partner. Before that, he needed a drink.

He sat at Millie's desk and willed time to speed up.

———

FINALLY, in the bar with the returning crews, Rob recognised JR from the Maintenance Unit with a few of his colleagues. In another corner were the air traffickers. It looked like a special occasion, but then he noticed one woman with puffy eyes.

"Bright's girl," Brunson said. "Steve Bright. He was walking out with her. June's her name. I think."

The enormity of the crash washed over him again. A young woman, whose name he didn't know, in tears, her life torn apart.

The smell of the beer and smoke made him nauseous.

He was an interloper. He shouldn't be there.

"I have to go. Sorry."

He got up and hurried to the door.

———

AFTER DINNER, when Rob had left for the mess to plan Millie's wake, Mary finished the washing up and prepared to go out for a walk.

She needed to clear her head.

As she folded her apron and put it into a drawer, there was a polite tap at the kitchen door. She opened it.

"Hello, Mary."

It took her a moment to place Janet Laverstock. But the bouffant of blonde hair, without a strand out of place, triggered her memory.

"Hello, Janet. Is it my turn for the flower rota at church?"

Janet smiled. "No. I just wondered if we could have a chat."

Mary made Janet a glass of squash and they sat in the garden. Janet looked nervously around, as if checking they wouldn't be overheard.

"How are things?" she asked. "How is Rob coping?"

Mary sighed. "Honestly, I don't really know. He's clammed up a bit. I think he's still in shock and maybe... I think it's affected him more than he wants to admit. Admit to me, anyway."

Janet sipped her drink. "Does he have any other confidants who might help him through this?"

"The fellows at work, I suppose. He's at the mess now, as a matter of fact."

"Is he?"

"Yes, he is. Janet, what is this all about?"

"Does he have any female friends? I mean, beside Georgina and the other RAF wives? Someone younger, perhaps?"

"Janet, I don't know what you mean. If you have something to say—"

"Look, I didn't want to be the person to tell you and Mike and I have wrestled with it, but—"

"But what, Janet?"

"Mary, on Thursdays, Mike and I sometimes go to The Bell at Wyle."

————

Susie left the B&B and headed into town. She wandered past red brick terraced houses, some with front doors open. Children played in the scraps of front gardens.

An elderly man sat outside one house, on a faded wooden chair. He had sharp creases in his trousers, a moustache and side-parted wisps of hair. His eyes followed her. She gave him a smile and he nodded in return.

Susie let her mind wander. Where was the man a couple of decades ago? Did he have a good war?

As she got to the busier part of Salisbury, she found a phone box and called the Service.

"It's our very own Twiggy in the field."

"Can we dispense with the nicknames, please, Roger? I was never in your rugger team. Firstly, I'm about to meet May again. Secondly, anything from Blackton's in Cambridge?"

He rustled around with some papers.

"Your hunch is wrong. Their computer was out of action until the crash. According to our man, they resurrected it from deep maintenance to read one tape. But, as I say, that was after the crash, so it's unlikely to be your man on account of him being dead."

Her heart sunk. "Are we sure?"

"Yes, we're always sure, dear. The place has been on annual shutdown since 8th June, which means your theory doesn't work."

"Damn it."

"Time to come in from the cold. Or the warm."

"I'm about to meet May. He might have something for me."

"Well, it had better be good. All things being equal, I expect to see you in the canteen the day after tomorrow."

———

ROB ARRIVED EARLY and parked on St Ann Street before walking along the cobbled road toward the cathedral spire.

As he entered the manicured grounds, he looked up. The tallest church in the UK made even him, an experienced pilot, feel dizzy.

Scanning the area, he saw couples holding hands, a group of children kicking a ball. The sporadic benches were only sporadically occupied.

To his right, a demure figure walked casually toward him.

Still with her blonde hair, today in fawn miniskirt and a red blouse, she both stood out and blended in. Susie could have been a department store worker who had just finished for the day.

"Hello, Mr May. Shall we walk?"

She set off, he followed.

"Shall I start?" he asked, but she made a shushing noise without looking at him.

They walked on around the cathedral toward a quieter walled area on the far side. They sat down on the grass. Susie took out a cigarette and offered him one. She lit the cigarettes, using the movement to scan the surrounding space.

"I need to tell you, we were wrong about the tapes going to Cambridge. The computer's been out of action since the last official batch at the beginning of June."

"Are you sure?"

"Certain. Sorry. We're back to square one. So, I'm afraid unless you bring news of a breakthrough, I'm probably heading back to London."

"I thought we were going to do this together. You can't leave me on my own."

"We don't have anything, Rob. One sheet that hints at something, nothing more."

"Kilton's sped up the project. It will be signed off on Friday."

"As in four days' time? Shit."

"Yes. And they think Millie produced sixty of the tapes, not the twenty we thought. Kilton is using that as the reason, actually. They obviously have no idea where they are. They want to rush it out the door before it loses commercial and military value. Get the American contract signed." He shook his head and looked down. "It was awful. I had to sit there and listen to it all. He more or less accused Millie of being a traitor. And everyone's just going along with it."

Susie sighed. "That's the military way, right? All Kilton's done is ensure he's not properly supervised. He's talking directly to ministers in a government that's running out of money, desperate for foreign orders. No-one above him really knows anything." She took a long draw on her cigarette. "So you can see how this happened. You can't blame your colleagues, Rob. They've been brought up to trust and obey. Kilton says Guiding Light wasn't to blame and somehow has the investigators fooled and... you're the only one left with any direct experience of it going wrong the first time. No wonder he's finding it easy."

"Only Millie was standing up to him. But that's why we've got to continue."

"Rob—"

"No. I can't just go home. I can't just say goodbye to you and let this lie. I couldn't live with myself."

Susie put her hand on the back of his. "You might have to. We can't fix everything."

He sat up. "But we've got four days, right? Let's at least bloody try."

Susie stubbed her cigarette out on the grass and shrugged. "What have we got to go on? The trail's run cold."

She pulled out a notebook covered in what looked like Arabic letters.

"What is that?"

"A type of shorthand. We had this strange guy in training who taught us a technique to access parts of our subconscious memory. It's not that strange, really. If I ask you to name as many prime ministers as you can think of, you'll miss a few."

"More than a few."

"Right, but when I tell you the names of the ones you couldn't remember, you'll recognise most of them."

"So?"

"So... they were in your mind all along, otherwise you wouldn't have recognised the names. You just couldn't access them when you were trying to. The theory is, if you let your mind wander freely, it sometimes goes off into those areas. It can work, believe me. It's a way of recalling something you may have thought odd but then forgot. I tried it this afternoon and came up with two things we might have overlooked."

"What?"

"The tapes, especially now that we know there's sixty of them. How on earth did Millie get them out? If we crack that, we might find an accomplice."

"That's funny, it's exactly what Hoskins said."

"Hoskins?"

"The security officer Kilton has investigating Millie. What was the other thing?"

Susie looked down at her notes. "Someone gave Millie our number. Someone who was authorised to do so."

"What does that mean?"

"There's a system. The caller's given a name to ask for, so we know they've gone through a handler. He used 'AW Strutthers'. It's an older name, been knocking about for years. Could have come from anywhere, which isn't hugely helpful."

"Do you think this could be the accomplice?"

"Maybe. But no-one's contacted us since the crash, which doesn't make any sense."

After a moment, she turned to him. "Why don't you try it?"

"Are you going to hypnotise me?"

She laughed. He noticed her freckles in the setting sun.

"It's closer to meditation, but yes, it's a little like self-hypnosis. Most of my colleagues are sceptical about it, but like I say, it works for me. There's a lot of interest in eastern transcendental meditation and, frankly, we should try everything."

"So what do I do?"

"First, you have to be silent and completely relax. Allow your mind to wander. Allow it to go wherever it wants. Don't think of anything specific to start with."

Rob sat stiffly, with his knees up.

"Lie down, for goodness' sake."

He shuffled forward and lay back.

"Just let your mind wander. Tell me what you see in the sky."

"Cumulus. Scattered, maybe two eighths. Could coalesce into an overcast."

"That's not exactly what I meant. Let's try with your eyes closed."

The air was warm. Rob was aware of heat reflecting off a wall behind them. Susie remained silent. Minutes went by. He noticed distant sounds. Boys playing football. A woman talking. The birds. One bird in particular with a beautiful sing-song call. He saw Mary in the kitchen, pinny on, washing up. She looked unhappy. He was neglecting her. Red Brunson in the bar. He should have talked to him.

"Now let's take you somewhere specific," Susie said, in a soft voice. "Let's start with the flight."

His mind filled with the sound of tearing metal, of chaos and blood. Of Millie, forlorn and dying.

He sat up, panting.

She put a hand on his back.

"It's OK, it's OK. Calm down. I'm sorry, that wasn't very clever of me. It's too raw. Let's leave it. Lie back down. Let's try after the flight. When you first realised something was up. Go back then, put yourself in the room and let your mind explore."

He lay down. For a while he didn't think about the moments after the flight. Instead, he listened to the birdsong again. The talking woman was gone, but the boys were still kicking a ball about.

He found himself back in TFU after the crash.

Red's squeeze of his arm.

Buddy, tough situation...

Other men avoiding eye contact.

Kilton.

Officious. Efficient. Barking orders.

We drink tonight for the men. You need to be there. So, come back. Understood?

He drove to Georgina's.

Georgina's.

The house.

The shaft of sunlight. The dust. Georgina being brave, but with sore, red eyes.

Mary, kind and tactile. Her hand on his shoulder the whole time.

And someone else. A man in a sports jacket.

Charlie.

In his father's hand-me-down.

The dining room.

A word floated into his mind.

Oxford.

Charlie said something about...

He sat up suddenly.

"Charlie."

"Who's Charlie?" Susie said, raising herself up.

"Oxford."

"What about Oxford?"

"At the Milfords' after the crash, I said to Charlie, their son, 'I am so pleased you got to see your father a couple of weeks ago', because I knew Millie had visited him. But Charlie said he hadn't seen him since Easter. It was odd. I double-checked with him and he looked at me like I was mad, questioning when he last saw his father. But Millie had been very clear. He went to Oxford to see Charlie. He missed a day out with us for it."

"And that was unusual?"

"It was. I think Georgina was taken by surprise that he suddenly went off to visit their son. Then Charlie tells me he never even saw him."

"This could be it, Rob. It sounds like a cover story. So, where did he actually go?"

"I don't know."

Susie patted him on the knee. "See, I told you this works. Let's do some more."

Rob felt exhausted. "I'm worn out."

"We don't have time to schedule a session for next week."

"Fine." He lay back down and closed his eyes, allowing his mind to wander a second time. But the adrenaline rush from his first discovery made everything cloudy.

He sat up. "It's no good. My mind's too busy now."

"OK, well, let's think this through. Millie fibs to his wife and disappears for a day using a cover story about visiting Charlie. Is this the day he delivered the tapes? When was it?"

"Quite a while ago. I remember it being not long after the first incident. I think that makes it far too early to have delivered the tapes. He wouldn't have had time to record sixty of them."

"It must be connected, though. We need to know where he went. You have literally no idea?"

Rob cast his mind back. He couldn't remember much about the morning. He thought maybe Georgina had told them Millie wasn't coming...

But then there was the evening...

"We went to a cocktail party that night. Millie drove. He acted odd."

"What do you mean exactly?"

Rob shook his head when he remembered. "The guards stopped us. He was nervous. Really nervous." His eyes widened. "*Christ*. He must have had the tapes in the car."

"Why on earth would he have the tapes, going into West Porton for a cocktail party? Wasn't he trying to get them out of there?"

"Don't know."

Rob thought through the evening. The crowded room, the heat. The mayor's wife.

"He went off at one point. Said he left his watch in TFU."

"Right, so he was returning something. Tapes, maybe. This is good, Rob."

"But that's it. I didn't question him."

"Did he ever talk to you about it? Did he ask for your help?"

Rob studied the grass. "Yes, but I closed down the conversation pretty quickly."

"Was there anyone else at TFU he would confide in?"

Rob shook his head. "No. Everyone liked Millie, but I think I was the closest. Funnily enough, Kilton was probably the next nearest. They served together in the war. At Tangmere, I think."

Susie offered Rob another cigarette and held out a lighter. He leaned forward and spoke with the cigarette in his mouth.

"He served everywhere, actually. All the old boys knew him. Even the graveyard—"

Rob stopped lighting his cigarette and looked up.

"What is it?" Susie asked.

"There's a man, an ancient fossil from the Maintenance Unit. We call it the Graveyard. JR. Nice bloke. Friendly, just Millie's sort. He said something odd to me. Something about Millie, but I can't for the life of me remember what."

"When, Rob? When did he say something?"

"The night of the crash in the bar. I was drunk. And upset. I remember being confused. Damn it, what did he say?"

Susie let him rack his brains in silence for a minute before speaking again.

"Well, why don't you ask him?"

"Is that safe? I've avoided saying anything to anyone at TFU."

"He's not at TFU, is he? And anyway, all you're doing is asking what it was he said to you."

Rob looked at his watch. "He lives in the mess. I could even catch him tonight."

"Then let's fly, flight lieutenant."

———

THE MESS BAR was busy for a Monday night.

Rob surveyed the room.

At the bar; a white-coated steward regarded him expectantly.

"Is Squadron Leader Richardson in?"

Without answering, the steward pointed to the far wall where JR sat with two others Rob recognised from his few dealings with the Graveyard.

As he approached, the three men stood up, as if he was a senior officer or a woman.

"Hello, Rob." JR reached out his hand, followed by the two other pilots who gave him a warm greeting.

"JR. Do you mind if I borrow you for a moment?"

JR gave the others a look, and they headed off to the bar.

"When we spoke on the night of the crash, you said something to me about Millie. Do you remember?"

Although JR's eyes were sunken well into his head, with bags that looked like rolled up carpets, he still had a twinkle. Just like Millie.

"I wondered when you would come to me."

Rob stared at him for a moment. "You're the accomplice?"

"Ha! I'm not sure I'm that. But, just to be clear, this isn't an official visit on behalf of Wing Commander Kilton, is it?"

Rob shook his head. "No, it absolutely is not."

"Good. You know what this place is like. What it's become since your lot moved in, anyway. Careless talk costs lives, and all that."

"Yes, sorry about that."

"Not your fault. Anyway, I know you and Millie were close."

"We were."

"And yet, it appears he kept something from you?"

"I think so, probably for my own good. But now I need to know."

JR looked more serious. "Is it true Millie's name is being dragged through the mud by that oaf Kilton?"

"It's nonsense, of course, what they're saying about him."

"We all know that." JR picked up his drink and looked around the bar. "But this is not a place to raise doubts about the truth unless you're well-armed."

"So, you were helping him?"

JR waggled his head. "Sort of. Just one trip. He'd officially asked to go to Wyton for some meeting, but he asked us to take him to

Abingdon instead. He obviously didn't want the visit on any official log."

"Abingdon? When?"

JR screwed up his face, which became a sea of wrinkles. "Early last week. Monday, I think."

"What did he do there? Who did he meet?"

"No idea, I'm afraid. Like with you, Millie didn't want to involve anyone else unnecessarily. I just waited for him."

"Abingdon..." Rob said to himself.

"He was there for nearly three hours, from memory. We decided not to make any logbook entries, so I can't be certain."

"Did he have anything with him? A large bag, for instance?"

JR thought again. "Yes. Like a holdall."

Rob sat back.

"I'd look through a list of units at Abingdon if I were you," said JR. "He must have met with someone there?"

"We will, thank you."

"We?"

Rob looked around the room and thought for a moment. JR was the picture of a trustworthy man. But he knew he couldn't take any chances.

"I probably shouldn't say too much. The same reason Millie didn't involve you more than he had to. You've been very helpful. Can I buy you a drink?"

"No need. The bar's about to shut. To be honest, Robert, if you're helping a cause that's close to Millie's heart and it pulls the rug from under Kilton, I'm happy. He's bad news."

"It's taken me a long time to see that."

They stood up. JR shook his hand. "It's not your fault, it's the way the system works. But Robert..."

"Yes?"

"Tread carefully."

———

SUSIE SAT IN HER CAR, exactly where she said she would be, opposite the church in Amesbury. Rob could see the red glow of her cigarette as he approached.

He opened the back door and climbed in.

She looked around in surprise.

"What are you doing?"

"I thought it would be better?"

"Well, it looks odd. Get in the front."

They both laughed.

"We'll make a field agent out of you yet, Flight Lieutenant May. But there's a way to go."

Once he was in the passenger seat, she drove off.

"Too suspicious, sitting in a parked car in the middle of the night. So, what did you find out?"

"The Maintenance Unit helped him, but just once. Last Monday. The old boy I mentioned. JR. He took him on an unrecorded trip to RAF Abingdon. And he had a large bag."

"Well done, Rob. Who did he meet?"

"They don't know. It was pretty much an air-taxi service. They waited for around three hours and then took him back. JR suggested I look up a list of the units at Abingdon as a starting point."

"And then what? We call them? That's fraught with danger."

"What else can we do?"

"Where's RAF Abingdon?"

"It's an old station near Oxford."

They looked at each other.

"Oxford!" Susie said.

"A coincidence?"

"My organisation doesn't believe in coincidences, Rob."

"So, Millie drove there at the beginning of June and then flew in with a large holdall last Monday."

"The tapes?"

Rob nodded. "Has to be. It was so clever of Millie. He *flew* the bloody things out. No-one searches us when we fly. Quite brilliant."

Susie smiled.

"What's funny?"

"My prodigy's outstanding work."

The car briefly mounted a verge and swerved back onto the Tarmac.

"Forget this. I can't drive and talk." She pulled over into the entrance to a field and parked the car completely off the road, masked by a break in the hedge.

"Let's have a walk and work out our next move."

She opened a five-bar gate and immediately recognised the field.

"Huh?"

"What?" Rob asked.

"Don't you recognise it?"

Rob looked across toward the airfield double fence. Pieces of discarded tents lay on the ground, along with the odd piece of litter.

They began walking toward a circle of logs in the centre. "What exactly did you do here?" Rob asked.

"What you might imagine. Listening, mainly. The services get an instinct for groups that can threaten national security, and the first thing is knowledge. We need to know what's going on. But, as you're finding out, we don't really intervene very much. It's more a case of tipping off the local police, which is what happened here."

The blackened remains of a bonfire sat in the centre of the log circle.

They sat down on the largest log.

"So, it was you who returned the Guiding Light material that was stolen?"

"Well, first I helped steal it, but then... Yes, I made sure it didn't go very far."

He laughed.

"It was wild. We cut the fence, scrambled across the airfield, and broke into the toilets. Took us a while to work out they were a dead end. It was a bit of a farce, but it was a pretty good job in the end, and well targeted. So, worth me being there."

"Like special forces, behind enemy lines," Rob said.

She lit a cigarette.

An eerie orange glow from the airfield lights softened her features and cast dim, elongated shadows along the ground.

"I've enjoyed it more than anything else I've done," she said. "Mind you, this is only my second year."

"At MI5?" Rob asked, still not sure she'd ever confirmed it.

"Yes, Robert. MI5. We tend to call it Box Five Hundred. Box for short, or the Security Service. They say MI5 in books and films, so we don't use it."

"Box Five Hundred?"

She shook her head. "Don't ask me. I've no idea where it comes from. No doubt one of the boys I trained with would be happy to lecture me on it if I ever asked. But I'd rather be here in a field than sitting in a cramped office in Mayfair with them. Even if they do know every second of the Service's history."

"Why did they choose you to send out?"

Susie shrugged. "I'm a young girl who looks like she might be a hippie peace campaigner. That's the sole reason. Still, it's worked out well. I'm on to my second job now, thanks to you. Thanks to Millie, to be precise." She looked around before stubbing out her cigarette. "Right, to business. We know Millie has a contact in the Abingdon area. If we find that person, we can learn whatever it was he found out. We may then have the evidence needed to blow the whistle."

"I can get a list of units from an Air Force directory tomorrow."

Susie shook her head. "No. We can't just start calling and using Millie's name. As soon as that gets back to Kilton, we put him onto the same trail. That would be a world of complication we don't need."

"Then what?"

She faced him. "You have to retrace his steps."

"What?"

"I'm serious. It's the best way. The most accurate, and the one that involves the fewest other people. Could you land at RAF Abingdon? Would that be a normal thing to do?"

Rob exhaled. "Maybe. If I was in a single seater. Something like a Hunter. I could call it a practice diversion. The trouble is, I'm down to fly the Vulcan this week. Every day."

"What about JR? Can he fly you in? That would be better. He can take you exactly where Millie went. That's what you need to do. You need to stand where he stood. You're bound to find something. Some clue to where he actually went."

"But how would I do that? I'm expected in work every day, all day."

"Aren't you ever sick?"

He put his head in his hands. "Christ, Susie, you're asking a lot. You're asking me to call in sick, then sneak onto the station, fly off with a Maintenance Unit pilot, land at another RAF station and then... god knows what."

"It's no more than Millie did. Alone. Without your help or anyone else's at TFU."

He sat in silence for a while.

Susie touched his hand. "Rob, why are you doing this?"

"For Millie, I guess."

"And for you, right? You're also doing this for yourself."

"What do you mean? I'm being selfish?"

"Not at all. I'm just pointing out that you're carrying a lot of guilt and I think this is a way out, at least I think you've convinced yourself it is. Try to imagine for a moment that you back down now, before we've tried everything. You'll have the rest of your life to reflect on that decision and, believe me, that stuff can eat away at you." She gestured to the remnants of the peace camp. "There was a woman here who had some sort of regret inside her. Something she didn't want to think about. I was never sure what it was, but I think she lived with it every day. She was cold and distant most of the time. You could mistake it for confidence, but when that gas bomb hit, she crumbled. Unable to cope. Funnily enough, it was the most human I ever saw her. And let me guess, it's the same for Mark Kilton? Cold and distant? His generation, from the war, they bury so much that after a while they bury themselves. It's no way to live, Rob. This choice today, it could affect you for the rest of your life."

"It's such a gamble. So much could go wrong," Rob said quietly.

"It could. True. But living with the consequences of doing nothing and letting Kilton walk all over Millie's name and reputation might be worse for you. Save yourself from a lifetime of not being able to think about Millie and your role in his death." He winced in the shadows. "Rob, trying and failing is very different from not trying at all. You can stand up high and tell Millie you did everything in your power to honour his legacy, but giving up... That's another matter. You would be choosing to comply with an authority you know to be wrong. You'd find it hard to look in the mirror ever again."

She looked away across the field to the fences that surrounded the airfield. "My father came out of the First World War like that. Part of a generation of British men who don't look in the mirror. This whole head-down, get-on-with-it, stiff-upper-lip stuff. It has a function because it allows you to carry on in desperate times, but believe me, it's not without consequences. You'll pay the price with the rest of your life." She turned to him. "And so will your children."

The Moon crept up beyond the trees; the orange glow gave way to a silvery light that played across her face.

She reached across and brushed a tear from his cheek.

"I'll need to go back and talk to JR as soon as possible," said Rob. "This is going to take some planning."

Headlights swept across the airfield to their right, and a vehicle approached the fence. She grabbed Rob's hand and lowered him to the ground behind the trunk.

They lay still, next to each other. He basked in the warmth of her body, his heart thudding in his chest. Susie wrapped an arm around him.

The vehicle moved away and they stood up.

"You can talk to JR tomorrow. We're running out of time so don't dilly-dally."

"It might actually be easier if I go and see JR now. I've got a front door key for the mess at home."

––––––––

ROB PULLED up in front of the house; there was a light on downstairs.

He breezed in, picked up his mess keys from a set of hooks just inside the back door.

He looked across to the lounge where the light was on, and hesitated.

On the kitchen table was a half drunk cup of tea. He touched it. Still warm.

Rob stood and listened carefully, but the house was silent.

He turned and left for West Porton.

———

AFTER FIDDLING with the mess side door, he made his way along one wing to the central lobby to identify JR's room number.

First Floor, Room 12.

The place wasn't completely quiet; he could hear some laughter coming from somewhere. A few of the boys playing cards, no doubt.

Next to a batting room on the first floor was a door with the number '12', and the label *SQ LDR JL RICHARDSON DFC*.

Rob tapped gently, but got no response and tried again more firmly.

Eventually, he heard some movement. The door opened to reveal a surprised-looking old pilot in a red silk dressing gown.

"Flight Lieutenant May." JR glanced down the corridor. "Twice in one night. I suppose you want to come in?"

JR's room was large, with two single beds and a basin.

"Nice," Rob said, looking round.

"I bagged it when TFU was just a twinkle in Mark Kilton's eye. They'll get me out of it in a wooden box. Smoke?" JR offered him a silver case, opened to reveal about twenty filter tipped cigarettes.

"Thank you." Rob took a cigarette and a box of matches from the engraved case.

He took a seat in an armchair; JR perched on the end of his bed.

"What are the chances that you could replicate the trip to Abingdon with me on board?"

JR thought about it. "I don't see why not, but it's risky. A lot could have gone wrong and Millie could have ended up in very deep water. Are you happy to take that risk, even in this febrile atmosphere at West Porton?" JR raised his eyebrows.

"Yes. I am."

"Well, we've still got the Anson; but I fear it's in a few pieces at the moment. Might have it ready for Friday."

"That's too late. Can you do Wednesday?"

JR shook his head. "Not Wednesday. Station Commander's annual inspection. No flying. We'll be standing by our beds saluting. I dare say we could encourage the engineers to have it ready for Thursday, though. Best I can do."

"There are no other options over there?"

"Not really. We have a Beverley destined for the scrap heap, but it's a team effort to get that airborne and not quite the discretion you're looking for. The Twin Pioneer's dead, and I can't see it being resurrected this month. No, sorry, it's the Anson or bust, and they'll need tomorrow at the very least to get it back together. So with the inspection on Wednesday, Thursday's the best I can do."

"It's fine, JR. Incredibly kind of you, actually."

"So. How will this work?"

Rob puffed out a breath. "I haven't got that far yet. I'll have to call in sick. I can't think of anything else that would excuse me for the day."

JR nodded. "OK. But you live in the middle of a married quarter patch, surrounded by TFU officers. Won't they see you?"

"I hadn't really thought of that."

"And the main gate? Lots of eyes as the cars crawl through at that time in the morning."

Rob sagged in his seat. "As I say, I hadn't really thought it through."

JR drummed his fingers on his thigh for a moment before sitting up. "We can do this. How about I pick you up? You drive that red Healey don't you?"

"Yes."

"Far too conspicuous. Nestle into the passenger seat of my old banger. I'll come and get you. Let's choose somewhere you can walk to, away from the patch. How about that shop on Church Street? Do you know it?"

"The newsagents? Yes."

"I'll scoop you up, drive you onto the station and around to 206. Your Healey can stay in front of your house. It's not perfect, but it's better."

"Thank you, JR. You really are a different breed across that side of the airfield."

"Chap, when you've delivered thousand pounders to a heavily defended Berlin a dozen times, the odd clandestine trip around here doesn't seem so bad."

Rob stood up and held out a hand. "I don't know what to say."

"I'm looking forward to it. Nice for an old warhorse to be on operations again."

―――――

As Rob switched off the car lights in the driveway, he noticed a vehicle parked across the road with a man sat at the wheel.

He stared in his wing mirror but couldn't make out any features; just the outline of a figure.

As he locked the Healey, a terrible thought occurred.

He was being watched.

Had they followed him everywhere?

Or was this man with Susie? Protecting her? Monitoring him?

He stood by his car, unsure what to do.

If it was West Porton security, he was done for, surely?

"Bugger this."

He marched across the road.

As he approached the car, the man turned toward him and looked alarmed.

He wound down the window.

"Can I help you?" Rob said.

The man stared, mouth open, apparently at a loss.

"Who are you?" Rob said.

"I'm Derek Laverstock. We met at church a few times. My wife knows your wife."

"What are you doing here, Mr Laverstock? Are you watching me?"

Laverstock shifted in his seat.

"I think you need to speak to your wife."

Rob looked back at the house and then back to Laverstock. "What's going on?"

"Just speak to Mary, Mr May."

Rob slowly turned and walked back to their married quarter.

He found Mary exactly where he'd left her, on the sofa.

"What's going on, Mary? Why is a man called Derek Laverstock outside watching us?"

Mary stared at him for a moment and then said, "What's her name?"

"Whose name?"

Mary's face creased up into tears. She dabbed her eyes with a tissue.

Rob took a seat opposite her in the armchair.

"Oh, Mary. No. It's not what you think—"

"Really? You lied to me, Rob. You lied tonight, didn't you? I called the mess. There was no meeting to plan the wake."

"No, there wasn't. But it's not what it looks like."

"You lied on Tuesday night as well, didn't you? You weren't at the mess then. You stood in our kitchen and looked me in the eye and you lied. You lied to me."

Her voice trembled.

He stood up.

"Keep away from me."

"Mary, you've got it wrong—"

"No, Rob, I haven't." Her voice settled. Now she sounded steady, defiant. "They saw you. You've been caught. Janet and Derek from church saw you last week in a pub with her. Just the two of you. Janet thought it might be innocent, but she saw you kissing." She began to sob. "For Christ's sake, Rob. Just down the road from us, for everyone to see? And just when... just when I thought you were back. Back in our relationship. But you've betrayed me in the worst possible way."

"No, Mary, no. That's not right. It's not what you think."

As he stepped back from her, he noticed a suitcase by the front door.

"For Christ's sake, Mary, you're not going to leave, are you? You haven't even heard what I've got to say. She isn't a lover. She's helping me. The kiss was a cover. It's how she operates."

Mary stood up and snorted her contempt.

"Helping you? With what?"

"The box. She stole it."

"It's her? The CND woman? Bloody hell Rob, have you lost your mind?"

"She's not CND. She's working against them. She's helping me now. She works for..." He hesitated. If Mary was determined to leave, what if she told the Laverstocks? What if they told someone else and it got back to Kilton?

"I'm waiting, Rob."

"Look, I can't say too much and you mustn't say anything to anyone. But Mary, please trust me. *Please.*"

Mary glared at him. "How old is she? Twenty? You expect me to believe a bloody twenty-year-old girl is somehow helping you? And by the way, you don't tell me anything anyway, Rob. Not one thing and now..." She sobbed harder. "And now you're telling this twenty-year-old everything?"

Rob knelt down in front of her. "I don't know what to say, Mary. I know it looks bad, and I can see how that's hurt you. But please believe me. I haven't told you to protect you—"

She stared at him. "I'm hurt, Rob. You've betrayed me. But even before this, I was unhappy. I don't suppose you noticed, because you were never here, but things haven't been right for a long time. I thought you'd changed after the crash, but all you've done is create another life that doesn't involve me."

She walked to the front door and placed a hand on the suitcase.

"It's time to reap what you've sown, Rob. You had your chance to involve me, you chose someone else."

"Mary, no. You've got this wrong. She's helpful to me and I need help at the moment. It will be done this week, I promise, and then I'll be back. I'll never see Susie again, I promise."

Mary's face changed. The hand holding the suitcase was shaking.

"'Susie'. How lovely. I hope you and that little slut will be very happy together. How could you, Rob? How could she? Does she know what she's done?"

He moved toward her; she flinched and took a step back.

He was crying now. "Please don't back away. I'm not going to hurt you. Don't leave me. I love you, Mary."

She opened the door. This time Rob held back.

"You know what hurts the most, Rob? That's the first time you've told me you loved me in two months. Something happened to you when you joined this place. First you dumped Millie and now you've dumped me."

"That's not fair. You don't know what you're saying."

"I don't know anything, remember? Perhaps I should ask Susie what my husband's thinking."

Before he could respond, Mary disappeared into the night. He watched through the small window next to the front door as she walked to Laverstock's car. She pushed her suitcase onto the back seat and climbed into the front passenger side and held her head in her hands.

As he pulled away, Laverstock glanced back towards him.

29

TUESDAY 5TH JULY

"You're planning *what?*" Roger asked.

"It's the best way," said Susie. "He retraces Milford's steps. There's a limited number of places he could have got to from an aeroplane on the Tarmac at Abingdon."

"This is irregular. You're supposed to be keeping it low-key. You know they're jumpy about this. I can't see them going for it."

"Well, your job is to persuade them, Roger. There's something rotten here. Milford got the evidence before he was killed. We just need to identify who he was working with and the whole thing's blown open."

"Blowing the whole thing open is precisely what they're trying to avoid, Susie."

"Even if there's corruption at the centre of a UK arms project?"

"Obviously not. If that's the case, then bring it in, but you'll need irrefutable, solid evidence. Nothing less will do."

"We'll get it, if we retrace Milford's steps."

She heard shuffling at the other end of the line and then a muffled conversation. Roger must have his hand over the phone.

Eventually he came back on. "I'll ask. That's the best I can do. But don't expect them to say yes. When exactly are you planning this little jaunt?"

"Tomorrow, hopefully."

"Bloody hell. You are a firecracker."

———

TFU WAS the last place Rob wanted to be.

He pulled over while they searched his car. Guards shuffled around the Austin Healey.

Sleep had come to him eventually, in the early hours. But it was fitful and he ached with exhaustion.

"You can go, sir."

He sat motionless in the driver's seat, staring ahead.

"*Sir!*"

At TFU it was business as usual. Pilots and air crew hunched over charts and flight planning paperwork.

Men in orange vests and light blue coveralls heading out to shiny jets.

"Hey, Buddy. Wales OK?"

Red held a chart in front of him. He'd drawn a familiar line through the central valleys to Aberystwyth.

"Fine." Rob turned away.

"Don't be too enthusiastic," Red called after him. "It might catch on."

Like a robot, he pulled on his coveralls, dressed for the Vulcan and headed out.

He was co-pilot for the trip, which suited him.

At the aircraft, he waited for a member of the ground crew to open the hatch. While he did so, Rob walked around, pausing at the glass-covered laser mounted under the nose. He peered in at the swivel head, noticing for the first time an intricate series of small mirrors set inside the mechanism. A delicate system that decided their fate.

Arriving back at the hatch, he climbed in. Red strapped into the left hand seat, the mirrored visor on his USAF helmet and oxygen mask giving him the look of an illustration on the front cover of an Isaac Asimov novel.

He pulled the mask away to speak.

"All good?"

"Sorry?"

"The walkaround, Rob. All good?"

"Oh, yes."

Red's stare lingered. "You OK?"

Rob pulled on his straps. "Yes. Let's get going."

"OK, then."

Rob busied himself with procedure: checklists, radio calls, liaison with Berringer in the rear bay.

Brunson got them airborne and put the Vulcan into a smooth ascending turn to the west.

By the time they'd let down over the borders, Rob had taken the controls, glad of the distraction.

As they handed the jet over to Guiding Light, he monitored the ground ahead, noting every approaching rise and fall of the green and brown landscape.

Ready to disengage.

If something went wrong now, even at the relative safety of one thousand feet, it would save a lot of trouble. With testimony from Brunson and the others, that would surely prompt a stay of execution for the project.

But the equipment performed flawlessly, and they climbed out over the Rheidol estuary.

Rob banked the jet one hundred and eighty degrees and Brunson took over for the transit home.

Another forty minutes low-level ticked off. Another step toward the United Kingdom presenting the United States with a system to beat the Soviets and maybe even end the Cold War.

———

ROB FLEW a repeat of the track in the afternoon. This time Red supervised the low-level and he handled the transits.

At 4.45PM he walked the completed reels over to the safe, returned to his car and drove home.

He called the operator, who put him through to the Laverstock's.

"Hello?" Derek's voice.

"It's Flight Lieutenant May. Can I speak to my wife, please."

There was a pause.

"Mr May?" Janet Laverstock's voice came on the line.

"Yes. Can I speak to my wife, please?"

"She's resting."

"Can you tell her I'm on the line? She's my wife."

"I'm sorry, she's had a very difficult day and I don't want to wake her. I'll tell her you called and if she wants to speak, she will call you back."

"Excuse me, Mrs Laverstock—"

The line went dead.

He kicked the telephone table; it collapsed to the ground, taking the phone with it.

———

FOR A CHANGE of scenery and because of the outside chance she was being watched, Susie walked all the way across Salisbury and found a different phone box for her afternoon call.

The greeting with Roger was more perfunctory than normal. He wasted no time in passing on the bad news.

"Sorry, my dear. They just can't have an agent involved in such a flagrant breach of rules and with such flimsy evidence. Well. No evidence, in fact."

"For Christ's sake, Roger. Did you even try?"

"Of course I did. You know me, I can be very persuasive."

"I want to talk to them myself."

"Why? They've given their answer."

She should have gone back to London to present the case herself.

"Damn it, Roger. This is bloody ridiculous. We're onto something."

"You could have gone to Oxford to sniff about. But instead you've dragged this poor pilot into it. You weren't even supposed to contact him and yet, here we are."

"The answer's most likely at RAF Abingdon. He can get in. I can't get in."

"Well, it's academic now. They want you here tomorrow to debrief."

"Tomorrow?"

"It is a Wednesday, my dear. Sorry, did you have plans? Oh, that's right, you were going to commandeer one of Her Majesty's aircraft. Maybe you could fly home?"

She slammed the phone down and closed her eyes, struggling not to scream.

Outside the phone box, a waiting young woman gave her a startled look. Susie pushed the door open.

"Men!"

She brushed past and walked along the river toward the meeting place with Rob. She was early. A few ducks swam hopefully toward her as she took a seat on a bench facing the river. "You're out of luck," she said to them. "If it helps, you're not alone."

For ten minutes, she watched the world walk by, trying her best to calm down.

But she was angry. Undermined.

Worst of all, she knew they were wrong.

She checked her watch and walked along to The Old Mill Hotel.

Inside the low-ceilinged building, she asked for two teas and found a table outside, overlooking the mill pond.

Rob appeared along the river path from Salisbury.

He looked terrible.

"You OK?" she asked.

He shook his head, looking as if he was about to cry.

"Christ." She stood up and led him away from the hotel.

"What's happened?"

"Mary left me."

"What?"

"We were spotted, you and me. Some busybody from the church. Mary waited up for me last night. I think she'd spent the evening stewing, getting herself all worked up about it, and of course I was out with you."

"God, I'm sorry, Rob."

"What do I do?" He stopped walking and faced her. "You can fix this. You can tell her."

"Haven't you told her?"

"I said you were helping me, but she didn't believe me."

"Then what do you want me to say?

"Can't you fix it?"

"I'm not a marriage counsellor, Rob."

His face fell.

"Please talk to her for me." He sounded pitiful, in actual pain. "I don't think I can go on Thursday unless she's back."

"Thursday?"

"We can't go tomorrow. Has to be Thursday."

"Shit."

"Is that a problem? Maybe we should call it off?"

She studied him. "Let's sit down." She walked him over to the bench.

"You've changed your tune, Rob. Is this because Mary's left you, or has something else happened?"

Rob looked across the river in the direction of the cathedral. The ducks fidgeted about in the water, diving for scraps. In the distance, the cathedral clock rang for 6PM.

"It just hit home today. At TFU, it's just me. Everyone else is just carrying on as normal. Maybe I'm wrong. Is it worth it, Susie? Is it worth my marriage?"

"Rob, you're the only one left because the others are dead. Or sent to the gulags by Kilton."

He chewed a nail. Susie noted the dark bags under his eyes. It reminded her of those images of Battle of Britain pilots smoking after a flight; drained of energy and ageing by the minute.

"So many things can go wrong on Thursday, Susie. It could ruin everything and achieve nothing. And where would that leave me with Mary? I could be out of the RAF or worse." He gave her that forlorn look again. "What if Mary never comes back?"

"And what if you don't go? You stay and sign off the project and it goes into production with the same flaw that killed Millie. Can you live with that? You know Mark Kilton's done his sums. He's not an idiot. He knows people will die while this thing enters service. Even now, he's probably planning how TFU will be involved in the inquiries, quick to rule out the secret technology and blame the crews. We've already seen it with Millie. That crash should have been the end of the project, but if anything, it's emboldened him. It's shown him he can get away with the worst case scenario. And you're right. You're alone now. Millie's gone. It's down to you." She looked up at the sky and sighed. "We all have to make choices in life, Rob. As a matter of fact, I'm in a similar position."

He gave her a quizzical look.

"I wasn't going to tell you this, but the Service doesn't want us to go ahead with the flight. In fact, I've been recalled."

"So we can't go, anyway?"

"I didn't say that. I was never going on the flight. So that's still a matter for you."

"But you wouldn't be there to help me."

"I didn't say that, either. But I'm not staying around if you're half-hearted about it."

She let the statement hang in the air for a minute.

The ducks appeared to have lost hope on being fed and paddled off downstream.

"It's easy for me to walk away," said Susie. She tapped his shoulders. "But there's a lot of weight on there. I'm not sure there's any other way of shifting it."

She looked at her watch. "Look, do one more thing for me, before you make your final decision."

She pulled out her notepad and flicked through the pages of shorthand, before settling on a couple of scribbled lines. Tearing off a fresh sheet, she used a ballpoint pen to translate it.

73 Sunrise Avenue

Totton

"What will I find here?" Rob asked.

"A reminder why we're doing this."

———

THE A36 WAS QUIET. Rob pushed down on the accelerator and opened up the Healey, braking heavily as he came to a series of bends on the outskirts of Totton.

It took him several minutes to find Sunrise Avenue.

He crawled along the road, peering out of the passenger window at the odd numbers. 31, 33...

He gently sped up. 57, 59...

He glanced forward and stared at Millie's car.

Climbing out, he let his hands brush across the distinctive fins on the burgundy Rover.

He recalled the occasions he'd been in the passenger seat. The thing rolled around corners like a boat. Not great with a belly full of beer.

A door opened to his left. Georgina stood in the entrance of a small bungalow with an overgrown front garden. She wore a red pattern dress. Even among the shabbiness of her new home, she looked wonderful.

Tears welled in his eyes as he made his way up the path, stepping over long discarded children's toys.

"Hello, stranger," she said. They embraced.

She pulled back. "It's lovely to see you, dear Robert. But as I'm on the naughty list, I'm guessing this isn't a sympathy visit."

"Can we have a chat?"

She led him through to the garden. The interior of the house was in dire need of repairs. Peeling wallpaper and wonky radiators. He glanced into the kitchen as they passed and saw a small, two-ring cooker.

Charlie sat at the kitchen table nursing a mug of something.

The teenager sprang to his feet and beamed.

"Hello, Mr May."

"Please call me Rob. How are you?"

"Not great, to be frank with you."

"And that's OK, Charlie. It's OK not to be OK."

Charlie's eyes were warm as he looked at Rob. "Thank you."

"Look, when this is all over, why don't you and I spend some time together? I can tell you a bit about your father at work. Maybe a few stories he'd hope you didn't hear."

Charlie smiled. "I'd love that so much. Thank you."

Rob followed Georgina out into the garden where he was offered a cheap plastic chair. Georgina sat on a wooden stool.

The fence at the back of the garden leaned forward, having been attacked by unkempt undergrowth on the far side.

"It's not ours," Georgina said. "It's my brother-in-law's. He rented it out, but the last family left it in rather a state. I think he's hoping Charlie and I will help do it up in return for a little rent-free stay."

"They just threw you out of the married quarter?"

"They said it was a crime scene. Can you believe that?"

Rob shook his head.

"They told me while the investigation took place, everything was on hold. Including the pension."

"How are you for money?" Rob asked. Georgina gave him a look that said it all.

"It's hard enough for me, but it's been terrible for Charlie. Can you imagine what he's thinking? He adored his father. He was his hero. But now? I hate that he thinks Millie could have done anything wrong." She dabbed her eyes with a hanky.

"He did nothing wrong, Georgina. But it's... complicated." He waited for her to recover herself. "Can I ask you some questions? Do you remember that Saturday when Millie went to Oxford to see Charlie and we went shopping?"

"I do. And I know he didn't go. I suspected as much, but knew better than to ask. It's funny, after he died I didn't think so much about the conversations we had. I thought more about the ones we didn't have. I barely knew anything about his work these last few years. It must be hard to hide so much. Damn Kilton and his vale of absolute secrecy."

"So, you didn't ask him anything?"

"No. I let it go, like so much. Charlie told me you asked him, though. I didn't know what to say. Do you know where he went?"

"Not exactly, no. Was there anything odd about him, leading up to the crash?"

She thought for a bit and looked off in to the distance. "There was something off, I could sense it. In fact, I thought it was about you."

"Me?"

She smiled. "He loved you, Rob. Loved having you around. You made him feel young. He was so pleased you'd picked him out as a friend, when you had all those glamorous flyers queuing up to rub shoulders with.

"But then, something changed. You drifted away, which was fine of course. Understandable. Ultimately, I think he understood it. He was good like that. A man without ego. But for a few weeks, it was hard."

Rob tightened his hand around the thin plastic arm of the chair.

Georgina tilted her head. "Oh, darling, he still loved you and you were still friends, weren't you?"

"I wasn't a friend when he needed me."

Georgina handed him a tissue.

"I have plenty of these!"

Rob took a moment to steady himself.

"Was there anything else, Georgina? Just something he may have mentioned in passing that sounded odd?"

Georgina put her hand to her chin and stroked it for a moment before shaking her head. "I can't think of anything. I mean, he was wrestling with some maths problem at one point, but I can't see that's got anything to do with anything."

"Maths? Tell me exactly what he said."

"Well, I don't remember much. He just said he had a maths problem. We laughed a bit about Charlie having all the maths brains in the family."

Rob stood up and took a few steps around the area of grass that had been cut enough for a couple of chairs and a table. "But he didn't ask Charlie? Unless Charlie was lying. Maybe he asked Charlie to lie?"

"I'm sure he would have told me by now, but let's ask him. *Charlie!*"

He appeared at the back door.

Rob faced him. "Charlie, do you remember our conversation at your mother's?"

"About me seeing Dad in Oxford?"

"Yes. I want to check that you're not covering up for him. That he didn't ask you not to say anything. I promise you I'm on his side. I'm not here for TFU or the police. I'm here to clear his name."

Charlie shook his head. "I would tell you, Mr May, I promise. But I never saw him. God, I wish I had. But he didn't visit me."

"Or call you?"

"No. Nothing. I last saw Daddy at Easter."

"Thank you, Charlie."

"Will you clear his name?" Charlie asked, glancing across to his mother.

"I'm doing everything I can, I promise."

Georgina stood up. "We're so alone here, Rob. This means everything to us. Thank you."

She showed him to the front door.

"God, I miss Mary. How is that gorgeous wife of yours?"

"She's fine."

"Well, send her my love from Siberia."

Rob smiled. "We'll see you on Friday. After that, you won't be able to get rid of us."

30

WEDNESDAY 6TH JULY

I n their final chat on Tuesday evening, Susie had dubbed it 'Normal Wednesday', urging Rob to play the part of the TFU lackey. Toe the line. Head down.

"Throw Kilton off the scent. He'll be writing up your special commendation for delivering the project rather than worrying what you'll do next."

At the tea bar, he was nervous. He couldn't believe that his colleagues didn't know Mary had walked out.

But he drank tea, laughed when he could, and threw himself into the planning for two more Guiding Light trips.

According to the truncated project timetable, they had nine hours and twelve minutes left to log. Kilton wanted the jet in the air morning and afternoon. Log four hours today and four tomorrow, leaving the ceremonial final flight with around sixty minutes to complete the minimum requirement.

After an uneventful morning trip to Yorkshire and back, Rob took himself off to the mess for lunch.

JR was at a table by himself. It would be too out of the ordinary for Rob to join him, so he loitered by his side for just a moment as he passed with his drink in hand.

"All ready?" He kept his voice low.

JR looked up and nodded.

"She's fixed and waiting for you, Flight Lieutenant. I'll pick you up at 7.30AM."

Rob nodded.

He avoided the bar after work and went home, remembering to casually mention to Red and Jock that he wasn't feeling one hundred per cent.

Twice he picked up the phone and dialled the Laverstocks'. On both occasions he hung up before the line connected.

It was unbearable, not speaking to Mary. But Susie had warned that any contact might upset him. Throw a spanner in the works at the wrong time.

The light faded. He finished a bottle of wine as a distraction from the silence. At 10.30PM he went to bed, praying for a good night's sleep, although he knew it was unlikely to come.

He turned onto his side and closed his eyes, imagining Millie sitting next to JR in the cockpit of the Anson. Holdall behind him.

Alone on a mission to save lives.

31

THURSDAY 7TH JULY

The alarm unleashed its urgent clanging. Rob's eyes flickered open.

His first thought was surprise. He'd slept.

He turned over and faced the space where his wife should be. He rested a hand on the undisturbed pillow, before rolling out of bed.

He put on his uniform and packed a civilian change of clothes in a holdall.

It was just after 7AM.

He walked downstairs, picked up the telephone receiver, and, with nervous fingers, dialled the switchboard at West Porton.

"Commanding officer, Test Flight Unit, please."

A short pause.

"Kilton."

"Sir, it's Rob May. I'm afraid I've been rather unwell in the night and I'm not fit for work or flying today."

"You can come in, though?"

"No. I'm unwell."

"This is very inconvenient, May. You have two trips today. Important ones. I'm about to reassure the government we'll sign off tomorrow."

"I'm sorry, sir."

"Fine. I'll take your place."

Rob said goodbye but found himself speaking to a dead line. Kilton was gone.

———

TEN MINUTES LATER, Rob slipped out of the house and walked at a brisk pace into the village.

He didn't look left or right, but just prayed his fellow TFU colleagues were too busy dressing or eating breakfast to glance out of the window.

As he entered the village, he spotted an old Hillman Minx outside the shop. JR was cramped into the front seat, his head tilted forward to avoid the low roof.

He gave Rob a wave.

As he approached the passenger door, a man in RAF uniform swept out of the newsagent, paper tucked under his arm. He nodded at Rob, smiling.

Rob forced a smile back and studied the man's stripes; a squadron leader with a medal ribbon.

He climbed in next to JR.

"Do you recognise that officer?"

JR nodded.

"Deputy on Handling Squadron at Boscombe. Worry not."

The car pulled out and Rob sunk lower in his seat.

He felt exposed, but short of hiding in the footwell, he had no choice but to remain on view to anyone who cared to look.

They entered West Porton through the main gate. Since the security clampdown, it was the only way on or off.

"We used to have our own airfield gate," said JR. "It was on the other side and led directly to the unit. No-one bothered us. Halcyon days."

"Sounds idyllic. And then TFU came along."

"Indeed. Still, the mess is a lot livelier."

They turned onto the approach road to the gate and joined a short queue. Rob found himself sliding down in his seat. He scanned ahead and recognised a couple of the cars. It looked like Red Brunson in the distance, but he didn't recognise the white Rover immediately in front of them, although he did notice a pair of eyes in its rear-view mirror.

"I keep thinking I'm being watched."

"You're fine," said JR. "It's the morning. No-one's alert."

It was their turn. The officers ordered JR out of the car. Rob put his hand up to his cheek to mask his face from anyone who might drive by.

The guards also stopped the vehicle in front.

Out stepped Dave Berringer.

Rob leant all the way forward, as if tying his shoelaces. With heart thudding, he kept his head down.

JR got back in the driver's seat.

"Everything all right? Do you think you've been seen?"

"Is the person in front still out of their car?" Rob asked.

"There's no car in front of us."

Rob unfolded himself. "OK. Let's go."

They turned immediately right after the gate and separated themselves from the main station and TFU traffic.

JR drove up to an airfield entrance beyond the officers' mess and they made their way around the peri-track.

At the Maintenance Unit, JR led Rob to the flying clothing store: a series of cardboard boxes that wouldn't have looked out of place at a jumble sale.

He picked through until he found coveralls that just about fit him. He also picked out a tatty leather flying helmet with earphones built in. It smelt musty; maybe it had seen action in the last war.

They headed to the aircraft as quickly as possible. Rob had no desire to line up and taxi anywhere near any TFU aircraft.

JR took command. Rob scanned the pilots' notes.

In a small cloud of black smoke, the two engines fired up one after the other. After waiting for the temperatures to rise, JR made the radio calls and they taxied out.

————

"MR STAFFORD FOR YOU."

Jean's cheery voice grated with Kilton's mood. He snatched the receiver.

"What?"

"Good morning to you, too, Mark."

"I'm busy."

"I need to know we're on for tomorrow. The minister's meeting the Board this afternoon and he'll want reassurance."

"I told you, we're doing it," Kilton hissed. "I've already assured Buttler. The government want this more than you do and they're not in the mood for hearing bad news."

"And the missing tapes?"

"Milford's dead. We can assume that inconvenience died with him. Look, I haven't got time for this. I'm going flying. Just be here tomorrow. We fly after the funeral."

"Right, and Rob May? I know you had your concerns about him."

Kilton paused.

"Don't worry about May. He'll do as he's told."

"Good. General Leivers is waiting for the word, and the UK is waiting for the money. Can I be assured there'll be no more surprises?"

"Just be here tomorrow, Stafford. You'll get your signature."

He hung up and pushed open the adjoining door to Jean's office. "No more calls. I have to go flying."

In the planning room, he found Red. "I'll take Rob's place. He's ill, apparently."

"Well, we're getting ready to go. Do you want to see the route?"

Kilton looked over the chart; it looked straightforward. Departure to the west, runs at two thousand and then one thousand.

"Can we get going? I've got a lot on."

"Sure thing, boss."

Red looked around for Berringer and Smith. "*We're going!*"

Berringer looked surprised to see Kilton standing next to him. He put his mug down and came over, along with Smith, a young navigator.

"Ready."

Kilton worked in silence to pull on his coveralls, before he walked to the airfield door with Red. Together they waited for the others.

Impatient, he led Red out onto the apron. The marshallers towed a Victor out of the hangar to the right, while straight ahead was their Vulcan, hunched on its main gear, waiting.

A whine of props drifted over the wind and Kilton watched as an old Anson rumbled along the opposite taxiway.

"Bloody people. Make the place untidy."

"The lineys?" said Red, watching the junior ranks busying themselves around the jets.

"The Graveyard. After Guiding Light, I'm going to expand our operations. We'll need that space."

Eventually, Berringer and Smith appeared next to them.

The crew walked to the aircraft.

Kilton hauled himself up the yellow ladder into the belly of the bomber, leaving Red to do the walkaround.

He settled into the co-pilot's position on the right, happy to let Red do most of the work.

Outside, the Anson wound up to full chat and started its laborious roll down the runway. The captain looked like JR; he must have been older than the bloody aircraft he was ferrying to the knacker's yard.

Kilton squinted.

Some youngster with him?

Unusual for that lot to be working with someone who didn't have one foot in the grave.

Red appeared. He strapped in, and donned his US-made helmet.

"You look ridiculous," Kilton said, appraising the mirrored visor.

Red laughed and pulled on his oxygen mask. Between them, they brought the Vulcan to life.

With the four engines at a roar, Brunson taxied to the westerly runway and accelerated into the sky.

They settled into the cruise, ploughing through the air for fifteen minutes.

As they began their descent, Red made some notes and Kilton noticed the Guiding Light panel light up; clearly, Berringer was getting ready.

"What's wrong with him?" asked Red.

"Who?"

"Rob. You said he was ill. What's wrong with him?"

"I don't bloody know. I didn't ask him."

"Who's ill?" Berringer piped up over the intercom from his position in the rear crew bay.

"Rob May."

There was a pause before Berringer spoke again. "He looked OK this morning."

Kilton's head turned. "What do you mean?"

"At the main gate. He looked fine. He was with that old bloke from the Maintenance Unit."

"Turn the jet around," Kilton barked into his oxygen mask.

"Sorry?" Red said, but Kilton didn't wait any longer.

"I have control," he said, and grabbed the column and throttles, throwing the jet into a steep bank.

"What's going on?" Red asked.

Kilton levelled on an easterly heading and released the controls.

"Just fly us back, and tell ATC we're a priority."

———

EVEN IN THE LUMBERING ANSON, the trip to Abingdon was a short hop.

JR positioned them to the south-east to join the downwind leg for the southerly runway. Rob did little more than help with flaps and settings. As they lined up, he looked across the RAF airfield to the town, and just visible about ten miles beyond was Oxford.

JR's experienced hands nudged the throttles as he fine-tuned their final descent; smooth as silk, the wheels caressed the runway. A perfect three-point touchdown for the tail-dragger.

"Nice landing," Rob said.

"You have to treat these old girls with care," JR replied, without taking his eyes off the white lines disappearing under the nose as they rolled out.

Rob let JR make the radio calls and they headed toward the clusters of hangars and buildings.

"Where exactly did you drop Millie?"

JR pointed to an apron to the right of the largest hangar. "It's used for visiting aircraft, and we have to sign in over there." He nodded to a single-storey structure on the other side of the apron. "It's 47 Squadron. Friendly bunch."

After he'd shut down the two Cheetah engines, JR ran through the checklist.

"You can go, Rob. I'll wander over to the squadron later for a cup of tea. Good luck."

Rob entered the 47 Squadron building and approached what looked like an operations desk.

The place was busy, but each person who bustled past said a cheery good morning.

"I need to sign in a visiting aircraft, please."

The desk sergeant smiled. "Welcome to RAF Abingdon," he said, as he turned a visitors' logbook around in front of him.

Rob opened it and made his way to the last entry.

29/6/66 – Lightning 1A – XM184 – Fl Lt RWA Meakins – Diversion (fuel)

He fished a pen out of his coveralls and recorded an entry for their flight. He wrote slowly, waiting for the right moment, as the sergeant turned away.

He quickly flicked the page back and scanned the list of entries. His eyes stopped as he read the name.

Sq Ldr CJ Milford

He brushed the entry with his finger.
The rest of the line read:

Anson – TX183 – MT

Rob tapped the desk for a moment. MT only stood for one thing as far as he knew.

He completed his own entry in the log, adding 'X-Country Navex' as a vague reason for his visit.

He pushed the book back toward the sergeant. "I wonder if you could point me toward MT?"

"Have you booked some transport, sir?"

"Actually, no. I was hoping they'd be able to help me?"

"I can ask." The sergeant picked up the phone. "Where are you headed?"

"Just local."

The sergeant furrowed his brow.

"Got an officer in need of car at 47 Squadron. Can you oblige? No, I'm not sure." He cupped the receiver and looked at Rob. "Do you have a requisition?"

"Yes," Rob lied.

The sergeant finished the call. "Someone will pick you up from here shortly."

He pointed at an old sofa that lined the wall opposite the desk. Rob walked over, but before he sat down, he removed his flying coveralls and folded them into the holdall.

He crossed his legs and did his best to hide his nerves.

After a few minutes, a corporal appeared at the desk holding his cloth beret. The sergeant pointed at Rob and the man came over.

"You need a transport, sir?"

"Yes, please, Corporal."

Rob stood up and walked out. A grey Austin 10 staff car sat next to the entrance. Rob winced; it was the sort of official vehicle normally reserved for senior officers.

As the corporal opened the door for him, he tried to summon his most casual tone.

"Actually, Corporal, I have a slight problem, in that I've only gone and lost the actual address I need to visit. I wonder if you could help?"

"I'll try, sir. Do you know the name of the person? Or is it a company?"

"My colleague visited the place at the beginning of last week and I think the MT section provided the transport. Maybe you have a record?"

The corporal didn't look best pleased. "We have records in the office, sir. Do you know exactly when this took place?" He spoke slowly, clearly reluctant to have to go back to his office and rifle through the cards.

"20th June, in the morning. Squadron Leader Milford."

"Right. Perhaps you could write that down?"

The driver sat behind the wheel and turned, handing Rob a notepad and pen. Rob wrote Millie's name and the date, and they made the short journey to the MT office.

———

KILTON FIDGETED while Red brought the Vulcan onto a short final.

By the time the last engine had shut down, he was out of his seat and disembarked through the hatch, leaving the others scratching their heads.

Still in his coveralls and Mae West, carrying his helmet and oxygen mask, Kilton marched into the planning room and headed straight to his secretary's office.

"Get me security, now."

At his desk, he fell into his seat, crashing a fist onto the table.

The phone rang; he snatched at the handset. "Kilton."

"Squadron Leader Hoskins for you."

There was a click.

"Hoskins, Rob May called in sick this morning, but I've had a report he entered the station with a dinosaur from the Maintenance Unit. I don't know what he's up to, but there's a good chance he's trying to interfere with the project. I need him tracked down and arrested immediately."

"OK. Are you sure? Shouldn't we check his house first?"

"Check everywhere!"

Kilton hung up and stared at the phone for a moment.

He left the office and walked through the planning room out onto the apron.

Looking across the airfield, his eyes rested on the ramshackle nest of huts and hangars that made up the Graveyard.

"Damn this."

———

AFTER A SHORT TRIP in the TFU Land Rover, Kilton marched into the MU crew room.

Two men—one slumped into an old sofa and one at a desk—stood up as he entered.

"Who's in charge? Where's JR?"

"He's flying," said a pilot by the sofa.

"Where? Who with?"

Furtive glances between the men.

"*Tell me!*"

"He's taken an officer to a meeting, I think."

"Which officer? What meeting? Come on, don't you keep records?"

The man by the tea bar pointed at a sheet on the wall.

"It just says 'transport'. Not sure of the destination. But he'll be back at some point. I can have him visit TFU if you like, sir?"

Kilton walked up to the sheet and scrutinised it.

Anson – TX183 - Transport

"Who was the officer?" he barked.

"Not sure."

Kilton turned and walked toward the man; he wore squadron leader stripes.

"Do you have any idea how much trouble you're in? Now, I'll ask again. Where have they gone?"

"I'm sorry, Wing Commander Kilton. I don't know. As I say, I can send them over when they return."

"You won't need to."

―――――

As the car pulled away from the MT compound and toward the exit from RAF Abingdon, Rob turned a small square of paper over in his hand.

Rhodes Cottage, *Merton Street, Oxford*

The main gate was a lot more relaxed than West Porton's. He wound down the window and sat up.

If Susie was watching, he needed her to see him.

They passed through the gate. A blue MG turned in, blocking his view. The corporal swung left onto the main road and sped up.

Rob shifted in his seat, craning his neck to look back at the entrance.

Susie was at the wheel of her Herald, parked about fifty yards away from the airfield entrance. She was reading a newspaper.

As they left her behind, he willed her to look up.

She didn't.

They reached a roundabout, maybe half a mile from the gate. The Herald still hadn't moved.

"Everything all right, sir?" said the corporal. Rob looked forward to see the man staring at him in the rear-view mirror.

"Fine, thank you."

Rob kept his eyes fixed ahead. Why the hell hadn't she spotted them leaving?

Thirty seconds after they navigated around a roundabout, the distinctive blue car flashed across the wing mirror.

He whipped his head around and saw Susie, with her black bob of hair returned, about fifty yards behind.

Before long, they were on the outskirts of the city.

Rob had never been to Oxford; he felt like they were driving onto the set of a film. Sandstone college buildings as far as he could see; spectacled men in corduroy jackets on bicycles, gliding around the car.

The car slowed to turn into a narrow road. Rob looked back and could just see Susie's car two vehicles behind.

"Are we close?" Rob asked.

"It's just down here, sir. Next left."

"Actually, Corporal, I think I might walk the rest of the way, as it's a nice day."

The driver pulled over and looked back at him. "Are you sure, sir?"

"Yes, it will be good to get some fresh air."

"What time should I collect you, sir?"

"I won't need a lift back, thank you, Corporal."

"Very good, sir."

Rob climbed out and watched as the Austin drove off in a cloud of smoke.

He turned to see Susie walking toward him.

"Nice hair."

"So, I assume you've spotted some breadcrumbs, Flight Lieutenant May?"

Rob pointed ahead. "Merton Street. It's along here. The address Millie was taken to."

———

RHODES COTTAGE WAS a terraced Tudor house with a gated drive to one side. The ancient walls were crumbling in places.

Rob and Susie stood at the front porch.

"Let's see what's behind the green door," Susie said, as she knocked.

It was a quiet street; the odd student cycled past.

An elderly woman with a shopping bag ambled along the pavement toward them.

They leant in to the door, trying to detect any sounds of life from within.

Rob knocked again.

"Can I help you?"

The woman with the shopping bag stopped by the door.

"Ah," said Rob. "Yes."

She put the shopping down and produced a small bunch of keys.

Susie leant forward and held out her hand. "Hello, I'm Susie, and this is my colleague Robert. We were friends of Christopher Milford. I believe you may have met him?"

The woman gave them a puzzled look and shook her head.

"I don't think so. You must have the wrong house."

With that, she pushed her key into the door and picked up her shopping.

"I'm sorry," said Susie. "Maybe he used a different name. Rob, why don't you describe him to Mrs...?"

The woman shook her head again and pushed the door open.

Rob gabbled out a description of Millie. "Fifties, balding, bit of middle-age spread. Moustache..." He tailed off, before adding, "and the nicest person you will ever meet."

The woman hesitated as she crossed the threshold into the cottage. She turned and gave Rob a polite smile.

"I wish you luck in finding your friend."

She closed the door.

Rob looked at Susie; she bent down and opened the letterbox.

"We won't find him. He's dead. And that's why we're here."

She stood up again. After a moment, the door opened a crack.

An eye appeared in the gloom of the doorway.

"Maybe you had better come in then."

———

INSIDE THE DARK KITCHEN, the woman unpacked her shopping. She paused and looked over her shoulder.

"How did he die?"

"In an aeroplane crash," Rob said. "I survived, but I'm afraid the other three men didn't make it."

"I'm sorry to hear that. The professor liked him very much. I'm Mrs Lazenby." She turned back to her unpacking. Rob watched as she piled up three jars of fish paste before opening a cupboard.

"Mrs Lazenby, can I ask you what your husband does?" said Rob.

The woman laughed. "Not much. He died in 1944."

"Then who—"

"Professor Belkin lives here, and that's who I suspect you need to speak to. I'm just the housekeeper." She put away the last of the shopping as the clock in the hall struck the half hour. Rob looked at his watch; it was 10.30AM.

"But you'll have awhile to wait, I'm afraid. He's not here and won't be back for another week."

Rob's heart sunk.

"We only have today, Mrs Lazenby. Perhaps you could tell us where he is?"

"Would you like a cup of tea?"

Susie smiled at her. "That would be lovely."

With great deliberation, Mrs Lazenby took the kettle from the draining board and filled it with water over the sink. She placed it on the stove and then spent a long time fiddling with the gas and box of matches.

Rob looked across at Susie with impatience, but she put a finger to her lips.

"Mrs Lazenby, do you know why we are here?" Susie asked.

The housekeeper pulled a chair from under the table and sat down opposite them.

"Was it an accident?"

"I'm sorry?" Rob replied, even though he had heard her clearly.

She turned to face him. "The aeroplane crash. Was it an accident?"

Susie answered, "We don't know. Why do you ask that?"

Mrs Lazenby looked vague for a moment, as if recalling a dim memory. "It's not my place to discuss this. You really are best waiting for the professor."

"I understand that, Mrs Lazenby," said Susie, "but we are in a rather desperate position. As I think you realised, Mr Milford took a great risk in coming here and now that he's gone, we are all he has left to ensure that risk wasn't for nothing."

The kettle whistled. Mrs Lazenby stood up.

Susie continued. "We think Professor Belkin is the only person who can help bring to a conclusion the work Mr Milford was doing and we need to speak to him today."

Mrs Lazenby slowly poured the boiling water into a teapot which she then covered with a knitted cosy. Without turning around, she asked, "And who are you again?"

Rob watched her lift the teapot onto the table.

"I took a significant risk coming here today, Mrs Lazenby. If you telephone RAF West Porton to confirm my identity, I guarantee the next thing that will happen is that police officers will arrive at this house and arrest me. I have a career as a test pilot at risk. And a wife." His voice cracked with the words. "I realise you only have my word on this, but please, Mrs Lazenby, I would give everything I have to ensure that Squadron Leader Milford's discovery does not die with him. Please help me."

Mrs Lazenby reached into a cupboard and retrieved three cups, followed by three saucers.

Finally, she returned from the refrigerator with a jug of milk.

"I see," she said, and sat down. "I'm afraid you won't want to hear what I'm about to say. The professor is a long way away. More than a day, I fear, with the ferry crossing times."

"Is he in France?" Susie asked.

"No, not France, but he may as well be. The professor takes his summer holiday on Lundy, and he has done every year that I've known him."

"Lundy?"

"An island off the north Devon coast," Rob said. He looked at Mrs Lazenby. "I didn't know anyone lived there."

"I believe there are some holiday cottages. The professor has an arrangement with a gentleman. Mr MacPherson."

Susie had visibly slumped.

But Rob was already thinking about their next move.

"We can get there today."

Mrs Lazenby looked doubtful. "I can give you the address, but it takes the professor more than five hours to drive to the port, and then I understand there's only two crossings a day. You'll be lucky if you're there before tomorrow lunchtime. So, unless you brought one of your fancy aeroplanes with you, I'm afraid you're out of luck."

Susie looked at Rob with an eyebrow raised.

He was smiling.

———

THEY STEPPED onto the street into bright sunshine. Rob turned back to Mrs Lazenby at the door.

"You've been extremely helpful. I can tell you guard the professor's privacy closely, but I believe you've done the right thing."

"Mrs Lazenby," Susie said, "did the professor take any work related items with him on holiday?"

She shook her head. "Not at all. He goes to get away from all that. He tells me he doesn't even read the newspaper."

"That explains why he hasn't contacted us."

They walked back to Susie's car. Rob studied the brief address.

Old Light Cottage, Lundy

They pulled over at the first phone box and Rob dialled the Ministry operator, asking to be put through to the operations desk at 47 Squadron.

They quickly found JR.

The old pilot laughed when he heard the plan.

"In for a penny, I guess. I'll do some planning and see if we can't beg some paraffin from the good people at RAF Abingdon." He paused. "I'll have to look at the strip carefully. Getting in is one thing, but we'll need to get out again."

"Thank you, JR."

Susie steered them onto the main road again, and they headed back toward Abingdon.

"I can't believe we're doing this," Rob said.

"Don't get ahead of yourself. We need irrefutable evidence, remember. I was hoping we'd be poring over results from the sixty reels by now, preferably with the tapes themselves still intact." She shrugged. "What are we going to find in Lundy?"

"The truth?"

Susie changed into top gear. "Unfortunately, the truth isn't usually enough."

"But we have to try."

"I agree. But flying across southern England is a lot more than we bargained for. You're certain you want to do this?"

Rob stared out of the window as the colleges gave way to countryside. "I have to," he said quietly. "We've got hours left on the project before it's too late. Millie worked with Belkin. I've got to talk to him, Susie. I've got to give it a chance. It's the least I owe Millie."

They drove on in silence for a few minutes.

As RAF Abingdon's main gate came into view, Rob turned to Susie.

"You don't have to come if you don't want to."

She smiled. "The chance of a flight? I'm not missing that! Plus, they ordered me not to go to Abingdon, but they didn't say anything about Lundy."

————

"WITH RESPECT, sir, I think that's naive." Kilton stood in front of Group Captain Periwinkle's desk.

"Calm down, Mark. I'm sure there's a logical explanation."

Kilton shook his head in exasperation. "The evidence is clear. May lied about his illness. I'm certain he flew with the Maintenance Unit. In fact I think I saw him in an Anson."

"You think? But you're not sure?"

"I'm sure, sir."

"Might Rob just be at the doctor's? Didn't the police say that the house was empty? Mary must have taken him off."

"No, sir. He's up to something, I'm sure of it."

The phone in the outer office rang. A moment later, the call was put through to Periwinkle.

"Station Commander," he answered. "I see. And that's as much as you can tell us, is it?"

He said a polite thank you and hung up. "ATC say the only MU traffic this morning was indeed an Anson. There was no flight plan, but the aircraft departed to the north-east."

"North-east?" Kilton looked around the office and pulled a southern England chart from a shelf, spreading it open on the conference table. With his finger, he drew a line running north-easterly from West Porton. It led to Cambridge.

He looked up at the station commander. "Get your corporal to call Cambridge Airport and ask them if they've had a visitor this morning. Anson TX183." He wrote the serial number on a scrap of paper and handed it to Periwinkle. The station commander moved from behind his desk.

Kilton stood by the chart and listened as Periwinkle relayed the message in the outer office.

"*Oh, and could we have a pot of tea, please?*"

"Call Cambridge first!" Kilton shouted.

Periwinkle walked back into the office. He eyed Kilton as he dealt with some correspondence on his desk. Kilton stood in silence, gazing down at the chart. Why Cambridge?

After a few minutes, the corporal appeared at the door.

"Nothing, sir."

"Nothing?" said Kilton. "Really?"

"No, sir. Cambridge confirms they've had no visitors at all this morning."

"*Bollocks!*" Kilton stood up and hunched over the chart again. "North-east. Could just have been their initial heading." His eyes moved either side of an imaginary line to Cambridge. RAE Bedford was a common destination for test crews; the place hosted a lot of aeronautical engineers.

The corporal stood next to him, also looking at the chart.

"RAE Bedford, corporal. That could be it. Call them, will you?"

"Yes, sir. Would you like me to make a list of the other airfields along the route? They could have gone beyond Cambridge, of course?"

"Quickly then," Kilton snapped. He watched as the corporal scribbled at speed.

Marham

Wyton

Alconbury

RAE Bedford

Bicester

Brize Norton

Abingdon

As he returned to the outer office, Kilton shouted after him. "Start with RAE Bedford."

He paced the room.

"Cup of tea, Mark?" asked Periwinkle.

––––––

RED BRUNSON STOOD by one of the planning desks and drummed his fingers. He'd been watching the comings and goings since their abrupt return to West Porton, including the order of the police to Rob May's house.

Jock MacLeish appeared beside him.

Red looked over his shoulder to ensure no-one was too close.

"First, they came for Brian, then they came for Millie."

"And now they've come for Rob." MacLeish finished the thought.

"Did he ever say anything to you?" Red asked.

Jock shook his head. "Nope. I wondered if he would, but he seemed happy with the project."

Two West Porton security men in uniform marched into the planning room. They tapped on Jean's office door. Red and MacLeish watched as she led them to the wooden lockers and handed over a set of keys.

It didn't take them long to tip the contents of Rob's locker into a bag.

MacLeish shook his head and went back to his planning, but Red loitered for a moment, before heading over to Jean.

He tapped on the glass window in the door.

Jean looked up and beamed, waving him in.

"Well, hello, Captain Brunson."

"Hi, Jean. I need to check a few items for the funeral. Do you have the contact list, please?"

"Of course," she said brightly, then delved into a file, handing him a sheet with the names and telephone numbers.

"Thank you. I won't be long."

––––––

ROB WENT into the Abingdon guardroom at the main gate and filled out a visitor form for Susie, making up a name. One of the smaller illegalities of the day.

At the 47 Squadron operations desk, JR explained they would have a female VIP passenger, and Susie was duly treated like royalty with offers of cups of tea and biscuits.

JR filled out the departure details, and he sat on the sofa next to Rob as they ran through a copy of the Anson pilots' notes.

They hadn't been able to contact anyone at Lundy. Apparently, the island wasn't connected to the mainland by wire. However, JR had found a description of the strip; it was one thousand four hundred feet long, which was tight.

The more they read in the notes, the better they felt their chances were. The handling instructions for take-off at eighty-five knots had a considerable margin of error, as the actual stall speed was closer to fifty knots.

During his test pilots' course, Rob had placed various aircraft in all sorts of marginal situations. He felt this was acceptable.

JR agreed.

He shrugged. "Well, we'll find out one way or another."

Rob donned his flying coveralls and the three of them headed out to the waiting aircraft.

———

A FEW MINUTES AFTER JR, Rob and Susie had left, a phone rang on the 47 Squadron operations desk. The duty desk sergeant picked it up.

"47 Squadron Operations. Sergeant Wilkes... Thank you. Put him through."

As he listened, he jotted down an aircraft serial number.

TX183

"I think so. Stand by, I'll check."

Wilkes could have done without this extra task on a busy morning. Cupping the receiver, he looked across to his corporal.

"Those VIPs? Were they in an Anson?"

"I think so."

"Serial?" He waited as the corporal opened the visitor log and ran his finger down to the last entry.

"Tango X-Ray one-eight-three"

"What time did they leave?"

The corporal looked at the wall clock. "Ten minutes ago."

The sergeant uncapped the phone. "You've just missed them, sorry."

A new voice appeared at the other end of the line and the sergeant had to hold the receiver away from his ear.

"Yes, sir." He dropped the phone and shouted at the corporal.

"Stop the Anson!"

———

ROB SWITCHED on the main magnetos in the aircraft and switched off the starting mags. He scanned the rest of the checklist while a member of the ground crew outside waved to confirm he had screwed down the priming pump and closed the priming cock.

He watched as JR opened the engine up to one thousand RPM.

"Pain, but we have to warm the engine for a minute or two."

Rob monitored the engine temperature gauges. The white needle inched slowly around the dial.

Susie appeared between them.

"You're best to keep seated," Rob shouted above the engine noise, but she pointed out of the window.

An RAF police car was driving toward the air traffic tower. They watched it pull to a halt before a policeman jumped out and looked toward them.

"For us?" Rob said.

"I think so. Perhaps we should get going?"

JR didn't need asking twice. He released the park brake and gave a wave to the ground crew, who showed him three chocks. He pushed the throttles and the aircraft crept forward.

Rob kept his eyes on the policeman. He was running toward them.

"Are you going to radio the tower?" JR asked.

"I think that would be futile now."

"Agreed."

JR swung the Anson onto the westerly taxiway and taxied as fast as he dared.

The radio burst into life. "Anson, Shorthand one-three, you are requested to shut down ."

Rob watched through the side window as the policeman, reacting to the plane's movement, stopped and ran back to his car.

The radio shouted at them again. "Shorthand one-three you are ordered to stop taxi and shutdown immediately.'

"Shall we turn that off?" Rob said.

"Good idea." JR turned the rotary dial.

The crossing point for the main runway was straight ahead, about halfway along its length.

"Plenty of space for this old girl," JR said.

Rob selected a take-off flap setting and craned his head around. The police car swung onto the taxiway and disappeared behind them. It must have been doing fifty MPH; they were doing about twenty. The policeman would be level with them, or worse, in front of them, in moments.

The turn onto the main runway was still a hundred yards away.

But they were facing into wind.

"Just go," Rob said.

JR looked at him. "What?"

"Use the taxiway. We've run out of time, JR. *Let's just go!*"

JR pushed the throttles forward, and they both monitored the engines, which should have had more of a chance to warm up.

The airspeed indicator lumbered slowly up.

"Come on, come on..." Rob willed the aircraft to accelerate.

He looked around, pressing against the window, trying to glimpse the police car, only to see it had caught up with them and was now attempting to overtake, one set of wheels on the grass.

"Shit, he's going to get in front of us!"

Forty-five knots, fifty knots.

The needle was agonisingly slow to respond.

The police car came level with the leading edge of the wing, just as the nose of the Anson was lowered by JR, lifting the tailwheel off the ground…but still more speed needed to get airborne.

The policeman seemed to find a burst of energy from the car engine and it moved ahead, level with the nose.

"Oh no," Rob muttered.

Sixty-five knots.

JR eased the yoke back.

But the aircraft stayed planted.

The police car inched further ahead.

"If he gets clear, he'll pull in front and we're done for!" Rob shouted.

Susie stood up again, gripping the back of the two cockpit seats.

"COME ON!" she yelled over the din of the engines.

The Anson's wings finally began to bite and the aircraft lifted slowly into the air, leaving the police car way behind.

JR kept the nose close to the horizon, allowing the airspeed to build, before nudging it up, teasing the vintage aircraft into a gentle, if reluctant, climb.

"Better keep your chart out and radio off," said Rob. "We're going to navigate old-school."

JR continued the gentle bank. Rob scanned the scene below. Two more police cars caught up with the one that had been chasing them. A crowd of men in various uniforms stood around the base of the tower.

"This is it now. We're committed."

JR laughed. "You could say that."

The Oxfordshire countryside slipped by. JR kept the battered silver Anson just below the clouds, with the nose pointing south-east.

Rob tapped the compass heading.

"Let's throw them off the scent a little, leave the west until Reading when we're well out of sight."

"Good idea."

Rob studied the chart.

"That's Didcot ahead." He pointed. "See the brown sprawl beyond? That's Reading."

"Got it," JR confirmed.

Rob retrieved a pencil from his coveralls pocket and drew a rough line from Reading to a point between Bristol and Bath.

From there, they would follow the Severn Estuary and north Devon coast until they were visual with Lundy.

He showed the new lines to JR, who nodded in appreciation at their simplicity. He roughly measured the distance, checked their cruise speed, and noted the duration of each leg, just in time to start the stopwatch at Swindon.

After the navigation exercise, there was little else to do.

Rob sat back. With no distraction, lost in the rhythmic drone of the engine, the full enormity of what had happened started to sink in.

"You OK?" JR called over the intercom.

Rob pushed off his headset.

JR leaned across and tugged at his harness until it released.

He manoeuvred himself out of the P2 seat and staggered back. Susie caught him and helped him into the torn leather seat next to hers.

Susie's breath next to his ear.

"It's OK, it's OK. Just breathe."

He closed his eyes and folded himself forward. Her voice was soft and kind, and the breath on his ear was warm. He smelt her sweet scent.

Slowly, he took deeper breaths; the worst of the panic was passing.

Opening his eyes, still doubled over, he studied the dirty floor of the old aircraft.

The dust of a thousand troops transported around the world.

Some to their deaths. It could be worse.

Susie's hand stroked his head; he sat up.

"Sorry," he said.

"No need to apologise."

"It feels like I've crossed the Rubicon." He turned to her. "My old life, it's gone, isn't it?"

"We're doing the right thing, Rob. Remember what Millie must have gone through, sitting in these very seats, terrified, lying to Kilton. And why? It must have been the most urgent thing in his life, and that's why we're here."

Rob thought of Millie, alone in the back of the Anson, JR up front, helping but unaware of his real task.

"But what if we don't get what we need? Like you said? I can't go back now. I have nothing to go back to, except Kilton's fury. He'll have me arrested."

"Let's hope we'll get what we need. And when we do, Mark Kilton will be the one under arrest."

The aircraft banked and he looked up to see JR with the yoke in one hand and the chart in another.

"I have to help him." Rob rose from his seat but turned back to Susie. "I've got no wife, no best friend and no career. I hope you're right."

Back in the cockpit, he apologised to JR, who dismissed his words with a wave and patted him on the back.

The Severn Estuary was directly ahead. Rob made sure JR was following his line on the chart to keep them clear of Bristol Lulsgate Airport.

———

THE SUN CAME and went as clouds drifted across the sky. Mary stared into the blue spaces between.

Standing in the Laverstocks' front room, cup of tea in hand, in front of their large bay window, the wound of Rob's betrayal still hurt.

But in the long night hours, with little sleep, she'd had her doubts.

And she had been surprised by another feeling creeping in.

Guilt.

"Why on earth should you feel guilty?" Janet Laverstock said, over breakfast.

Mary didn't know the answer, but that didn't stop the feeling nagging at her.

Three nights of quiet crying in a strange bed had taken their toll.

After breakfast, she decided she needed to take action.

She tried her best to put aside the emotion that clouded her thoughts and remember what exactly Rob had said.

Not much. But enough for her to believe she was missing something.

Something that involved Millie. Something that began a series of events which ultimately led her here, living with a snobby woman and her compliant husband.

The type of happy marriage she couldn't begin to contemplate.

Janet had insisted that Rob be given no more chances. But she hadn't really given him one chance.

She was losing him, even before Janet Laverstock had called with her shocking news. She knew that. But in the clear light, Mary found it hard to believe she'd lost him to a young lover.

His insistence, full of clichés about it not being what it seemed, played over in her mind.

But what to do? She didn't want to simply arrive back at Trenchard Close.

She needed to embrace something that had been absent from their marriage for some time.

Truth.

And there was only one place she could start.

Only one person she could truly trust.

A noise came from the kitchen as Janet hung up the phone. She appeared, with her trademark bouffant of perfect hair.

"Good news," she announced. "I've found her."

———

JR TOOK them low over the island while he and Rob scrutinised the strip.

"It looks smooth enough, but then it would from up here," Rob said.

They searched for clues to help them with wind speed and direction, eventually spotting a bonfire that showed a fairly stiff southwesterly.

JR descended on the dead side of a left hand circuit and set them up for a slow approach.

The Anson banked onto final. Rob gave JR full flaps. He slowed the aircraft down to sixty knots. With the stiff breeze that gave them a pleasingly slow ground speed, he felt confident that the short strip would accommodate them.

Rob watched as JR skilfully applied thrust with the nose attitude up, holding the aircraft just above the ground, and enabling him to drop on the first part of usable strip.

He glanced back at Susie, who gazed out of the window.

They landed with a thump and JR immediately pulled the throttles back to idle and gently applied the brakes. The ground was indeed rougher than it looked from above. They bounced in their seats before slowing enough to turn.

It didn't look like they had much of an area to park, but JR carried on down the strip until they saw a small portion of cut grass off the westerly end.

After bringing the aircraft to a stop, pointing into wind, JR shut her down. Susie appeared behind them.

"We have a visitor."

She was looking out at a man, maybe in his sixties, walking with a limp toward the aircraft.

Rob unstrapped and went to the door, opening it and lowering the folding stairs to allow Susie to leave first. He pulled off his flying coveralls before following her.

"This is Mr Bonner," said Susie, raising her voice over the stiff breeze. "He knows where Professor Belkin's cottage is."

Rob leant back into the aircraft.

"We're off. I hope we won't be too long."

"No problem," said JR. "I'll sit here and contemplate my next career."

They walked from the grass strip, along a plateau that covered most of the island. Ahead of them lay what looked like a stone lighthouse, isolated and exposed to the prevailing wind.

"The old Light Cottage in the garden." Bonner pointed at a small stone building. "The MacPhersons own it now. He's staying there."

Susie thanked him, but before they could walk off, the man asked them, "Who did you say you were again?"

"Oxford University business," she replied. "Very urgent."

Bonner didn't look convinced.

"An urgent maths problem?"

"Yes!" said Susie brightly, and they set off.

———

THE COTTAGE WAS TINY. As they approached it, Rob looked for signs of an ageing maths professor, but it appeared empty.

They arrived at the small wooden door and glanced at each other before Susie gave it a few hefty thumps with her small fist.

No sound from within, but the wind carried a new voice to them. They whipped around.

"Are you looking for me?"

A grey-haired man, with woollen jumper and baggy red trousers, lowered himself down the grass bank with the aid of a walking stick. A pair of glasses hung from a chain around his neck, and he carried a pair of binoculars.

"Professor Belkin?" called Susie.

He didn't immediately answer, but concentrated on the last few steps. Rob went forward to help him down.

He steadied himself on the flat ground that ran around the cottage.

"I am he. To what do I owe this pleasure?" Belkin said, and gave them a warm smile.

"I'm Robert May and this is my colleague Susie. Perhaps we could go inside?"

"Yes, if you like. I have little to offer, I'm afraid, but I could rustle up a cup of tea. Or maybe something stronger?"

He opened the door, which wasn't locked.

"Arrive in that thing, did you?" Belkin said, motioning toward the airstrip.

"We did. I'm afraid it's rather urgent."

The professor took a seat by the door, next to a small cabinet. "Perhaps one of you would be kind enough to make the tea? The fresh air does rather take it out of me. But I enjoy feeling tired. It's one of life's pleasures when you get to my age."

Susie got up and moved to an old range at the side of the room. She found a stainless steel kettle and a china teapot.

"Professor Belkin, we've taken a considerable risk to visit you today. In fact, believe it or not, the RAF is currently looking for that aeroplane we arrived in."

"I see," the old man said.

"Can I ask you if you have ever met Squadron Leader Christopher Milford?"

The professor considered the question for a moment. "Perhaps you should tell me why you're here."

Rob glanced at Susie; she gave a small nod.

"I'm very sorry to tell you that Millie died in an aircraft accident on the 24th June."

The professor bowed his head. "Oh, dear me. That is terribly, terribly sad. I am so very sorry to hear that."

"Thank you, Professor. He was a good friend. But I'm afraid I rather failed in my duty to him. We're here to make amends."

"Did the bastards kill him?" the professor asked with nonchalance, as if this was a perfectly reasonable question in the circumstances.

Rob again looked at Susie.

"We don't know," she answered. "Maybe."

The professor nodded, appearing to accept this as a potential outcome for Millie.

"After Millie died," Rob continued, "they found out what he had been up to. They're currently trying to portray him as a traitor, but we know better. We know he was trying to prove a new guidance system was fatally flawed, and that the trial to see it into service was a sham. I believe you may have helped him?"

The professor didn't answer. Susie left the tea-making and moved from the kitchen area, pulling a piece of paper from her pocket. She unfolded it and handed it to Belkin. He put his reading glasses on and held it up to catch the light from the window.

Susie sat down at the table.

Eventually, the professor relaxed his hand, let it drop to his lap and looked at them expectantly.

"So, what do you need to know?"

"What does it mean? What did you find out?"

He looked across to Susie. "I can see that Mr May is with the Royal Air Force, but may I ask about your role, miss?"

"Attenborough. Susie Attenborough. Can I assume it was you who passed a certain telephone number to Mr Milford?"

A flicker of recognition passed across his face. "Ah, yes. And can I assume you answered it?"

"Well, I don't work on the switchboard, but it did eventually come to me, yes."

He seemed satisfied and turned back to Rob, with Millie's notes still in his hand.

"This appears to be a combination of notes taken from a telephone call I had with Mr Milford. Oh, must have been... well, the day before he died, I believe." He looked at the paper again. "But also, some of his own subsequent conclusions."

"Millie brought you tapes?" Rob asked.

"Yes. Mr Milford brought me a series of magnetic tapes. I facilitated the reading of the reels and provided him with a list of statistical anomalies. We also carried out some interpretation of the data based on its operational use. These are the results."

Susie leant forward. "Statistical anomalies?"

"Yes. Sections of data that didn't fit into the surrounding context."

"I'm sorry, could you explain a bit more?" Rob asked.

"Well, let me put it in more practical terms. Now, as I understand it, the data was gathered by a new form of height-measuring device on board an aircraft? A laser beam?"

"Millie really did trust you." Rob smiled at the thought of the two men together.

"In the end he had to, otherwise I would have found it difficult to complete the tasks he set. Anyway, you would expect the height readings to look consistent with an aeroplane travelling across the land, but let us say that within a time period of less than a second, the height reading showed a difference of one thousand feet. Well, your aircraft would be physically incapable of manoeuvring at such velocity, and therefore the data must be wrong."

"So you proved that the system was faulty?"

Belkin considered this for a moment. "We have to be careful drawing such conclusions. Mr Milford thought it possible that small inaccuracies might happen very often, but they would not likely interfere with the flight, as true readings would flow through before the aircraft's autopilot would have time to make any changes. What he wanted to know, therefore, is how often inaccuracies lasted long enough to affect the flying. We provided this answer. We also used those numbers to make projections using actual flying statistics."

"And the conclusion?" Susie asked.

"You have it on this piece of paper. Here..." Belkin pointed at a figure on the sheet. Rob leant forward:

0.9816%

"That's how often we saw some sort of deviation. But this figure is the more interesting one."

0.014%.

"That's how often the figures could be wrong long enough to affect a flight. One and a half tenths of one per cent."

"That doesn't sound very often," Susie said.

"True. If you only flew, say a hundred times a year, it would statistically never occur. However, the Royal Air Force flies rather more than that. And as I understand it, we should also consider the flying carried out in the United States of America?"

"Yes," Rob said. "We should. So how often are we talking?" He looked at the figures again. "I'm sorry, my maths isn't quite up to it."

"Quite often. Without a pencil and some graph paper I can't tell you exactly, but maybe a hundred times every ten thousand hours flown."

Susie leaned forward, hands on the table. "You're telling us, this system would cause one hundred crashes in ten thousand hours?"

"No. Again, there is another layer below this. For the vast majority of those occurrences, the incoherent data would cause a small deviation, but not enough to be a major problem. Mr Milford was keenly interested in very specific circumstances. Low-level, high speed and banked or approaching rising ground, and for the deviation to instigate a downward deviation rather than cause the aircraft to rise."

He picked up the paper. "This, I believe, is his conclusion."

$$262 \ ll/day$$
$$100/TFR$$
$$5 \ dys$$
$$250/y$$
$$= 25,000$$
$$0.014\% = \underline{3.5}$$
$$2.5 \ Cr/ = \underline{8.75}$$

Rob crouched down next to Belkin and peered at the sheet. "I still don't understand the figures."

"This is a classic application of statistics. Mr Milford has started with the number of flights, here..." He pointed at the number 262. "And down here is an extrapolation from the data of the more serious anomalies. As I recall, it was a very low number and yet because of the sheer volume of flights every year, it appears that 3.5 flights annually would be critically endangered. I must say, from my recollection of our findings, this is about right."

"Hence the 8.75 figure at the end. He's averaged the crew size across the low-level fleet and come up with 2.5."

"2.5 times 3.5?" Susie asked.

"8.75," Rob confirmed. "The number of lives in danger annually if Guiding Light goes into service. Here it is, Susie. Here's the evidence, in black-and-white."

Susie turned to Belkin.

"Professor, where is the actual evidence? Do you still have the tapes and the data?"

"I'm afraid we destroyed them, on Squadron Leader Milford's instructions. But there is something else rather important here. These conclusions are not reliable. There simply wasn't enough data. Not nearly enough. The true figure, that number at the end, has much that is assumed and extrapolated from a very small sample size. I imagined this would be the beginning of an investigation, not the end."

Rob didn't reply; Susie rested a hand on his shoulder.

"I'm sorry if that's unwelcome news."

They sat in silence for a while. Rob toyed with the sheet of statistics. He stared at the final figure.

<u>8.75</u>

"Shall we have that tea now?" Belkin said.

The three of them drank from old mugs that looked like they'd seen service in the war. Belkin told them he'd stayed on Lundy with his wife Winifred the year after they were married in 1931. She was hit by a bus and died, crossing the road in Edinburgh in 1942.

"I thought she was safe up there."

"Where were you during the war?" Rob asked.

"I suppose I can tell you now. I worked at Bletchley Park. Have you heard of it?"

Rob shook his head.

"I have," Susie said. "Ultra."

"That's right. Your friends across the river."

"We had a couple of lessons on it during training," said Susie. "It was amazing. They captured the German code machines and cracked them. For most of the war, we were one step ahead. They never did find out."

"So this was child's play in comparison," said Rob.

"Yes, it was a tough assignment. Much pressure on our shoulders and frequent setbacks. Rationing the information was the biggest challenge. If we used too much of it, it would be obvious we'd cracked the Enigma machines and the precious supply would suddenly end." He poured himself another cup of tea as he spoke. "I never did get used to the idea that we would let a ship sink and all those men die, just to keep our secret safe."

"But it was the right thing to do," Susie said.

"Yes, it was. It shortened the war considerably and saved many more lives in the long run." Belkin stirred in another sugar.

"You think this is how Kilton sees Guiding Light?" Rob asked Susie.

"Undoubtedly. He's done these figures. With more data, his numbers will be more accurate, no doubt. Maybe higher than 8.75 men a year, maybe lower. But either way, he clearly considers it a price worth paying for the advantage gained."

"But Mr Milford did not think it a price worth paying," Belkin said. "And neither do you, Mr May, do you?"

"No."

They finished their tea quietly.

Just after 5PM Belkin saw them to the door. "I'm sorry I could not provide you with the firm evidence you require. But I think you must ask yourself this. If this is, as your superior must think, a price worth paying to win the Cold War or whatever, why has he felt the need to cover it up? Is that not something you can use to change the minds of those who need persuading? Surely there is enough you have uncovered to at least raise a question mark over the project?"

"Maybe," Rob said, without conviction.

As they stepped out, Susie turned back to the professor.

"How did you know the number and code name, to contact us?"

"I've been at Oxford since 1945. I have my fair share of geniuses passing through my study. It's always been in the interests of certain organisations to remain in touch."

Susie smiled. "The Oxford recruiter. You're a legend at Leconfield House."

"I doubt that."

———

MARY THOUGHT HERSELF A CONFIDENT DRIVER, but encouraging the Laverstocks' Armstrong Siddeley Sapphire to stay in one place in the road was a challenge. The old car leant around corners and seemed to sway even on the straight.

On the passenger seat was an address near Southampton. Mary was glad of Janet's officious nature, and she had done well in prising Georgina's whereabouts out of the vicar.

The sun was still high in the afternoon sky as she reached the outskirts of the city. She turned toward the village of Totton.

It took her a frustrating ten minutes before she found the small close containing the Milfords' rented bungalow. The old car overheated, and Mary left the vehicle to cool as she approached Charlie and Georgina's temporary home.

She tapped on the door and waited, looking around at Millie's car and the small, unkempt front garden.

There was movement inside; she heard a familiar voice call out.

"Charlie! Can you get that?"

He opened the door.

"Hello, Mrs May."

"Hello, Charlie." For a moment they just stared at each other. He looked uncertain.

"May I come in?"

Charlie appeared to relax. "Of course. Sorry."

Georgina appeared behind Charlie. Composed, made up, wearing a red chiffon dress. Positively glowing.

"Mar! Darling!" She raced to the door, brushing past her son. The two women embraced and Mary clung tightly to her friend.

IN THE GARDEN, Georgina poured two glasses of sweet German white wine. Mary wasn't a connoisseur, but it tasted cheap.

"How are you?" Mary asked.

"I can't pretend it's easy, Mar. I try to stay strong for Charlie, but once the bedroom door shuts, I'm a mess. I miss you all so desperately."

"What did they say to you, Georgina? Why did they ask you to leave?"

"Oh, they considered our house a crime scene, or some such nonsense. I think Rob's doing his best for us, but Millie obviously got himself in a muddle about something... I just can't believe they're taking it so seriously."

"When you say Rob's doing his best, you mean that box of papers?"

"I suppose so. He got them away, so the police never actually found anything, but they know something's missing. What I don't understand is why Mark can't put a stop to it all."

"Kilton?"

"Yes! He's in charge, isn't he?"

"Georgina, do you have any idea what's actually going on?"

"I don't have the foggiest, Mar. People keep asking me, but as always, the wives are the last to know anything."

"What 'people', Georgina? Who keeps asking you?"

"Rob, of course. Yesterday—"

"You spoke to Rob?"

"Well, yes. He was here yesterday. Didn't he tell you?"

"No. He didn't. I'm sorry I had no idea he'd already spoken to you."

"Well, I couldn't tell him much, but he asked a lot about what Millie was up to, running up to the crash. I'm afraid I wasn't much help." She shrugged. "I said the same thing to Red."

"Red was here, too?"

"Not here, but he telephoned a couple of hours ago, asking all the same questions." She took another drink of wine. "I'm surprised Rob didn't mention it to you, Mary!"

"Georgina, did Rob say anything about us?"

"You and me?"

"No, I mean about me and Rob?"

Georgina looked at her, puzzled. "No. What are you talking about?"

Mary shook her head and looked away. "I can't believe he didn't say anything." She looked back at Georgina. "I left him on Monday."

"What? Why?"

Mary hesitated for a moment, before deciding on her answer. "I was told he was having an affair..."

Georgina stared at her, open-mouthed for a moment. "Are you being serious?"

"I just don't know, Georgina. Yes, I was told categorically. He was with a young woman. The Laverstocks saw them at a pub, kissing."

"Janet Laverstock? That busybody... She must have been mistaken. What did he say?"

"He said it wasn't what it looked like."

"Well, there you go, then."

Mary toyed with her wine glass and tried to recall precisely what Rob had said as she left, but the memory was clouded with rage.

"To be honest, I think it fitted my mood to believe it. He's drifted off in the last few months, and I've been feeling cut out. So it made sense to me, I think, that he had someone else he was sharing his life with."

"Yes, darling. It's called the RAF. We have to share our men with the flying club. Now what exactly did he say about this supposed other woman? What was his explanation?"

Mary looked around the garden, noting the poor state of everything.

"I was so angry. I didn't really let him get that far. Her name's Susie, and she's helping him. That's all I can remember. Of course I dismissed it all. But now... I'm not so sure. Something's going on, Georgina, and I think Rob's rather desperate about it all, trying to fix whatever went wrong for Millie. Maybe he's trying to fix it for you and Charlie?"

"That's exactly what he said to us. Mar, you need to talk to Rob."

"But there's so much bloody secrecy all the time. No-one talks to anyone."

Mary took a long drink of the wine.

"What did you say to Red Brunson? And why's he involved?"

"I told him about the box." Georgina spoke quietly. "I wasn't going to. Rob asked us to never mention it. But there was something about his manner. He was whispering on the phone. I got the feeling he's looking out for Rob."

Mary bit her bottom lip.

"I think I need to go home."

"Good. Mary, darling. You have no idea what it would do to me to see you two fall apart."

———

JR WAS APPARENTLY asleep in the shade of the wing.

Rob and Susie climbed the bank onto the plateau. With the aircraft still a hundred yards away, Rob stopped.

"I'm frightened. How do we do this? They'll be waiting for me."

"You'll have to face that music, I'm afraid. But remember, it will help you if it involves the police. Even this strange branch of the RAF police Kilton seems to have occupying West Porton will have a degree of independence from TFU. They are the people you need to convince. You know everything you need to know. Just hedge your bets about the evidence. It's our weak point. Tell them the evidence is out there somewhere."

It sounded easy, coming from Susie. He would reveal Guiding Light was fatally flawed and that Kilton was ignoring the evidence.

"Will you help me?"

"My job is to get my lot to intervene at a much higher level. We report to the Ministry or even Number Ten and tell them we believe the project has been compromised by Kilton, and that will tip the balance for us. As soon as they ask questions, Kilton will be in trouble. As long as I can persuade them to ask questions."

"Will they?" Rob could see from her expression that she was unsure.

"Mark Kilton has played a good game here, Rob. From the moment he set up TFU, the odds were stacked heavily in his favour."

Rob closed his eyes.

"Look, you've done brilliantly. How far have we come in just a few days? All we can do is give this last push. You do your bit, I do mine."

JR was up, carrying out the pre-flight walkaround.

"I can't fly back with you," she announced.

"What?"

"If I get arrested at West Porton, things will get messy very quickly and the boys back in Mayfair won't be happy, not least because they don't know I'm here. And right now, I need them on my side."

They walked toward the aircraft.

Susie looked around the island. "There's a ferry somewhere, Mrs Lazenby said."

"We can drop you," Rob said. "But I'd be reluctant to divert to another RAF station. How about Eastleigh at Southampton? It's a civil aerodrome."

"Really? That would be amazing." She gave Rob's arm a little rub.

They climbed on board. JR joined them, and took the diversion to Eastleigh in his stride.

Rob planned the route.

A few minutes later, with Susie in the front row of tatty seats, Rob as co-pilot, JR as captain, they fired up the Anson's two engines. Once they warmed up, JR taxied beyond the official end of the runway to give them a little extra in the roll.

"I walked it while you were gone. It looks firm and dry enough for us to steal a little extra."

JR stood on the brakes and brought the engines up to take-off power. As he released them, he worked to keep the Anson in the centre of the grass strip. The breeze was a little across, but also, helpfully, it was mainly over the wings, giving them some extra airspeed.

The needle crept up slowly; at one point, the right wing dipped as they hit a rut, but JR kept her steady. He got the tailwheel off the ground at the earliest opportunity and waited for the speed to build on the main gear. Rob tensed his fists as they fast approached the end of the usable grass.

Finally, JR eased them into the air.

A moment later the ground beneath them dropped away and the silver aircraft swept over the craggy cliffs of Lundy, banking toward the mainland.

Once they were established on the first leg, Rob considered unstrapping and talking to Susie. But was there anything left to say? She had made clear what his role was. She had her own task.

It was the end of their time together. It felt as if he'd known her for months, not days.

As they got closer to Southampton, JR called ATC and explained they had no flight plan or booking, but could they carry out a practice diversion with full stop.

The tower agreed.

On the ground, they were marshalled into an area close to the new passenger terminal. Susie disembarked and Rob stood in the doorway, ready to pull the steps back in.

"You'll be fine on your own," said Susie. She paused for a moment and took his hand. "I have great faith in you, Robert May. Millie would have been proud of what you've achieved in the last forty-eight hours. You've picked up his torch, Rob."

"God, it's his funeral tomorrow," Rob said.

"A lot's going to happen between now and then. Good luck, Flight Lieutenant May."

"Thank you. I'll be listening for the sound of the cavalry charge from MI5."

She smiled at him. "I told you, it's passé to use that name."

Susie stepped off the aircraft. Rob watched her walk toward the terminal. Would he ever see this enigmatic and beautiful woman again?

He withdrew back into the aircraft, feeling vulnerable and alone.

Minutes later, they had the wide, long Eastleigh runway in front of them. Rob asked JR if he could fly, believing it might be the distraction he needed.

He advanced the throttles, levelled her onto the main gear and at seventy-five knots, raised the nose and she released her grip on the runway.

West Porton was mere minutes away and soon after they reached five thousand feet, JR called them up.

"Shorthand one-three, you are cleared to land. Please taxi immediately to TFU apron."

JR acknowledged and gave Rob a sympathetic look.

"JR, tell them you know nothing. I asked for the flights, telling you it was official TFU business, and you simply flew us where I requested."

JR laughed. "They'll never believe me, but I like your optimism."

Rob could only admire JR and his laid-back approach to impending doom. He saw the same twinkle in his eyes that he'd seen so often with Millie.

Rob descended and joined downwind, trying to minimise the time between now and whatever would greet them on the ground. He just wanted it over with.

The Anson flew over the West Porton double perimeter fence; he glanced out of his window. A collection of police vehicles were parked on the apron, with men standing beside them.

He looked ahead and brought the aircraft down onto the runway, knowing that whatever happened, this would be his final flight as an RAF pilot.

I'm not even thirty years old.

He turned onto the taxiway and brought the aircraft parallel to TFU before turning in. The official reception would happen in clear view of the planning room.

JR helped him shut the aircraft down. They unstrapped and looked at each other.

"Let's do this together," JR said. They both left the cockpit. Rob opened the door and JR folded the stairs out.

Standing in front of them were four uniformed security force officers, one of whom Rob recognised as the man who interviewed him, Hoskins. He stepped forward.

"Flight Lieutenant Robert May, I am placing you under arrest on suspicion of disobeying direct orders, the unauthorised use of RAF equipment, and breaching the Official Secrets Act. Do you understand?"

He looked beyond the men in front of him and saw Kilton, lurking in the gloom of the doorway to TFU. Squinting, he could just about make out some faces staring from the planning room.

He looked back at the squadron leader who had announced his arrest.

"I have urgent information about a TFU project—"

"There'll be time for that later." Hoskins turned to one of the other uniformed men. "Sergeant, please take the flight lieutenant to the station."

As the sergeant stepped forward, the senior officer turned to JR. "We're arresting you on suspicion of aiding and abetting."

JR shrugged.

They ushered Rob into the back of a car by himself and drove from the apron. He looked across at TFU to see Kilton return inside as the faces at the window withdrew.

———

SUSIE WALKED through the empty passenger terminal building at Southampton. She called her desk officer from a public telephone just inside the main doors.

"We have what I believe is grounds to intervene in the Milford case."

"I see," Roger replied. Two words that dripped with scepticism. "Just to be clear, you did not intervene as discussed?"

"May carried out the task of his own volition. As I said, he was going whether we liked it or not."

"You better talk to them upstairs." The line went quiet.

Susie pulled her notepad from her purse.

The line stayed quiet.

At her level, tasks involved staying unseen and making reports, yet here she was, running an entire operation.

And now what? What happens next?

"Miss Attenborough?"

"Yes."

"I'm putting you through to Mr Collingwood."

The department head. A man she'd been introduced to on her first day and had not seen since.

"Miss Attenborough. How was your day trip?"

"Hello, sir. I'm sorry I ended up doing a little more than we planned, but I really had no choice. Rob May was determined."

"I see."

"But we have made a significant discovery. We have the knowledge required to challenge the conventional wisdom that seems to surround Guiding Light."

There was a pause. "Go on."

"The system is flawed. It's a small, often inconsequential error from the laser rangefinder to the autopilot. But with the number of flights planned both here and in the United States, it will claim aircrew lives."

"Quite a bold statement. May I ask how you know this?"

"Before he died, Christopher Milford managed to smuggle a good number of tapes from West Porton to the maths department at Oxford University. That's how they found and quantified the flaw."

"And that's where Professor Leonard Belkin comes in?"

"Yes, he allowed use of the mainframe computer. But he wasn't aware of the details. He was able to extrapolate the numbers, though. He carried out important work, albeit unknowingly."

"That's as may be, but even before we present it, this theory has been thoroughly dismissed by those with access to the actual project recordings. TFU are content to continue with Guiding Light and that's been backed at the highest level in government."

"I know, but I believe a cover-up is in place, led by Mark Kilton. It possibly involves DF Blackton as well."

"It sounds elaborate."

"Sir, I've seen the results in black-and-white." She pulled a piece of paper from her pocket. "8.75 crew members a year would die. That's just from a 0.014% rate of error from the laser beam."

"Fine. So we ask West Porton to examine these tapes that Milford, as you say, smuggled away. I think that's the best we can hope for. With the extra scrutiny they won't be able to disguise the results."

Susie sighed.

"We don't have the tapes, sir."

"Where are they?"

"Incinerated."

"I see. So you have no evidence for these rather extreme allegations which have already been batted away by TFU?"

"You have to understand the position Milford was in, sir. Mark Kilton's all powerful. Milford was scared of him. That's why the evidence was destroyed. But even without the tapes, we know enough. We need to take action."

"I'm not sure I see that, Miss Attenborough. Not without evidence. What action do you suppose we should take? Give me your precise recommendations."

She took a deep breath.

"Kilton operates with an autonomy that does not fit with the armed forces hierarchy. I believe he has lines of authority to government which allow him to bypass the usual checks and balances. Ultimately, he's used this to press into service a potentially dangerous aircraft system."

"I understand the case you have made, Miss Attenborough, but I asked you for your recommended actions."

"Guiding Light needs to be halted and independently investigated."

"And who do you suggest does that?"

"I'm not sure. The existing trials units at Boscombe Down?"

Collingwood spoke calmly, with a sing-song, matter-of-fact voice. "That would undermine TFU and the point of its existence. It would also expose a Top Secret project to an intolerable number of witnesses, which would be in breach of the United Kingdom's undertaking to the United States. And I don't need to remind you that a great deal of investment is at stake."

"Then we concentrate on Kilton—"

"Have him arrested?"

"Yes."

"On what charge?"

Susie had a sinking feeling. She could imagine Roger laughing in the background.

"Falsifying aircraft trial results. And I believe that would just be the start. We should also look carefully at the crash that killed Milford."

"An inquiry is already taking place into that. Its conclusion is likely to rule out Guiding Light as a culprit."

"That's a cover."

He sighed. "You understand the problem I have, Miss Attenborough. Your word against an independent Board of Inquiry and a decorated senior officer in Mark Kilton. What we need is hard evidence. Irrefutable. Something the director would have no choice about. I'm afraid we are a long way from that point."

"What about the statistics I gave you? Derived from actual flying data, straight from the aircraft."

"I am trying to help, Miss Attenborough, but your evidence is the word of a septuagenarian who tells us the tapes and papers were burned. Remind me again why the only hard evidence was destroyed?"

"This was just the first sample. Milford intended to continue gathering data, but he was killed."

There was a silence at the other end of the line and Susie realised she had just undermined her already weak case.

"Just a first sample, from which conclusions were extrapolated, and on that basis you would like Her Majesty's government to halt a billion dollar export deal?"

She should have had this conversation a week ago.

"Miss Attenborough, you have worked hard and with diligence, but not for the first time in the career that lays ahead of you, I am sure, you have come up against the rather cruel realities of our service. We can act only when the evidence is overwhelmingly criminal, or there is evidence the national security is in immediate danger. I'm afraid, that contrary to your expectations, neither of those tests have been met. We have no direct evidence of cover-up, no reliable evidence of project mismanagement. In fact, the only evidence we actually have of wrongdoing are the actions of Flight Lieutenant May and Squadron Leader Milford, both of whom are already under investigation, one posthumously—"

"Of course they are, sir. Kilton has an iron grip on the unit. Milford and May risked everything."

"I wonder, would May have risked all without your prompting?"

She saw an image of Rob stuck inside some dank police station, his career over.

"You see, Miss Attenborough, if we attempt to intervene on such feeble evidence, we open ourselves up to the type of criticism the Service very much wishes to avoid."

He continued to speak with a gentle manner, but the message was clear.

You've screwed up, Susie.

"I think it's time to come home. We'll find something better suited to your particular talents."

She shuddered as she imagined Roger asking her to make his tea.

"But what about Rob May? His wife left him, he's at the mercy of Kilton—"

"And you believe it's all your fault?"

"I believe it's the result of us doing what needed to be done, sir. And I believe we have a duty toward him."

"We do not, Miss Attenborough. You may feel that, but I would advise you to disengage your emotions. They let you down and cloud your judgement. The Service has a duty to the country, not an individual junior officer in the RAF. If it's any consolation, we believe, due to the nature of the project, any kind of public hearing such as a court martial is out of the question. Of course that won't spare May from the wrath of his superior. A man who can effectively end his career, no doubt.

"Try to see this as an opportunity for personal and professional growth, Miss Attenborough. Don't get too close to your marks in the future. I'm sure we briefed you on that point in training. Now, we've come to the end of the line and that's that. I expect to see you back here on Monday morning. You can take tomorrow off."

Susie stood upright in the phone box and took a deep breath.

Rob had shown so much courage to take that Anson back to West Porton, knowing he would be arrested.

Now it was her turn to be brave.

"I'm sorry, sir, but this is not the end of the line. We would be derelict in our duty to allow this project to proceed and leave a good man hanging out to dry. You may find yourself content to write off lives, but I am not."

"Miss Attenborough..."

She raised her voice. "Christopher Milford died for this cause. And I'm buggered if I'm going to abandon him. I'm sorry I didn't work out to be the agent you wanted. Let's face it, I'm the wrong sex for that. No, I won't take tomorrow off. And no, I won't be in the office on Monday. I have work to do."

She slammed the phone down, her hand shaking.

She turned to the doors at the front of the terminal building and walked out into the warm evening light.

For a moment she stood and stared at the sinking sun. Thin clouds drifted across its surface.

Susie wondered what the hell she was going to do next.

———

STRIPPED OF HIS WATCH, belt and shoelaces, Rob sat by himself in a makeshift cell, with a camp bed and a blanket.

They had ignored him since his arrest.

The entire police station set-up appeared to be inside RAF West Porton, in an adapted office block on the far side of the camp.

It felt more like Soviet Russia than the United Kingdom.

Eventually they led him into a smaller room, with a single desk. Squadron Leader Hoskins arrived, clipboard in hand, and took a seat opposite.

Hoskins took Rob through a torturous recap of the entire day, making extensive notes. Rob hid nothing. They'd already made it clear they had identified Professor Belkin from the address given to them by Abingdon.

As the interview went on, the experience became more and more frustrating. The senior officer was only interested in where he went with the Anson, what time they had landed, what time they had taken off.

Every time he explained what they had discovered, the investigator went back to the logistics of the unauthorised flights.

Rob's mood passed from impatient to desperate in a matter of minutes.

"Please. Sir. You must understand that a computer has extrapolated a terrible accident rate from the data."

"So you keep saying."

"Maybe I should talk directly to Wing Commander Kilton?"

The squadron leader raised an eyebrow.

"Impossible. You're accusing him of either negligence, or some-thing much worse."

The room smelled of fresh paint.

Rob had a horrible thought: had this police station been prepared exclusively for him?

And the uniform Hoskins wore; it looked like a branch of the RAF police, but was subtly different.

Everything at West Porton was subtly different.

The reinforced fence didn't just keep CND out; it kept everyone out.

"We'll check your assertions against the official trial records," Hoskins said. "If you can give me some specific occasions to look at?"

Rob huffed. "It's not like that. I don't have those specifics. But I do have the conclusions. We'd need to conduct a lot more safe height trials to prove the issue properly."

"So, it's not proven? It's just... speculation?"

"No. No, it's real." Everything was slipping through his fingers. "You have to believe me, the computer calculated this. Millie gath-ered the data and the computer found the problem."

"And where is this data now?"

Rob hesitated, remembering Susie's advice not to dwell on the fate of the data.

"It's been through the computer at Oxford. But we need more to identify the problem fully."

The squadron leader's pen hovered over his notepad. "So, do you have the evidence or not?"

"We don't have that specific evidence anymore, no. Millie was gathering more. He thought he had more time."

His voice caught on the words.

The squadron leader put down his pen and stopped making notes. "So, you have the conclusions to a study, but no evidence. You accuse a decorated commanding officer of conspiracy on the basis of a scrawl of notes written in fountain pen. You can't even tell me where to look, because you say that only a computer can see the truth. You can understand the difficulty I'm having with this, Flight

Lieutenant? The only actual crimes I have evidence for are those committed by you. And Mr Milford, of course. Now that you confirm to me he was secretly gathering data and taking it off West Porton."

"Our plummet to the ground, on the 7th June, about 2.30PM, in a Vulcan, mid-Wales. Check the data."

"We have a report from DF Blackton on all the data from the early trials. It shows no abnormalities."

"What if they're lying?"

"You have evidence for that? Then show me."

"What about our crash? The system caused the ground strike. Last Friday. Check that data."

"But Guiding Light had been disengaged some time before the impact."

"No, no, you're wrong. And what about the professor who looked into it all? I can give you his details."

"We're not authorised to discuss this project with outsiders. I can ask for permission, but that would have to come down the chain and have Wing Commander Kilton's approval."

Rob stared at him.

"If there's nothing else?" Hoskins asked, shuffling up his notes.

Rob slumped forward, bowing his head, exhausted. "What will happen to me?" he asked, his voice weak.

Hoskins studied his notes for a moment. "They'll make a decision whether to prosecute you for disobeying orders, the unauthorised use of government property and breaching the Official Secrets Act. Quite a collection of charges."

"Will I go to prison?"

The man averted his eyes. "Probably."

"And you're happy with this? That I go to prison because I found out that a secret system is fatally flawed?"

He stood up, sighing as he did so. "I think we've been through this, Flight Lieutenant."

As the man walked toward the door Rob sprang to his feet. The man looked briefly alarmed. "What about Millie's funeral? I need to go."

Hoskins half-turned, with what looked like an understanding expression. "These are serious charges."

He left the room, and a moment later a corporal escorted Rob back to his cell. He lay down on the old camp bed and curled up.

He thought of Mary and began to cry.

————

SUSIE PAID THE TAXI DRIVER, stepped out onto the kerb and assessed the scruffy bungalow. It was a far cry from the neat married quarter patch at West Porton.

The death of Christopher Milford was real; here was his widow and fatherless son.

The crash, the secret guidance system, deciphering the equations, tracking down ancient professors... The whole thing had a surreal, disconnected quality to it. And yet, somewhere in the background, was an unimaginable human loss.

It was inside these walls: the suffering.

She knocked. Through the frosted glass, a diffuse red shape grew larger, and a woman in a striking chiffon dress opened the door and gave her a quizzical look.

"Mrs Milford? My name is Susie, I'm a friend of Rob May's. I wonder if I could talk to you?"

A wry smile crept across the woman's face as she appeared to assess her.

"So, you're the floozy?"

Susie hadn't expected the news to have travelled here.

"I'm guessing all is not what it seems," said Georgina. "Which is what I told Mrs May this afternoon, and Red Brunson. And now here you are. I've never felt so popular. Perhaps you'd better come in."

Over the next half an hour, Susie tiptoed her way through the truth, giving Georgina a hint of who she was and what had happened. Millie's widow laughed a couple of times as Susie explained how he had been courageously taking on the establishment. But then her face turned very serious.

"Is this why he died?"

Susie thought carefully before answering. "Maybe."

Georgina told Susie what she knew, which was not much for her to go on.

"At the door you mentioned another name?"

"Red Brunson?"

"That's it. Tell me about him."

"Tall, handsome, adorable." She saw the look Susie was giving her. "Well, perhaps more pertinently, a colleague of Rob and Millie's. I think he's someone else having second thoughts."

"What do you mean?"

Georgina thought for a moment. "They don't talk very much, that lot. It's not encouraged. If you're on a secret project, you keep it to yourself. So it doesn't surprise me that the chaps would have no idea what Millie was up to. But I can tell you, it's caught Red's attention."

"Do you think he's going to do something?"

Georgina shrugged. "I don't know. But he's sniffing about."

They sat for a while. Susie turned the events of the day over in her mind.

Rob was behind bars. Belkin had told them as much as he could.

Chris Milford was dead.

That only leaves one person, whose name had suddenly entered the conversation.

She looked at Georgina. "How would I get back to Porton from here?"

Georgina smiled at her. "We have a lumbering old red car, if you'd like to borrow it."

"Your husband's? Are you sure?"

"Well, I suppose it's mine now. And yes. I think I am sure. Mr Kilton has arranged official cars for us tomorrow, although now I come to think of it, I wonder if that's so we don't hang about afterwards and talk to the wrong people."

"Possibly. You really wouldn't mind? It would be tremendously helpful."

"It's a tank to drive, I'll warn you now."

At the front of the bungalow, they shook hands and said their goodbyes. Susie stepped out onto the road and with a scrap of paper and a scribbled address, she set off back to West Porton.

As she pulled out of Totton, she glanced around the car. The red leather seats were worn and tatty, and the engine complained at every use of the accelerator. And yet the car had warmth to it. She inhaled the smell of the interior; how much of it was the scent of Christopher Milford, a man she had never known. Yet somehow, they were now colleagues in the same fight.

————

At 7PM Mary told the Laverstocks she needed to pick a few bits up from her married quarter, waving off the overbearing offers of help.

As she pulled into the drive, it was clear their quarter was dark and empty.

She looked down the road. The street lights were just coming on. Her eyes settled on a row of cars parked directly outside number 27.

The Brunsons.

She walked the hundred yards or so and approached the front door.

Men's voices inside. She hesitated, but then took a deep breath and knocked.

Red answered quickly. He was in his USAF uniform, looking anxious. Beyond him into the kitchen, she could see Jock MacLeish and a gaggle of other officers, each man with a serious look on his face.

"Mary." He said it as if he was expecting her. "Come in." He glanced up and down the road as he ushered her over the threshold.

"Has there been a crash?" she asked as she stepped into the kitchen, crowded with Rob's colleagues.

"Have you heard from him?" asked Jock MacLeish.

"From Rob? What's happened, Jock?"

Red stepped forward. "Have a seat, Mary. Jock, get this woman a glass of scotch."

Jock stood up and offered Mary his chair.

She looked around the grave faces. *"What's happened?"*

"We assumed you knew."

"Knew what? What's going on, Jock?"

"The details are sketchy, but Rob has commandeered an Anson, flown it god knows where and back, and has been promptly arrested."

Around her, the men ran through their theories.

Mary listened, bewildered. Something radical had changed. These men, usually so concealed and secretive, were talking freely in front of her and Sarah Brunson.

The room filled with smoke, and Sarah opened some windows.

It dawned on Mary that a secret war had been taking place around them.

First between Millie and Kilton, and then Rob and Kilton.

No-one had discussed it with anyone else.

The men had ignored the signs, but they reserved some blame for Rob. Why had he not enlisted their support? Why had he acted alone?

Her heart ached at the thought of her husband languishing alone in a cell.

She spoke up. "I think the time for keeping secrets is over."

The voices in the room stopped. All eyes turned toward her.

"Rob found something at Millie's. After he died. I don't know the details, of course. But he was frightened. Secret details of a project. He protected Georgina by removing the evidence from the house, but I don't think he knew what to do next. Then, matters were taken out of our hands, literally."

"What do you mean?" Red asked.

"The box was stolen. By a young woman. She was in our house when we returned from the dinner party."

"The night Rob got drunk?"

"He sobered up pretty quickly, I can tell you. He chased her over the fields. But lost her."

"A young woman?" said Jock. "Are you sure?"

Mary nodded. "He said he recognised her. She was from the peace camp." She suddenly put her hand to her forehead. "Oh, bloody hell. Christ, I've been an idiot. That's who it was! I've been so stupid not to see it." She looked around the room. "Some silly woman from the village spotted Rob and a young woman in a pub and she convinced me he was having an affair. But it must have been her. They must have been working on something together. Rob told me it wasn't what it looked like. A likely story I thought, but now... now I believe him."

"So who is she?"

"All I know is she goes by the name Susie."

Mary suddenly felt hot and faint.

"I need some air."

Sarah rushed to her side, scooped her up, and led her out of the room.

She opened the front door, and Mary stepped into the garden.

"I'll put some tea on," Sarah said, and disappeared back into the house.

Mary walked to the small wooden fence, unsteady. Her eyes ran down the uniform row of married quarters. Even in the street light, the grass looked yellowed and thin after the heatwave.

Each lawn had the same dimensions and the same borders cut, with the only variation being the choice of flowers.

Was this outward impression of uniformity and order just an illusion?

Her eyes settled on a car a few doors down.

A red Rover she knew well.

A car she'd last seen outside the bungalow in Totton.

"What on earth?"

She looked up and down the street, searching for Georgina.

A figure stepped out of the shadows.

Mary clutched her chest.

"You scared the life out of me."

The young woman looked directly at her.

"Mrs May?"

Mary stared back.

"Susie, I presume?"

––––––

SUSIE FOLLOWED Mary to the kitchen.

"Gentlemen, we have a visitor."

Mary stepped aside.

Susie took her cue and walked into the small, smoke filled space. The men in uniform parted, their mouths open.

A woman at the sink let a tap overflow into her kettle, apparently unable to take her eyes off her.

"Well, well," said a man in an American accent.

"You must be Red Brunson?" Susie said.

"And you, my dear, must be the mysterious Susie."

She surveyed the room: a short, plump man with red cheeks; another who looked a couple of years older than Rob; another who was closer to Millie's age; three more younger men, one with a classic handlebar moustache.

"Gentlemen, ladies. Mrs May tells me there is discontentment in the TFU ranks? Just so I know, can we all agree that we have a friend in need and a senior officer of dubious method, out of control?"

"I think that about sums it up," Red said.

"Good. My name is Susie Attenborough. I work for a department of Her Majesty's government. I can't tell you any more, so you'll have to take my word for it. If it helps engender your trust, you might like to know that I was due to meet your colleague Christopher Milford on Saturday 25th June. A meeting he requested to pass on certain information. Subsequently, I have been assisting Robert May to uncover what it was Milford found. Because of his diligence and commitment to his late friend, he is now under arrest, with little prospect of being believed. Unfortunately, we don't have hard evidence, because Millie ensured it was destroyed to protect others. But we know the results. Under normal circumstances, that would be enough. But in Kilton we're up against an operator who has been one step ahead throughout this process.

"As it stands, he's won. Rob will be dealt with harshly. Any credibility will be stripped away. And to make matters worse, I've been told by my own superiors to back off." She gave a grim smile. "I can't say I'm keen on that idea. So I've decided to stay."

"And do what?" one of the men asked.

"Well, that's why I'm here." She looked around, taking in her new partners. "I'm hoping we have the brains and ability in this room to come up with something."

The men stayed silent for a moment.

"So, who's with me?"

32

FRIDAY 8TH JULY

Susie groaned. It felt like she'd only dropped onto the bed a few minutes ago.

With an effort, she pulled herself upright and allowed her mind to wake up.

Snatches of conversations came back to her, along with sketchy details of the plan.

Her doubts also returned

It was too complex. There was too much that could go wrong. The outcome was uncertain.

It was 8.05AM. She needed to go shopping.

———

AN HOUR LATER, Susie was the first customer of the day at Turner's department store in Salisbury.

She strode past the sofas and mahogany desks until she reached Ladies' Wear.

Briefly distracted by the new stock from Mary Quant, she pulled a miniskirt from the rack and held it to her waist.

An elegant, middle-aged woman appeared.

"I can see madam has the figure for the skirt."

Susie smiled and placed it back on the hangar.

"Thank you, but I don't think it's what I need today."

She turned to look at an area of more conventional clothes, spying a David Windsmoor dress her mother might well have worn.

The assistant followed her gaze. "Is madam shopping for a particular occasion?"

"Yes. A funeral."

————

THE FULL LENGTH mirror in the hall was cracked, and the dim light from the single bulb above made it barely usable. But Georgina managed to draw on a thin layer of eye-liner and a thicker layer of bright red lipstick.

She pulled on her wide brimmed navy hat with a cream trim to match her dress.

Standing back, she noticed how pale her skin looked, accentuated by the lipstick. Or maybe it was the low wattage bulb.

A low wattage bulb in a low wattage house on the edge of nowhere.

How had it come to this so quickly? How could Millie have let her down so badly?

Carrying on with something, gambling with their future.

And losing.

It was such a pleasant Friday afternoon, when Mark Kilton had arrived to take her life away.

A movement behind her. She turned to see Charlie hunting for a piece of mirror to help fit his tie.

She turned and took over the task.

"You look so handsome, darling."

He grimaced, and didn't reply.

"Come on, the car will be here in a minute. Let's be brave together."

———

MOST OF THE men arrived into the planning room in their full service dress.

The chat around the tea bar was subdued.

Red Brunson stood on one side of the room and watched Kilton emerge from his office, medals in place.

He looked the picture of authority; a steady rock in the uncertain world of the test pilot.

Red should have known from his time at Edwards that appearances can be deceptive.

Jock MacLeish was hunched over a chart; one of only two pilots in working clothes. They were drawing a line, not on an air chart but on an Ordnance Survey map; the sort of detailed map a walker might use. Red peered at the initial point MacLeish had selected: a crossroads on the A345 three miles south of Amesbury. He nodded his approval and patted Jock on the back, confident he would do Millie proud.

Red felt the men next to him stiffen as Kilton looked over.

"It's odd now, isn't it?" MacLeish said quietly to the others. "Looking at him now?"

Red didn't reply, but he followed Kilton's progress out of the door.

For good measure, he moved into the entrance area to TFU and watched as the boss got into the back of a black staff car complete with flag.

The car pulled away and turned right, not left toward the main gate.

Puzzled, Red checked his watch. Still two hours until the funeral.

———

ROB ROLLED himself off the camp bed and struggled to his feet.

The walls glistened with moisture; the room clearly wasn't designed to hold a sleeping man. The unventilated, moist air clung to his skin.

A plate of breakfast sat on the table; he had barely moved when the corporal brought it in.

He'd heard nothing following his interrogation.

By the early hours, alone in the silence, any lingering hope vanished.

They'd given him a set of exercise clothes to wear as pyjamas.

They even had his watch; he had no idea what time it was.

They were going to bury Millie without him.

The cell door pushed open; Rob stood up.

"Corporal, please let me go to—" He cut his question short when the corporal stepped aside and ushered in Mary.

He ran forward, like a toddler to his mother. The guard looked startled.

"It's all right," said Mary. "I'm here to take you to the church," she whispered into his ear.

The corporal ushered them both out of the temporary cell.

"There are showers in the gymnasium if you want to use them," he said. "But you haven't got long."

The guard picked up a pile of clothes from a trestle table next to the entrance to the building.

Next to the clothes was a document with a fountain pen on top.

The corporal handed him his dress uniform, and his spirits rose at the thought of Mary retrieving his clothes, back in their home.

There was so much he wanted to say to her. But she backed away, apparently unwilling to have a conversation.

"I'll wait for you."

The corporal ushered him out of the building and marched alongside as they walked the short distance to the station gym.

"Is it strictly necessary to guard me to the showers, Corporal?"

"Just my orders, sir. You no longer have a pass to West Porton. You're a visitor and must be escorted."

He undressed in the changing room and stood under one of the silver heads in the empty communal showers. He closed his eyes, letting the water flood over him.

He screwed the tap shut. The water became a dribble and then a series of drips. He leaned with one hand on the cold tiled wall. The shower had felt like an oasis, a haven.

He wrenched himself away and stepped out to see Mark Kilton standing in the centre of the room.

Medals gleaming, RAF hat tucked under his arm.

Rob was naked, with water pooling around his feet. Kilton stood between him and his towel and clothes.

"You have a choice, May. Put your signature to the completed project today and I will not prosecute you. We will record nothing that occurred yesterday or in the previous week on your file. You will be transferred to Transport Command and posted to Hong Kong, with Mary. It's a staff job, but you will retain your General Duties branch status and be available for a flying position in the future. I shall see that you receive a favourable evaluation from your time here.

"You'll be sipping G&Ts on the veranda in the Far East with all this behind you. And you'll be free to attend Millie's funeral, under escort of course."

"Or?"

"You'll face a court martial. Your views on the project will be inadmissible under the Official Secrets Act. You will have no defence to a series of detailed charges that include insubordination, unauthorised and unsafe operation of both Royal Air Force and Ministry of Aviation aircraft, and breach of the Official Secrets Act. We are also considering a charge of treason. Either way, the sentence for your inevitable conviction will be around twenty-five years in prison. Oh, and by the way, Guiding Light will be in full service regardless of your choice, of course."

"Then why do you need my signature?"

"I don't."

Rob stood in silence. The only power he had over Kilton was to make him wait for an answer.

He walked past the boss to his towel and wrapped it around his waist.

"8.75."

"What?" said Kilton, irritated.

"8.75. That was the conclusion Millie reached after the analysis. 8.75 aircrew every year."

Kilton's expression didn't change.

"I'm interested. What was your figure? After all, you had a lot more data to go on than we did."

"May, either sign the document and attend Millie's funeral, or refuse, and you'll be back in your cell while we arrange the charges. The choice is yours."

Rob stared at Kilton, impassive.

Kilton turned on his heels. "I'm not playing your games. The papers are at the police station. The corporal will escort you."

––––––

A POLISHED BOOT rose into the air and came down with a crunch on the gravelled church path. Sergeant Nigel Woodward's steps moved in unison with those of his fellow pallbearers.

Like many of the TFU NCO's, he had volunteered immediately to carry Squadron Leader Milford's coffin. With shining buttons and medals in place, he did his duty with as much precision as he could muster.

Ahead, the vicar waited, white surplice flowing in the gentle breeze.

They reached the door and paused.

Following some unseen communication, the organist began to play 'Abide With Me'.

They marched into the church with slow, measured steps.

Every pew was full. Uniformed men, and women with large hats stood, facing forward as the pallbearers turned into the aisle and continued to the side of the pulpit.

Two wooden stands, ready for them.

After reaching the front, they began their choreographed routine to lower the coffin from their shoulders to its temporary resting place.

Woodward glanced at the others and, with a barely perceived nod, they turned in unison to face back down the aisle.

The pallbearers marched to the back of the church and joined the mourners who had arrived too late for a seat.

An elderly gentleman appeared and pressed an order of service into the vicar's hands.

————

THEY HAD NOT ALLOWED Rob time alone with Mary. She sat alongside him in the back of a plain RAF car, accompanied by a police sergeant in the passenger seat.

The slow draw of his signature on the papers had felt like the final betrayal.

Everything that followed was demeaning.

Stripped of his security papers, Rob was officially not welcome at RAF West Porton. The only exception was that he could attend the wake in the officers' mess as a guest. But they would escort him on and off the station.

They arrived late at the church, but a space had been saved in the second pew, directly behind Georgina and Charlie.

As they walked down the aisle, Rob gazed at the ground, unable to make eye contact with anyone else.

"I shouldn't be here," he hissed at Mary. "What will they think of me?"

The only face he caught as he shuffled into the pew was Kilton's. Two rows back, eyes staring straight ahead.

The victor picking over the bones of the vanquished.

He took his seat. Mary bowed her head and appeared to be praying.

He thought of Millie. An image came into his mind: Millie with Belkin, poring over statistics.

All that work he had completed alone.

How different would it have been if they'd collaborated?

He imagined the two of them meeting with Susie, explaining what they had found and planning the gathering of further evidence.

That is not what happened.

There had been no meeting with Susie.

There was no usable evidence.

There would be no cavalry charge from MI5. He was certain of that now.

She would be back in London; on to her next task.

He studied the order of service.

It included his name. Had Kilton tried to influence that?

But there it was: the first reading. A short section of the Bible given to him by Jean what seemed like a year ago; but it was just a matter of days.

He turned the page.

Wing Commander Mark Kilton DFC would give the eulogy.

He felt sick.

"I can't do this," he whispered to Mary.

She shushed him, with a strange urgency in her eyes. *"Act normally."*

It must have been a show for Georgina. Mary still hadn't forgiven him; she still believed he was having an affair, but she wanted to put on a front, just for today.

The organ stopped and the congregation stood up. Charlie supported his mother in her attempt to rise. Rob and Mary put out their hands to help.

Georgina rose, unsteady.

He wanted to sob, but he was in uniform, stifled by all those years of maintaining a stiff-upper-lip.

After a moment, the coffin appeared in his peripheral vision and Mary broke down, lifting a hanky to her eyes.

He fought back his own tears, tilting his head up to keep them from falling.

Not in uniform.

The stifling, suffocating uniform.

Nigel Woodward caught his eye. The sergeant who'd almost ended his flying career by releasing that gas bomb.

Everyone loved Millie.

Rob concentrated on the precision of the pallbearers.

Anything to stave off the tears.

The vicar appeared and, after a brief word, they launched into a hymn.

Christopher Milford and everything he stood for was writ large in every line:

> "I vow to thee, my country, all earthly things above,
> Entire and whole and perfect, the service of my love;
> The love that asks no question, the love that stands the test,
> That lays upon the altar the dearest and the best;
> The love that never falters, the love that pays the price,
> The love that makes undaunted, the final sacrifice."

Rob sang with his eyes fixed on the order of service. He kept his head bowed, humiliated by the words.

In that moment, he had an awful realisation that he would go to his own grave knowing he had failed in the only task that had truly mattered to him.

There would be no absolution.

Kilton had ensured the victory was complete by leaving him no choice but to sign Guiding Light into service.

But the real punishment was the guilt: already crushing him, and now a life sentence.

The singing stopped. He sat down, consumed with his own thoughts.

It was a moment before he realised they were waiting for him. The vicar motioned with his hands for Rob to take to the lectern that held the large bible.

He stood and shuffled along the pew. The vicar put a hand on his arm as he passed.

"The bible's open at the right page."

Rob stepped onto the wooden plinth at the base of the lectern and found the start of his passage in the church's ornate King James Bible.

He took a deep breath and looked up.

Straight into the eyes of Susie Attenborough.

His mouth dropped open. He faltered, and snapped his head back down.

Had he really seen her?

She sat upright in a black dress and black-brimmed hat, next to Red and Sarah Brunson.

He looked up again. She smiled at him, looking serene.

Kilton sat directly in front of Susie, glaring at Rob.

He recovered himself and looked down at the reading. But he couldn't stop himself from looking again.

This time, Susie had an admonishing expression on her face. She mouthed some words.

"Get on with it."

The congregation shuffled at the awkward silence.

Clearing his throat, and hoping his voice would carry further than the front pew, he read aloud, bringing as much measure and authority as he could muster.

To his surprise, his voice sounded strong.

"The righteous perish, and no-one takes it to heart; the devout are taken away, and no-one understands that the righteous are taken away to be spared from evil.

"Those who walk uprightly enter into peace; they find rest as they lie in death."

He reached the last word and allowed himself a proper look at the congregation. His eyes swept across the packed church.

He wasn't sure exactly what to expect from his former colleagues.

Judgement? Disappointment?

What he saw was sympathy. Warmth, even.

Red Brunson looked directly at him, confidence in his gaze.

He returned to his seat.

They sang 'Jerusalem'. During the second verse, Mark Kilton made his way promptly to the lectern.

He recounted tales of World War Two. Millie as an engineer who worked miracles to keep them flying day after day.

He drew laughs with his accurate descriptions of Millie's inability to hold his beer, and his natural clumsiness. He paid a warm tribute to Millie's patriotism and sense of duty.

Kilton's eulogy went down well; had it not been in church, he may have received a round of applause.

After he returned to his seat, the vicar's voice shifted. He spoke with deep solemnity, in a serious and authoritative tone. Woodward and the pallbearers reappeared. As they manoeuvred to raise Millie to their shoulders, an overwhelming sense of grief and finality swept across Rob, and he couldn't force back the tears any longer.

Damn the bloody uniform.

As the coffin was walked past, he turned. Red Brunson also had tears streaming down his face, as did Dave Berringer, George Taffter, Henry Wiseman, Leslie Owens...

In fact, all his colleagues were weeping.

Why had he even tried to keep it in?

Georgina and Charlie followed the coffin, Millie's widow slumped against her son. Rob and the others in the second row moved out to follow them.

Within a few minutes, the large congregation had filled one half of the graveyard. Rob and Mary stood close to Georgina, staring at the coffin which was now on the ground next to the freshly dug grave.

Rob looked around again, desperate to see her.

Eventually, he spotted Red, towering over the crowd, leaning down, talking to someone.

He wanted desperately to join them, to find out who Red thought she was.

And why was she here?

The congregation closed around the grave. A breeze flapped at the dresses and the women held one hand on their hats.

The vicar projected his voice to the furthest reaches of the graveyard.

"I am the resurrection and the life, saith the Lord. He that believeth in me, though he were dead, yet shall he live. And whosoever liveth and believeth in me shall never die."

Millie had been a more regular churchgoer than he or Mary. Rob could only hope this meant something more than a few stirring words.

The pallbearers stood either side of the grave and lifted the coffin. Rob's legs wobbled and he clutched at Mary. She squeezed him tight and tears fell freely from his eyes.

Goodbye, old friend.

As the vicar spoke, a low rumbling began behind them.

"We therefore commit his body to the ground. Earth to earth, ashes to ashes, dust to dust. In sure and certain hope of the Resurrection to eternal life."

A thunderous noise erupted above them, and the sun was blotted out as a huge Avro Vulcan swept over and pulled up, climbing toward the clouds.

"Christ, that was low," he said to Mary.

They were all hit by a blast of following air. Hats flew off in the swirling vortexes, grit and dirt kicked up from the ground, and men and women plugged their ears, too late against the roar.

The flypast had been recklessly low, and the vicar and crowd had ducked. But as they rose up again, gathered their hats, and picked the dirt from their eyes, laughter and cheers rippled forward from the back of the crowd.

Georgina turned, smiling at Rob.

"What fun!" she mouthed at him, and he broke into a broad smile.

The coffin was lowered. The vicar picked up a clump of earth and dropped it. Georgina and Charlie did the same.

Mary used her hand to guide Rob a step forward; he bent down to scoop up his own fistful of soil.

"I'm sorry," he said, with a cracked and weak voice, as he released the earth onto the coffin of Christopher Milford.

————

AS THEY WALKED from the grave, Rob pressed himself close to Mary, wrapping an arm around her, pulling her tightly against him.

"I've never needed you more," he said.

She pushed her arm around his waist; it felt good.

"Are we back together?" he whispered.

She looked at him, their faces an inch apart. He smelt her sweet breath and wallowed in a moment of intimacy.

"Everything's changed. Just act normally, follow along." She snapped her head forward and unentangled her arm, looking nervous.

Confused, Rob looked around, searching for Susie. Finally, he spotted her next to Red Brunson. They were already through the gate, ahead and beyond the policemen who were waiting for him.

He couldn't take his eyes from Red and Susie together, but as he and Mary arrived at the police car, a door opened, and they were ushered into the backseat.

The security men climbed into the front, and the sergeant in the passenger seat turned to them.

"You'll be dropped at the officers' mess. We will wait outside until you wish to leave, at which point we will escort you off the station. We can give you a lift somewhere nearby."

Before Rob could answer, Mary spoke up. "I've arranged a lift from the mess with Captain Brunson."

"Fine, but we'll still have to escort the vehicle off the station. It's our orders."

"I understand," she said.

Rob stayed silent.

They passed through the gates to RAF West Porton; the car drove directly to the front door of the mess.

Rob climbed out, as mourners walked past from the car park.

Inside the mess, they made their way to the large anteroom, securing the early pickings at the buffet and wine. But Rob wasn't hungry.

The room filled quickly and the chatter level rose.

Rob tried to talk to Mary again, but she warned him off with a stern look and a shake of the head.

Before he knew it, the room was packed, and Rob could see only the few people directly around him, and there was no-one he knew well.

Red Brunson appeared, pushing through the throng.

Brunson's eyes locked with Rob's but then darted to his left, urging Rob to look behind him.

Mark Kilton followed him.

Rob stiffened.

Kilton stopped to talk to a group; he was only a few yards away.

From behind Red's frame, Susie Attenborough stepped out.

Red ushered her forward.

"This is Susan Wilson. She worked with Millie at Boscombe Down."

Susie put out her hand. Rob stared, eventually taking the cue and shaking it.

"Hello," he managed.

"I'm so sorry for you all. I hadn't seen Millie for some time, but he was the perfect gentleman and we are all very upset."

"He was," said Red.

A waiter appeared with a tray of white wine. Susie took a glass, along with Mary. But Red Brunson sipped from an orange juice.

"I'm flying later," he told Rob, and looked at him, apparently waiting for a reaction.

The final flight of project Guiding Light.

Rob stared at Susie, but she was looking elsewhere.

There was some shuffling in the crowd to their right as Georgina arrived into the room with Charlie. Kilton left the nearby group to greet them.

A moment later, a cheer went up, and Rob turned to see Jock MacLeish arrive, all smiles as he received several slaps on the back.

"What's that about?" he asked Red.

"The flypast," Red said, beaming.

"Low, loud and probably illegal," one of the TFU pilots nearby said. "But just about the best thing I've ever seen."

"Millie would have loved it," Rob said, laughing.

A couple more men from TFU joined them, ushering their wives away.

Rob got a few polite greetings from his former colleagues. But no-one asked him where he had been or what was happening to him.

The temperature in the room rose. He felt dizzy.

He stood alone in a crowd.

Red was talking to Susie. Mary moved away.

Either it was his imagination, or the other chaps around him were turning their backs on him, one by one.

He was now boxed in with Red and Susie.

Red grabbed his arm to get his attention.

"How you doing, buddy?"

Rob's head swam. "Not good. I think I might faint."

Red's grip on his arm became firmer. Susie moved alongside him.

"Susie..." His voice cracked.

He leant forward, but she pushed him away.

"We don't have time for that. Listen. My people. They're not going to do anything."

"I know."

"You should have told me," Red said to him. "You shouldn't have done this alone. What were you thinking?"

"I'm sorry. I didn't think I could say anything to anyone. And now it's too late."

Susie's hand appeared on his arm. "Not necessarily."

Rob looked back at Red. "But the final flight. It's today, isn't it?"

One of the men with his back to them leaned over.

"Kilton!"

Red spoke with a sense of urgency. "Do you want a last chance? It won't be easy and it's risky, but it's up to you, buddy."

"What do you mean?"

Red continued. "Say yes. You're going to have to trust me. And I tell you now, it might not work. In fact, I don't think it will work. But it's all we can think of. Only Kilton can stop the project. That's how it's all set up. That's how everything at TFU is set up. So you have to change his mind."

"I can't do that."

"What if you could take him flying? Him and Ewan Stafford?"

"What?"

Susie slipped away; the three men turned and faced in, and immediately fell into conversation about Millie's obsession with scotch.

Kilton walked past, nodded at the men, but didn't make eye contact with Rob.

Red looked back at Rob.

"You need to be ready and you'll need to do exactly what we say, when we say it. OK?"

He was pushed over to a new group to talk to. He caught up with Jock MacLeish and congratulated him on the flypast. Jock winked and downed another glass.

————

AFTER ROB HAD BEEN THERE for an hour, two security force officers appeared in the doorway. He watched as they made their way to Kilton, who pointed directly at Rob.

Red came across.

"Time to go, buddy. Are you ready?"

"What for?"

"You'll find out soon, I promise. For now, just do what we say. This is gonna be tight."

The wives appeared. A group of TFU officers moved toward the door. In the lobby, they waited for the security men.

Rob stared at the oil paintings of senior officers standing beside fighters and bombers of years gone by.

Each one staring proudly into the distance.

The men who had nursed new aircraft into the world.

Wartime aces and post-war test pilots.

Heroes of the work, whose diligence ensured the safety of ordinary squadron pilots and crews; the men who would climb into the machines for decades after those first tentative flights.

Mary looked worried.

"Are you OK?"

"I lost my way, Mary."

"What?"

"This is what we do here. We make things better, not worse. That's what Millie was trying to tell me."

She held his hand.

"I know, darling. And the boys want you to have one more chance." She paused. "But you don't have to do it. You don't have to if you don't want to. And if you do, you promise one thing, Flight Lieutenant May?"

"What?"

"You come back to me," she whispered.

A security officer reached Rob. "Let's go."

The group followed into the car park.

Red's estate car was parked back to back with an RAF Land Rover. A couple of men in fatigues were working at its rear, pulling a canvas over and tying it down.

As they got to the car, a few things happened at once.

With the security guards watching, Rob was ushered into the back of Red's car. Confusingly, the back seat was completely folded flat, and he wasn't sure where to put his legs.

Then there was a scream.

He whipped his head around to see Susie on the floor, holding her ankle. The security guards bent down to help her.

At that same moment, Rob felt a firm grip on his arm. He looked up to see one of the NCOs in the back of the Land Rover pulling him roughly back through Red's car. He landed with a thump in the dark interior of the wagon. As the canvas came down over the back, Rob glimpsed the back seats going up and someone he didn't recognise, but who was about the same size as him, pulling on his RAF cap and settling into Red's back seat.

It was the last thing he saw before the Land Rover engine started and the vehicle pulled away.

One of the men with him peeped through a tiny crack in the rear canvas.

"OK. The women are now getting in. Police are watching. Stand by."

There was a tense pause.

"They're going for it. Yes. They've got into their wagon, and Red's pulled away."

"Superb!" one of the men in the back said. "You owe me a pound."

After several minutes of driving, the vehicle stopped.

Rob heard the Land Rover doors open at the front. Light flooded in as the canvas at the rear was pulled to one side.

An ageing warrant officer looked in.

"Your stop, Flight Lieutenant May."

Rob climbed out and found himself at the back of the ramshackle Maintenance Unit. The men led him inside, where a small team had assembled to greet him. He glanced around; there were eight or so men looking at him, but no-one he knew well.

JR was not there.

"I'm Ted Durrant," said a man sporting RAF wings and a moustache. "I'm one of the pilots here. It's my job to brief you for your flight. JR apologises for his absence."

It took Rob a second to process what he'd heard.

"My flight?"

The men looked at each other for a moment before the warrant officer stepped forward and addressed the MU men.

"None of you have to be here for this. If you choose to stay, you're implicating yourself in a deception. It's your choice, boys. No-one will think less of you for leaving. On the other hand, if you want to end the empire of that scheming bastard Kilton, then maybe you should stay."

The men laughed and not a soul moved from his position.

Durrant guided him by his arm. "OK, then. Rob, if you'll step over here..."

They moved to an old wooden table with a typical TFU tasking sheet and a chart with drawn-on lines. Next to the chart: the unmistakable sight of Red Brunson's elaborate flying helmet and mirrored visor.

"Now, I should tell you, this wasn't my idea," Durrant said. "I believe it was cooked up by Brunson along with a couple of your colleagues at TFU, with the help of that young woman."

"Susie?"

"Is that her name? Anyway, the idea, my friend, is to get you inside the Vulcan in place of Red for the final project flight." He looked at his watch. "Which is due to launch in an hour. So, we don't have long to get this right. And believe me, a lot needs to go right."

"How will this ever work?" Rob said.

Durrant continued with his brief. "The two key elements are Red's suggestion to Kilton that Stafford observes the flight from the co-pilot's seat, not the rear bay. They've gone for it. Kilton will be at the navigator radar station. The second element is this."

He picked up Brunson's helmet.

"The mirrored visor," Rob said.

"Correct. With the oxygen mask, it could be anyone under there. Brunson thinks Stafford would be unlikely to spot the difference."

"But what about everything else? What about before the flight? Walking out together, the brief?"

"Red will use the fact that Kilton wants him to fly the Vulcan alone as an excuse to get in the cockpit early." Durrant looked across at his colleagues. "Now, there is some choreography to carry out on the apron. Basically, swapping you and Red over. But we managed to smuggle you from the mess, so who knows? It might even work."

"And if it doesn't work? When I get back they'll arrest Red. And you lot."

"Then it'd better work," Durrant said, with a flash of a smile.

Rob looked uncertain.

"Look, on the ground, every officer at TFU will back you up. The idea is to give Kilton a chance to personally reverse his decision about Guiding Light. He's not a man to be overruled, but he should see the way out of the mess." The man shrugged. "It's all they could come up with. Red doesn't know enough to persuade him."

Rob stared at the chart, the brief for the trip, and Red's flying equipment.

"Will I see Red beforehand?"

"Not for long. He's created an additional checklist for you." Durrant shuffled through some papers and handed Rob a handwritten list.

It included four circuit breakers with instructions to open them before he took his seat and a small power switch to locate on the rear Guiding Light panel. The function of the breakers and switch wasn't clear, but it was obvious that the whole operation had been thought through.

He finished studying the list and looked up; the room was silent.

Durrant looked at him. "You don't have to do this if you don't want to, Rob. No-one will judge you here."

"Thank you, Ted. But it would be out of character for me this week not to do something very stupid indeed."

Durrant nodded with a smile. "Well, just make sure you come back. Either you'll get your point across or you won't. There's no point in taking unnecessary risks."

"What about my voice? Won't that be a giveaway?"

"Only speak via the intercom and make it monosyllabic. The intercom makes everyone sound the same. Hopefully. I'd get airborne quickly. Once you're up, you can reveal yourself, I guess. Not much they can do about it then."

Rob looked at the sheet and notes; it was not a complex flight. The lines on the chart were mainly for show, as Red had written *VFR* —Visual Flight Rules—next to the flight description. Basically, go out west, drop to one thousand feet, briefly hand over control to Guiding Light, let the passengers see it working, then return.

Not a thorough test; just a pleasure flight for Stafford before he gets his sign-off.

"We have forty minutes. Rob, you need to get into Red's coveralls."

————

IN THE MAINTENANCE UNIT LAND ROVER, Rob was starting to overheat; Brunson's flight suit was thick. As a precaution they'd decided he should have the helmet on with the visor down at all times.

He sat on a tin shelf under the canvas as the vehicle sped along the peritrack. Two MU pilots came along with him, including Durrant in the passenger seat up front. They both looked about Millie's age.

After he'd first signed up, it was easy to get bored with the war stories from the veterans in the crew room, but now, in an old military vehicle, driving around a former World War Two dispersal airfield, about to climb into an aircraft with an unknown outcome, he felt he had a small glimpse of their once daily routine.

Eventually, they came to a stop.

The canvas at the back parted and Durrant's face appeared.

"OK, we're in position." He looked at Rob. "When Red gets around this side of the jet, he jumps in and you jump out. Got it?"

Rob tried to nod, but the helmet moved slightly over the leather inner. Would it give him problems in flight?

They waited. After a few minutes, Durrant spoke again. "He's on his way."

Rob shuffled to the back of the wagon, waiting for his cue.

His heart was beating fast, but time slowed down.

"Come on," he urged Red Brunson under his breath.

The canvas parted, and there he was. The tall American climbed in.

"Are you ready for this, buddy?"

Rob raised the visor and met Red's intense gaze.

"Yes."

"Make your case, convince them, scare them even. But don't do anything stupid, OK? We need you back here in one piece. We'll back you up, every one of us."

"Really?"

"Everyone, buddy. Now listen, in case Kilton tries to override, I've added some steps to the checklist—"

"The circuit breakers?" Rob interrupted.

Brunson smiled. "Yep. Flip those breakers and only the captain's side panel will work. No-one else will be able to engage or cancel."

"They're coming." Ted Durrant spoke with urgency from the front seat.

Brunson looked back at Rob, eyes wide. "He still might try something. Your number one responsibility to me, Mary and everyone else is to stay safe. You understand, Rob?"

Rob dropped the visor and jumped out of the back, clutching his checklist and air chart.

He looked across. The short and stout Ewan Stafford waddled around in oversized flying coveralls, looking like a sack of potatoes. He and Kilton posed for a photograph by the TFU door. They were a couple of hundred yards away, which gave him just a minute or so.

The Vulcan stood proud on its landing gear; Rob ducked and walked underneath to the yellow crew ladder.

Once in the rear crew bay, he searched his paperwork for the additional checklist steps from Red, and located a small fuse block on the left side of the panels. He tried to open the fuse marked '7a'.

It wouldn't budge. He lifted his visor to get a clear view.

The fuse case was flush with the wall; he needed a small flathead screwdriver.

He patted his coveralls, hoping Brunson kept a tool of some description in his pockets.

Nothing.

Rob looked around, as he heard Kilton's voice carried on the breeze.

"*Shit.*"

He tried the trouser pockets of the suit and found a fountain pen. It would have to do. He pulled off the lid.

Placing his gloves and paperwork on the AEO's station, he pushed the pen nib into the outside case of the fuse holder. Using the nib as a lever, he got the holder completely open and tipped out the fuse, before pushing it back in. His fingers were now covered in black ink.

He consulted the list again, smudging the paper with black as he did so. He opened two more traditional circuit breakers on a panel above the radar operator's station before finally disconnecting a small wire underneath the Guiding Light readout panel.

Just as he had completed his extracurricular tasks, a shadow appeared below him.

He snapped the space-like visor back down and pushed the oxygen mask back into place, then quickly moved to the small steps, up to the cockpit itself.

He settled into the left hand captain's seat while Ewan Stafford climbed fully into the rear crew area and stood aside to let Kilton up.

Rob hurriedly consulted Red's list again. He opened two more circuit breakers above and to the left of his seat.

He exhaled, just as Stafford appeared next to him.

"Hello!" the managing director said cheerily. Rob pointed at the empty co-pilot's seat on the right and Stafford made getting into it look like a trick Houdini would have struggled with.

Kilton appeared below him between the two seats, his head poking up into the cockpit.

Rob froze.

Kilton continued up the pilots' ladder until his head was level with them.

"Red, you carry on with the pre-start, I'll strap him in."

Rob exhaled quietly and turned away from the pair to busy himself with the checks.

Kilton's hands reached over Stafford, pulling on his straps, and in the process, he pushed against Rob.

The Vulcan cockpit suddenly felt more cramped than he was used to.

Kilton told Stafford which pins to remove to make the seat live and then where to store them. Meanwhile, Rob brought the Avro aircraft to life and prepared to start the engines.

To his relief, Kilton shuffled back down the ladder. An engineer stood on the crew-access ladder, ready to help him close and seal the hatch.

Once done, Rob craned around to see Kilton move to the Guiding Light position and strap himself in.

He quickly began the quick engine start sequence; he had a few seconds before Kilton would connect his PEC and access the intercom. Each of the four Olympus engines fired up, utilising a built-in procedure for the Vulcans that sat on standby with Britain's nuclear deterrent on board. Something else Brunson had arranged in advance; no waiting for ground power units.

Rob was grateful for the noise and distraction of the auto sequence.

He got a good start on all four engines and continued with the after-start checks.

He would have to talk to ATC.

The engine noise whined in his head through the intercom and he considered taxiing without permission.

He looked down at the intercom control panel and realised with relief that he could isolate the rear crew. He set the switches, keyed his own press-to-transmit switch and requested taxi.

He exchanged hand signals with the ground marshaller and set about shifting the large aircraft from its resting place.

As he swung the Vulcan around and headed for the eastern end of the runway, Mark Kilton appeared next to him, again.

Rob kept his eyes front, but Kilton tapped him on the shoulder. He reluctantly looked around; Kilton tapped the side of his helmet and shouted over the din.

"Intercom's not working!"

Rob nodded, and Kilton went back down into the dark.

He flicked the switch to bring the rear crew back onto the circuit.

"That's better. I need to talk to Ewan. Red, power the laser on now, Ewan can watch the reading as we climb out."

Without replying, Rob reached down to the Guiding Light panel on his left. He flicked the power on, ensuring the flight computer was not yet engaged with the autopilot.

The single height reading lit up on the small meter fitted above the main panel between the two pilots. He used his hand to direct Stafford's attention to it.

"Great to see it live," said Stafford. "It's only ever been a simulation on a workshop bench for me."

Rob remained enigmatic, trying to look busy and occupied, which was easy, because he was.

As he rounded the final turn to face the runway at ninety degrees, he realised he was going to have to push his luck again with the intercom. He isolated the rear crew once more and made the quick call to ATC for take-off permission, advising them that he would head west after climb out.

He switched Kilton's intercom back on, to pre-empt another visit up the ladder, and he acknowledged the clearance with a curt, "Roger."

That was it. He was seconds away from getting airborne and nearly over the first significant hurdle.

Rob looked across to Stafford and out of the side window to check the approach to the runway, ensuring they were safe to line up.

He needed to know the civilian had armed his ejection seat correctly.

More talking.

"Pins?" he said quickly.

Stafford pointed at the removed pins, now in their stowage position.

"Switch?"

Stafford pointed down to his side and gave a thumbs up. "Armed!"

Rob turned back and checked the approach lane to the airfield again. All clear.

He made quick work of the line-up and advanced the throttles to a take-off setting. The engines responded well; they rolled, gathering pace. A white needle climbed around the airspeed indicator.

The noise level rose. Rob's nostrils had already filled with the familiar smell of the Vulcan's interior, filling his mind with unwanted images.

For a moment he imagined the ghost of Christopher Milford watching Kilton in his seat, and then chastised himself for not concentrating. He closed and opened his eyes as the centre lines disappeared under the nose at an increasing rate.

Rob eased the stick back, allowed the nose to rise to the horizon, and held it there as the four-engined, large delta wing bomber left the ground.

He tapped the wheel brakes and moved the landing gear handle up.

Loud whirring and bangs from below as the gear tucked itself away.

He banked right and headed west.

The tasking called for a gentle flight in the area immediately west of the airfield, but that didn't suit Rob's purpose. He needed a full demonstration, deep in the hills.

Somewhere their lives would depend on the integrity of the Guiding Light system.

That wasn't the downs around Wiltshire; he needed to get them into Wales.

Kilton spoke to Stafford, taking him through the height readings.

Rob climbed the Vulcan to expedite their transit.

Eventually, Kilton called to him. "When you're ready, Red, let's get down to one thousand feet and begin the demo."

Rob ignored him and continued to climb.

Kilton didn't seem to notice at first. He and Stafford discussed how the equipment would be installed in existing aircraft.

Rob kept the aircraft moving fast. It was a perfect day for visibility and he tried to pick out Bath ahead, aiming for the city as a convenient run toward the Severn Estuary.

"Come on, Brunson, let's get this thing down."

Rob managed to get them to twelve thousand feet. The ground speed was pleasingly high in the thin air, but he could sense Kilton's patience being stretched. He levelled off and then tipped the aircraft into a very gentle descent. He hoped it would placate the CO.

"Brunson?" Kilton urged again, a couple of minutes later.

They were already over Bath; he'd done well to get them in spitting distance of the hills. Finally, Rob lowered the nose another ten degrees and edged the throttles back as gravity added to their airspeed.

He levelled out at one thousand feet between Newport and Cardiff. The Brecon Beacons were on the nose.

He pushed the nose down and let the Vulcan settle at five hundred feet. Looking down to the Guiding Light panel, he selected three hundred feet as the target height and, using a waypoint that was about two hundred miles north, in Anglesey, he engaged the system.

There was a familiar jolt as the autopilot took over, fed from Guiding Light.

The nose wrenched down and the aircraft repositioned three hundred feet above the ground. The auto-throttle was busy with the four levers to his right. Rob checked they'd reached the target speed of 320 knots.

The aircraft started to complain as it heaved through the turns. The physical nature of the flight had changed significantly from the relatively genteel cruise. Guiding Light was working hard.

"This is low," said Stafford next to him, although he seemed nonchalant.

It was taking Kilton a while to register that Rob had deviated significantly from the flight plan.

Meanwhile, aware of the frailty of the system, Rob kept his eyes fixed on the terrain ahead, ready to intervene.

Kilton finally spoke over the intercom. "Hey! Up please, Brunson."

Rob ignored him.

"Red. Up. Can we get back to one thousand, please? We're at bloody three hundred."

Rob was breathing heavily; the combination of anxiety from his situation and a fierce focus on the flying was straining his energy levels.

"Red!" Kilton shouted.

Rob raised his hand away from the control column he was shadowing. He pulled his oxygen mask away from his face. Cooler air washed over him and he raised his visor and turned toward Ewan Stafford.

The stout businessman's eyes bulged over his own mask.

"What's going on?" Kilton shouted over the intercom from the back. "For the last time, Brunson, climb this aircraft to a safe height."

But the next voice he heard was Stafford's.

"Mark. Red Brunson isn't here. I think we have a problem."

Stafford didn't take his eyes off Rob, and Rob continued to stare back at him, no longer covering the controls. Any serious problem from Guiding Light now would consume all three of them.

Rob raised his hands up to emphasise the situation.

He pushed his loosely hanging oxygen mask over his mouth and spoke, with no attempt to disguise his own voice. "I think we'll stay low," he said, slowly and deliberately.

The aircraft continued to clank about in the thick surface air, but despite the rough ride, Mark Kilton had unstrapped. His face appeared between Rob and Stafford at the top of the pilots' ladder.

Rob moved his right hand to the control column; his left hovered over the Guiding Light control panel by the side of the seat.

Rob reattached his oxygen mask and faced front. "If you try to take control, I'll push us into the ground. If you try to cancel Guiding Light, I will push us into the ground."

He could hear the desperation in his own voice.

Kilton shook his head, contempt burning in his eyes.

"Are you out of your mind, May? How the hell did you get in here? Where's Brunson?"

"Red thought it best that I got a final chance to demonstrate Guiding Light to the only two men who can stop it."

"Did he? Well, that's another career ended. What is wrong with you stupid people? Now, for Christ's sake, get us away from the ground."

"Is there a reason why we shouldn't be putting Guiding Light to the test, sir? Do you need me to climb away and leave this to some other crews?"

"Climb the bloody aircraft to one thousand feet as ordered. That's a final warning, May."

There was the merest edge of desperation in Kilton's voice. Rob enjoyed it. He saw an image of him standing naked in front of Kilton in the changing room.

"I'll ask again, boss. Why do you need me to climb? Is there a problem? Is there a specific reason why we shouldn't trust Guiding Light to keep us safe at low-level?" He looked across at Stafford as he spoke and then noticed Kilton looking at the flying controls. Instinctively, he turned back to the front and covered the throttle and control column with his hands.

They swept left into a valley, then rolled right. The hills had become steeper. So far, the nimble airframe was coping well.

"Ewan, pull the stick back," said Kilton.

Rob looked across at the Blackton MD. "We're doing three hundred and twenty knots at three hundred feet. If you try to fight me for it, it will all be over in an instant."

Stafford's eyes were still bulging; the man looked terrified. He looked down at the stick and then back to Kilton and shook his head.

"Right," Kilton said. "Stafford, get out of that seat."

Kilton stripped off his rear crew harness.

Rob looked across, alarmed to see Stafford actually unstrapping. Eventually, Stafford's hands moved to the five-point quick release; he seemed to be having trouble.

The TFU boss heaved himself up the ladder, shoving Rob in the process. Rob held the stick firmly, ready to fight physically for control if necessary, but Kilton ignored him and fumbled with Stafford's straps, eventually freeing the civilian.

Stafford extricated himself from the cockpit and disappeared behind into the gloom. Did he know how to put on the rear crew harness that Kilton had discarded somewhere? No time to brief him now.

Kilton clambered through and got himself into the co-pilot's seat.

While the TFU boss fiddled with the ejection seat pins and switches, Rob tried to anticipate his next move.

He needed to make it too risky for Kilton to attempt to take control.

He moved his hand down to the panel by his left side and dialled the target height down to one hundred and fifty feet. The aircraft suddenly lurched down and Kilton looked up in alarm.

The ground flashed past, and Rob realised he had set the Vulcan on a flight path at the extremes of its abilities; he could not afford to take his attention away.

"Robert," Kilton spoke calmly, with a softer tone. "I know you're upset. We can talk about this. In a moment, I'm going to take control and I need you to keep your hands away from the controls."

"Sorry, sir, I don't think the promise of a talk is enough."

The aircraft continued its descent. Rob saw Kilton in his peripheral vision, tensing himself, just as the jet levelled again. The manoeuvre sent both men up in their straps.

Rob heard a clunk behind. He craned his neck around to see Ewan Stafford recovering himself, after being knocked off his feet.

An image of Millie flashed into his mind.

"We're at the mercy of Guiding Light, now."

Rob nodded ahead at the unreal sight of mountain sides looming above them and the aircraft rising and falling to avoid the higher trees.

"Even the slightest aberration from the laser and we'll be dead in an instant. You might get a chance to eject, I suppose." He looked back toward Stafford, who had now got himself into a seat, and had managed to connect his PEC. "But as you've taken Mr Stafford's ejection seat, he will of course go down with the jet, should Guiding Light have any issues."

"For Christ's sake, Mark," Stafford squawked over the crackly intercom, "take over control. I've had enough of this."

"Then you agree there's a problem?" Rob asked.

"Shut up, Ewan!" Kilton barked.

Kilton twisted in his seat, his eyes burning into Rob.

"This is simple, sir. If this system is safe, as you and Mr Stafford have told us, then there will be no issue. We have full tanks and we can fly for three hours at this height, just as RAF jets would be required to across the Soviet Union."

"This is dangerous, May, and you know it."

"Dangerous, sir? Is it?"

Kilton stared at him.

"I'm waiting," Rob added, liking the way he sounded in control.

Kilton shook his head, smiled and grabbed the co-pilot's control column, wrenching it back toward him.

The Vulcan's nose pitched up.

"NO!" screamed Rob, and he rammed his column forward in an explosion of anger.

He must have taken Kilton by surprise, as the column moved all the way forward, Kilton's hand slipping from its grip. Suddenly, they were plummeting again, the ground filling the windshield.

Shit.

Rob eased the stick back and looked across; Kilton was pale, his hands in the air.

"OK, OK, OK. For Christ's sake, May, you nearly killed us."

Rob looked down to check that Guiding Light had remained engaged. It had.

He looked across in time to see Kilton's hand move back to the control column. Rob shook his head, and flexed his fingers, as if to demonstrate his readiness to dive them into oblivion.

But Kilton simply pressed the autopilot cancel switch on the far side of the column.

Nothing happened.

Rob felt the control move. The autopilot was still in control, still connected to Guiding Light.

Red's tricks with the circuit breakers had worked. By following the scrawled checklist, he had disabled all the safety systems that would normally cancel the automations.

"It's no good, sir. You're along for this ride whether you like it or not."

He released his grip and let the Vulcan sink again, settling into its bumpy ride at one hundred and fifty feet.

The hills loomed around them. The Vulcan banked right, then rolled left, with extra power fed in. It wrenched them around an outcrop into a narrow valley.

Rob looked ahead and wondered if they would eventually fly into a position the aircraft was simply not capable of getting out of. Even a fully working Guiding Light had its limits.

He glanced back at the TFU boss. The blood had drained from his cheeks, and he stared back.

"You know this system is flawed," said Rob. "You know it killed Millie and yet you expect us to sit back and watch you roll it out into service?"

"Us? Who else is in on this lunacy, May?"

"Are you still trying to work out who to punish, sir? You'd be surprised how few friends you have left."

The aircraft rose sharply. They were pinned in their seats for a couple of seconds before it rolled right and descended, sending their stomachs floating up. Rob felt sick again.

"You're pushing it too far, May. Climb and let's talk."

"I don't think so, sir. Let's talk now. Tell me about the 8.75 figure. We derived it, thanks to Millie, from the mainframe computer operated by the maths department at Oxford University. But you must have your own version of this figure from the hours of tapes sent to Cambridge. What is it? A number low enough to disappear into the background of statistics. Was that part of your calculation? A price worth paying. Just like the V-Bomber rear crews at low-level without an effective escape system? The same thing all over again. I wonder if you still think it's a price worth paying, now that it's *your* life?"

Kilton stared at him.

"So bloody what?" he said, eventually. "That's what you flew halfway across southern England to find out? Who the hell cares? No system is one hundred per cent safe, May. Aircraft crash. Men die. That's what you signed up for. You're a fucking wet blanket, and if I didn't know it before, then I do now. You have no place in the military."

Rob was momentarily lost for words. He had expected some sort of argument about the facts, not a callous dismissal of the consequences. He turned his head back to try and make eye contact with Stafford in the rear crew compartment.

"You as well, Mr Stafford? Are Guiding Light crews expendable for your success?"

Stafford didn't reply; he was too busy being terrified.

"You're a fool, May." Kilton spoke calmly. "A cowardly, ill-advised fool. Real men take risks every day for what we believe in."

The aircraft hit a pocket of air and thumped down before recovering.

"For Christ's sake, Mark." Stafford's voice croaked from the darkness behind. *"End this."*

The aircraft rolled, sweeping into a larger valley complex. It looked like a dead end ahead, but Rob had been here before and knew it opened up at the last minute. He'd never flown this low before. He hoped the aircraft was not about to be taken beyond its performance limits.

"Maybe we'll all die?" Rob said quietly, while looking at the tight passage ahead. "It would serve my purpose, wouldn't it?" He looked across at Kilton. "The boys know enough now, and this crash would be the final nail in Guiding Light's coffin. You wouldn't be around to cover anything up."

"You'd kill yourself to prove a point?"

"I don't think you realise what I'm living with, boss." The walls of rock were fast approaching dead ahead. "I ended it for Millie, didn't

I? I played your game. I took us back down to three hundred feet, against his wishes. I ignored him, even belittled him, with you. You really got me, didn't you? But now, in a simple moment, I can make it right."

The Vulcan reacted to the sharply changing relief. The wings rolled just as the valley opened up. Kilton's hands moved to the panel in front to steady himself, and the huge Vulcan banked steeply left, then immediately right to negotiate the tight channel.

There was no bang, no sudden moment of black.

Rob moved his hand to the control panel, and this time dialled them down to a hundred feet.

The aircraft shifted down among the trees and meadows; the ride became bumpier and more violent.

"That's enough, May!" Kilton bawled. "We're lower than the bloody wingspan, you fool!"

Rob stared straight ahead, still covering the controls.

This is why Susie, Red and the others were urging caution from him.

They must have known it would come to this.

"Look, maybe I was too harsh on you," said Kilton. "I can reverse the transfer. Have you back at TFU. But you're wrong about Guiding Light. If we wait for perfection, it will never get released. We'll never equip with it and we will lose the chance to take the Soviets down. Think about the bigger picture, for Christ's sake. Take us up, Rob. You've proved your point."

Rob didn't move his head. He kept his eyes on the flight path ahead.

"I don't think so."

"Christ, Kilton, that's it," said Stafford. "Get us out of here. I don't care what it takes. May, I will personally stop production of Guiding Light. I promise."

Rob looked across at Kilton. "I need to hear it from you."

The aircraft plunged, and Rob grabbed the control column, but it was just the laser guiding them down a gully. Rob released his grip and allowed the computer to continue.

"I'll say no such thing. You think I'm scared, May? I faced death every day in 1940 and didn't back down once. Your generation don't know the half of it. You're a coward, and you don't deserve the freedom we fought for. And you're a naive fool for thinking the enemy is not coming for us again. And when he does, you'll be begging for Guiding Light to keep you safe from his missiles." Kilton turned his head around, although Rob doubted he could see Stafford in the back. "And as for you... You were never cut out for the front line. Shut the hell up and speak when spoken to."

Rob's blood pumped around his body, his legs shaking with adrenaline. He concentrated as hard as he could on keeping the aircraft flying.

"I don't think you understand," Rob said. "I can't go back having failed. I don't care about my job, or even prison. The only thing that scares me is going to sleep every night for the rest of my life knowing I failed Millie in every possible way."

"Take us back up, May. This is your final warning."

"Or what, sir? I think you're out of options."

"He's right," Stafford shouted. "Give in, for Christ's sake, Kilton."

The aircraft rolled right, and the nose pulled around, wrenching them into a wider valley with a lake.

Rob's left hand squeezed the control column while his right hand rested on the throttles.

A strange sense of calm washed over him. Kilton had nowhere to go; he would know that any attempt to interfere with the flying controls would end in disaster.

The Vulcan shot over the end of the lake, then rose and fell over a small hill.

The wings rolled left and they headed toward the deepest section of Welsh hills.

Rob's mind turned over, trying to work out how to bring this to a conclusion.

But Kilton was on the move, unstrapping from his seat.

The TFU boss lunged across the cockpit. His hands landed with a thud on Rob's stomach.

Rob grabbed the stick, ready to fight for control.

But Kilton's hands didn't go to the control column or the throttle.

Rob looked at Kilton's head, his dark eyes just inches from Rob's as he leant across at full stretch from his seat.

"What the hell?"

Kilton smiled.

Rob lowered his head to see what Kilton was holding.

Both his hands were on Rob's ejection seat handle.

"*Shit.*"

Terrified, he stared back at Kilton. "It'll rip your arms off!"

"No, Rob. I'll have one second. You should read the pilots' notes more carefully."

The aircraft rolled into a steep right hand bank; an ejection now would surely be fatal.

Rob grabbed Kilton's fingers and attempted to prise them off the yellow-and-black cord.

"No! Not now!"

Kilton actually laughed at him and yanked the handle firmly up.

There was a loud bang above them, and Rob looked up to see nothing but grass.

With that sight, he knew his life was about to end.

No more decisions to make; it was over.

The seat erupted underneath him.

33

FRIDAY 14TH JULY

One Week Later

MARY HADN'T MOVED for some time. She let her eyes rest on the changing morning sky. The fiery reds of dawn had replaced the first rays of pale white light.

Over the past week she'd become an expert at mornings. She now knew her blackbirds from her greenfinches just by their call; the birdsong that had for so long just been a background noise in a busy life.

A busy life, until time had stopped. One week ago.

There was a tap at the door. It opened, and a small, pretty woman with a black bob of hair entered the room.

Mary smiled, glad of the company.

"Morning," they said to each other, and Mary went back to studying the sky.

"Newspapers?"

Susie offered a small pile of the dailies, but Mary couldn't bring herself to read anyone else's news.

"The story's appeared," Susie said.

"Oh."

"The local MP is a bit rattled. He's spilled a few beans." Susie proffered the papers again.

Mary struggled to focus on the print.

"Would you mind reading it to me?"

"Of course."

Susie sat on the edge of a high-backed, green-cushioned chair and opened *The Daily Telegraph*.

The headline at least was clear.

MP TO QUESTION MINISTERS OVER SECOND RAF BOMBER DISASTER.

Susie read the article aloud. *"Wiltshire Central MP, Sir Alan Giddings, is to raise the recent brace of fatal RAF crashes with ministers in the House of Commons, later today. Yesterday, it emerged that the Vulcan bomber crash, which occurred in mid-Wales a week ago, was the second such loss from the same RAF station in the space of a fortnight. The spot-light is now on the secretive RAF West Porton, north of Salisbury and in the heart of Sir Alan's constituency.*

"Details of the accidents are scarce. An official spokesman for the MOD has told The Daily Telegraph *that due to the nature of the work carried out at West Porton, they would release no formal details; however, the public can rest assured the trial that linked the two accidents has been halted.*

"Sir Alan says RAF West Porton is cloaked by an 'unhealthy amount of secrecy' and he 'wishes to see a broom swept through the organisation'.

"Sir Alan is expected to question the secretary of state for defence at 2.30PM.

"The Daily Telegraph understands one of the dead from last week's crash was the commanding officer of a previously unknown unit, referred to as RAF-TFU. Wing Commander Mark Kilton DFC was laid to rest in Amesbury on Thursday."

Susie rested the paper on her lap.

Mary pondered the reform of West Porton, one week too late.

A shaft of sunlight streamed into the room, falling on Mary's face. She closed her eyes and tried to enjoy its warmth.

"I'm surprised it's taken this long to appear in the press," said Susie. "I thought there might be some reporters at the funeral."

Mary kept her eyes closed. "It was strange, wasn't it? The funeral. So much unsaid."

"Isn't that always the way at these things?" Susie said. "They do seem adept at not saying things, these men. God knows it may have turned out differently if they'd only had a few more conversations, early on."

With her eyes closed and the sun warming her face, Mary listened to the remnants of the dawn chorus. The blackbirds were always the last to finish their song.

An unfamiliar sound.

A low murmur.

Her eyes flicked open as she swung off the chair.

Susie was already standing at the hospital bed.

"Was that him?" Mary asked.

"Yes, he moved," said Susie. "I'll get the doctor."

Susie left the room and Mary cupped her hand on the side of Rob's face, careful to avoid the stitches that ran from his chin.

He moaned again and turned his head a millimetre, but it was a millimetre more than she had seen him move since he had been scraped off the side of that hill.

"Can you hear me?"

For a while, nothing happened. Then his head turned a fraction more.

A moment later, Robert May opened his eyes.

34

MONDAY 5TH SEPTEMBER

Two Months Later

ROB YAWNED at the breakfast table.

"I told you we'd set the alarm too early," Mary said. "I mean, 5AM. It's for the birds."

Rob raised another spoonful of cereal to his mouth. He was becoming good with his left hand.

"You try getting ready for work with an ankle and arm in plaster."

She leaned across the table, placed her hand on his white cast and kissed him on the cheek.

"That sounds good, doesn't it?"

"It's taken a long time."

"Getting you out of that blasted hospital was the best thing we did."

Mary cleared a couple of bowls from the table and rinsed them at the sink. "Are you nervous?"

"Going back to TFU? Not really. It's not like I haven't seen Jock and Red already." He manoeuvred himself from under the table. Reaching for his crutch, he hauled himself upright. "I know it's changed. That's the main thing."

Mary turned to him. "And what about flying?"

Rob looked at his two limbs in plaster and laughed. "I don't think I'll be on the roster today."

"You know what I mean," she said and playfully flicked some soap bubbles at him. "Do you still want to do it?"

Rob reached for his second crutch and hobbled out of the kitchen. "Bloody right I do."

Outside, in the last days of an English summer, Rob climbed into the passenger side of Millie's old Rover. He'd tried getting into the Austin Healey, but his inflexible plastered leg was having none of it. Georgina, back in her married quarter for 'as long as she needed' was pleased with the swap, and Rob had to admit she suited his little sports car.

Mary climbed into the driver's seat.

"No driving, no flying," he said. "It's going to be a long winter."

"On the other hand, you're alive, Mr May."

He smiled at the love of his life and leaned over to whisper in her ear. "I love you, Mary May."

She laughed. "So you keep telling me."

"Sorry," he said, in mock protest.

"That's OK. You can tell me again."

She backed out and they set off toward West Porton. Minutes later, they arrived at the barrier which was rising as they approached.

"Good morning, Mrs May, Flight Lieutenant May. Are you happy you know where you're going?"

Mary told the guard that she knew the way to TFU and they carried on into the station.

"Doesn't feel like entering a prison anymore," Rob said.

As they approached the edge of the airfield and the TFU buildings, Rob noticed one or two of his colleagues walking in. He was hoping to arrive early, ahead of everyone else, but it looked like he was the last.

They parked. Mary quickly made her way around the outside of the car. But as he went to open the door, Rob found it being opened for him by somebody else.

"Good morning, Flight Lieutenant. It's good to have you back."

Wing Commander Jock MacLeish greeted him with a beaming smile.

"Thank you, sir," Rob replied to his new commanding officer.

With Jock and Mary's help, he pulled himself upright and tucked the crutch under his arm.

They made their way to the double doors of TFU.

"I hoped we'd be the first here," Rob said, again alarmed at the busy car park.

"No chance of that, Robert."

Jock pushed open the door to the planning room.

"Welcome back, Rob." Red Brunson was the first to greet him.

"Welcome back," said the next man, and the man after that.

Each officer stood by the planning desk made the effort to personally greet him.

The admin team, including Jean and a group of young corporals —men and women—who Rob didn't know were lined up on the way to the CO's office.

"Welcome back, sir," each one said as he passed.

Rob finally made it to the office. Jock closed the door behind him.

"So, this is your office now?"

"Certainly is," Jock said.

"Feels odd, doesn't it?" Rob looked around at the room that was once Mark Kilton's lair.

"I'm used to it now. We're working hard to move on."

"It feels different," Rob said. "Just walking in here."

Jock took his seat behind the desk. "Good. We nearly lost TFU, but a few of us argued it still has a role. It just needs to do things... differently. Boscombe oversee us now. Projects are ultimately signed off by them when they're happy. We're free to concentrate on the flying, testing and evaluating. Leave the politics to the others."

"Sounds ideal."

MacLeish turned serious as he pulled a foolscap report out of a desk drawer.

"How was the Board interview?"

"I couldn't tell them much. I remembered snatches of it but... nothing solid."

MacLeish nodded. "They did their best to piece it all together." He opened the report. "You told them you were low, very low, and that you think Kilton and Stafford swapped places?"

"Yes, it's a strange, cloudy memory. Quite surreal, actually, but I can see Kilton unstrapping Stafford."

"They think you were ejected," MacLeish said, then seemed to study him for a reaction.

It took Rob a second to understand the meaning of the sentence. "I *was* ejected? I didn't choose to eject?"

MacLeish shook his head. "It's a best guess, but Kilton had a badly fractured right arm and smashed up hand. The best theory they've got is that he was withdrawing it just as your seat fired and it suffered a glancing blow. It would have been very nasty for him. As for your route out of the aircraft, you appear to have missed the summit of a hill, floated for a bit under the canopy, and then bounced your way down on the other side. Bit of a mess when they found you, but you don't need me to tell you that."

"Why didn't Kilton eject?"

"They can't be sure, but they think a combination of his excruciating injury which took one arm completely out of action and the fact that as you ejected, it pushed the nose down from what was already a treetop-skimming height. As you know, you were found less than a mile from the crash site." MacLeish paused for a second before adding, "It's not in the report, but the chairman of the BOI did wonder about Mark's mental state. I think we all know he carried some scars from the war."

"And poor old Ewan Stafford?"

"A hapless onlooker who paid the price for getting into bed with Kilton." MacLeish closed the report. "Of course what's also not in here, and I doubt will ever be in any official capacity, is the fact that a young technician at DF Blackton has confirmed that Stafford was aware of the flaws of Guiding Light and he actively covered it up. We have to assume Kilton was in on this, rather than a victim of Stafford's scheming, as it explains his extreme behaviour toward Brian Hill, Millie and then you."

"All the same, quite a price to pay."

MacLeish tapped the desk idly with his fingers. "The technician told us they calculated the odds of causing a crash if Guiding Light went into service with its gremlin. They worked out, with future crewing, it would lead to as many as 14.25 aircrew deaths a year. And yet these men were prepared to roll it out and hope for the best."

A flash of a conversation on board the Vulcan came back to Rob. "I remember confronting him with the figure Millie had deduced. 8.75. So the real figure was even higher?"

"It would seem so." MacLeish handed over a copy of the report.

Rob picked it up, it was just a few pages on thin white paper marked *Her Majesty's Stationery Office*.

"I'll let you read it in your own time. A censored summary will be released more widely. But I'd draw your attention to the recommendations at the end of that version. A thorough system for examining any reported deficiency or concern, regardless of the rank or position of the person raising it. And a requirement that every project is signed off by every team member, again regardless of rank. We thought about calling it the May Check." He smiled.

"How about the Milford Agreement?" Rob said.

MacLeish nodded. "That would work."

Rob opened the first page of the report. It was perfunctory, to say the least. His eyes caught the crew list.

Flt Lt Robert May (Captain) – Seriously injured
Wg Cdr Mark Kilton – Deceased
Mr Ewan Stafford – Deceased

He thought about Kilton, the larger than life character who had steered him and dominated him for so long.

"You know Millie told me he used to be kind," Rob said.

"Who?"

"Kilton. Back in the war. They worked together at Tangmere. Millie even said he was shy, but always polite and unassuming. Hard to imagine."

"The war changed many people, Rob."

"He went on to Malta, then took part in D-Day and the aftermath. I guess there wasn't much kindness left by the end of that."

"Are you suggesting he somehow wasn't responsible for his own actions? That his death on a Welsh hillside in 1966 was just another victim of the war?"

Rob shrugged. "I don't know. But we're shaped by our experiences, aren't we?"

"We are, Robert. We are. And how has this experience shaped you?"

"I've made a few vows, that's for sure. A man in plaster has a lot of time lying on a bed to think."

Jock studied him for a moment. "Good."

———

FOR THE REST of the day, he discussed his duties and Jock gave him an initial plan for getting him back in the air, once the plaster could be removed.

"I can't wait, boss," Rob said, as he looked at the programme.

"And I can't wait to sit alongside you, Rob."

At the end of the working day, or 3.45PM to be more accurate, the men helped Rob down to the mess bar.

It didn't take long before he felt decidedly squiffy, having fallen out of practice.

He looked at the clock above the bar, expecting it to be nearly 10PM, only to find it was 6.30PM.

The new TFU boss got up to replenish glasses.

"Just one more for me," Rob announced to mock jeers.

Red nipped out to the hall and called Mary to pick him up, assuring her they were having just one more.

MacLeish came back with seven tumblers of whisky.

He placed them on the table in front of the six men.

"To absent friends," Jock whispered in his soft Scottish accent.

It took a moment before Rob noticed the empty chair with a glass of scotch in front of it.

THE END.

AFTERWORD

Released under the UK Government's 'Thirty-Year Rule' - would you like to read the official Board of Inquiry summaries for the two Vulcan crashes in this story?

Head to jamesblatch.com/thefinalflight

ALSO BY JAMES BLATCH

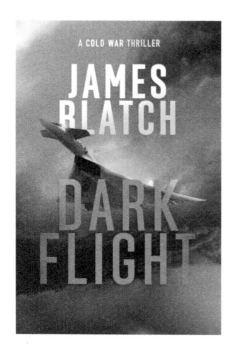

jamesblatch.com/darkflight

Captain Red Brunson starts his life as a test pilot at Edwards Air Force Base. But his cautious and safety-first approach to flying sets him at odds with his no-nonsense boss.

As the high-flyers are picked off for Apollo, he finds himself promoted to a seat on a highly sensitive, highly secret mission.

There's just one problem: at the heart of America's darkest project, is a traitor.

Red Brunson's world is about to collapse.

Turn the page for a free preview of Dark Flight.

DARK FLIGHT - PREVIEW
CHAPTER 1

Rosamond, California

May 21, 1947

The baseball disappeared into the blinding white of the midday sun. Red squinted, and held up his mitt in an attempt to block the light. The ball was smeared in the orange dust of the desert; he should be able to see it.

Instead, something else caught his eye.

High in the cloudless blue sky: a series of rapid bright flashes.

He lowered his arm, staring in wonder at the pulsing light.

"Damn," he muttered under his breath.

Behind him, the baseball thudded to the ground.

"Jesus, Red!" Joe called from the pitcher's mound.

The kid who'd hit the fly ball reached first base and stopped, staring at the distracted fielder.

But Red was on the move.

He threw his mitt to the ground and bolted, glancing up at the twisting, falling shape as he ran.

He reached his bike, scattered with the others on the ground.

"Goddamn!" Joe shouted. "Where you goin', Red?"

"Joseph. Language!" Mr Brookland admonished him from behind home plate, but Joe, too, was on the move.

"Red Brunson. Joseph Keel. The game's not over." Joe ignored Brookland and reached for his bike, threw himself on, and pedalled furiously after his friend.

With Joe a few yards behind him, Red swept out of the rustic, uneven patch of desert that Mr Brookland laughingly called a baseball field and on to the main road.

The falling shape was nearly down.

They gathered speed; thin, prefabricated homes flashed past on either side.

Amy Goodyear stopped skipping and stared at them.

"Hi, Red," she called with a beaming smile. Red looked and briefly considered pulling over, but he was on a mission.

He snapped his head back to the tumbling aircraft. The nose careened through the air. He knew enough about g-forces to wonder if the pilot could remain conscious.

It was also silent.

Why couldn't they hear it?

The aircraft grew larger.

Then it was there, just a few hundred yards away, filling the sky, until it disappeared behind the water tower.

A beat later, they heard a WHOMP, and an orange fireball rose high above the light blue tower.

The boys stamped on their brakes and came to a puncture-risking stop.

Red panted. He looked across at Joe. Without saying a word, they took off again. They turned right onto a path that ran between two of the houses. The lumpy dirt road became a lumpier dirt track.

"Boys! No!" A shout from an unseen adult; they ignored her.

The orange fire had been replaced by a thick plume of black smoke.

They got to the small wire fence that surrounded the faded water tower and dumped their bikes. Red took a running jump, and Joe followed.

They pushed through a thin row of trees and, for the first time, got a clear view of their target.

The wreckage was contained in a small area. A silver fin remained *upright. The centre of the fuselage was mangled, the front cockpit area broken and scattered.*

Flames licked around the remains of the jet fighter.

Red gulped and walked slowly towards the burning debris.

————

Aircraft Test and Evaluation Center

Edwards Air Force Base, California

June 10, 1965

"I'd like to say I'll be thinking about you all at A-TEC when I'm walking on the moon. But I can't lie to my friends."

Red leaned against the wall at the back of the room and peered past the short haircuts. He picked up a doughnut from a table at the back and took a bite as the farewell speech came to its conclusion.

He'd heard it before. Three times. And apparently there were four last year. So, that was seven men NASA had tempted away from Edwards's various test and experimental units.

He looked at his watch, frowned and tapped it. The military clock on the wall said 1710. His watch was misleading him as usual.

"You persisting with that thing?"

Red turned to find Jay Anderson laughing at him.

"Seriously, Red, you're the only test pilot I know who wears a broken watch. Look at it! It's falling apart."

"It's not broken," Red said, and rolled his sleeve down.

"Well, you must have been issued an IWC like the rest of us. You sold it?" Jay laughed again.

"I prefer this one. Now leave me alone." Red gave his friend a gentle push.

"Not before I have one of these boys," Jay said, as he reached down for a doughnut.

He took a bite and immediately spat into a napkin. "Damn. These things are stale." He threw the debris into a nearby wastebasket. "I bet they don't have stale doughnuts at NASA."

Red looked back at their departing comrade. "So, another one gone to Apollo. We'll be the only ones left soon."

"You can't blame him. Who wouldn't want to walk on the moon?"

"If they ever get there," Red said. "Long shot, if you ask me."

"You're just jealous."

Red shrugged. "Maybe. Even if I had the experience to apply, I'm not sure they'd have me."

Anderson didn't respond, but he gave Red a sympathetic smile.

"You've got the experience, Jay. Why don't you apply?"

"Who said I haven't?"

Red scrutinised him for a second. "Bullshit."

Anderson laughed. "I tried. Two years ago. Didn't make it."

"You never said anything."

"Guess I was embarrassed."

The room broke into applause as the speech ended.

Anderson put his hand on Red's shoulder and leaned into his ear. "They'll take you one day, Red. But you need to spread your wings a bit, buddy."

Red turned. "What do you mean?"

"You're getting a reputation for caution."

"Isn't that good?" Red felt a flush of disappointment that a fellow test pilot felt the need to speak to him like this.

Jay nodded slowly. "It has its place, but we need to press on with some of these projects. You've come back a couple of times having not completed the mission. Fine, you're worried about something or other, but—"

"But?"

"Maybe it's happening a bit too much with you."

Red thought back to his last couple of project flights. "But the B-57 had a shake. A vibration."

"You were testing a new camera housing on the belly. Of course it felt different." Jay stared at him.

Red spoke carefully. "It was getting worse. I curtailed the flight and wrote it up for the engineers. It felt like the right thing to do."

Again, Jay nodded and looked sympathetic, but it was clear he was letting Red know he'd made a mistake.

"You could have taken it to altitude and probably even to limit speed. The vibration measurements would have been a lot more useful."

"Even if I thought it was dangerous?"

"That's the thing, Red. We're test pilots. You want safety, join Pan Am."

Red thought his caution and safety-conscious approach to flying was an advantage. He assumed it was the reason he'd won his place at Pax River.

No-one had spoken to him like this before.

Jay must have seen the hurt look on his face. "Look, it's fine. You're new to test flying. You're trying hard, but it's probably time to start pushing things more. You're never gonna get to fly the black stuff until you've proved you can handle it. Time for a new start?"

"They'll never let me near an A-12."

"*Red!*" A bark came across the room. Both men turned to see Colonel Tucker Montgomery pointing at his corner office.

Jay stared. "Uh-oh. Chickens coming home to roost for you so soon?" He gave Red a friendly slap on the back.

"This can't be good," Red said, as he pushed his way through the dispersing crowd.

Two sides of the colonel's office were windows that looked out onto the unit's little corner of Edwards. As the boss shuffled into his seat behind his desk, Red watched as the mechanics pushed the last of the silver machines back into the dark recesses of A-TEC's hangars. Each aircraft was unique at Edwards, and it usually had its own team of engineers.

His eyes rested on two armed guards posted outside the nearest building.

Montgomery followed his gaze, twisting in his chair. He turned back and smiled. "We have some new toys to play with."

"Toys that have their own armed guards?" Red said.

Montgomery studied him. The silence became uncomfortable. After a while, he opened a folder and began reading. "Project Xenon. Camera housing. Flight One curtailed because of excessive vibration. Modified Aim-9 fins. First flight curtailed due to . . ." He squinted at the report. "Unusual drag characteristics. Project completed by Jay Anderson. I could go on." He looked up. "You've had an interesting first six months as a qualified test pilot."

"I'm sorry, sir. I made the best call I could."

"Those were expensive calls. Each project delay gets my ass kicked from above. The camera on the B-57 was for the National Reconnaissance Office, and believe me, those guys are not used to delays."

Red bowed his head.

Montgomery held his tone. "We're test pilots, son. We need to push the envelope before we give up. If you're gonna make it at Edwards, you need to grow a pair. Understood?"

"Yes, sir."

Montgomery lifted himself from his chair and moved to the front of his desk. "You've had a tough start in life, I know that. It's why I stuck my neck out for you after you graduated from Pax River. I understand why you're scared. Who wouldn't be, with your background? But you gotta pick things up. Start paying me back for the trust I've shown in you. In short, Red, I need you to cut the crap and start flying."

"Yes, sir."

"Yes, well. I've got another problem now."

Red looked up as Montgomery leaned behind him and picked up a phone. He covered the handset for a moment. "We're running out of test pilots." He reacted as his call was answered. "Tell Johnny to get in here with that Mississippi article." He replaced the receiver. "We've lost three to NASA this year, and A-TEC is always last in the pecking order for the new boys from the schools. We're gonna be short for a couple of years. When I explained this to the Nation Reconnaissance Office, well, let's just say they weren't very supportive."

The door opened, and Johnny Clifford, A-TEC's chief test pilot, came in with a newspaper under his arm.

"They've got something big coming down the line," Montgomery said. "Something high-priority big. The NRO know we're stretched, and they're worried. Now, I can't tell you what's coming, not yet, anyway, but it's the type of project this unit was created for." He paused as he opened the newspaper. "So, there's a plan to fill the pilot vacancies. It's a terrible plan, and I want to be clear, it was the NRO's idea." He gave out a long sigh. "But we figure we have no choice. Tell him, Johnny."

Clifford spread the opened newspaper on the table.

"We're going to establish a new role. Utility Test Pilot."

"What does that mean?" Red said.

"The UTPs will do the grunt work. They need to be engineering-minded, of course, to fit in around here. But we're reducing the need for them to have graduated from the test-pilot schools."

"We're gonna take on regular pilots? As test pilots?"

"They'll work alongside the test pilots. They can ferry the aircraft for maintenance and positioning. They can even fly the routine trials. Straight and level, instrument calibration stuff. I hate to say it, but the NRO's right. We send highly qualified TPs on a lot of routine flights."

"You want me to be a Utility Test Pilot?" Red said quietly.

"Of course not," Montgomery barked. "We want you as a reliable, fully qualified test pilot, we can trust."

"You can trust me now, sir."

"Can I?"

The room was quiet for a moment.

The colonel reached forward and tapped the inside spread of the *Mississippi Clarion*. "What do you see?"

Red examined the pages.

A photograph of a man in dungarees standing next to a biplane. Headline: *THE FLYING HILLBILLY.*

A second picture of a crop duster and a middle-aged man with a leather flying cap in the open cockpit.

Red shrugged. "A farmer in a Boeing Stearman."

Clifford and Montgomery exchanged a quick look. "Check again, son," Clifford said.

Red looked closer; the picture quality wasn't great.

But now he saw it.

The wings were swept. The engine was a radial, but not the usual for a Stearman. Actually, lots of small things were different.

"What is this? I don't recognise it."

"That's because he built it," Clifford said. "From parts thrown out by a couple of flying circuses. And when he couldn't find the parts, he milled them from scratch."

Montgomery lit a cigarette and leaned back. "He redesigned the wings. Albert out there reckons he's given the Stearman a shape that is thirty percent more fuel efficient and fifty percent faster. Although how the hell he gets it airborne on a short grass strip is anybody's guess. Maybe he's added rockets."

Red stared at the face of the farmer, who looked back through the grainy image. Serious but unthreatening. A run-of-the-mill advanced aircraft engineer working on a backwater farm in the Deep South.

"Raw talent," Montgomery said, waving his cigarette in the air. "He was an unremarkable USAF jet pilot. Flew Sabres in Korea but came out when he got back, to run the family farm."

"Jet experience and an eye for aerodynamics and engineering," Clifford added. "These guys are rare. We want him recruited."

Red finished studying the pictures and looked up. Both senior men stared at him.

"We've written to him," Montgomery said. "Eventually got him to agree to a meeting. But he was a no-show. Red, we want you to take a shot at it. Let's recruit Brandon Dupont as our first UTP." Montgomery had a smile on his face.

Red looked between the two men. "Me? Sir, you want me to recruit him? With the greatest respect, I think my best role here is as a pilot. I'm not sure I'll—"

"Son, you're on thin ice with me and Johnny. You know that, right? You're costing us budget, and you could end up costing us an entire project. But we need you. Not just to fill a seat, but to excel in your role as an experimental aircraft pilot. You need to learn to push that safety-first thing down a notch." Another wave of the cigarette from Montgomery. "And we think this little job might help broaden your horizons a bit. And give you some time to think. Take you out of the cosy little world you seem to inhabit."

It was little more than an admin task. And Montgomery's concerns about Red's abilities were unnerving him.

"Think of it as a punishment for bailing on two major projects, if you like," Johnny Clifford added.

Red stared back at the picture. The farmer's face gave nothing away. Where would he start?

"Fly down to Shitsville, Mississippi, and bring me this farmer." Montgomery paused and waited until Red looked up. "Then we can talk about the NRO project."

Montgomery's looked expectantly at Red.

"You want to talk to me about the NRO project?"

He noticed a quick exchange of looks between the colonel and Johnny Clifford.

"That's way we're going to do it. Johnny will take the lead, and we'll assign a junior test pilot alongside him. That could be you."

Red looked down to the newspaper. "If I recruit this guy?"

"We need to know we can rely on you. We'll start with this little task." He tapped the newspaper. "Sign up Brandon Dupont, then we'll talk."

Red wasn't sure if Montgomery was being completely serious. But he thought better of challenging the notion that he needed to recruit a farmer to work at A-TEC before he was assigned to a major project.

He was gonna have to suck it up and head across America.

Clifford stood up. "One other thing. We're up against the Defense Intelligence Agency on this one. They issue the security clearances, and they hate the plan almost as much as we do. So, some DIA guy's gonna hold your hand. We can't sign Dupont without the clearance, so you'll need to be very persuasive."

"Don't piss him off," added Montgomery.

DARK FLIGHT - PREVIEW
CHAPTER 2

The T-38 Talon sat gleaming on the line outside the A-TEC hangar, factory fresh, like a Mustang straight off the line. Ready to purr.

Red climbed up the ladder and laid his helmet and charts on the seat, before climbing back down to walk around, as a technician strapped his holdall into the vacant rear seat.

Minutes later, he climbed away from the California desert and set his heading due east. He allowed the jet to settle at thirty thousand feet and three hundred knots indicated. As he passed over Barstow, he reached forward and activated the timer built into the panel.

It was the least challenging navigation exercise he could think of. A straight line east to a refuelling stop at Kirtland, New Mexico, and then a further hop east on to Columbus Air Force Base, Mississippi.

Five hours in a small cockpit with no one to talk to.

He had his notes on Brandon Dupont tucked into his flight suit, but they were sparse. Dupont was unreachable by telephone, and pretty much unheard of since he'd left the air force.

Below, the shades of brown gave way to green tinges as he crossed into Arizona. The jet was trimmed nicely; he took his hand off the stick and relaxed.

He rolled up his sleeve and inspected his watch, running a finger along the curved outline of the Omega. Each irregular dent and scratch was as familiar as the lines on his own hand.

As the T-38 passed over Flagstaff, he looked out to the left. In the distance was an area of forest with a distinct tear in the earth beyond.

He exhaled at the sight of the Grand Canyon.

"Would you look at that?" he said to no one.

A couple of hours later, he began a descent to his refuelling stop.

Landing at Kirtland was an interesting experience. The air base shared its runway with a civilian airport, and Red had to hold ten miles west of the field. He quickly leafed through the charts to find holding pattern "Zulu."

Once on the ground, he had to work hard again to take the correct taxi route to the refuelling area.

He stepped onto the apron and stretched his legs. It was warm.

As two men emerged from a fuel truck, Red headed off to find a telephone. He needed the latest weather.

On his return, he was disappointed to see the refuelling operation was still ongoing. Tutting to himself, he climbed up to the rear seat of the T-38 and unzipped his holdall.

He took out a small wad of briefing notes and passed the time by familiarising himself with what would greet him in Mississippi.

The Defense Intelligence Agency guy he was to meet at Columbus was called Leo Rodriguez. Durden Creek Yard was the address they had for Dupont. Red looked at an overhead photograph of the place: a small collection of run-down farm buildings, a few pieces of rusting machinery. These folks were poor.

The only thing that stood out was the landing strip that ran close to the farm. It looked neat and well maintained, just about the only thing that was.

"You're good to go, sir," came the call from one of the refuelers.

"Thanks. Is the huffer nearby? I've got some bad weather coming in to my destination."

The kid looked confused.

"The huffer? The air blower to start the jet?"

"Ah! On its way, sir," he said, but Red couldn't see it anywhere close.

He stretched one more time then climbed back in, tucking his paperwork into the gap between the canopy and the panels. Ten frustrating minutes later, the ground crew finally arrived with the huffer, connecting the hoses to give him the pressurised air he needed for the start.

Air Traffic were helpful, and he went through the start, taxi, and line-up procedure in five minutes. A moment later, he accelerated the Talon back into the clear sky.

Just another nine hundred miles.

Ninety minutes later, the earth changed again. From the flat, featureless deserts of west Texas, the land became green at Oklahoma City. By the time he crossed into Arkansas, Red was mesmerised by the swirling rivers and forests.

As he passed into east Mississippi, the clouds began to build. Out to the south, he saw a collection of ominous Cb. Cumulonimbus. Thunderstorm clouds that would eat a small airplane like the T-38 for breakfast.

He plotted the path of the cloud build-up and realised he needed to get down quickly.

Edging the throttle forward, he increased his cruise to four hundred twenty knots, keeping an eye on his reserve fuel. He needed to land with thirty minutes in the tank. Unit rules.

He got on the radio with Columbus as soon as he could, and they cleared him in for a straight approach to runway thirteen.

Red adjusted his heading to take him northeast, calculating the minimum turn he could make to get the jet on the ground. Clouds began to gather beneath him. He chose a gap and dived the T-38. At five thousand feet, the ride became bumpy, just below the lowest layer of thick cumulus.

He crossed a wide river about two miles from the threshold and looked up to see his first lightning strike, around five miles south of the field.

"This is going to be tight."

After five hours sitting on an ejection seat, he really did not want to divert. But the desire to press on had killed many before him.

He made the finals turn, careful to keep enough power on through the buffet the Talon was famous for. He dropped the flaps and gear as he rounded out and held the jet at one hundred fifty-five knots.

Another lightning strike to the south.

Concentrate, buddy . . .

Red held the nose up, and the aircraft came down firmly. He stepped on the wheel brakes and held the stick back, killing the speed as efficiently as he could.

Turning off the runway, the tower told him he had about two minutes before they were shutting the airfield down, so he'd better make this bit quick.

He parked but didn't wait for the chocks to be in place before setting the throttles to cutoff and quickly shutting the Talon down.

The rain started as the stairs were pushed alongside, and by the time the crew chief released his holdall from the rear seat, it was torrential.

He left the chief to close the jet up and ran across the flight line, diving into the nearest building, pursued by another strike of lightning.

As he signed the visitors' log, an airman handed him a telephone message from Leo Rodriguez. An order from the agent to check into a motel eight miles south of the base.

Red climbed into his air force-allocated Chevrolet Nova and drove out into the apocalyptic rain. Water seeped in on the driver's-side window.

The motel was small: about ten years old, and already down on its luck.

Behind the counter, a middle-aged woman with a cigarette hanging from her lips stared at a small TV set. As Red arrived, she pushed a registration form towards him. He filled it in, passed her eight bucks for the room and incurred her disdain by asking for an invoice.

"Sorry, ma'am, but I'll be darned if I'm going to pay for this."

"Quite right" came a voice from behind.

Red swung around. A short, balding man sat on a small couch. He wore round spectacles and clutched a briefcase.

The man stood up. "Captain Brunson, I presume?"

Red nodded. "Leo Rodriguez?"

Rodriguez held out a hand, and Red shook it.

The DIA agent caught the look of surprise on Red's face. "You were expecting me, Captain?"

"Yes. Sorry. It's just . . . your name. I was expecting someone different."

The agent leaned closer and whispered, "We don't always use our real names."

"Of course. Sorry."

"No problem. And I hope you don't mind me dragging you away from the base? We prefer to operate away from the crowds."

"Well, I was looking forward to a steak in the Columbus O Club. But I'm sure we'll find somewhere better."

Rodriguez smiled. "Not on, my allowance, we won't."

Red dropped his bags in the room, peeled off his flight suit, and stepped under the weak shower.

Thirty minutes later, dressed in his civilian clothes, he walked out to meet Rodriguez, the humidity hitting him full in the face. The rain had stopped, and the sun had reappeared. Steam rose from the ground as the moisture quickly condensed.

Rodriguez waved from the parking lot, standing next to a gleaming Chevy Impala.

"There's a diner a couple of miles that way." Rodriguez pointed at the highway.

"Good with me." Red ran a hand over the car, admiring the sleek lines. "You travel from Washington in this, Leo?"

"Yes, sir. They do look after us at the agency."

"Apart from the food and accommodation?"

Rodriguez glanced at him. "Like I say, in our jobs, it doesn't do to become too familiar."

Figures from all the agencies turned up at Edwards from time to time, but this was Red's first close encounter with a bona fide field agent. A spy? Is that what they were? He didn't want to sound stupid, so didn't ask.

They pulled up to a diner: a single-storey, powder-blue building set back from the main road. Rodriguez parked and Red peered out his window, wincing at the puddles of water in the parking lot.

As the NSA agent got out, Red nodded to a large stain that ran across both seats. "You gonna get billed for that?"

Rodriguez turned around and looked back. "Stupid milkshake. Went all over me. I'll hand the car back with seat covers. They'll never know." He laughed.

Inside, they both ordered burgers and lemonade.

The agent looked out the window, and Red felt awkward. Leo Rodriguez clearly wasn't much of a conversationalist.

"So, the Defense Intelligence Agency, right?" Red said eventually.

"That's right." Rodriguez replied but didn't elaborate.

"Hmm. I get confused by all the different agencies up there in DC."

"It's easy. The National Security Agency has nothing to do with security, and the Defense Intelligence Agency has nothing to do with intelligence. The important thing to understand is that no one talks to anyone else, and we all hate each other."

"I see." Red replied, unsure if he was supposed to laugh.

To his relief, Rodriguez smiled.

"Anyway, you're not here for a lesson in government departments, Captain Brunson. You want me to clear your farmer to work at Edwards?"

"Yes, please."

They stopped talking as the food and drinks arrived. Once the waitress was beyond listening range, Rodriguez stuck a fork into a pile of fries and held them briefly in front of his mouth.

"I don't think we're gonna be able to clear him. Sorry." He ate the forkful.

Red put his own cutlery down. "I've flown a thousand miles for nothing?"

"Like I say, sorry if it's a waste of your time."

"What's the issue? My boss is pretty excited about him."

Rodriguez tapped his briefcase and rested it on the bench.

"I've done as much as I can. There's nothing on him, outside his service career. He has no civilian background to check. He started in the army, somehow got a college degree out of them before transferring to the air force. Right time, right place. He was fast-tracked onto jets. Converted onto the F-86 Sabre and shipped to Korea. But then, that's it. He came back, got out as fast as he could, and disappeared. We have his Social Security number, but he hasn't popped up on government paperwork for five years."

"So, what's the problem?"

Rodriguez shrugged. "The agency likes to know who we're dealing with. Clearing someone to work at Edwards and Groom Lake is a big deal. We're not comfortable that this guy is outside the usual career path."

"So, what do we do?" Red tucked into his own burger and took a slurp of the cool lemonade. Rodriguez had a calmness and a straightforwardness about him; he'd expected more mystery and distance.

"We go see him tomorrow, it's only ninety miles, although the roads get pretty poor the further you get from here. We talk." Rodriguez shrugged. "He might not want to join, anyway."

"And if he does? That leaves me with a big problem. I can't go back empty-handed."

Rodriguez toyed with his fork. "I'll do my best to fill in the blanks on his resume. After that, I can make a call. But don't get your hopes up. It doesn't look great at the moment. And I'm at the end of three-week road trip, so I'm going home after tomorrow either way."

The car jumped, and Red woke with a start.

"Good nap, flyboy?" Rodriguez was laughing at him.

"Where are we?" Red looked out on the rough dirt road. Trees, fields, nothing else.

"We're about ten miles north of Coffeeville, which is in the middle of nowhere, so we're beyond that point."

"Hicksville, USA."

"You got that right."

Red leaned forward and rubbed his lower back. "You weren't joking about these roads."

Progress was slow, but as they rounded a sharp bend in the road, they were greeted by the sight of a large barn, two smaller farm buildings, and a ramshackle wooden house with most windows boarded up. Rusting machinery littered a wooded area to the left of the house. The place looked abandoned, nothing like a viable farm.

But standing out from the ruins was a gleaming airplane. A big, beautiful Stearman-like biplane. Significantly more striking in real life than in those grainy newspaper pictures.

Red whistled, and his eyes went to the wings. They were quite something: swept and beautifully engineered. "Hey, stop the car a second."

They drew to a halt, and Red got out. The cicadas were in full voice, and it was about ten degrees hotter than Columbus.

He undid a button on his shirt—strictly against regulations—and walked over to the biplane, resting on its tail wheel.

The wings had been machined to perfection. They were definitely narrower than a regular Stearman. He ducked under and ran his hand over a strange line set back from the leading edge. A break in the surface a few inches from the leading edge. Metal rods ran from two hinges.

"This thing has slats," he said to himself.

A strong southern accent called out. "Can I help you, son?" Red sprang up.

A tall man in his early forties walked towards him. His hair was neatly parted to the side and slick with something. Otherwise, he looked like a poor southern farmer: oil-stained pants, a blue check shirt, and worn leather boots that may have seen service in the war.

"I was just admiring your airplane."

Red glanced at Rodriguez, standing by his car. Watching, evaluating.

He stuck his hand out. "I'm Captain Red Brunson of the United States Air Force. And I'm guessing you're Mr Dupont?"

Brandon Dupont nodded, but didn't step any closer.

Red withdrew his hand. "Mind if I call you Brandon?"

"Okay, sir."

"Please, call me Red." He turned to the aircraft. "Hey, Brandon, does this thing have slats?"

Dupont moved slowly around to the front of the modified Stearman; Red followed. The older man ran his hand along the hinged break in the wing. Through the yellow frame of the aircraft, Red noticed an elderly man in dungarees standing in the gloom of the doorway of the house. He might have been anywhere between sixty-five and one hundred years old.

Noticing Red's gaze, Dupont turned around. "It's all right, Pappy. Go on in." The farmer turned back to the aircraft. "Flaps on the front, if that's what you mean by slats. They create drag and lift. Enough to see her up safely from the strip and not get dragged down by the trees over yonder."

Dupont motioned to the start of the grass runway about fifty yards away. Red studied the ground; it looked the best-maintained piece of land on the farm. Red guessed he had four hundred feet of usable strip, followed by a ditch, some undergrowth, and then at maybe eight hundred feet, a small cluster of trees. It looked tight.

He looked back at the slats. The hinge was lubricated with shiny metallic parts and a tight wire, exposed over the top of the wing, trailing back to the cockpit.

"Did you make these yourself?" Red asked.

"Yup. Built them in the shop here. She was okay until I put the new wings on. Smaller, faster in the air, but longer takeoff roll. I learned the scary way she'd outgrown the strip." Dupont laughed.

"I can imagine. And so, this was your solution. Brandon, you invented a leading-edge, high-lift device, presumably without knowing what it was."

Dupont shrugged. "I knew what it was. Never understood why the Sabres didn't have something similar. We used a whole lotta runway getting those in the air."

"Korea?"

"Yep."

Red looked over the rest of the aircraft. An additional strut seemed to have been added to the landing gear on each side. Again, beautifully engineered.

"You got a lathe somewhere?" Red said, while crouched under the wing.

"Got some old forge tools."

Red shook his head at the thought of this man handcrafting precision aero parts in a rustic blacksmith's shed in Mississippi.

He looked back; Dupont was staring at him.

Red took a step closer. "Brandon, you're probably wondering why we're here?" The farmer didn't respond. "Well, I work for a very special unit based in California. And I've got something very exciting to offer you."

Again, Dupont, didn't move or respond. Red stayed silent, returning the stare.

Eventually, the farmer nodded slowly. "Uh-huh."

"We need people like you."

"People like me? Farmers?"

"No, Brandon. We need aeronautical engineers who can fly."

The farmer's expression didn't change. "How much do you weigh?"

"I'm sorry, what?"

"How much do you weigh, Captain?"

"About one sixty."

Dupont moved to the aircraft and reached into the cockpit, retrieving a leather helmet. He turned back to Red with a wide grin.

"Wanna go for a ride?"

Red studied the aircraft and considered the offer. He knew Dupont might invite him up, and he'd dismissed the idea of flying in an aircraft built in someone's backyard. But now that he saw it in the flesh, it was clear this machine was a labour of love. The machining was precise; the engineering looked sound.

And there was something deliberate and methodical about Dupont himself. If that's how he approached flying, it was going to be a safe ride.

"Okay."

Red helped push the biplane around until it was clear of the barn and facing into the gentle breeze. Dupont handed him the battered leather helmet.

He looked across at Rodriguez and gave him a wave. The DIA man shook his head, but Red ignored him and climbed into the front cockpit.

As he strapped himself in, he checked the anchor points. They looked secure, possibly original from Boeing.

Dupont appeared on the wing next to him, crouched down, and pulled on his straps to ensure they were tight.

He had to admit, the man knew what he was doing.

"There ain't no flying controls in the front, so it'll be up to me if we get in trouble. Sit tight. I'll get her down. Once we stop, get out quick as you can. She's full of gas."

Red nodded at the ad hoc emergency brief. "Got it."

"Well, all right."

Dupont climbed into the rear cockpit, and Red listened to the sound of pulleys and wheels being pulled and turned. Moments later, the engine turned over twice and burst into life. The air buffeted above the plexiglass as the engine noise increased and they started to move.

The ground was smooth for the short journey to the cut landing strip. With the aircraft sitting on its rear wheel, Red had to stretch up in his straps to see the tress ahead.

He was about to find out if Dupont's makeshift high-lift actually worked.

A sheet tied to a metal pole flapped gently at one side of the strip. Wind sock. Slight cross breeze.

Before they entered the runway, Dupont turned into the wind and wound the engine up a notch. He was doing his power checks, another sign that his military flying training was embedded in his routine.

The leading edge of the lower wing was on the move. Red imagined Dupont winding a handle for his improvised slats.

They dropped down by maybe twenty degrees; it was clear that they would add considerable lift.

Dupont moved the Stearman until it faced down the strip. The engine wound up to full power, and they began to roll.

The aircraft pitched forward as the tail wheel came up and, almost immediately, they floated into the air.

"Jesus, this thing wants to fly."

They swept over the trees with plenty of clearance and continued to climb. Dupont put them in a gentle left bank, and Red watched the slats winding back in, followed by the flaps.

They continued the bank and climbed higher. At five thousand feet, in the cool air, they cleared a large lake south of the farm. Dupont began his show.

There were no comms between them, and Red found it difficult to twist in the harness to look back. He figured he was along for the ride and that was that.

The nose pitched up, and Dupont led the aircraft into a smooth and accurate barrel roll. All the way through, Red felt an even 1g holding him in his seat. If he had been an examiner, he would be extremely happy with his student.

The nose dipped, power came on, and Red felt the grunt from the modified engine. Dupont heaved her up into a three-sixty-degree loop. This time Red felt pushed into the seat, impressed at the energy the aircraft sustained.

Between each manoeuvre, Dupont climbed back up to five thousand feet, ensuring a good margin. This was no cowboy pilot.

The demonstration grew progressively more complex and included a vertical stall. Dupont them pitched down, gathered energy, and then pulled them into a steep climb, raising the nose until it was more or less straight up. The energy fell off quickly. For a second they hung in the air high above the Mississippi farmland, before the home-built Stearman began to fall backwards.

This was the sort of position an aircraft could fail to recover from in the wrong hands. But Dupont had the aircraft just offset from the vertical, and with full deflected rudder, she smoothly fell through one eighty degrees into a nose-down attitude for a perfect recovery.

It was an alarming manoeuvre for a passenger, but Red had to admit, the farmer had the skills.

As they descended, Red looked at the smooth rivets in the airframe; he ran a finger over the bright silver buttons, not a scratch, shard or notch to be seen.

Pilot skills and engineering proficiency. He could see why Montgomery wanted him at Edwards.

The aircraft descended and gathered speed. The wind became a roar over the small windshield as they reached the treetops.

Red tried to estimate their speed. One hundred seventy-five knots?

He held on to the sides of the airframe as the modified Stearman began to buffet.

"Jesus." He breathed into the tornado of air crashing into them.

His stomach went south as Dupont pulled them up through what Red figured was around 5G.

Off the top of the pull-up, the Stearman fell around into a curved approach. Dupont touched down with a firm thud and rolled them out on the grass before killing the engine as the aircraft drifted to a halt.

Red removed his leather flying helmet and straps and stood on the seat, holding out his hand.

Dupont looked surprised, but shook it all the same. "Glad you enjoyed it, son."

"I did, very much, thank you. Now, Brandon Dupont. How about that chat?"

The house was dingy and smelled of rotting timber. Gaps in the boarded-up windows let in only the odd shaft of sunlight, illuminating swirls of dust.

A discoloured mirror hung over the fireplace. No photographs, no paintings, no ornaments. Nothing that said it was a home to anyone.

Pappy sat in a rocking chair, in the shade at the back of the room. Dupont stood in the centre, with folded arms.

"So, what do y'all wanna say?"

Red looked around at the old sofa and chair and thought better of trying to sit on either.

He pointed to a dining table behind the sofa. "Could we sit down?"

The three men took their seats, but not before Red and Rodriguez tested the rickety chairs with a quick prod.

Dupont sat at an angle with an arm resting on the table.

Before Red could say anything, Rodriguez fired off his first question.

"Why'd you leave the air force, Brandon?"

The farmer didn't flinch at the directness. Instead, he studied Rodriguez.

"Done my time."

Rodriguez waited, but clearly no further illumination was coming. He made a note. "You have a pilot's license for that thing?"

"*That thing* has its own license. Yes, sir. From the FAA. I have my own license, too. That what this is about? You come to ground me?"

"No, Brandon," Red said quickly. "Quite the opposite."

"You have any other relatives alive?" Rodriguez said.

Dupont shook his head. "Just me and Pappy now."

Rodriguez studied his notes and opened a brown file. "Says here you served in Korea. In Kunsan?"

Dupont nodded.

"But you didn't want to stay in and keep flying?"

"Ma died. Jo died. I had the farm to look after."

"Jo?" Red asked.

"My sister. Died of fever in '53."

"I'm sorry," Red added.

Dupont looked at Red and smiled. "Thank you, Red."

Red felt the warmth in his sympathy. The older pilot had a deep maturity and calmness about him.

Flying experience and a little worldly wisdom. Wasted out here.

He glanced at Rodriguez. The agent was leafing through his notes. Red turned back to their host. "Brandon, I want to make you an offer."

On the edge of his vision, he saw Pappy turn his head very slightly.

"You're exactly what we're looking for at Edwards Air Force Base in California. Have you heard of Edwards? Chuck Yeager? It's where he broke the sound barrier, in an X-15."

"Damn nearly killed him," Dupont said, and leaned back in his chair. "They didn't understand the pressure wave."

Red laughed. "That's right, they didn't. But they modified the wing and controls, and they got there. And that's what we do. We test and revise until things work. Now, you wouldn't be a qualified test pilot, but we would get you fully certified as an engineer and a commercial pilot. You'd be a key part of the team, moving aircraft and helping the qualified TPs like me with our workload. You'd have a nice house, access to the base facilities, including a medical centre. You and your father would be well looked after."

"Uh-huh . . ."

"Uh-huh, yes?"

Dupont lowered his gaze.

"This is an incredible offer, Mr Dupont," Rodriguez said. "Why aren't you biting his hand off?"

More silence from the farmer.

"And you know what?" Red said. "We have a great time. Lots of drinking and fun and the flying, well it's the best in the world. Of course, you'd have to pass the clearance process from Mr Rodriguez here, and there'd be a refresher course to pass in the T-38. But even that would be quite something. I can tell you, the Talon is a helluva ride."

"Them that fly out of Columbus?"

"That's right. We have a few just for us pilots to get around. It'd be your regular jet. It's supersonic, Brandon. Beats an old biplane any day of the week."

No answer, but a hint of a smile.

Red glanced at Pappy, who remained as still as a shop dummy.

Rodriguez lifted his briefcase onto the table. "Son, can I ask you a couple of more questions?"

"Uh-huh."

The DIA agent lifted out a small wad of papers and took the lid off a fountain pen.

"Did you go to school?"

"Sorta. Miss Honeybeach taught us for a couple of years. Then I had to pull my shifts here."

"Ok, so you didn't go to college."

"Not until I joined the army. They sent me."

Rodriguez looked down at his forms. "Did you ever apply for anything after you left the air force? Are you registered with a doctor?"

"Doc comes here to see Pappy, but we don't pay. He does it for free."

Red smiled to himself at this family living in the nineteenth century in the middle of modern America, like pioneers arriving in the West. He pictured bath night once a week in front of the stove.

Yet, somehow, he was perfect for them. A natural engineer and pilot, and so confident, assured. The army gave him an education, found his potential, lifted him up. Now he was falling back down. Red wanted him to join A-TEC, not just because it was a waste leaving him on the farm, but because he was good. He couldn't imagine him ever getting flustered in the air.

"Brandon." Red put his palm on the table. "Whaddya think? You want to move to California and work with the latest flying technology in the world?"

For the first time, Dupont looked across at Pappy. "Well, that's mighty kind of you, and I sure do 'preciate you comin' all this way.

But I don't think I can just leave here. With or without Pappy. We got four fields now. I do most of it by myself." He shrugged as if that was that.

Red sat back in his chair. His chance of progressing to the NRO project had hit a wall of obstinance.

Rodriguez shuffled his papers and leaned forward. "Son, I don't think you fully understand what's on offer here. This is a once-in-a-lifetime opportunity. You'll never get a chance like this again."

There was a movement to the side, and Red looked around to see Pappy stand up and leave the room. Maybe this was his chance to hear what Dupont really thought.

"You and me flying together in California," Red said. "You want to say yes!"

Dupont looked down at his shoes and scratched the table with his dirty fingernails. "I'd better say no, sir. But like I say, I sure do 'preciate the offer."

"C'mon, man. This is silly. You worried about the fields and whose gonna farm them? You'll be on a government salary of . . . Leo, what's the salary?"

Rodriguez scanned a document in the papers on the table.

"Four thousand two hundred twelve dollars. That's nearly three hundred fifty dollars a month, son."

"He said no."

Red whipped his head around to see Pappy standing in the middle of the room with a shotgun aimed at them.

"Shit," Red said.

"Pappy . . ." Dupont spoke in a tone someone would use to gently chastise a cat. "No need for that. These people were just leaving."

Rodriguez leaped to his feet. "Sir, please put the gun down. We're here on official government business. You're committing a felony."

Red stood up slowly, keeping his eyes on the old man.

Pappy took a step forward and kept the gun levelled at them. "He said no. Now get out."

Rodriguez looked panicked. He stuffed his paperwork into his briefcase.

But Red slowly turned back to Dupont and whispered, "Is this what you want, man?"

"Now!" Pappy shouted.

Dupont avoided Red's eye, as he followed Rodriguez past the snarling father and into the brightness outside.

It took a second for Red's eyes to adjust to the bright sunlight. He paused, but felt a prod in the back. Pappy was an inch behind him.

Protecting his son from a better life.

Refusing to show any fear, Red walked slowly to the car. Rodriguez was already stuffing his case into the back before climbing in.

As they pulled away, Red glanced back to see Pappy standing steadfast in the yard. In the shadow of the doorway behind him, he could just about make out the figure of Brandon Dupont.

They stopped at a diner in Coffeeville. The adrenaline burst prompted by the sight of a levelled 12-gauge had subsided, and Red felt tired.

Rodriguez looked pale. How much time had this pudgy guy actually spent in the field?

"What do we do now?" Red asked.

"I'm tempted to report him to the locals," Rodriguez said. He stirred his coffee and looked lost in thought.

"But you're not going to?" Red asked, prompting him.

Rodriguez exhaled. "I doubt they'd do anything. This probably counts as normal behaviour around here. In any case, that would be the end of it for Brandon Dupont."

"So you think it's not over? There's still a chance?" Red was surprised.

Rodriguez shook his head. "No. We're done." He stopped stirring and looked directly at Red. "It's a damn shame, but that's that."

The food arrived. Red's mind was turning over. "I don't think we should give up so easily."

"We don't have a choice, Red. The old man chased us off with a shotgun. I'm not going back there, that's for sure."

"But you saw Dupont. He's a genius, living in a cow field. He could be at Edwards, at the centre of it all. A pilot among the best in the world."

Rodriguez stuck a fork into his hash browns. "You can't save everyone you meet, Red Brunson."

Back at the motel parking lot, Rodriguez shook Red's hand as he climbed into his car.

"You heading back north?"

Rodriguez tapped his briefcase "I've gotta little paperwork to do, then I'll get on the road. I prefer to drive overnight." He gave a weak smile. "I'm sorry it didn't work out for you, Captain."

"Yeah. Me, too." Red heaved his overnight bag from the trunk.

"Where will you be tonight?" Rodriguez asked.

"In the Bachelor Officer Quarters at Columbus."

"Sleep well and safe flight tomorrow."

Rodriguez disappeared towards the motel.

At the base Red was happy to be allocated a good-sized room. He lay on the bed, closed his eyes, and tried to nap.

It was hard to shift the image of Dupont from his mind. The man with so much promise, left to rot in the fields.

It didn't feel right. There was a connection there.

He drifted off eventually and was woken by a sharp rap on the door.

Red swivelled off the bed, noticing it was dark outside.

On the other side of the door was an airman.

"Arrived at the main gate for you, sir."

Red looked down to see a large, brown government file.

"Thank you."

He rubbed his eyes and sat on the bed. Inside the cover was a handwritten note.

Just in case . . .

Leo.

He realised he was holding one hundred pages of completed and signed security clearance for Brandon Dupont.

The O Club was filled with young lieutenants on their advanced jet training, drinking and laughing. Red could only dwell on what Brandon Dupont had given up.

A lieutenant colonel approached his table. Red sprang to his feet and stood to attention, but the senior officer waved him to sit down.

"No luck today, huh, Brunson?"

"No, sir."

"I'm Bill Ryman. I head up training here. Agent Rodriguez called me. Said we're to provide any support we can, but I guess you're going back empty-handed?"

"I'm afraid so, sir."

"Too bad. Sorry we couldn't have been of more service. I used to fly with Tucker Montgomery. So you give that old bastard a kick from me."

Red smiled. "I might not kick him, sir, but I'll pass on your regards."

"You do that, son. See you in the morning. Your jet will be on the line and full of fuel."

The clanging alarm clock once again intruded on Red's attempt at a full night's sleep.

He silenced it and picked up his watch, winding it carefully.

After breakfast, he entered the training squadron close to the flight line. In his case was Dupont's security clearance to work at Edwards. But with no Brandon Dupont to go along with it, the trip had been an expensive waste of time and money.

The squadron was a busy, bustling place. To one side was a large, open locker area with men who looked like boys changing into flight gear, nervously glancing at their brief for the day's sortie.

Red went to the ops desk ready to file his flight plan and grab the latest weather. Another refuelling stop in New Mexico and another straight line across the continent.

As he read through the notices for his route, he heard T-38s firing up outside. The noises and smells brought back his own days at Columbus. Sometimes two sorties a day, each filled with a series of tasks. Mistakes were allowed, but only once. A failed sortie meant a recheck. Two failures and you were in front of the review board. Often, that was it for dreams of being a fighter pilot.

For all the glamour and excitement, jet training was a physical and mental grind like no other.

And yet Red missed it. The camaraderie that comes with navigating an ordeal. Making bonds that will last for life. Plus, the T-38 is an awesome jet, every child's dream idea of what a fast airplane looked like. Sleek and purposeful.

If only he could get Brandon Dupont up in one.

Red paused his form filling, put his pen down, and looked around the unit. He tapped the table, mind turning over.

He looked up to the admin officer on the other side of the sign-out desk.

"Excuse me. Is Lieutenant Colonel Ryman in today?"

The officer pointed at a corridor that ran down to Red's left. He wandered down until he found Ryman's name on a door. It was ajar.

He gingerly leaned into the room. Ryman was at his desk, in flight suit.

"Brunson? You off?"

"Actually, sir, I've had an idea."

Minutes later, he was in his flight suit, walking to his fuelled and ready Talon.

As he ran through the start-up procedures, Red pulled out some notes he'd made from the T-38 flight manual. He committed the slow flight parameters to heart.

Climbing out of Columbus he headed southeast and made a climbing right hand turn until he captured the reciprocal heading, aiming the nose at Coffeeville.

He kept the speed at a slow two hundred knots, but still, he was approaching Coffeeville in less than twenty minutes. His first task was to find the farm.

He spied the two large grain towers that marked the edge of the land, and lowered the nose, feeding in more power. In the distance, he spotted the small grass strip, surrounded by crumbling buildings. The yellow Stearman sat right where Dupont left it the day before.

Red lowered the nose a little more. Scanning the forward view for cables or high trees, he let the aircraft sink to one hundred fifty feet. The earth flashed past him, and the T-38 ate up the mile or so left to run.

A final nudge on the throttles; he didn't want anyone to miss this.

He flashed directly overhead the house with the engines at full power. He must have been within one hundred feet of the roof.

He pulled up and banked over as the Talon screamed into the sky.

Looking back over his shoulder, he saw a figure run from the house.

Bingo.

He swept back around in a wide arc, pulling the throttles back to idle. The speed bled away quickly, and as he rolled out with the farm two miles away on the nose, he dropped his flaps and landing gear.

The jet slowed to one hundred forty-five knots, and he fed in a good handful of throttle, with a little allowance for how slowly the engines spooled back up from idle.

He found himself with a distinct nose-up attitude, but the aircraft held its height.

Red crept closer to the farm, engines howling to keep the metal jet airborne.

He gave himself a small adjustment so he could see the buildings below. Dupont was there, smiling and shouting.

"You gotta follow me up, old man. *C'mon.*"

He made sure he passed all the way over the farm at one hundred forty-five knots before feeding in the last inch of throttle he had to spare. The Talon responded with a gentle climb, and as the needle swept through one hundred sixty knots, he raised the gear, followed by the flaps, and entered the same pattern as before.

Sweeping around a second time, he was disappointed to see the Stearman still on the ground.

"Don't you get it? I'm flying like this so you can join me."

He set the jet up for another slow pass. Everything down and dirty.

This time he allowed the Talon to sink even lower. He gave the jet the gentlest of nudges to ensure he flew between the house and barn. Straight over the strip.

There was no way he could put down on the grass and expect to get up again, but he could come close.

Seventy-five feet as he crossed the property boundary.

Finally, Dupont was on the move. Running towards the strip.

Red brought his concentration back inside. He descended to just fifty feet before pushing the throttles to max again. A slight lag as the engines wound up. He nudged the nose down to tease the airspeed up. The cockpit view filled with trees as the jet continued to sink, but eventually the needle moved, and he raised the nose as much as he dared.

With what must have been a deafening roar below him, the T-38 pulled up into a spectacular climb.

As the speed picked up to something normal again, he banked and looked over his shoulder.

The Stearman's prop was turning.

"Ha ha. Let's go!"

As Red flashed across the farm, Pappy emerged from the house and stared up. Red was relieved to see no gun in his hands.

He set up an orbit a couple of miles north and waited.

"Come on . . ." he urged Dupont under his breath.

A burst of yellow appeared, climbing above the trees. Red smiled under his oxygen mask and studied the hastily written notes on his kneepad.

He reckoned the Stearman's top speed was about one hundred twenty-five knots, but Montgomery told him they estimated Dupont's modified wing gave him a fifty percent increase in top speed.

"Well, let's see about that."

He continued in the orbit as the Stearman approached from the east, slowing the aircraft to one hundred fifty-five knots, which was the basic approach speed for a fuel-light Talon. It gave him good enough manoeuvrability, and he rolled out, facing southeast, and looked over his shoulder. Sure enough, the farmer was coming up on him. Just a few knots in it, but enough to close up.

Red kept the jet steady and straight. The Stearman got closer, and eventually, a yellow shape appeared in Red's side vision.

He looked across to see Dupont giving him a wave in the back seat.

Red gestured forward with his hand, hoping Dupont would recognise it as a *follow me* sign.

They stayed in loose formation, and Red called up Columbus to warn them that the Stearman had no radio and the pilot might act unpredictably.

For twenty-five minutes they travelled in a rare formation of aircraft separated by thirty years and what felt like a century of innovation.

As they approached the air force base, he turned gently, giving Dupont plenty of space and time to follow. He lined up the T-38 just offset from runway 13, allowing Dupont the extended centreline. He lowered his gear and went to full flap extension.

Looking across, he pointed down for Dupont, indicating they were going to land.

He led the farmer down the glide slope, and was pleased to see Dupont's trademark leading edge slats winding out.

As they crossed the threshold, Red banked gently away and let Dupont land and roll out as he came around for his own landing. By the time he brought the jet to taxi speed, Dupont was shutting down outside the squadron.

Red taxied in as the squadron boss and two other pilots greeted Dupont. Instructors, he assumed.

He brought his Talon to a stop and scribbled the times on his kneepad. By the time he climbed out, Dupont was already on the tarmac surrounded by a small team, which included Lieutenant Colonel Ryman.

Red observed from a few yards away, listening to the farmer explaining his new wing and leading-edge modification over the distant whine of jet engines. Dupont's confidence was striking.

"You seen this, Red?" Ryman called him over.

"Quite something, isn't it?" Red replied.

He watched as Ryman completed a tour of the Stearman, and he made a note to let Montgomery know just how useful he was being.

Eventually, they emerged back at the nose of the prop aircraft.

"Colonel, do you think we have flight gear that would fit this young man?" Red said.

Ryman smiled and looked at Dupont. "How about it? Want to get back in a jet?"

Inside the locker room, an equipment specialist appeared, tape measure in hand. He checked Dupont's head, thigh length, and weight. He gave Red and Colonel Ryman a subtle nod. Dupont was good for the ejection seat, heavy enough to arm it and thighs short enough to ensure he wasn't kneecapped in the event of an emergency exit.

After fifteen minutes of pulling on increasingly heavy layers of flying clothing, Dupont began the transformation from farmer to fighter pilot. He settled his helmet's inner ear cups like a pro before strapping his oxygen mask over his mouth and nose, and checking for leaks. He was confident and efficient.

Ryman slapped him on the back. "Well, go enjoy yourselves and listen carefully to Captain Brunson. He's one of our best."

Red led Dupont out to the jet, where a marshaller had lined up a fresh set of steps with the rear cockpit. He ushered Dupont up and told him to step on the ejection seat, before watching him lower himself into the cockpit. The farmer immediately started to run his fingers over the instrument panel, quickly identifying the main dials and controls. Red took him through some systems he might not be familiar with.

"F-86 Korea, wasn't it?" Red asked.

"Yeah."

"Well, the Talon's a little more up to date. I think you'll enjoy it."

Red helped him with the straps, pulling them tightly over his shoulders so he wouldn't lose Dupont through the canopy when they inverted.

Finally, he plugged the farmer into the aircraft—oxygen, air for the g-suit, and communications—and took him through the procedure for arming the ejection seat.

He gave him a friendly pat on the shoulder before disappearing down the stairs and up into the front cockpit.

Red lowered the canopy and signalled for the pressurised air from the huffer. He waited patiently, watching the revolutions rise on a small dial, before moving the throttle an inch or so forward, firing fuel into the engine. It caught and he set the throttle to idle. The ground crewman diverted the flow into the second engine. It was now about a hundred degrees in the aircraft, and Red quickly selected a blast of cool air before he had to shut the air conditioning off again for the takeoff.

"You secure?" Red asked.

"Yup."

"Okay then, I need you to look to your left. You'll see a metal pin with a red label dangling."

"Got it."

"Remove it—"

"—you want to remove both, then set the seat live?" Dupont asked, interrupting him.

"Ha. Yeah. You've not been gone that long, have you?"

Red noticed a ground-crew member give a thumbs-up to Dupont behind him. Clearly he'd held up the pins to be counted. A good safety drill.

Red then worked methodically through the checklist, despite his familiarity with it. A lot had gone into this flight, and Red was conscious of having senior officers such as Colonel Ryman doing his bidding.

No mistakes now.

In his small mirrors, he watched as Dupont checked out his surroundings. The farmer had slipped back into the unique world of the military jet pilot, with ease.

"You ready?"

"Yes, sir" came a drawl from behind him.

Red taxied them out, lined up on RWY 13 and stood on the brakes, while bringing the engines up to a scream. After waiting for the instruments to stabilise, he released the brakes and pushed the throttles into afterburner. The jet jumped forward before accelerating hard as the burners kicked in.

He raised the nose, allowed the aircraft to creep into the air. As the airspeed needle swept past one hundred fifty knots, he raised the gear, quickly followed by the flaps. Red held the nose around three degrees as the speed wound up. When it got to three hundred knots, he snapped the stick back, pulling 5g on the Talon as the rocketed skyward.

Dupont let out a "Yee-haw!" over the intercom.

Red watched the speed carefully; he lost a lot of energy in the pull-up but judged he had enough left to get them all the way over. Once inverted and facing back the way they came, he rolled them upright to let the aircraft accelerate through three hundred knots again, hoping he wouldn't get in trouble for busting the T-38's limit below ten thousand feet. Once at three fifty, he performed a second zoom climb, this one slightly shallower but no less impressive. He glanced over his shoulder and saw Columbus growing smaller. As the speed got down to two hundred knots, he used the last of the energy to perform an aileron roll, turning them upside down, before levelling out, building speed once more.

Dupont made more whooping noises from behind.

"You enjoy that?"

"You bet! Pretty smooth through the range. No buffet?"

Red shook his head at the farmer's need to analyse the T-38's aerodynamics.

"It's a great jet. You wanna have a fly?"

For the next ten minutes, Dupont took the controls. Red observed as he got used to the throttles and engine response, the aircraft's handling, and even the buffet close to the stall.

As with any new student, Red covered the controls with his hands, ready to take control. But there was a proficiency to Dupont's flying that gave him confidence the jet was in good hands.

He talked him through the procedure for landing, and they carried out a three-hundred-knot join in the overhead, breaking into the pattern with a seventy-degree roll. The farmer flew it okay, but he needed prompting. They would have to effectively put him through flight school to bring him up to scratch and issue his military licenses.

Red kept hold of the stick and throttles as Dupont attempted to set the T-38 up for an approach. It was tricky without experience; the aircraft required some amount of anticipation. But he got there in the end, and it was a safe and satisfying plonk onto the runway at Columbus.

After taxiing to a stop, Red shut the aircraft down and popped the canopy up. He made his seat safe, unstrapped, and stood up, looking down on his smiling passenger.

"Okay, farmer. Time to make your mind up. You wanna be paid to fly the latest military aircraft? Or do you want to grow soybeans for the rest of your life?"

Dupont was still strapped in, his arms resting on the rim of the fuselage. He looked around just as two T-38s took off as a pair on the main runway. After the noise subsided, he turned back to Red.

"Three fifty a month, you said?"

DARK FLIGHT - PREVIEW
CHAPTER 3

Red was woken by an urgent hammering on the door.

"Jesus, what time is it?" He tried to focus on the alarm clock.

0645.

He staggered out of bed, aching from the long trip home in a cramped cockpit.

"Captain Brunson?"

A man in a white shirt and tie stood on the other side of his screen door.

"Yes?"

The man held out a government ID badge. It had his photograph and a seal Red didn't immediately recognise.

"I'm Agent David McInery from the Federal Bureau of Investigation. Sir, may I come in?"

He led the man into the kitchen and offered him coffee. McInery looked around doubtfully at the empty kitchen.

"Actually, I have only water," Red clarified.

"I'll pass. Thank you, son." The agent placed some papers and forms on the breakfast bar. "You met with a Defense Intelligence agent called Leonard Rodriguez the day before yesterday?"

"Yes, sir, in Mississippi."

"Mississippi. That's right," McInery said, opening a notepad. "And when exactly did you last see him?"

"Late afternoon. In a Motel America near Columbus Air Force Base."

The agent nodded and made a note. "You see anyone else around?"

"Um, I mean, there were other cars in the parking lot, but I can't recall anyone in particular. Mind telling me what's going on?"

"Agent Rodriguez is dead. Murdered."

"What?"

"His body was found close to a rest area off I-75. Couple of miles north of Chattanooga."

"Jesus." Red pulled a chair out from his small kitchen table and sat down. "When?"

"Yesterday, morning. But, the body was pretty badly burned, and they don't know exactly when he was killed. So, they're keen to know his precise movements."

Red shook his head slowly. "I can't believe it."

"When he left you, where did Agent Rodriguez say he was heading?"

"Said he was going straight back to DC. He wanted to drive overnight."

The agent nodded and made more notes. "That would fit with his route."

"Poor Leo. Was he married?"

"Yes, sir. Two boys."

"Damn."

"Son, was there anything unusual at all about your time with Agent Rodriguez. Did you get the feeling you were being followed, for instance?"

Only one image popped into Red's mind.

"Not followed, no. But someone did pull a gun on us."

McInery stood up straight and stared at him. "What did you say?"

"Actually, it wasn't that big a deal. It was this elderly hick farmer in Coffeeville."

"Where the hell's that?"

"Nowhere, is where it is. About a hundred miles south of Memphis."

"What exactly happened?"

Red pinched the bridge of his nose. "He basically chased us off his land for having the audacity to offer his son a job."

"He threatened you with a gun? An actual weapon?"

"An old twelve-gauge, I think. Probably wasn't even loaded."

"You don't think he was serious? That he couldn't have come after Leo later?"

Red shook his head. "No. This was just some crazy old man on a farm in the middle of nowhere who wanted to keep his son by his side. Besides, how the hell would he have known where Leo was?"

"He didn't follow you?"

"Definitely not."

"How can you be so sure?"

"We drove out on a dirt road for about two miles. There's no way he was behind us, believe me. Plus . . ."

"Plus?"

Red hesitated. "Plus, I saw him the next day."

"You went back?"

"Not exactly. I flew over, in a T-38. I saw him outside the house."

"What's a T-38?"

"It's a military jet. It's a long story, but I flew over around ten thirty. He was definitely on the farm then. I doubt he ever leaves it."

McInery made a note. "You're sure of the time?"

"Yes, sir."

"I guess that makes it impossible it was him, then."

A horrible thought came into Red's mind.

"Agent Rodriguez gave me the signed security clearance for the guy we met. Is that still valid?"

The FBI man riffled through his papers. "Brandon Dupont?"

"Yeah."

The man shrugged. "That's not part of my investigation.

Rodriguez was at the end of a long road trip. I understand this was a small job added on at the last minute."

Red wrote the location of the Duponts' farm in McInery's notepad and showed him to the door. "What do you think happened, Agent McInery?"

"Local cops think he was taking a nap in a rest area and was jumped."

"Christ. Poor Leo. He probably didn't see them coming."

"Lucky for them he didn't. He would have torn them limb from limb."

Red smiled politely.

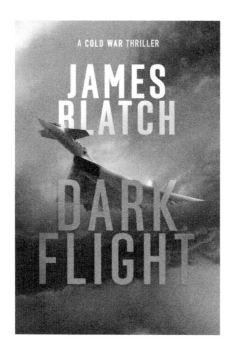

Available now

jamesblatch.com/darkflight

ACKNOWLEDGMENTS

HUNTINGDON,
Spring 2021

Novel writing may look like a solitary career, and perhaps for some it is. But The Final Flight felt like a collaborative effort to me. It involved a cast of thousands, in fact, as I shared my writing journey with the author community. The book also benefitted greatly from the specific help of several writing professionals, who skilfully equipped me with the means to produce a coherent story and hopefully, an entertaining read.

Mark Dawson, my business partner and friend, encouraged me to blow the dust off the draft manuscript I wrote back in 2010 as a November novel writing challenge. He gently and not-so-gently encouraged me to complete the project over the next few years. I am grateful for every nudge and occasional kick up the backside.

Jennie Nash was the person who made me confront the essential question of why I needed to tell this story. The answer surprised even me. It was deeply personal, but once identified, the writing process had the focus it needed. Jennie is a hugely experienced book editor based in LA. I am lucky to have had her on my side.

Lizette Clark steered me through the long form version of the book and it was Andrew Lowe, here in the UK, who helped me over the line.

Andrew is another experienced editor I am lucky to have worked with. He helped me turn a wordy and clunky manuscript into a much tighter and focused novel, while keeping those themes I identified with Jennie, central to every chapter.

Finally, on the writing front, my many writing friends who have cajoled, encouraged and occasionally pushed a little harder to ensure this book made it into the world. A few friends kindly read early versions and gave me the benefit of their thoughts. Thank you John C, Bob and Nathan in particular. I also received some valuable last minute help with the nitty task of proofreading. Thank you Paul Eddleston, Tracey Pedersen and Tom Feltham.

It is a wonderful time to be a writer, thanks to the changes in publishing, and I'm lucky to be at the centre of this quiet revolution.

For the story itself, I am grateful to the many former Royal Air Force men and women who gave me their time and thoughts as I worked to recreate an environment that was, a little before my time.

Foremost is my father. A test pilot at Boscombe Down, 1960-1966. Squadron Leader John R. Blatch, AFC, flew the Vulcan, Canberra, Hunter, Javelin and many, many others during his time and it was a luxury having him at the end of the phone to answer questions such as whether Vulcan pilots could isolate the intercom from the rear-crew, how the autopilot cancel worked and which pubs did the officers drink in?

Alas, my mother will never read this book. We lost her on May 31st, 2005. She was an air traffic controller at Boscombe when she met my father. She enjoys a cameo in this book, but you can find her bright and unmistakable character on the pages that involve Georgina and Mary.

Ray Cotton was a test pilot colleague of my fathers at Boscombe and I am very grateful for an hour I spent on the phone picking his brains about the day-to-day operations. It was Ray who told me of the drinking culture. So bad at one point that the Station Commander ordered the bar closed at lunchtimes... He also told me of the times they switched off the oxygen in the V-Bombers and had an in-flight smoke. Times have changed.

Besides my father and Ray, many others have helped with the authenticity aspect of the book, including the operators of the preserved Vulcan XH558. I spent a highly informative afternoon at Robin Hood Airport (formerly RAF Finningley), learning how to operate and navigate a Vulcan bomber to its target in deepest Russia.

I'd also like to thank the ever helpful and witty former military aircrew who inhabit the PPRUNE online forum, for their patient answers to my questions.

However, I should point out that this is a work of fiction. I have in some cases deliberately introduced unrealistic working practices, simply for the story, and I am certain I have also made mistakes in portraying 1960's RAF life. If you have any observations, I would love to hear from you, but please accept my apologies in advance.

My wife Gill was an early reader of the manuscript, and she gave me invaluable advice. I'm grateful for her practical support. I'm also grateful for the emotional support she gives me as we navigate life together.

To get in contact, please join my occasional newsletter. It's a place where you can learn a little more about the real-life incidents that inspired The Final Flight.

jamesblatch.com/thefinalflight

ABOUT THE AUTHOR

James Blatch is a former BBC defence reporter and a former BBFC film examiner.

James covered British military matters around the world including stints on the aircraft carrier, HMS Invincible, as well as reporting from Ali Al Salem (Kuwait), Gioa Del Colle (Italy) and Bardufoss (Arctic Circle, Norway).

He was lucky enough to fly twice with 1 (Fighter) Squadron in a Harrier MkT.10 as well as with 41 Squadron in a Sepecat Jaguar.

Today James lives near Huntingdon in the UK with his wife, two children and two dogs. He works in publishing and other ventures.

The author, after a flight in a Jaguar, Royal Air Force Coltishall, 2003.

© Crown Copyright

facebook.com/jamesblatchauthor

twitter.com/jamesblatch

instagram.com/james_blatch

Printed in Great Britain
by Amazon

82318718R00304